Swimming with Tigers
Kathy Hopewell

First published in 2024

by Pen-y-Bryn Press

Wales, UK

ISBN 978-1-7385442-0-2

eISBN 978-1-7385442-1-9

For David, and for Liz.

The problem of woman is the most marvellous and disturbing problem there is in the world.
André Breton

I cannot be reached.
Nadja

Chapter One

Paris, January 1938

P enelope Furr dived into a café on Rue du Four, shaking off the melting sleet from her mane of black hair. Once inside, she took in a solitary male drinker who looked up and ran his eye down her figure. At another table there was a group of fashionable women with their discarded fur coats slung over nearby seats like slaughtered animals. She could feel these bourgeois wives disapproving of her flea market clothes: a slash-sleeved emerald-green velvet jacket worn over a paint-stained white lace blouse and arranged so that the cuffs spilled out frothily to resemble an Elizabethan courtier's costume.

Scanning the room, she noticed a table at the front of the café that reminded her of a window seat in one of the pubs she knew back in Oxfordshire, and experienced a flash of homesickness. But surely, after six months of living here, hadn't she earned the right to call Paris her home? She sat down and gazed out at the street as occasional weekend traffic passed back and forth in front of the hoardings advertising soap powder and nerve tonic. No longer obliged to wear uncomfortable stockings or elegant footwear, she enjoyed the sensation of her naked thighs against the fabric of her skirt and gloried in the sturdy Cossack boots that had taken her so steadily and so far from the stifling expectations of her upper-class family.

She was alone today because her partner Rolf and the other members of the surrealist group were all at the planning meeting for the new exhibition. Deciding that coffee was what she wanted on such a cold winter's day, she tried to attract the waiter's attention by calling out '*Café au lait*?' but he ignored her. Rolf had explained that one either sat at a table and waited to be served, or one stood at the bar: the prices were different. So Penelope had learnt to wait to be asked, just as she had waited for one of the artists in their group to invite her to today's meeting or ask her to contribute a picture to their exhibition. Was her art simply not good enough? Rolf praised her work, though never in public, and it was impossible to ask outright why she was being excluded in this way.

With a jolt she saw that a woman outside had rested her forehead against the window of the café just inches away from her. The woman's eyes were closed. Was she sleeping? How tired she looked. Her breath on the glass grew and shrank like ghostly wings beating. Then, without warning, the woman opened her eyes and stared.

Penelope stared back.

As the woman outside straightened up, a man with burly arms collided with her. The woman fell to her knees and the man moved away with a halting, furtive motion. Penelope leapt up from her chair and went outside, throwing back the glass door so that it banged on its hinges.

She helped the woman back onto her feet, feeling her thin shoulders shaking under the coarse material of her red coat.

'Are you all right?' she asked, but the woman ignored her and searched frantically through her pockets.

Understanding immediately, Penelope turned and ran after the man, yelling 'Stop, thief! *Arrêtez*!'

He halted, looked down at whatever was in his hand and dropped it to the ground. Then he sprinted up the street and disappeared around a corner.

In the gutter, lay a knitted beige cloche hat, decorated with yellow and red flowers. Penelope took it back to the woman who was now motionless and dazed.

'This belongs to you, I think,' she said.

When she held out the hat, the woman grasped it and staggered, looking as if she might fall down again.

'You've had a shock,' said Penelope. 'Come inside for a moment.'

The woman allowed herself to be led into the café and guided into a seat.

Penelope strode up to the bar and asked for brandy. She stared out the waiter's disapproval then waited while he milked the optics. She returned to the woman, placing her drink next to the dowdy, old-fashioned, cloche hat.

The woman's thin fingers clasped the collar of her garish scarlet coat in one hand as she reached for the brandy. Penelope guessed that the woman was older than her: probably around thirty. Her face was delicate and fine-boned but her green eyes had shabby vestiges of kohl, from the night before perhaps, and her straw-yellow hair was badly cut to shoulder length.

'What did he want with your hat?' Penelope asked.

'It was my mother's,' said the woman in a tired monotone.

So she spoke English. Good. 'But why steal it?'

The woman shook her head and gazed at the table. 'He thought it was a purse, I suppose.'

'He'd have had a shock when he got it home' said Penelope, and at last the woman cautiously met her gaze. 'And,' she added, risking a smile, 'it wouldn't have suited him anyway.'

'No,' said the woman. She threw back the last of the brandy. 'Not his colour at all.'

3

Taken by surprise, Penelope barked out a loud laugh but the woman's expression remained the same.

'I'm Penelope. Penelope Furr,' she said.

'Suzanne,' said the woman, allowing her stiff, cold hand to be clasped briefly.

'Suzanne what?'

'Just Suzanne.' Immediately, the woman's shoulders hunched again. She cast a look around the café and out into the street then grasped the horrible hat as if to leave.

'Wait. Please stay,' said Penelope. 'Some coffee perhaps? Or more brandy? Please, don't go.'

Returning with the drinks, she watched Suzanne get out a squashed packet of cigarettes and light one.

They sat in silence.

Penelope looked again at her companion. Her red coat had a dropped hem and beneath it she wore a much-washed black crêpe dress. Her face could do with a wash and there was a faint smell of tomcat about her, overlaid by a cheap, sharp perfume. It was impossible to place her. Even if she was just posing as a penniless bohemian or artist, no self-respecting woman in 1938 would wear a 1920s cloche hat. She was somehow both naive and streetwise at the same time with her childish, short dress and sophisticated way of holding her cigarette at head height. Finally, Penelope realised there was nothing for it but to behave as if she was back at one of her mother's agonisingly dull tea parties for the wives of the managers at the factories her father owned.

'Are you from Paris originally?' she asked.

'No.'

'You speak English very well.'

'Yes.'

Penelope sat back in her chair and sipped her drink. At least she had tried.

'My mother was Scottish,' said Suzanne at last. 'Her name was Ailsa Gold and she was a singer. My father saw her perform at the Opéra-Comique in 1902. She never went home.'

'And does she still sing?'

'She died.'

'Oh, I—'

'But yes, she still sings to me.'

Penelope wasn't bothered by this strange claim. Her own mother had once been to a psychic who said that one of her children would be famous in one hundred years' time. At Christmas, Penelope had hoped for a card, or some sort of communication other than the cold, official letters confirming the amount of her monthly allowance, but there had been nothing. Rolf, who had long since lost touch with his family, told her it was for the best.

'My mother won't speak to me,' said Penelope, noticing that Suzanne was looking restless again.

'Why? What have you done?'

'I ran away to be with Rolf, a penniless artist and a German too. They can't forgive me.'

'I see.' Suzanne took a long drag on her cigarette and continued to gaze distractedly around her. There was a blunt, almost aggressive quality to her silence.

Then, without warning, she began to sing, very softly: '*Je vois une rose dans les ténèbres.*'

'What's that?' asked Penelope.

'Debussy. *Pelléas et Mélisande*. Mélisande has married Golaud, an old, violent, jealous man who hits her.'

She finally looked at Penelope. 'My mother was singing this part when my father first saw her. He was a respectable man, a baker with his own shop, and so she escaped the story of Mélisande. But I did not.'

'What do you mean? Does your husband hit you?'

'Let's not talk of these things,' she said.

Another awkward silence descended.

'How did you meet this man, Rolf?' Suzanne suddenly demanded.

'In London, the year before last, at the First International Exhibition of Surrealism.'

At this, Suzanne's eyes widened and she stubbed out her cigarette.

'I don't expect you've heard of it.' No response. 'It caused a real sensation because, of course, not many people in Britain had heard of surrealism.'

'Tell me more about the exhibition,' said Suzanne, leaning forward. 'I knew some of the surrealists once. One man in particular, I ...'

'Really? Who?'

'It was a long time ago. Did you like the exhibition?'

'It's the reason I'm here in Paris. Surrealism turned me inside out. It was as if someone had suddenly turned on the lights in my brain and in my heart. It changed everything for me. First, I met Rolf and he introduced me to the others: Fabien Sadoul and Alain Girard, the poet.'

Penelope waited to see if Suzanne would recognise the names but she said nothing.

'Tristan Müller was exhibiting one of his obscene dolls, and Louis d'Argent, although I didn't know who he was then, was giving a talk about a De Chirico picture.'

Suzanne's face fell; it was as if she had suddenly heard terrible news. Penelope hesitated.

'Go on,' Suzanne whispered. 'Please, go on.'

'It was at the exhibition that I first saw Rolf's picture of a young girl with a large knife fending off a tiny nightingale. And I remember saying to myself, "I know what this is". I had never really understood any painting in that way before. Rolf says that surrealist art is meant to defeat the rational mind by forcing the viewer to entertain a contradiction.'

'And does that make sense to you?'

'Completely. One of the exhibits was an iron with nails stuck to the base, pointing outwards, where you would iron clothes.'

'Perhaps a man made it; one who had never used an iron,' said Suzanne.

'And he thought that the nails would keep it hot for longer?'

The ghost of a smile passed over Suzanne's face. 'Or that the nails would hold the clothes steady while you ironed them.'

Penelope returned her smile.

She thought again of the meeting going on at D'Argent's apartment. Had they expected her to turn up? It suddenly occurred to her that she had misread the situation and that she was snubbing them by not attending. Perhaps they were waiting for her to offer a picture.

Suzanne drained the last of her brandy. 'Are you happy with Rolf?'

'What do you mean?'

'Do you enjoy living with a man, sharing his home?'

'You mean do I enjoy picking up his socks, ironing his clothes and putting up with his snoring?'

'If you love each other, surely that is all that matters?' said Suzanne, screwing up her face.

'My aunt Carys used to say that living with a man is less about love than doing his laundry. And of course you need to feed him – I mean, cook for him.'

'You make it sound like having a dog. As if it was nothing but a nuisance.'

'Yes, I mean why would you want to have the trouble?' said Penelope. Then she grinned. 'You have to remember to put down fresh water every day.'

'Check his fur for fleas,' Suzanne returned.

'Take him to the vet.'

'Train him to fetch sticks.'

This time they were laughing together. What on earth was this unexpected woman going to say next?

'Let's have another drink,' said Suzanne.

Chapter Two

'Mademoiselle.' The waiter placed a glass of red wine in front of Penelope. She watched him take the other glass from his tray and put it down at Suzanne's place without a word.

'He doesn't seem to like you,' Penelope murmured, once the waiter was out of earshot.

'He thinks I don't belong here,' said Suzanne, taking out another cigarette.

For the first time, it occurred to her that Suzanne might be a prostitute. What would Penelope's mother say if she knew that her precious debutante was out in public with a woman of dubious reputation?

Suzanne was shifting awkwardly in her chair. No, she didn't look like a prostitute, not exactly; she looked displaced.

'Do you live in Paris?' asked Penelope.

'No.'

Oh, hell. Back to this game. Penelope sipped her wine. The door to the café opened, letting in another gust of icy air. Looking out of the window, she saw a feathering of snow drifting down to coat the pavement and it took her back to the winters of her childhood when the roads were blocked and her governess couldn't come to the house. Snow meant freedom at home, but here she was suddenly fearful that she might lose her footing on the smooth city pavements.

'I have never belonged,' said Suzanne abruptly. 'Even when I was very young, I was alone. I have never been part of any club or group. I cannot be.'

'Did you ever try to join in?'

'Only once.'

'And what happened? Did they throw you out?'

'No, it was much worse than that.' Suzanne fell silent again.

Penelope was getting fed up with all this cryptic stuff and she wondered if Suzanne was one of those people who would not help themselves. Some were just born victims and hugged their persecution. She noticed that Suzanne was holding her collar closely around her throat again and that her hands were shaking. Maybe she was a drug addict?

She wondered if Rolf was back from the meeting. Immediately after waking up this morning he had gone into the curtained-off alcove which served as a makeshift darkroom. By contrast, Penelope felt like an animal in captivity in the city. She craved light and open air and her new painting was going to show a horse leaping from inside a room through a window to gallop over open fields.

'Shall I tell you about my paintings?' asked Penelope

'If you like.'

'Since I came to Paris I've been painting horses, probably because I miss my own so much. My painted horses are having a riot: they climb trees and eat feasts at long tables full of fruit and pies. Then they run across fields and turn their necks like beautiful women and look back at me with long eyelashes, challenging me to catch them.'

'These horses,' asked Suzanne, 'are they wild and free, or does a man follow them with a bridle?'

'It would take an unusual man to subdue such a wild creature,' said Penelope.

'And is Rolf that man?'

Shocked by this question, Penelope looked out across the street and there, as if in answer, was Rolf on the other side of the road. 'My goodness, there he is. Wait here, I'll be back in a moment.' Penelope kicked back her chair and once again threw open the door to run outside.

Rolf was strolling along, studying the ground intently.

'Rolf!' she cried out. He turned immediately at the familiar voice.

Penelope joined him, arresting his forward movement and causing the crowd to part and flow around them.

'Has the meeting finished?' she asked.

'Yes, everything is arranged.'

She watched tiny, wayward flakes begin to descend in zigzags and settle on his hair. At forty-eight, Rolf was almost twice her age, but his hair had been white since his thirties. He made as if to guide her onwards, back in the direction of his flat on Rue Jacob.

'Wait a moment. Can you come with me? I've met a very strange person and I think she needs help.'

'What kind of help?'

'I think she may have run away from her husband.'

'Then she is to be congratulated.' Rolf followed the surrealist line on marriage: an outdated notion that was only occasionally necessary for financial reasons.

'I think she was being brutalised. Her name is Suzanne, and she said she had some connection with the surrealists in the past.'

'This could be Suzanne Müller. Maurice said he saw her yesterday. It is her first time back in Paris since she ran away from Tristan ten years ago.'

'Tristan Müller's wife?' Penelope brought to mind the man who made ugly, life-size dolls. 'Come and talk to her, please.'

As they approached the café, which was called Le Parisien, she could already see that the table in the window was empty.

'She has flown away,' said Rolf, once they were inside. 'There is nothing to do. You must come along with me to Alain's. He has completed the words for our collaboration.'

'No, I'm going to wait, in case she comes back.'

'Why not speak with Tristan? She will go to see him, for sure. Then you can continue your gossiping with her.'

'I don't know if she wants to see him. She was very nervous.'

Penelope sat back down and stared at the half-empty glasses and still-smouldering cigarette. Rolf joined her.

The waiter immediately came to their table and took out his little pad to take Rolf's order. When Rolf told him he wasn't staying, the waiter gave a slight bow and retreated.

'I—' But Penelope got no further with asking for the coffee she still craved before the waiter's back was once again turned.

'So, she is saying he mistreated her?' asked Rolf.

'Didn't he?'

'I was not here then, but Maurice painted a different picture: that she ran off with another man, a richer man.'

'That doesn't sound right. She was more or less dressed in rags.'

'Never mind, then. I need to see Alain. Come with me and you can keep Una company while we talk.'

'I'm not your pet dog, you know. If Suzanne doesn't come back, I need to go and get on with my new painting, not sit about with Una while you work with Alain.'

'As you wish,' he said and got up to leave.

He did not kiss or touch her in farewell. At the door he paused and came back. Penelope thought for a moment that he was going to apologise. Instead he said, 'Here, you forgot these,' and put her keys to the apartment on the table.

'Thank you,' she said. As usual, it was impossible to know what he was thinking.

Penelope pocketed the keys. It was almost as though Rolf had not believed her, being concerned only with making sure that she would fit in with his plans. She began to feel angry, whether with Rolf or with Suzanne, who had seemingly abandoned her, she wasn't sure. Probably both.

Had she been taken advantage of? Suzanne had had three drinks at her expense; for all she knew, the burly man in the street and Suzanne were running a racket together. But she had seemed genuine.

Penelope threw some coins onto the table and got up.

The toilets were down a flight of wooden stairs and, as she searched in the gloom, she saw a blotch of red against the wall under the coat hooks. Suzanne.

She was sitting on a ledge, bent over, hiding her face in her hands.

'What are you doing here?' Penelope crouched down in front of her. 'Are you ill?'

'I couldn't let him see me,' said Suzanne, still shielding her face.

'Rolf?'

'Yes.'

'Why? Is it because of Tristan? I'll protect you. I won't let him hurt you.'

Suzanne looked up, her face streaked with tears.

'Look,' said Penelope, 'here's a clean handkerchief. I'm going in there and then we'll go and get some fresh air, shall we? Will you wait for me?'

She nodded.

'Promise?'

A weak smile at last. Really, thought Penelope, she's like a child, but if Tristan thinks he can knock her around again, he'll have me to reckon with.

They left the café and set off along Rue du Four.

The snow had stopped falling and the cars and bicycles were already clearing the surface of the road.

'Have you heard any news of Spain today?' she asked Suzanne, who trailed along behind her in an infuriatingly slow fashion.

'Spain?' she asked.

'The war. I have a cousin who's gone to fight Franco,' Penelope said.

'Fight who?'

Penelope could scarcely believe her ears. 'Do you really not know what's going on in Spain? This is our chance to end fascism for good and let those jumped-up idiots know what we think of them. Communism is the future and the artists will be in the vanguard.'

'But that's nothing to do with me,' said Suzanne, rather sulkily.

'Surely you don't admire those psychopaths, do you? Like that ugly Mr Hitler and his exhibition of so-called *Degenerate Art*. It was a real crowd-puller and more people saw Rolf's work than ever, so that shows you the sort of imbecile Hitler is.'

Penelope waited for a woman with a pram to mount the pavement. 'Seriously though, I saw a newsreel about the huge rallies at Nuremberg and it was the worst kind of sabre-rattling stuff. A school friend of Rolf's has joined the Nazi party.'

'Nar-zee?' repeated Suzanne.

'Oh, for goodness sake. Where have you been all this time?'

'In Lille.'

'Lille?'

'Yes, where my father's bakery is,' said Suzanne as if this fact, unlike the politics of the world and its wars, was known to all.

On Boulevard Saint-Germain the crowds thinned out.

'Where are we going?' asked Suzanne, hesitating.

'To the river, and then I'll show you where I live,' Penelope answered.

'I don't want Rolf to see me,' Suzanne said, standing still.

'Don't worry, he's gone to see a friend of ours. They're planning a new book. Look,' she said, 'there's some blue in the sky.'

Suzanne tipped back her head and her tense shoulders relaxed. For a moment she closed her eyes and Penelope studied the grey tear stains on her face as the wind blew the uncombed hair across her mouth. She put her hand inside Suzanne's thin elbow and they went on, arm in arm.

'I wonder what we look like,' Penelope said.

'You could be a lion tamer at the circus with your jacket and your boots. All you need is a whip.'

Penelope laughed. She liked it when people noticed her clothes. 'And what about you?'

'I am the lady in the cage about to be eaten by the lions.'

Penelope slashed her imaginary whip to left and right. 'See the beasts retreat at my command, ladies and gentlemen!'

'Thank you,' said Suzanne, very quietly.

When they reached the Tuileries the sun came out, making the remaining snow crystals sparkle on the grass. The heat from the sun was weak but Penelope sat down by the edge of the lake and opened out her arms to catch all the rays. The gardens were nearly empty. In the thin winter light, the gravelled space might have been a junkyard for rejected aristocratic garden ware. Each statue had a pigeon on top, like a grey cherry on a mouldy cake.

Suzanne went slowly from figure to figure, pausing at each one to study a face, an arm or a representation of drapery. She stood for so long in front of one of the statues – Ceres, holding a sheaf of wheat – that Penelope got up to join her.

'It reminds me of my mother,' said Suzanne. 'She used to bring me here when I was a little girl.'

'When did she die?' asked Penelope.

'Nine months ago. She was driving the delivery van far too fast and hit a tree. The next day they wouldn't let me see her. It was as if I was still a child and they thought that death would frighten me. But I have seen death. It was so much worse to imagine her dear face somehow changed. In my dreams I take away the coverings but her face is blank, like unformed clay.'

A pigeon crawled over the statue's head and dropped a foul, green liquid on its cheek.

They walked back slowly and stood contemplating the grey water of the lake.

'I have to go now,' said Suzanne.

'But when will I see you? Where are you staying?'

Suzanne shifted her feet and stared at the ground. A cloud covered the sun.

The thought of returning to the flat to wait for Rolf on her own was too much to bear. 'It's the opening night of the exhibition on Monday,' she said. 'Why don't you come? We could go together.'

'No. I couldn't.' There was a look of pure panic on Suzanne's face.

'Don't worry. Tristan's going to be away in Frankfurt or somewhere and I can get you in as my guest. Why don't we meet at 9.45? It's at the Beaux Arts gallery on Faubourg Saint-Honoré. Oh, do come. Rolf is always so busy; there are always so many people wanting to talk to him. Suzanne—'

But she had turned away and was putting on the old hat. 'I have to leave now,' she said.

'Don't go,' pleaded Penelope. 'I haven't shown you our apartment.'

'No, thank you.' Suzanne began to walk off.

'The exhibition,' Penelope called after her. 'Promise you'll meet me there. I'll wait for you.'

Chapter Three

London, June 1936

It was eighteen months earlier, on a sweltering hot day at Burlington Gardens, that Penelope had encountered surrealism for the first time. She had told her mother that she was at the hairdresser so, on reaching the gallery, she went first into the ladies' bathroom. Gathering her hair into one fist, she chopped off two inches. 'There,' she said to her reflection. In the deserted hallway, she turned the doorknob of the oak-panelled door, took a deep breath, and launched herself into the first surrealist art exhibition ever to be held in Britain.

Instead of the usual reverent hush, she was immediately surrounded by an absolute roar of voices coming from the crowded room. She bent to examine a photograph of a chalet in the mountains which had a picture of a giant Swiss roll superimposed on top. In the centre of the room there were free-standing exhibits, including one unidentifiable object about a foot high which was completely wrapped in a brown blanket and tied with hairy twine. This was nothing like the prestigious classical tradition that Penelope studied at art school, or indeed the dry abstractions of cubism. It was art as a children's party, a champagne-fuelled, fairground ride. Was this the answer she had been seeking? For some time now she had been disillusioned with her course. The training was formal, painfully conservative and, astoundingly for 1936, female students were still prevented from working from the nude model.

At one end of the room, a man in a bright green suit was giving a talk in French. Penelope went closer and peered through the crowd. The picture he was pointing at was a completely deserted street scene done in brown and grey, which contained shadows of pillars and had an uncanny, dreamlike, quality. Across the way, she saw a man holding a kipper in one hand and a hammer in the other going from picture to picture and eyeing them up. From another doorway came someone in a diving suit and helmet, and there was a fat man weaving through the crowd offering something to people who were shaking their heads and smiling. When he reached her, Penelope saw that he had a mug of water with string floating in it.

'Do you like it weak or strong?' he asked her. Then he moved on without waiting for an answer.

She felt slightly dizzy and headed out of the teeming main room. What would her father say to all this? Penelope, the most striking debutante of her year, was determined to avoid the insipid life that her parents expected her to lead. Her mother had tried to listen but her father literally couldn't understand what she wanted. To him, pictures were what you put on walls where there was a gap, and as for his daughter devoting her life to art, it was incomprehensible; the women in his family bred dogs.

She slipped into a small side room which was, for the moment, empty. One of the pictures immediately captured her attention. In a garden, near a shed, a young girl lay apparently unconscious on the ground while a second girl waved a knife angrily at a bird in the sky. On the roof of the shed was a man in a black suit making off with a third girl. He carried her close to his body and was reaching towards a real, not-to-scale and hence enormous, wooden doorknob as if to escape to another dimension outside the painting and take the little girl with him.

This was it: something that was akin to her own vision; something in the same visual language that she used. There was fear in this image, though, and she felt an irrational panic rising that made her reach out, like the sinister man on the roof, to grasp the wooden doorknob on the painting in a cabbalistic repeat of her entry to the exhibition.

She was just about to grasp it when she heard the voice of a man with a German accent behind her.

'Do you wish to enter my painting or escape from it?'

Penelope spun around. He might have been anything from twenty-five to fifty: a lean, bony man with a beaked nose and completely white hair which, perversely, gave the illusion of youthfulness rather than age.

'You painted this?' she asked.

'I did. Many years ago, when girls like you were easy prey.'

Penelope frowned and turned back to the painting. One of those types of men, she thought, and muttered 'insufferable' just loud enough for him to hear.

'Forgive me,' he said, moving to her side. 'My name is Rolf, Rudolf Gantz. I would be honoured—'

'Penelope Furr.' She held out her hand stiffly but instead of taking it, he reached up and placed his hand on her mane of wavy hair.

His hand rested there for a moment, as if in blessing, and Penelope was unusually aware of the shape of her skull as a dome: a sphere of bone. Then he tilted his head to one side and looked more closely at her springy hair. He rubbed a lock of it between his fingers as if to appraise it in a gesture that recalled the examination of some pedigree animal. Then his hand fell to her shoulder and she had a sense of her frame, her physical shape comprehensible as a whole, as if from an outside view. She felt an extraordinary peacefulness. She had seen this quietening done with horses; some trainers she knew had the knack of subduing the most awkward case. Like a nervous yearling, she became pacified and trustful, so it was neither unwelcome nor alarming when his hand slid around her waist. She stepped obediently forwards and he embraced her, burying his face in the heap of hair on her shoulder.

The embrace was at first somehow ceremonial but then most definitely carnal. A wave swept over her and she broke away. To distance herself from what had happened she thought desperately about his artistic identity, his gifts, and his contacts.

'I expect you know all the important people here,' she said. 'I paint too, you see.'

'Yes. Come with me.'

As they returned to the main gallery, Penelope realised that he had taken her hand but found that she had no real objection to this. He began to lead her around the exhibition talking about the artworks as if she were a fellow artist as yet unfamiliar with the styles, names and philosophy of the surrealist movement.

'This is by my countryman, Tristan Müller. As you see, he celebrates the perverse and the misshapen.'

He pointed at a grotesque collection of life-size doll parts which were joined together in an anatomically impossible way: there were too many legs. The limbs had Mary Jane shoes and schoolgirl socks, and once again Penelope felt unstable and confused. Not waiting for her response, he led her to the next exhibit.

As well as the artworks, Penelope studied her companion. His eyes were unnervingly blue and never fixed for long on one point. His restless fingers sought out every texture: he stroked his clothes, poked and cupped things. If nothing was, literally, to hand, he would massage and mould his own cheekbone or hip; there was a continual need in him for form and surface, like a physical hunger. And, after every sensual journey, his hand came back to rest in hers, giving her again and again this infusion of warmth and peace. It made her feel like a child to be led around in this manner, but soon she stopped caring how it looked and started to imagine what it would be like for his warm, intelligent hands to explore her naked body.

They had returned to a canvas of globular figures she had seen earlier, called *Atlas*, but Rolf had spotted someone just outside.

'Ah, here he is,' said Rolf, moving into the hallway towards a badly dressed man and towing Penelope behind him.

'May I introduce Fabien Sadoul, creator of the world of *Atlas* and lover of many men.'

The man blushed as he shook her free hand, then gave such a bashful smile that Penelope immediately warmed to him. His hair was closely shaven at the back and merged into a gorgeous blond quiff, which set off his thickly lashed, liquid-brown eyes.

Next to be presented to her was a patrician, expensively turned-out man, also French.

'And this is Alain Girard.'

'Is your work on display here, monsieur?' asked Penelope, trying out her rather basic French.

'Alain's work is with words only,' explained Rolf. 'His poetry book is in the little shop.'

'Yes, mademoiselle, the surrealist adventure began on the page, as I am sure you know.' He had switched to English for her benefit.

'I didn't, actually. I really don't know much yet.'

'And you would like to know more?'

She enjoyed the caressing sound of Alain's voice so much that she was slow to absorb the meaning of his words. 'Yes, I would.'

'Rolf, there is room for another next month, if you wish?'

'Of course,' said Rolf. 'We are going together for a week to a house by the sea in Corn–wall.' He pronounced it as two words. 'You would be welcome to join us.'

Just at that moment, a crack of thunder ricocheted like a pistol shot through the hallway. They all paused to listen, hoping for the sound of rain, but the tension continued.

'So?' asked Rolf.

'I'm sorry, it was tricky enough to get away for two hours today; I don't know how I'd manage a week.'

Both Rolf and Alain seemed visibly to lose interest at this but Fabien gave her a kind, sympathetic look. She noticed his ragged-hemmed jacket and his stained fingers; maybe his problems were different to hers but just as intransigent.

'In fact, I shall have to leave now,' she said.

Rolf accompanied her to the ground floor.

At the main entrance he made her stand still and said, 'Paddington Station, 4 July, 10 a.m., platform 1.'

'Pardon me?'

'If you wish to join us in Cornwall, this is the arrangement. Repeat, please.'

She chanted it all back to him. 'But I can't go, I really can't.'

'And yet you would like to?'

'Yes, of course.'

They were outside now and a flare of lightning whitened his already-pale face.

She stared, fascinated.

Chapter Four

Penelope invented a cover story to tell her parents and caught the train to Cornwall with Rolf. Their days in Padstow consisted of early morning cliff-top walks followed by hours at an easel or crawling on the floor making collages. Penelope spent the afternoons in bed with Rolf, and then there were meals cooked and shared with everyone else. In the evenings they played word games and went sea-bathing late at night. The moon's light turned the surf on the waves into silver lines in the darkness.

One day in bed, Rolf drew a fantastic creature. It had two powerful legs that merged smoothly into generous women's breasts and ended in a horse's head with a long, wavy mane.

'One of your old loves?' she joked when he showed her the sketch.

'No,' he replied, 'this is how it is when we are together. You were married to the wind before me.'

Then he grasped the hair at the nape of her neck and the drawing slid onto the floor. She experienced their love-making as a journey of increasing, exhilarating speed.

After the holiday, she returned to her parents' house and began to lay her plans in secret until finally, a year after that life-changing visit to the exhibition in London, she made her break for freedom. In the early morning light, the whinnying from the stables pierced her heart and tested her resolve to the limit. Then the taxi loomed into view and took her through lanes and green fields into the dull grey of a London not yet woken to the working day. Then came hours of pacing on the platform at Victoria Station, waiting for the night-ferry train.

What sleep she had that night in the carriage, as it swayed nauseatingly aboard the ferry, was flooded with nightmare pictures of rabid horses chasing her across red fields and then drowning agonisingly in the dank water of the Channel. On waking, she saw lights from the port of Calais ahead. It was as if these countless bright jewels, set in the soft grey of the approaching harbour, represented her future. Never had she felt more alone, or more exhilarated.

When she stepped out at Gare du Nord, a cathedral of blue ironwork with softly cooing pigeons greeted her. Then Rolf sprinted into view. He took her to his apartment on Rue Jacob, a high eyrie on a busy street where Fabien and Alain were waiting to welcome her. Fabien embraced her and presented the traditional Jewish gift of a loaf of bread and a twist of salt. Alain, once again in a formal suit despite the hot weather, gave her a bottle of Bordeaux. When they had gone, Rolf gave her a late-morning breakfast of coffee and croissants and then led her into the bedroom.

A few days afterwards, she was walking along the Boulevard Saint-Germain on her way to Café de Flore where the surrealists gathered daily at six in the evening. The blood was fizzing in her veins: she was on her way to join the surrealist group as an invited, approved member and would finally be introduced to the leader of the movement, Louis d'Argent.

The café had a revolving door: another door for her to push open. She took a deep breath for courage. Inside, the café was red and brown with oxblood-coloured seats, dark wood fittings, magnolia columns and fan-shaped, biscuit-and-cream floor tiles. In the left-hand corner, she saw Rolf first, then Alain and Fabien. In her haste to reach them, she tripped on the step to the back of the room and was saved by Rolf springing out to catch her. He laughed, but it was not the best entrance. Alain solemnly took her hand in welcome and Fabien arranged a seat for her on the banquette.

'Am I early?' she asked Rolf.

'No, perfectly on time. The others will arrive soon,' Alain replied in English.

'Ah, here is Jean,' said Rolf.

A man in tight navy trousers was introduced as 'Jean Morel, who works in leather'. He sat beside her, uncomfortably close, but seemed to be good-humoured.

Then a ripple of expectation ran through all the men and Penelope saw that D'Argent was approaching. She recognised him from the covers of surrealist journals and now knew that he had been the lecturer in the green suit at the London exhibition.

He shook the hands of Jean, Alain and Rolf and, as an afterthought, nodded to Fabien, then angled his glittering metal glasses to face her.

'May I introduce Penelope Furr, lately from England,' said Rolf.

D'Argent straightened in military style then grasped her hand at the same time as swooping down and kissing her fingers.

'Monsieur, I—' She began her pre-prepared speech in French, but he had already turned and taken the seat Alain had procured for him. He took out a bound notebook and a fountain pen and prepared to take charge, converting his place to the head of the table with every aspect of his regal posture.

Behaving like a vain old woman, he looked to the side as if he wanted to display his beautiful profile and lion-like swept-back hair.

The combination of nerves and excitement meant Penelope found this terribly amusing: his hauteur and magisterial egotism were hilariously funny in this bustling café. She laughed aloud and he looked at her not, as she feared, with displeasure but with a gentle, almost loving gaze. His face softened and seemed to glow with an inner light. She found herself transfixed and unable to speak.

Alain broke her trance by asking if she would like wine. He was speaking in French but using deliberately plain words and she answered gratefully that she would prefer coffee. Alain snared a passing waiter in an over-long white waist-apron to take their orders.

Penelope studied the men around the table. Alain's hair was receding a little and it gave him a rarefied look. He wore a dark, tailored suit made of superior cloth. It seemed that the surrealists, matching D'Argent's formal dress code, kept up standards to the point of having handkerchiefs showing out of their top pockets and Alain's was undoubtedly silk. In contrast, Fabien's proletarian origins were obvious: he had no jacket, just woollen trousers and a flannel shirt buttoned to the throat. Even Rolf, the most casually dressed of the men, had added a knitted tie to his assemblage of clothes which included braces and hiking boots.

'Where is Maurice?' asked D'Argent, apparently taking a roll call.

'Ill,' said Rolf, 'but the new man, Maurice's friend's son, he is coming.'

Penelope managed to grasp these preliminaries but as the meeting went on she began to panic over her slow comprehension and became increasingly irritated by the way in which she was being completely ignored by everyone, including Rolf, who was sitting opposite but didn't once catch her eye. She tried again to follow the discussion: something about a banquet or a hospital?

Then a young man came up to Alain. 'Excuse me, are you Louis d'Argent?'

D'Argent rose slightly from his seat and said portentously 'I am he.'

Again, Penelope could not help wanting to laugh at D'Argent's antiquated behaviour and looked across at Rolf to see if he shared her amusement, but he was frowning at the newcomer.

'You will be Gabriel Fontaine,' Rolf said. 'We are expecting you.'

'Thank you. And you are?'

'Rudolf Gantz, Rolf. Please, sit down.' He introduced the group one by one and described Penelope as his 'English friend'. 'So, Gabriel, you are the son of Maurice's friend Yves.'

'Actually I'm his nephew. Uncle Yves met Monsieur Poulin in the country. My uncle is a chef in a big house.' Gabriel seemed to be talking to Penelope and squeezed his hands into fists as he spoke. 'He has travelled the world and knows many people. My father has never left Nantes and—'

'What is your father?' D'Argent's voice rang out across the table.

'He's a farmer, monsieur.'

'Tell me about your work.'

'I ... It's ... Oil. Dark oil. Bodies, repeated, or arms, legs. It's dark. It's very dark.'

Penelope couldn't help but feel sorry for this new victim.

'I see, and you live by selling this *dark* art?'

'No, I'm a clerk, here in Paris – a legal clerk.'

'Like Bob Cratchit in *A Christmas Carol*,' said Penelope, not really meaning to speak out loud.

'You like Dickens?' Gabriel switched his attention back to her. 'I love him. They say it is different in French, but I never met an English person who read him. Is it so different, do you think, in French?'

'Monsieur Fontaine,' D'Argent cut in again, 'we are here for our meeting. You may talk some other time about these ... novels.' There was a sneer in the word when he said it: novels were vacuous, Penelope remembered, from reading the *Surrealist Manifesto*.

Gabriel looked first surprised, then deeply hurt. Penelope gave him a smile and he dipped his head to look down at his lap.

After another half hour of debate, during which Penelope was completely silent, D'Argent rose to leave. Shortly after, Alain and Jean also set off, together. Penelope understood from Rolf that Alain and Jean lived with a dancer called Una and that the three of them shared one bed. Fabien lived in the same building, separately, on the upper floor.

Rolf took their departure as a signal for the start of serious drinking and ordered a bottle of red wine.

Without D'Argent, their gathering ceased to be a meeting and became simply four people around a table. They sat companionably without talking for a while, as booming conversations went on all around them. What do all these people think of us, sitting here discussing our ideas so solemnly? wondered Penelope, and felt again the soaring exultation of her good fortune at being one of the elect.

Gabriel still looked very ill at ease, however. 'Did I say something wrong?' he asked Rolf, in English. 'Monsieur D'Argent seemed not to be pleased with me.'

'Don't be concerned, my friend,' said Rolf, 'it is always a while before a new man finds his place with D'Argent.'

And what about a woman? thought Penelope, reaching for the glass of wine Rolf had poured for her. The wine, hitting an empty stomach, went straight to her head.

Rolf refilled her glass. 'You are lucky, Gabriel, to escape the Truth Game,' he said.

'What is that?'

'This is when someone, usually D'Argent, asks a question and you must answer truthfully,' said Rolf. 'For instance, what do you say at the point of sexual release?'

Gabriel looked aghast. 'You're asking me?'

'No, no, rest easy, it was an example only.'

Penelope allowed herself to voice a wicked thought. 'I bet D'Argent says: "Ah, so this is what a woman is for."'

Rolf smiled and joined in: 'Alain would say, "Hmm, my feelings are of dark blue with serrated edges. I must remember to write it down."'

Gabriel laughed nervously along with them but Fabien was silent.

'Are you coming to the party on Saturday?' Rolf asked Penelope.

'Of course. Where is it?'

'It is a costume party, at Alain's apartment. You must come in fancy dress and naked to the waist. Will you come also, Gabriel?'

Gabriel thought for a moment, allowing his eyes to rest on Penelope and apparently forming a picture in his mind. 'Yes, why not. But if it's cold I'll keep my coat on.'

The others burst out laughing, then started up again when Gabriel looked at them with incomprehension.

It was past eleven when Penelope and Rolf left the café. Elated by the good red wine and companionship, she stumbled and giggled, holding on to Rolf's arm as the night sky revolved around her head.

A stiff-backed man intercepted them just outside the terrace.

'Mr Gantz!' he shouted in a clipped English voice. 'Such an honour, I'm sure. I saw your work exhibited in Berlin in, shall we say, not the best of circumstances.'

'No, indeed,' Rolf answered, 'I would prefer not to be classed as a German artist at all at this time.'

'But, sir, you soar above our times. You and all men of genius.'

'Thank you for your good opinion,' said Rolf, with a wry smile.

Then the man turned to Penelope. 'And what do you do, little miss?'

'Can't women be geniuses too?' she asked.

When the man laughed derisively into her face, she became immediately and fiercely angry and reckless. She reached up and took the hat off his head then turned it upside down on the ground, squatted and peed in it.

Both men stepped back instinctively.

'What on earth—?' the man began to say, as Rolf stood in front of him, screening Penelope behind him.

When she'd finished, she pulled up her knickers and sprinted away down the road without looking back.

Rolf caught up with her on Rue Jacob and captured her hand in his.

'I must take you to meet my father someday,' he said, with a completely straight face.

Chapter Five

Paris, June 1937

On the day of the party, Penelope burst into Fabien's bedroom flourishing a rather tatty grass skirt she'd bought in a junk shop. Fabien, who had been lying on the bed staring at the ceiling, snapped upright as if he'd been shot.

'My God, you scared me.'

'Sorry.' She started undressing and tossing her clothes on the dusty boxes that covered the floor.

'What do you think?' She spun around, feeling the ends of the stalks poking into her waist.

Fabien appraised her entire figure, taking in her loose hair, naked breasts and bare feet.

'It's unbalanced,' he said.

'Unbalanced how?' She craned her neck to see into the tiny mirror nailed to the wall.

'You need a garland, something round your neck to balance the shape. Some fruit, perhaps?'

'Bananas would be good,' said Penelope. 'I could be Josephine Baker in Tahiti.'

Fabien frowned. 'She wore bananas round her, you know.'

'Yes,' she said, smiling at his embarrassment, 'but they'd be perfect as a necklace.'

'I'll go and look in the kitchen.' He went downstairs.

Penelope crackled as she sat down on the bed. Fabien's room depressed her. His possessions were stored in packing cases that he brought home from the bookshop where he worked. It was a temporary place, not a home like Rolf's apartment that had pictures all over the walls, rugs on the floor and a squashy black sofa that he'd found in the street. Fabien's room had bare floorboards, an uncurtained window and a sloping ceiling that made the room dark all day. A garret to starve in all right, she thought and, in a rare moment of fondness for her father, felt sincerely thankful for her monthly allowance.

Fabien tramped back up the stairs and came in carrying a bunch of bananas and a bottle of red wine. He extracted some tumblers from one of the boxes.

'*Salut*,' said Penelope, raising her glass. 'What are you going to wear?'

'I have no idea.'

'Oh.' She scanned the room and lit on the pile of her own clothes. 'What about my skirt?'

Fabien obediently stepped into Penelope's brown skirt and zipped it up over his trousers.

She tilted her head to one side and narrowed her eyes. 'Take your shirt off.'

He presented his pale, hairless chest.

'A dervish, that's what you could be. Is it the same word in French? Spin around, with your arms like this.' Penelope held up her hands in a sort of Egyptian hieroglyph pose.

He executed a smooth turn.

'Faster. Yes. That's it. But you need a fez or something. Don't they have soft hats, quite tall?' She pounced on a hessian bag that contained paintbrushes and shook them out carelessly. She rolled the bag to the correct depth and planted it on Fabien's head, leaving his plume of fringe in place. 'Perfect. So that's us. Now give me some cotton, please, to tie my bananas. Or string.'

Obediently, he started to excavate one of the boxes on the other side of the room.

'So what have you been doing?' she asked, laying out the bananas on the bed.

'Nothing.'

'Not painting?'

'Only this.' He reached down to turn around one of the canvases that had been facing the wall.

She picked up her wine and came over to see it. Like many of Fabien's pictures, it was a discordant mix of bulbous shapes in an arid desert plain. There were suggestions of construction, a sort of organic scaffolding, but no enclosed spaces, no shelter. Fabien's pictures always made her feel lonely but she saw the authority of his vision.

'It's good. And there's more depth of field than in the last group.'

She was about to say more when she heard Rolf's voice downstairs. 'People are arriving. Quickly, help me with the bananas. I want Rolf to see the whole costume at once.'

By ten o'clock the apartment was heaving. The crowd was so densely packed that the strange decor of black crêpe drapery and horses' tails could hardly be seen. The light was kept low to persuade the more bashful guests to disrobe. Many of the women had cunningly managed to veil their breasts while still strictly in costume: one had a cape of feathers nestling around her nipples, one a sort of chain mail across the whole of her torso. A tall woman had simply added a yellow wig, which she wore backwards and had pinned aside to reveal her face while still covering her upper body. Una, with her soft blonde hair caressing her bare shoulders, proudly displayed her small breasts and looked entirely at home, as indeed she was. She was laughing and lounging on the upright couch with Alain's arm around her.

Alain appeared to be in his pyjamas, wearing expensive black silk pantaloons with drawstring bottoms. The cigarette holder and sleep mask that he wore pushed up on top of his head seemed to suggest a theme that Penelope could not determine. She was getting a bit bored. Someone had eaten one of her bananas, leaving the limp, blackening skin still connected to the rest around her neck.

'Are you enjoying yourself?' asked Rolf, taking long draughts from his mug of wine.

'Mostly,' said Penelope, reaching out to comb her fingers through his greying chest hair. In return, he cupped her breast with his free hand but she twisted away. He was dressed as a caveman and wearing a piece of mottled brown fur, probably once someone's prized doormat, which he'd lashed around his hips with leather belts.

'So what does Tarzan make of all this?' asked Penelope.

'He likes the wildlife very much,' said Rolf, making another drunken lunge at her.

'I'm quite hungry, actually. Shall we go home soon?' she asked, steadying him by the shoulders.

'Soon.' He turned away to hunt for more wine.

'Magnificent,' said a voice from behind. It was Gabriel, arriving late in a blue bib-and-brace overall.

'You cheated,' said Penelope, pinching his bicep.

'You didn't. You look amazing.' He was just about managing not to stare at her breasts.

'Come with me, Gabriel,' said Jean, appearing beside him, 'you need a drink,' and he led Gabriel through the crush leaving Penelope on her own.

All around, people were standing in tight knots and shouting at each other in order to be heard. Then she saw Alain snaking his way towards her and holding a tray aloft. He offered her slices of bread arranged with cheese and anchovies.

She ate greedily. 'I'm famished.'

'May I also offer you some champagne? I have something to celebrate.'

'Really. What?' She took another piece of cheese.

'Come to the kitchen with me,' he said.

They squeezed through the fleshy crowd. Over in the corner, she saw Rolf talking to the man he had pointed out earlier to her as Tristan Müller, the maker of the grotesque dolls. He had fixed Rolf into the corner with his staring eyes and shiny glasses, and his rotund figure looked quite repulsive when undressed. His stomach bulged over the top of his tight metallic trousers. Was he meant to be some sort of robot, perhaps? Penelope saw him drain his glass then take Rolf's and drink that too, but Rolf was so far gone he seemed to find this the funniest thing anyone had done all night.

In the kitchen, the respite from the noise was a great relief. Gabriel sat on the table in his dungarees grinning at Jean who was regaling him with tales of surrealist parties of old.

'Pah! This is a tame affair,' scoffed Jean. 'You should have been at the party when you had to be naked from the chest to the knee.'

'But that means ...' Gabriel struggled to process this information.

'Please, celebrate with me,' said Alain. He opened the window and produced from outside a chilled bottle of Moët. 'I have a publishing contract, and we together, as friends, shall share in the bounty of it.'

'You got it?' Jean embraced Alain with delight, which made Gabriel look away in confusion. Then he saw Penelope and opened his arms to her, hopefully. She gave him a smile but stayed where she was.

She looked fondly at her friends. Jean was wearing one of the most unusual outfits among the men. He had attached strips of fabric, ribbons and shiny, sword-shaped pieces of card to a belt, but the gaps between this array of objects revealed his naked bottom from behind and Penelope could not resist checking periodically at the front, in case parts of his own body were dangling alongside the rest of the paraphernalia. Earlier on, Jean had been teasing her by asking her to plait the ribbons for him. Jean had a very down-to-earth sense of humour, as her mother might have said.

'Is that what you wear on your father's farm?' she asked Gabriel, indicating the overalls.

'No, this is from a shop in Les Halles. Alain took me there yesterday.'

Alain handed them each a stemmed glass running over with butter-coloured foam.

'To good fortune!' said Jean.

Penelope took a sip. 'You've no idea how bad a head I have for champagne,' she said. 'Once at the races I got completely lost and ended up in the stables. But I had a much better time there. I always said horses were more intelligent than people.'

'Why don't you dance for Gabriel?' Alain said, pouring her some more champagne.

'Please, will you?' said Gabriel.

'Only if you sing.'

'We'll all sing,' said Jean. He took her glass and helped her up onto a chair and then the table.

Looking down on the men with the champagne racing through her veins, she suddenly felt very powerful. The men made a sort of whinnying, humming attempt at Hawaiian music and she began to dance. The wide straw skirt swayed and hissed and exaggerated the movements of her hips as she swivelled in time to the pulse of the voices. Jean started up a sort of African ululation and in answer she leant back, shaking her shoulders. The men began to clap and cheer and she went on dancing until, out of breath, she climbed back down.

'I need to cool down,' she said, and Alain opened the sash window to the top. Jean opened the window on the other side of the stove. On impulse, she stepped out onto the window ledge. It was just wide enough for her feet and the air was deliciously cold. Jean's comical face poked out of the other window and she did a pretend wobble to amuse him. Then she felt Alain's hand on her leg and he guided her back in.

'I could not bear to lose you,' he purred into her ear.

Jean roughly pulled Penelope away from Alain and placed a new glass of wine in her hand. 'Your payment for the dance.'

She felt a brief peevishness at being pushed to and fro between Alain and Jean. Gabriel's gaze was still flitting from her nipples back up to her face then down again. It made her laugh to see how simple these men were, how clumsy and obvious were their needs and wishes. Well, she was free to grant or deny them.

'I could watch you dance all night,' said Gabriel.

'I hear, Gabriel, that you are designing our next cover,' said Alain.

Gabriel smiled. 'Yes,' he said, with undisguised pride, 'D'Argent came to see me this morning.'

'Where is Rolf?' Alain asked Penelope. 'Will you ask him to join us?'

She drained her glass. 'I'll go and find him.'

The crowd in the other room had thinned out a little. Rolf was standing near the fireplace. He was trying to part the hair of the tall woman's worn-backwards wig to reveal the breasts beneath, but the woman was leaping back and forth to frustrate him.

Penelope hooked a finger into the waist of his caveman doormat and said: 'Come on, we're in the kitchen.'

Rolf gave the woman in the wig a silly grin and followed Penelope to the kitchen.

She was just about to get back up onto the table when she realised that Alain, Jean and Gabriel were deep in conference around it.

'Ah, Penelope,' said Alain. 'Una wants you. She came to find you.'

'Oh, all right.'

Although Penelope would rather have stayed to see what the men were talking about, she plunged back into the party, scanning the crowd for Una's blonde hair. It was only then that it occurred to her to question the speed at which Gabriel had been taken into the group and to wonder why she had never been asked to contribute to the magazine.

She stood in the centre of the room and took off her necklace.

'Who wants a banana?' she shouted, and everyone turned to look.

Chapter Six

Paris, January 1938

In the early hours of the day after she had met that girl from England called Penelope, who had rescued her mother's hat and tried to be nice to her, Suzanne sat on a bench in Place Dauphine. She scribbled words on a paper bag. *The eyes are pointed. The eyes have daggers*, she wrote, and then *I remember* six times, in smaller and smaller letters. Next to this, she sketched out a plan of the square with the two rows of houses that formed two sides of the triangle and the Palais de Justice, which had stone lions guarding it, forming the third.

She used to believe that ghosts were hiding behind these slender tree trunks and that if you stood in exactly the right position, they would be visible. She had heard them murmuring on early mornings like this and laughing too, late at night. But today everything was ordinary and the memories seemed more than ever to be those of another person. She had even believed that a tunnel began here that ran all the way across Paris. And why not, in this city of the underground dead where the tunnels of the catacombs, seeded with chalky knucklebones and femurs, forked and twisted under the pavements? She used to imagine the spirits searching anxiously for their mortal remains, now hopelessly mixed up with those of strangers. This magic triangle, which was always hushed, might easily be where those anguished ghosts, mourning their far-flung bones and melted sinews, met together to plunge and seethe underground.

There was a step behind her, a shuffling in the gravel. Suzanne's neck went rigid with fear, but it was just an old man. An old man in a cap coming to sit on the bench for his first cigarette of the day. Suzanne laughed at her fantasies, and the man glanced at her suspiciously before rolling and lighting a thin cigarette. Suzanne put away her drawing and took out her own battered packet of Celtiques.

'May I have a match, please?' she asked.

The old man tossed the box along the bench and Suzanne thanked him.

'Everything used to be a lot cleaner when I was a boy,' said the old man, after a while.

'Have you lived here all your life?'

'Just there,' and he twisted, with a grimace, to point at a house with a green door and a balcony with vertical iron railings.

The old man ground out his cigarette and got up to go. Suzanne was left alone once more with her memories and the sky made a further adjustment towards the full light of morning. Would today be the day she delivered her message?

She used to come here with him, all those years ago. He had listened patiently to the information that this was where the dead gathered. 'From how long ago?' he had asked. But he believed her. And then, because he looked so serious, she played a trick. They were sitting at a table outside a restaurant and she conjured up a red light behind a curtain in a window just above them. He was very quiet, truly awed by her powers, and she had laughed at his dumbstruck face. That was before the time when everything about him meant pain for her.

She stubbed out her cigarette under the worn heel of her old shoes and made her way carefully back into the roar of the morning traffic across Pont Neuf. She began to walk and, without really meaning to, she found herself back outside Le Parisien, the café where she had met that English girl yesterday.

Once again, she peered into the window, shading her eyes from the weak white daylight. The café was empty, of course, so early in the morning.

Then a man came out of the door to open the awning.

'We don't have your sort,' he said. 'I saw you here before.' He threatened her with his pole. 'Go away and don't come back.'

Suzanne forced her numb legs to move and began to walk, then run. She kept running long after the patron was out of sight and had covered half of Rue de Sèvres before she stopped. Her feet were on fire.

To her right was a small park and she stumbled in, feeling the wet grass through the holes in the soles of her shoes, and found a place to sit. There was no one around, so she stretched out on her back on the stone seat. The low clouds comforted her with their greyness and she closed her eyes.

She lay suspended between sleep and wakefulness, swinging from one to the other as if from foot to foot. Carefully, she allowed herself to remember that terrible time when she was bound to a bed and her whole body arched away from that man's invading hands, and his sharp fingers that could tear up her insides like a vulture's beak. In the same way as she used to then, she made her body hard. She threw back her head so that her neck extended into the segments of an insect's exoskeleton and her limbs became dry pods. Finally, every part of her was as hard and compacted as a muscle in spasm. One hand, connected to her arm by a rivet of steel, stiffened into a blunt, ovoid paddle. Her screams seemed to be coming from a long way off.

'Wake up,' said a voice. It was a little girl, a blonde girl, silhouetted by the grey sky.

Suzanne's first thought was relief: instead of being a monstrous metal thing, here she was, still a little girl with all future possibilities whole and bright.

But when the girl spoke again, Suzanne came back to herself. 'You were shouting,' said the child. 'It was probably a bad dream. I have those.' And she struck her hoop with a stick and trotted off.

A bad dream, thought Suzanne, sitting up and buttoning her coat. Yes, it did all seem like a disjointed nightmare after so many years. But this time it would be different. She stood up and smoothed her hair back into place. This time, she told herself, I shall be in charge.

She went back to her rented room.

For a while she sat and stared, picking at the fibres on the old bedspread. Then she rummaged around in the pungent wardrobe and found a left-behind workingman's shirt and rough trousers. Putting them on delighted her. She experienced a surge of entitlement and the remembered flavour of adventure. In the hallway, outside the door of another occupant's room, was a pair of heavy boots and she shucked off the flimsy, feminine shoes that had caused her such discomfort. Outside, she helped herself to a tweed cap left on the seat of a delivery van to complete the outfit and also solve the problem of her hair, which she tucked inside the hat.

She went to a café in Montmartre, drunk with the old Paris fluency. She was relearning to dance with the dipping, flowing movements of the city and its temporary, magical configurations. Once inside, she avoided speaking altogether: she pointed at what she wanted and issued a low grunt when served. The kitchen chairs of this workers' café were meant for men exactly like the one she was impersonating and she splayed her legs on either side of the three-footed iron table leg with actorly relish. Why not cross over completely? What better way to leave behind her unpleasant history as a victim than by converting to the opposite sex? She began to elaborate an identity as a school concierge with interminable war stories and, instead of a sense of fraudulence, the fabrications made her feel more solid, real and wedded to physical reality.

But every time she heard the creak of the heavy door with its familiar zinc handlebar running from top to bottom, or the ring of a shoe on the wide, pitted, metal step of the entrance, her past threatened to invade. Finally, she turned her head at the well-known sound of the café door and saw that, incredibly, it was him, actually him, coming in. Suzanne tried to banish this apparition from ten years back by gripping the drum-top of the table and imagining her hands as those of her assumed role: men's hands that were grimy, spatula-fingered and hairy.

Still, she couldn't stop herself from looking. In horror she watched him cross to the window, sit down and open his notebook, then gaze out at the street, pen poised affectedly against his pursed lips. He got out his gold glasses and positioned them halfway down his nose. It stung her heart to see these mannerisms of his again: things that she knew but had forgotten she knew. He scanned the interior of the café as if to challenge anyone to deny his right to embark on his task. Then he plunged, like a diver off of a board, into a frantic, scratching orgy of words. It was automatic writing: her own childhood game, now dignified, canonised and printed under his name.

This was it: the perfect opportunity. He was alone. She was not immediately recognisable in the dusty, alien male clothes and prickly wool cap. Don't think, Suzanne, she told herself. Just do it.

So she drank off the cold coffee, slammed down some coins and pushed back her chair. But at the same moment, Alain Girard walked past her and went to place a brotherly hand on his shoulder, then sit down opposite him.

Merde. Today would not be the day she spoke to him.

Nothing for it then, but to go back outside, back into limbo. She returned to the streets where no one knew her, or cared who she was.

Chapter Seven

Paris, January 1938

For Penelope, the building on Rue Jacob where she lived with Rolf was an enchanted place. It was a house out of a fairy tale in the middle of the city. The only one set back from the road, it had two pillars at the gate leading to a tiny courtyard where a tall conifer grew higher than the roof. Two-thirds up the tree was the window of the flat that she shared with him.

She turned the key and once inside climbed the steep, shallow steps, stubbing her toes in haste. Opening the door to the studio, she encountered some resistance because a pile of magazines had fallen off the printing press and slithered across the doorway. Rolf was at Alain's and would not be back for hours. She replaced her fancy jacket with a dirty laboratory coat and set a kettle on the gas flame. From among the scraps and brushes and drawing pins and pencils she unearthed a white teacup, saucer and spoon and took them to the bathroom to wash.

The water was tepid and the soap had been finished long ago so Penelope rubbed at the coffee stains with her fingers under the meagre stream. There was a curly black hair in the sink. She remembered the large draughty bathrooms of her childhood. There, the taps were gold and thick white towels were replaced daily by servants. It was not often that she thought of England; perhaps it was meeting that strange woman called Suzanne two days ago and talking about her home that had brought the memories into her mind again.

Back in the studio, she put the cup down on the table. Next to the palette knives and bottles of linseed oil was a heap of grey-brown gazelle fur that Rolf had picked up in the market for a few *sous*. She stroked the soft pelt and smoothed the skin on the other side with a pitying finger, then she tried bending, bunching and folding it to see how the fur stood out at angles, and ran her fingernail through it to make a parting as if on a head of hair. Then she reached for the scissors and paused for a moment to gaze at Rolf's photograph of her from the first few weeks after she had arrived in Paris. In the picture she lay naked on the floor, and the edges of her body were liquefied and oozing like molten flow. It brought back the way she had felt in those early days with Rolf when her skin was alive and soft with desire and her body seemed to be spilling over into his.

She began to carefully cut out a large circle from the pelt of the gazelle. That melting state was probably the reason why she never bothered about Rolf claiming the technique that produced this liquefied outline as his own discovery when in fact it was Penelope who had come upon it by chance. It happened one morning in the darkroom when, in a fright after something ran over her foot (it could have been a mouse), she had put on the light. Realising that it would ruin the picture in the developing tray, she hurriedly switched the light off again. Once Rolf had seen the results of this accident he immediately started to experiment with creating blurred edges around pictures of her face and hands and body.

She smoothed flat the circle of fur on the paint-splattered table and pictured it as a small dinner plate piled with steak and potatoes. On the floor there was a jar of flour and water paste and she looked around for something to stick the fur to. The kettle was whistling so she went to switch off the gas and picked up the saucer. She slathered the paste on the base of the saucer and pressed the fur onto it but the paste was too weak for the job. She wiped it off and went into the bedroom to find some glue.

On the unmade bed was D'Argent's book about Natalia, a beautiful waif he had met years ago. Natalia had gone mad and had to be locked up. In Penelope's opinion, Natalia was a whey-faced, whimsical fool who had let people walk all over her. Natalia's big thing was living spontaneously; she was a free spirit and D'Argent had been obsessed with her character and attitude as a template for the surrealist way of life. But when she went insane, he had completely abandoned her and had never been able to bring himself to visit her. Apparently Natalia was still locked away and D'Argent refused to hear her name spoken.

Penelope found a pot of hide glue that Rolf had used to fix a chair and took it with her. Once the glue was hot, she settled back to her work. As she cut and glued and cut again, her mind emptied. She went to retrieve the cup as well, and continued. The water cooled in the kettle.

An hour later, Rolf burst in, carrying two baguettes and laughing at some joke of Alain's. He threw down the bread as soon as he saw the fur-covered cup.

'Penelope,' he called out. 'Did you do this?'

She came over to stand next to him and looked at her work. 'Yes, do you like it? Shall I serve tea?'

'It is astonishing. Alain. Jean. Come and look at this,' Rolf said, switching to French for the benefit of his guests.

All four stood looking at the object on the table.

'May I?' asked Alain, in his suave voice, but Jean had already begun to stroke the cup. Then he seized the tufted spoon and ran it down the side of his cheek, grinning.

'There is still time to add it to the cabinet,' said Alain.

'Of course, it must be so. It must go into the exhibition,' said Rolf.

'Yes,' agreed Jean, replacing the spoon, 'next to the gramophone that swallows legs.'

'I will take it later but first we must eat. Have you eaten already, little one?' asked Rolf.

'No, not yet. You mean my cup is to be in the exhibition?'

'It is a masterpiece, Rolf,' said Alain, transfixed.

'Well done,' Rolf murmured into her ear. 'Now, food.'

There was sausage with the bread, the German kind that Rolf bought when he felt nostalgic for Munich. Jean and Rolf occupied the destroyed sofa while Penelope sat cross-legged on the floor and Alain knelt in an awkward but dignified manner beside her.

'Ah,' said Rolf, 'that wonderful cup of fur' (it sounded like 'cup of her' through the bread he was chewing) 'has made me forget about Fabien's troubles.'

'What's the matter with Fabien?' asked Penelope, tearing off more bread and leaning down to saw at the sausage with a blunt knife.

'It is the party congress in a week's time,' said Alain, 'and the delegate from Russia will not give D'Argent permission to speak.'

Penelope asked Rolf to explain the meaning of 'delegate', a new French word to her, then demanded to know why D'Argent had been refused.

'D'Argent will not concede, in writing, that the pursuit of art is a *subsidiary activity* in the struggle for revolution,' he told her.

'But that's just words.'

'You had better not say that in Alain's hearing, little one. His religion is poetry, as you know.'

Alain gave her a grave smile of absolution.

'I saw Fabien earlier,' said Jean, poking his finger into the loaf and pulling out wads of white dough. 'He had an appointment with the party secretary this afternoon. No doubt Fabien will try to use his charms on the poor man. Let's hope the commissar's aide is that way inclined.'

'D'Argent would not approve of those methods,' said Rolf.

'True, but you know what Louis is like,' said Jean. 'If Fabien is a homo, that's fine, as long as it isn't thrust in his face.'

'Hah!' snorted Alain.

'*Pardon*. But this is D'Argent's problem. He is so uptight. Not like our Penelope, here, eh?'

Penelope squirmed, trying to evade Jean's attempts to tickle her.

'Well, my friends,' said Rolf, 'I must get on with my work now we have eaten together.' He turned to Penelope. 'Will you pose today?' he asked, in English.

'Yes. Of course.' A session alone with Rolf would be a welcome distraction from the problem of the dog or cat or whatever it was that she was trying to fit into her yet-to-be started picture of the escaped horse. Penelope took her leave of Alain and Jean and hurried off to get undressed.

When she came back, wearing Rolf's old plaid bathrobe for warmth, Alain and Jean were still wandering about the studio, picking things up idly.

'Come,' said Rolf as he started to set up the camera on the wooden tripod, 'let's see what we can do with the press. Ah, perfect, Alain you may help me. We need to move this across into the centre of the room.'

'I'll clear the way,' said Jean, pushing the sofa aside.

Once the printing press was in place, Penelope slipped out of the robe. Alain and Jean threw themselves down on the sofa and called out advice to Rolf.

'The light is wrong.'

'You must have the camera higher.'

'Penelope, please go there, behind the wheel,' said Rolf.

'What am I to be? A blank piece of paper?'

'Very funny. This is a study of mechanism and I am using your beautiful body to make my paradox.'

'Look, I've been printed,' she said, and tipped out some black ink from a bottle into her hand then smeared it on her arm.

'That's enough, it's expensive. But this will work, I think,' said Rolf, as he ducked under the cloth.

As she posed, Penelope thought about the praise for her fur cup. Perhaps she had been accepted at last. She didn't like the way Jean was nudging Alain and gawping at her breasts, so she angled her body differently behind the press. Standing like this, the handle would seem to be sticking out from her groin, which was an amusing thought. She raised her dripping arm to her forehead and rested her elbow on the wheel. The aperture opened and closed with a slow metallic wink as Rolf adjusted the exposure. Then he stood next to the camera holding the cable release and scanned every part of her body in relation to the press.

Alain and Jean fell silent and Rolf's concentration filled the room. As he worked, the ink on Penelope's arm dried to a crust.

'I have finished,' said Rolf. He went off into the curtained alcove.

Alain got up to look at the press more closely and Penelope turned to retrieve the robe but Jean had snatched it up, grinning. He held out the robe to her then pulled it away when she put out her hand. Then he bunched it up and tucked it under his arm. Penelope stood, mildly annoyed, and waited.

All at once, Jean stopped smiling and reached out his index finger to touch Penelope lightly on the throat. Then he allowed his finger to move downwards and trace a line slowly between her breasts. Despite herself, Penelope felt her nipples tightening.

Alain was behind her and, always the gentleman, he stooped to pick up the robe which had fallen to the floor. She felt Alain's breath on her leg and inhaled sharply. Alain left the robe where it was and stood up again, then he placed his hands on her shoulders from behind and left them there for a moment. Very slowly his hands travelled down the front of her body.

Rolf wandered out of the alcove and studied the tableau of Penelope, naked, with Jean's finger on her belly and Alain behind her with both hands cupping her breasts. He gave her a questioning look. Then she twisted around to look at Alain which he interpreted as a signal to remove his hands. Jean also let his arm fall to his side, and gave a little laugh.

She picked up the robe.

Rolf looked at his watch. 'So late. I will take the cup to Saint-Honoré and meet you later at the café.'

'Shall we come with you?' asked Alain.

'No, please, stay and keep Penelope company.' Rolf put the furry objects into a paper bag, threw on his mackintosh and went out.

Penelope went to wash her arm. What did Rolf mean by deliberately leaving her alone with Alain and Jean? She put on her skirt, blouse and jacket and added a scarf. She thrust D'Argent's book into a bag in case of boredom.

'Come on, you'd better not be late,' she said brightly to the two men. 'It's already close to six.'

All the members of the group were trained to be at Café de Flore at six o'clock, no matter what. Persistent lateness carried the risk of expulsion, or D'Argent's displeasure at least, and she had often marvelled at the obedience of these grown men, each one a rebel in some way, whether to family, country or career, but all in thrall to this one man.

'D'Argent won't be there. He's putting up the last of the exhibits at the gallery,' said Jean.

'But he'll find out who was on time and who wasn't,' said Penelope.

'She's right,' said Alain, 'come on.'

Chapter Eight

As Penelope stepped into the revolving door at Café de Flore, Jean skipped on his heel to jump in with her. He put his hands on her waist and they did a slow, four-foot shuffle. Penelope found Jean's clowning reassuring after his piercing stare and insistent finger on her body earlier, an image which kept returning unbidden to her mind's eye, accompanied by the physical memory of Alain's soft hands. What might have happened next? Now, Jean was back to behaving like a rough and tumble younger brother, tickling her and linking arms.

They followed Alain as he threaded his way through the tables. The café was filled to the ceiling with roaring voices. The surrealist group had swelled in numbers this evening but occupied the same corner as usual. Penelope scanned the faces: she didn't recognise them all but she could see Gabriel, sitting primly upright on a stool to one side and, lounging on the rose-pink leather seating with his overcoat thrown over the rail behind him, was the ever-faithful Maurice Poulin, D'Argent's oldest compatriot (Rolf had told her that they went to school together). Penelope was surprised to see Josephine, D'Argent's tall, brown-haired wife, with Clara, their five-year-old daughter, sitting at the next table. Penelope was used to being the only woman present. Surely the child was not coming to the exhibition?

Penelope sat down opposite Maurice, thus depriving Jean of the opportunity of sharing the banquette with her because she knew that he would slide along and crowd her out. Jean had to content himself with sitting in a chair next to her which he dragged as close as possible, throwing his arm around the back of hers.

'Pernods for all,' shouted Alain at the harassed waiter who was trying to avoid catching anyone's eye. Penelope would have preferred wine, but it was easier to go along with the rest. Clara had been eating a meal and was now tearing up the bread which she started to throw at the members of the group.

Clara scored a hit to Maurice's cigarette – still in his mouth – and he smiled tightly. Josephine did nothing: she had an agreement with D'Argent that the surrealist principle of total freedom should also be applied to child rearing. Jean threw back the bread that Clara aimed at him and Penelope found herself caught between the yelps and lunges of the child and the man.

'Stop it!' she said, rather too sharply. 'Clara, let's see if we can make little people with the bread.'

Jean slipped out with his eye fixed on a dark-haired girl in black on the other side of the room and Penelope ended up in the domestic enclave, joining Clara and Josephine's table to play with the child. Josephine gave Penelope a deeply grateful smile as Clara bent over the table and carefully cut the bread into shapes, her tongue poking out of her mouth in concentration. I might as well have come to Paris as a nanny, Penelope thought to herself, but then remembered Rolf and looked around for him, forgetting for a moment that he was at the gallery with her fur cup. Why was she not there, deciding how best to exhibit her work instead of here looking after someone else's child? It had never even occurred to her to go. Had Rolf suggested it?

Clara began to tire of the game and maliciously cut off the heads of the bread figures then fixed her mother with a truculent stare. Josephine finally gave up and left, taking Clara with her. Penelope turned her chair back to face Maurice's table as Jean slipped back in again with a smug look on his face.

Next to appear was Miguel Púbol making a rare visit. His tense posture and immaculate brown suit had the effect of repressing the high spirits of the group. Things were strained between him and D'Argent since the fiasco a week earlier, when D'Argent had tried to expel Púbol from the group, but instead had been humiliated. Most of the young men who fell out of favour with D'Argent were deflated and ashamed and tended to slink away to lick their wounds, but Púbol had made a laughing stock out of D'Argent by waiting for the most public moment and then stripping off his clothes and literally throwing himself at D'Argent's feet like a spurned lover.

By turning the whole thing into a game Púbol had somehow nullified his own expulsion and D'Argent was now sufficiently nervous of further humiliation that he was pretending to forget that Púbol had committed any crimes at all. Rolf, who had told Penelope this story, did not like Púbol or his phoney political views, but he too was becoming weary of D'Argent's egotistical behaviour. The irony was that the accusation against Púbol – idolising Hitler – seemed almost like jealousy on D'Argent's part, since the devotion of the prodigiously talented Púbol was something D'Argent ardently desired for himself.

Púbol had clearly banked on D'Argent's absence to make this statement of continued membership of the group, but still he sniffed the air like a rat for signs of his adversary. He leant against the pillar and flicked his fingers at the soft ivory-coloured stone in an exaggeratedly casual way. Gabriel, star-struck, offered him his seat but Púbol merely gave that odd maniacal laugh of his that Penelope always found disturbing.

Jean then gave a loud cough, somewhat lost in the din of the café, and Penelope realised that he was, unconsciously or not, aping D'Argent's mannerisms. The peremptory cough brought the group to attention by force of habit and Maurice took on the deputising role.

Penelope saw Púbol slip away unnoticed by the others.

'Shall we continue our study?' Maurice looked over the top of his glasses like a professor. The impression was spoilt, not only by his salacious grin, but also by his prominent, sticking-out ears.

'Yes,' cried Jean.

'What's this?' asked Penelope.

'It's a truth game, for the magazine, about our lives ... at night,' said Maurice.

'More dreams?' said Penelope. 'Aren't the readers of our magazine getting tired with endless dreams? After all, there's nothing more tedious than hearing about another person's dreams.'

Maurice allowed this heresy to pass. 'No, my dear, it is the other, more enjoyable activity of the night. I mean, between the covers, or indeed anywhere you wish.'

'And not just at night,' chipped in Jean.

'You mean sex?' said Penelope.

'I mean sex,' said Maurice gravely. 'Who will begin?'

Maurice turned to Gabriel who looked plainly terrified. 'Gaby, you will be the scribe. Go and ask for some paper.' Gabriel's stool rocked with the speed at which he left it.

'I don't see why we have to talk about this,' said Penelope.

'Sex is the doorway to many worlds,' said Maurice.

'Yes, but I don't go through the doors in those places. It's only you men who visit them.'

Maurice gave her a sorrowing look. 'Sex without love is incomplete. We are all searching for the Elect One, who will begin in us the wave that changes the world into a place of light and freedom.'

'And I won't have the law or the priests telling me who I can fuck,' called out a small man whose name Penelope did not know.

The men laughed.

'Down with the church,' one said.

'Marriage is prostitution,' said Jean, although this idea seemed to please more than outrage him.

'So, shall we begin?' said Maurice. 'On the other hand, perhaps we should wait for Louis. And where is Rolf, by the way, Penelope?'

'With D'Argent ... I mean, with Louis.' Penelope found it difficult to use D'Argent's first name. She had once heard that he could not bear to be seen without his shoes on, which perfectly fitted the unremitting formality of the man.

Gabriel returned, eager to be of use, but Maurice had made up his mind. 'We shall wait,' he said. 'Time for more drinks.' He started signalling to a waiter.

Next to arrive was Tristan, back from Frankfurt. He immediately latched on to Penelope and quizzed her about Suzanne.

'Rolf says you saw her. Actually saw her.' His fiery green eyes bored through the nasty glasses and into her face.

Penelope had always disliked Tristan's manner, and the disjointed, distressing life-size dolls he made. The German accent she loved in Rolf grated on her coming from Tristan.

'Where is she?' Tristan actually craned his neck searching the bar as if Suzanne might be there.

'I don't know. And I don't know where she's staying before you ask,' said Penelope.

'What did she say? Did she talk about me?'

'Not much. I can't really remember.' Penelope was hazy after her second drink.

'Tell me.' Tristan grabbed her shoulder roughly. 'Tell me what she said.'

Jean broke off his conversation with Maurice to frown at Tristan.

Tristan released Penelope and let his hand drop, then sighed so deeply that she felt briefly sorry for him. She was befuddled by the Pernod and not entirely sure what she had against him. Perhaps she should try to help him somehow?

The café began to empty as the first wave of people left.

D'Argent finally arrived and produced the little bottle of food colouring with which he tinted his drinks. He added two drops to the Pernod that had been watered and placed before him. He raised the glass of cloudy, blueish, liquid and surveyed the entire group. They fell silent.

'I would like to announce,' he said, 'that Penelope Furr has committed an act of pure surrealism.'

All eyes turned. She struggled to assimilate the meaning of his words, delivered as ever in formal, flowing French.

'Later you will see,' he went on, angling the glittering light of his polished lenses towards her, 'that in the Cabinet of the Marvellous at the exhibition there is a new object of extraordinary surrealist beauty.' He smiled. 'As beautiful, in fact, as ...'

The whole group joined him in chanting Isidore Ducasse's well-known formula: 'The chance encounter of an umbrella and a sewing machine on a dissecting table.'

Everyone applauded. Drinks were brought for Penelope and the voices buzzed around her asking question after question about her new work.

'A cup? An ordinary teacup?'

She glanced across to D'Argent who gazed magnanimously at her, like a proud parent.

She basked in his approval, thinking of her own father, a man rigid in mind and body, who had been physically sickened by her artistic ambitions. He would not disown her but had gradually realised that the enchanting play of the little girl he loved, who drew and painted from morning to night, was not making way for a young lady's interests in gowns and dances. It was as though she was stunted in her growth: an embarrassment.

Her mother used to lead him to his chair like an invalid when he came back in the evening from touring his factories with that metallic, sour smell on his clothes. Her father would close his eyes for a few seconds and Penelope would watch the lines on his brow uncrease. Then all was well again, unless she had been careless enough to forget to change her clothes and he saw the paint staining her sleeves.

But Penelope did not delude herself that D'Argent would be anything but a capricious patron and protector; her time in the sun would probably be short. Well, why not enjoy it then? She drained her glass. Rolf had also returned and was deep in conversation with Alain on the other table: he never sat with Penelope at these events. Once she had asked him why not, and he said that he didn't want to imply ownership.

After a few minutes, D'Argent rose and informed them that he would meet them at the gallery, then left. The talk turned to the likely reception of the exhibition. Some predicted a breakthrough with the press (who they only affected to scorn) and an end to the repeated, humiliating attacks on their art and philosophy. Others forecast rioting in the old Dada tradition.

'Ah, those were good days, my friends,' said Rolf, 'when an axe was provided for the visitors to take part in the spirit of Dada and smash up the exhibits.'

'Not so easy to sell those exhibits afterwards, though,' said Maurice, who was so broke he was even considering returning to his job in the insurance business, despite D'Argent's pleading.

'And the smart set will be there, of course,' said Alain, 'to see Púbol modelling the dress of the season.'

'Púbol is wearing a dress?' asked Penelope.

'No, his mannequin,' said Alain, patiently.

Penelope did not understand and she couldn't hear what Rolf leant over to say to Alain, making him laugh. The Pernod was making the noise recede and then rush at her wildly like a young horse taking turns in a paddock. She got to her feet and steeled herself to negotiate the spiral staircase to the toilets. The black-and-white patterns on the triangular steps hanging over the abyss made her head spin and she gripped the handrail tightly.

When she came back, only Rolf remained.

'They have gone on ahead,' he said, starting to leave without waiting for her.

She threw a note onto the pile on the table and hurried after him.

Chapter Nine

The night was raw and Penelope wound her scarf around her face, obscuring her mouth, which Rolf found amusing. He drew her into the circle of his arm and she felt the alcohol in her blood transform into a steady inward warmth and contentment.

A particular quietness rose from the empty pavements of the city after long hours of giving back the echo of every footfall. From the buildings, too, came peacefulness, sated as they were with the roar of traffic that they had been drinking in all day.

Rolf saw Jean ahead of them and called out to him. Jean waited for them to catch up and they went on together. Rolf allowed his arm to remain around Penelope's shoulder and the support made her sleepy and sentimental. Jean walked placidly beside them.

When they reached the gallery, the entrance was hidden by a crowd of furred and feathered women in long, shiny dresses and men in black evening clothes. Penelope felt like a pauper at a feast and even wished, for a moment, for one of her coming-out gowns and some elegant sandals instead of her homely skirt and serviceable Cossack boots.

Alain gestured at Rolf who fought through the crowd like a strong swimmer to reach him. After a brief discussion, Rolf turned and shouted, 'The exhibition will open in ten minutes, ladies and gentlemen.'

There was a general milling about and some of the crowd moved off into the fashionable furniture shop next door which, even at this time of night, appeared to be open.

'Who will give the opening speech if D'Argent isn't here?' asked Rolf.

'Will you?' asked Alain.

'Yes, I can do this,' said Rolf, swallowing hard.

'Come on then, let's prepare.' The men went inside, leaving Penelope behind.

Gabriel stood nearby, looking as nervous and out of place as usual.

'Shall we go in?' she asked Gabriel and was rewarded with an enormous smile. He offered her his arm and they stepped over the sill. Behind the handsome wooden doors was a large courtyard. In the centre was a black taxi cab.

Then Maurice came out of the building and placed a large crate at Gabriel's feet.

'Gaby, you are to give one to every visitor. There are six more boxes and that's all.' He went back in.

Penelope and Gabriel peered into the crate. It was full of handheld Mazda torches. Then people began to pour in and she was jostled away; Gabriel would have to fend for himself.

A few minutes later, Rolf came out into the courtyard and climbed onto an upended crate, raising his arm for silence. Everyone turned their lights towards him and his bony face was lit from below like some screen vampire.

'Mesdames et messieurs,' called Rolf in a slightly hoarse voice, 'it is my pleasure to welcome you to the Second International Exhibition of Surrealism. Ladies of the night ...'

Rolf paused and smiled mischievously. He looked pointedly at some of the women in the crowd causing a ripple of delight, '... await you inside!'

Laughter erupted.

'For, my comrades,' this time he searched for the men, 'the greatest enchantment is the enchantment of desire. Beneath the world of daylight is the dimension of the dream and tonight these two realms are united in an explosion of bliss. Welcome to the Erotic Surreal!'

Rolf presented the black taxi: 'Your carriage awaits.'

The silly whispers and girlish titters died down as the crowd surged forward to surround the taxi. The little beams of light darted around, picking out the strange contents of the vehicle. The driver's head was grotesquely enlarged and had a wide-toothed, yawning jaw. There was an elegantly dressed woman in the back and it was soon apparent from the immobility of the figures that they were dummies. Then came the sound of water. The interior of the taxi was awash with its own internal weather system and the crowd pushed and craned their necks to see how it was done. After a while, water started to seep out from under the taxi, wetting the cobbles and soaking the soft, bejewelled slippers that some of the women wore. Exclamations of dismay mixed with the murmuring, and the crowd began to filter off into the open doorway where Jean stood, in the parody of a doorman, complete with top hat.

When most of them had gone, Penelope went up to the taxi and shone her light into the streaming windows. Little frogs hopped about among the greenery and the woman dummy had a mess of yellow eggy liquid on her lap which shocked Penelope and made her briefly nauseous.

Nearby, Rolf continued his lecture to a bemused couple. The man was elderly and had a monocle and the woman was fat and overdressed. Rolf was delighting in his role as scandalmonger.

'The Erotic is a sumptuous ceremony in a tunnel,' he chanted in a declamatory voice. 'The Erotic is the liberation of desire from the chains of morality. The Erotic is the imagination of the child in the body of the man.'

'And what about the body of the woman?' muttered Penelope, not loud enough for Rolf to hear.

'The loved one is the encounter with the Absolute,' he went on. 'The Erotic will tear down the repressions of Capital and Class!' But the couple had moved off.

'You can shut up now. They've gone,' said Penelope to Rolf, who was looking up to the dark night sky for further inspiration.

'They were suitably rebuked, were they not?' he asked. His inane, schoolboy grin reminded her of Jean and she woke up from the hazy romantic mood of the walk to find herself in a cold fury with Rolf.

'Tell me,' she said, 'why did you leave me with Alain and Jean today instead of bringing me here to display my own work?'

Rolf was about to speak but a voice came from the building calling his name.

'I shall be back in a moment. Wait for me.'

So she waited, abandoned as usual by Rolf, who had more important things to do. This was exactly what she'd been saying to someone a while ago. Who was it? Suzanne! She had forgotten about Suzanne. She was supposed to meet her. Penelope hurried out into the street again but it was deserted. She was furious at her own stupidity. What was the time now? Perhaps Suzanne was already inside. Maybe Tristan had come along earlier and found her and now they were in there together?

She walked back across the courtyard. The taxi, once again benighted, loomed like a black whale with glassy eyes. The water gushed on, running into the drains. Standing by the door was D'Argent.

'Where have you been?' Penelope blurted out.

'Walking.' D'Argent looked insubstantial in the moonlight and his voice was soft and strange. His shoulders were hunched and he had turned up the collar of his usually immaculate jacket.

'Penelope, please. Wait. I am afraid of so many people.'

This was a new and unknown D'Argent.

'But surrealism is more than just you; more than any of us.' She hoped she was using the right words; every shade of meaning was important and her French was still fairly blunt.

'The exhibition will be misunderstood. Once again our philosophy of freedom will be mocked by those whose chains are the heaviest.'

'You mean,' said Penelope, 'you are afraid of looking like a fool.'

'It is true. Pride is my greatest failing.'

This rare chance to see D'Argent emotionally naked, as it were, was fascinating. He did indeed look very crestfallen. She tried to rally his spirits.

'The exhibition will be a huge success. I'm sure it will.'

'They will laugh,' said D'Argent, staring at the ground and kicking his shoes like a shy little boy.

'Well then, they'll have a thoroughly good time and thank you for it.'

Finally, D'Argent looked up and smiled at her. It reminded her of Suzanne so forcefully that she was confused for a moment. Were they related in some way?

'Of course you are right,' he said. 'Let us go in. May I have the pleasure of escorting the creator of the Marvellous Teacup?' He offered his arm.

'Is that what they are calling it?'

'Do you have a name for it?'

'No,' said Penelope, 'I only made it this afternoon.'

'Good, because Rolf has come up with a title for the work and I think you will like it.'

As they stepped inside the building, Penelope was glad of the steadying support of D'Argent's arm because they were plunged into total blackness. There was no light except for a far-off glow from a group holding torches. Penelope fumbled for her light and switched it on then scanned her surroundings like a miner entering a new cave. They were in a narrow, seemingly endless corridor and along one wall, set at more or less regular intervals, were draped or decorated figures standing in stiff, doll-like poses. They were all shop mannequins.

'Here, this is Rolf's woman,' said D'Argent, who had no light but clasped Penelope's wrist gently and directed her torch to the blank eyes and exaggerated lashes of the first mannequin. Penelope ran the torch down the length of its body and then up again.

The dummy had a horse's tail and wore ankle socks and button-bar shoes like a schoolgirl. A man's tie was knotted around her neck and it hung low between the bare breasts of the torso. On her head was a wide-brimmed hat piled with bread rolls, bird's wings and spherical objects, plus a plumber's plunger.

D'Argent's arm slipped away and he melted into the darkness. She was alone. The figures regarded her. They were all female. What kind of nightmare was this? Penelope crept along in the darkness, afraid that they would come to life and grab her as she went past.

One dummy had a cage around the head, with glistening celluloid fish flicking in the air draughts and a mixture of animal fur and wooden clothes pegs around the throat forming a collar. The rest of the body was nude except for a G-string hung with thin chains from which jewels hung. When she stooped closer to see, the jewels turned out to be mounted on small tear-shaped mirrors, and Penelope was confronted by her own wide-open eyes staring at the nullified sex of the dummy.

One mannequin appeared to be wearing a man's jacket and Penelope went to it hoping for a change to this relentless procession of female anatomy on display. But this dummy, although untidily dressed in a man's jacket, shirt and tie, and wearing heavy men's shoes, was naked at the crotch. All that was added to the nub of the artificial female pudendum was the illegible signature of the artist, scrawled in ink.

Penelope thought about turning around and leaving. The parade sickened her but the excesses of the evening had made her brain soft and muddy and she could not get a firm grasp on her rational mind. She just knew that she didn't belong here and that it was not a good place. She felt unsafe and ashamed without knowing why, and she pulled the collars of her jacket together. It was exactly the gesture that she had noticed Suzanne make that time in Le Parisien and the sight of Suzanne, frail and nervous, flashed vividly in front of her. What would she say to all this? Perhaps together they could have laughed and stumbled along, arm in arm, giggly with wine. Penelope tried to conjure again the strong, wholesome ridicule they had poured on the iron with nails, but here she felt overwhelmed.

'What does it all mean, Suzanne?' said Penelope, out loud to herself.

'Penelope, is that you?'

It was Jean; the last person Penelope wanted to see at that moment.

'Yes, I'm here.'

Jean came bounding up and took her hand. 'Here is *mon amour*. Let me introduce you,' and he took her to a mannequin swathed in white with a cowl on her head which was topped with dead leaves.

When Penelope shone her light at the model's face she saw that under the hood the head was covered closely in a black leather mask and that the eyes were replaced by glittering zippers, shut tight.

'Jean, I have to go home. I'm not feeling well.' She dropped her head in her hands and her torch tumbled to the floor.

'Come, come. Here, I will hold you just for a moment.'

Jean clasped her, quite tenderly, and she felt his hot breath next to her ear. She allowed herself to abandon the weight of her head against his shoulder but then Jean's hands began to rove, stroking her sides and squeezing her breasts, and before she knew it his lips had fixed onto hers and he was forcing his tongue into her mouth.

She pushed him away and ran towards the lights ahead where the space finally opened out into a large, low-ceilinged room mercifully full of people. In the centre was a burning brazier next to a small pool of dirty water. There was a double bed with brass railings in each corner of the room. She stood still, breathing hard like a hunted animal reaching safety. She looked around desperately and located D'Argent then made her way towards him with the vague idea of seeking his protection.

A curious smell in the room caught the back of her throat. Underfoot, the floor was uneven and at each step something crunched beneath her boots. Penelope tried to follow the beams of the other lights to see what it was but most lights were pointing at the ceiling. Here was the source of the acrid smell: countless dusty coal sacks, grimy and bulging. Penelope was afraid they might fall on her head but the entire roof was covered in these pendulous egg-shaped bags and there was no escape.

Gradually the chattering died down and music could be heard but it was brief and unnaturally speeded up. The distorted music was quickly replaced by unnerving laughter, going on and on in hysterical cycles and echoing around the room. D'Argent lifted his head attentively and Penelope remembered a line from his book about Natalia: 'I shall never hear her unearthly laughter in that prison for the gifted' (he meant the insane asylum). D'Argent's expression was that of a connoisseur judging the quality of the sound as if it were a fine wine.

Next came a cockerel's crow and to Penelope's astonishment, since she had assumed it was part of the recording, a bird materialised in a flurry of feathers. Then, into a spotlight, hastily created by someone holding aloft a light on the end of a pole, came a wild, dark-haired woman wearing only a loose white shirt.

The woman swooped down to pick up the cockerel and then pirouetted towards one of the beds. She leapt onto the bed and tumbled around, still holding the cockerel which squawked with fright. Then she released the bird and knelt up on the bed. She leant back, and tore open her shirt to show her bloodied breasts beneath. Had she scratched herself, wondered Penelope, or was this the result of the cockerel's struggles? Then the performer climbed down into the shallow pool and curled up in a ball, motionless. There was complete, stunned silence until D'Argent began the applause. The clapping and laughing went on for some time until the tension was purged from the startled but delighted spectators.

Penelope spied a door at the back and slipped through the crowd into another room. This was the room with the Cabinet of the Marvellous and she eagerly sought out the familiarity of her own homely teacup. She remembered buying it from Monoprix in the first week she arrived in Paris. It was prominently displayed at waist height in the front of the glass case. The spoon was placed, oddly, inside the cup instead of resting on the saucer, but Penelope let that pass. Then she saw the handwritten label.

'Penelope Furr: *From One Hand to Another*.'

She felt her gorge rise.

Chapter Ten

Outside the gallery, Penelope cleaned herself up with her handkerchief then threw it in the gutter to hide the pool of vomit. She looked up and noticed a woman a little way off who was wearing a red coat and leaning against the wall smoking. A man went up to the woman but she shook her head and he moved on. Could it be her? Penelope started to walk and then broke into a run when Suzanne smiled at her in recognition.

'Don't tell me you've been here since quarter to ten?' said Penelope.

'No, I've been here and there. How was the exhibition?'

'Tonight was the worst night of my life. If you could see what was in there.'

'I can't go in.' Suzanne stiffened and moved slightly back.

'No, of course. Tristan might have arrived by now. Look, why don't we walk to the river? I need some fresh air. Unless you are too cold.'

'No,' said Suzanne, 'I'm not cold.'

They started the long walk along Faubourg Saint-Honoré. It was quiet in this wealthy residential area, apart from the knots of women clustered around the café doors waiting for the men to come out. Some looked like they might be from Les Halles, sent by their madams to tout for business in the richer quarter.

One of the women called out to Suzanne as if she recognised her. Suzanne walked on, giving no sign.

'Do you know her?' asked Penelope.

'I used to.'

Penelope expected one of Suzanne's abrupt, closed silences to follow but instead she went on.

'When I first came to Paris, in 1926, I worked the streets when I was hungry. But now I have a daughter, and I shall make sure she never has to do it.'

'A daughter?'

Suzanne smiled. 'Her name is Angélique. She is with my father and grandmother, in Lille. She ... she believes that I am her sister. My mother and father raised her as their own. It was better that way.'

'Better?'

'For her. For me. I had no choice, Penelope. I will tell her one day. She is so unhappy since *Maman* died. She has lost a mother too.'

'But Maurice said you had married a rich man.'

'What? Did Maurice say he had seen me?'

'No, it's just what Rolf told me he'd said.'

Suzanne had stopped walking. She put her hand on Penelope's sleeve. 'Penelope, promise me that you will not tell anyone that you have seen me, except D'Argent – and only then if he swears to secrecy. Do you understand?'

'Fine, whatever you like,' sighed Penelope. 'Nothing makes any sense today. Maybe the whole day is a dream and tomorrow I'll wake up and start it for real. Are you real?'

'More or less.'

Penelope laughed and they went on.

'So, tell me some more about the exhibition,' said Suzanne.

'It was ghastly. It made me sick.'

'Sick?'

'Yes, literally. First there was a taxi with rain inside. That was rather fun, actually. Then a long dark tunnel with shop dummies dressed like ... well, dressed like men imagine women when they are thinking about nothing but sex. Or cruelty. Or both.'

'Such as?'

'Never mind. But your daughter should see it. Surrealism has never before shown the true extent of its contempt for women.'

'But the surrealists worship women,' cried Suzanne passionately.

'What? You mean all that rubbish about Elective Love?'

'Perhaps it is different now, but this was what drew me to ... to seek them out at the beginning.'

'But Suzanne, if they worship women as you say, why did Rolf make a public joke out of me today?'

'How did he do that?'

'He advertised me as a whore! Oh Suzanne, what am I going to do?'

Suzanne put her slim arm around Penelope's shoulders and steered her wordlessly away from the road. Although Penelope knew that others, even on a night as cold as this, would seek out the cover of darkness for entirely different reasons, Suzanne seemed to know instinctively that she needed the comfort of being hidden, out of the streets.

At a fountain in a park, they found a bench under a dim lamp and sat down. Neither spoke. Penelope wondered where Rolf was now. Had he even realised she was missing? What would she say to him about that demeaning name for her fur cup?

'What are you thinking about?' asked Suzanne.

'There's a dream I have sometimes where I'm being chased by a tiger,' Penelope said.

'Does it catch you?'

'No, it tries to seduce me.' Penelope made a face at Suzanne who broke out laughing. It was infectious and by the time their laughter had subsided, Penelope had lost the need to cry.

'I will tell her,' said Suzanne, 'I will tell Angélique: beware of men in striped fur.'

'And men who paint pictures.'

'And write poems.'

'And dress up shop dummies like tarts!' Penelope shouted triumphantly into the night.

They settled into the silence of the night again.

'I once saw some tigers, when I was a little girl,' said Penelope. 'It was at London Zoo. It was the same summer that I learnt to swim and Mother told me that tigers were excellent swimmers. I remember imagining how exciting it would be to ride a tiger as it swam in the water. "One day," I said to her, "I'm going to swim with tigers." "Then you had better turn into a shark, Penelope," she said, "because tigers eat little girls for breakfast."'

'Not all tigers are killers,' said Suzanne.

'Have you ever known one who wasn't?'

'I thought I knew one once.'

'What happened?' asked Penelope.

'He betrayed me,' said Suzanne.

'I'm sorry. Who was it?'

'Come on, let's go to Place Dauphine. I will tell you there.'

Suzanne led her silently through the Tuileries and across Pont des Arts, then along by the river and up again. Penelope had never been into Place Dauphine before. It was eerie. The gravel hissed under their feet and the two rows of windows on the buildings either side seemed to be regarding each other, and them, with shy but attentive glances through the thin branches of the trees. They sat on a bench at the far end looking at the illuminated stone lions guarding the Palais de Justice.

'D'Argent spoke to me today,' said Penelope, when it was plain that Suzanne was not going to say anything yet. 'Really spoke to me, I mean, not as usual when it's like the king speaking to the grubby peasantry. He loved my teacup. Oh, but of course you don't know about that, do you? Today I found some fur and covered a teacup with it. The boys loved it. They were so delighted you'd think they'd made it themselves.'

'So what went wrong?'

Penelope got up and stood beside one of the thin trees. 'Rolf exhibited my teacup. And he called it *From One Hand to Another*.'

'I see. But perhaps Rolf meant that the teacup was a gift?'

'A gift?'

'Yes, something you had imagined and made, and given to the world.'

'But you didn't see the exhibition.'

She came back to sit down next to Suzanne on the bench. 'First there was the taxi, then the line of whores to choose from, and finally a room at the end with empty beds. People were paying to pretend to visit a *bordel*. Why don't they just go and have a look at the real thing? I hear that at the Sphinx you can bring the whole family. The children sit with their mothers and gawp at the naked ladies, and then Daddy chooses one and pops off upstairs for a while.'

'I can see what you mean about the exhibition, but why would Rolf describe you as a prostitute?'

'Because he saw me earlier with Jean and Alain.'

'Jean *and* Alain?'

'Yes, yes, I know how it sounds.'

'And Rolf says he loves you?'

'Constantly. But we are all supposed to be living according to D'Argent's religion of freedom.'

'Do you not want to be free?'

'Free to go with anyone I want? No. I love Rolf. He gave me my freedom and showed me I could really paint.'

'No one can give you freedom. You have to take that for yourself.'

Penelope smiled. 'And who made you so wise?'

'It was the man I promised to tell you about. I used to come here with him.'

'Who, then?' asked Penelope.

'It was D'Argent. We were in love. I met him on the street. No. Not like that. I was on my way to the hairdresser. He took me to a café and we talked. I knew of him, of course; I had read his poems. But I didn't tell him that. It was a strange time for me. I had run away from home, just like you, Penelope, and I didn't always eat every day, or have a place to stay. I suppose I was sometimes – how can I put it? – not in the real world. I used to see things and hear things. He was kind to me.'

'And what about Tristan?' asked Penelope.

'Why do you keep mentioning him?'

'Because you used to be married to him, of course.'

'You think I am Suzanne Müller?' Suzanne's eyes were wide open in surprise.

'Aren't you? Then who are you?'

'D'Argent knew me as Natalia.'

'The girl in his book? But she's locked up in an asylum.'

'In a way, yes, the person she was is locked away.'

Suzanne turned to look directly at Penelope and the lamplight cast a pale glow over her face. 'But I am her. I am Natalia.'

Chapter Eleven

S uzanne ran as fast as she could and Penelope's voice, calling out from the darkness, grew fainter. The cobbles on the way out of Place Dauphine punished her feet. Briefly cursing the arrogance of Henri IV up on his horse, she turned right at Pont Neuf and went down the steps to the river's edge, on the Quai de la Megisserie. She glanced around like a hunted animal then ran alongside the river, feeling the coarse sandy surface of the pathway through the soles of her detestable shoes.

A dull, wet bulk stopped her mid-stride. Instinctively, she knew it was death. She recoiled, panting. Yes. A man, lying on his back, bloated and inflated with moisture. His arms lay loose at his side with the eerie stillness of a body absent of life and soul, emotion and speech. The horror of it was paralysing. She stared at the dim shape in case it revived. After a while, she realised she was watching to make sure that it didn't. A picture from her dreams imposed itself on the corpse: her mother's disfigured, screaming face. Suzanne put her head in her hands and turned away.

She began to run again and when she glanced back the shadows had reclaimed the body of the man so it was difficult to be sure if he had been there at all. She hoped not, for his sake, but if she had imagined him, it meant that she had returned to that person of before when hunger and sleeplessness had conjured up so many ghosts. It was not what she wanted. She had Angélique to think of now. What would she be doing on a Friday night? Probably she was planning to sneak out to play with her friends in the morning. Suzanne enjoyed her daughter's rebellious nature and cultivated it in ways that a sister might, but a mother could not.

Was she mad, then? Was she *seeing things* again? Once, Suzanne had believed that her mind was broken, having been told so many times. Even D'Argent's book, apparently, had come to the same conclusion. But really it was a case of knowing when to dance and listening out for the music.

She had been running for a long time and needed to stop and catch her breath. She went to the edge of the water and gazed up at the silent night sky above the lead-grey water of the Seine. Quiet boats passed and stroked the water intimately, which roused to the touch of their bows. She calmed. La Megisserie: years ago there must have been a place here where the hides of animals were turned into leather. She too had been stripped of the skin of her disguise, because Penelope knew her identity now. She started to run again and reached the steps to Pont Notre Dame.

The last of the concrete steps was higher than the others and she stubbed her toe, fell to one knee and then onto her hands.

'Are you all right?' A voice. An English voice with a strange upward lift to it.

It was a young man, silver-haired under the streetlamp, which her eyes translated into a blonde colour matching her own. He put his hand gently under her arm and they rose together.

'Thank you,' she said.

He was slender, with gentle eyes. Kind eyes.

'Such a beautiful city,' he said, 'Is it your home?'

'It used to be, yes. Why have you come here?' she asked.

'To learn,' he said. 'Where are you off to now?'

'I don't know.'

'When I'm lost I follow the North Star.' He pointed over the river. 'Do you see? Find the Plough, then go down. It's at the tip of the tail of the little bear.'

'Yes, I see.'

'Bye, then.' He blinked his soft eyes and disappeared.

She stood for a while, watching him fade into the night. She had felt extraordinarily safe with him. Like when she was very small and her Scottish grandmother had come to visit. She was to call her Granny Campbell, she said, as she sat on Suzanne's bed last thing at night. Then she kissed her forehead and smoothed the covers. Angélique slept in that room now with the red and sapphire-blue curtains that Granny Campbell had made during her one and only visit to meet the baker who had captured her daughter's heart and ended her singing career.

Suzanne often felt at peace in the streets of Paris, especially Paris at night. And sometimes she would be given the gift of a caring stranger, like the young man with his restful manner, or Penelope, the English girl, who she could never see again. Being with Penelope at the table at Le Parisien and on the bench tonight in the *place* had given her the same feeling as when Granny Campbell had said, 'Sleep, now, Susanna, sleep'.

She relocated the star in the clear velvet sky, and began to walk, speaking her spells for good luck and protection out loud as she went: 'Granny Campbell, Penelope Furr, North Star.'

She was on the Rue de Rivoli already. Seeing the Tour Saint-Jacques pierced her with remorse. He had loved it so. But the entrances to the Métro were hers; the beginnings of stories about magical caverns and worlds under the ground. The Hôtel de Ville was right here, with its gorgeous, exciting fan of glass spread wide with iron spokes and, beneath it, glowing, jewel-like beads on the walls at the start of the descent. Her favourite, the Porte Dauphine (that name again), was a long way off and it was the one she loved the most because it was enclosed: a safe, hidden entrance to anywhere her imagination could take her. Why not go there and escape? No, Suzanne. That was then and this is now. You must protect yourself.

She continued on to the Marais, and went back to her hotel room where she packed up her things. It was impossible, now, to stay: if she was found, they would send her back.

In the corridor, Suzanne found some wonderfully sensible women's ankle boots. They had laces all the way up the front and were only just a little too large. The chestnut leather was beautifully soft and very expensive, so they wouldn't be missed. She carried them down the hallway, tiptoeing her way out.

Still faithfully following the North Star, she made her way to the Gare du Nord. She stared at the information board and there it was: the *Etoile du Nord* on platform two. The North Star had transformed into a train to carry her onwards and away. With supreme confidence she boarded, just as the whistle blew, and walked through the richly furnished Pullman carriages. She soon found the baggage car where she curled up into a ball and threw an empty sack over her head.

She dreamt that a lemur sat comfortably on her left shoulder. Its elongated claws pressed gently into her face, marking her cheeks and lips and gently pulling down the rims of her eyes.

Morning woke her. They had arrived. She slipped quickly into the next carriage and alighted, pleased by the stability of her newest footwear. Outside the station there was a smell of pink ointment, just like her mother had used on her cuts and grazes when she was little. She felt safe again. The early daylight was even and open; there were no stories in the streets and buildings here. Amsterdam Centraal, said the sign, but it did not speak out loud to her. Instead she heard the words inside her head, in her own voice. This was a good place.

An old man in a shabby coat walked past and a package fell to the ground behind him.

'Wait!' she shouted. 'You have dropped something.'

He turned around and looked up. He was half a head shorter than her at least, and his face was creased and dry.

She handed him the package which was surprisingly heavy, about the size of a small suitcase and wrapped in sacking secured with leather straps. The weight of it pulled his shoulders and head even lower, and his white beard threatened to touch the ground.

'Shall I carry that a little way for you?' asked Suzanne.

'Your kindness is God's gift to me,' he said in a rasping, papery voice.

'Yes,' she replied, taking back the parcel.

They walked slowly to a bridge over a straight, narrow river. Of course, she thought, this is a canal.

'It's a canal,' she said.

'Your perception is God's gift.'

She began to wonder if this was all the old man ever said and whether he was simple.

'But,' he said, pausing for breath, 'only a fool would be surprised to find a canal in Amsterdam.'

Suzanne looked at him and saw the mischief in his smile. She laughed.

'I am Suzanne, sir.'

'Isaac Room.' He briefly doffed his little skullcap.

A gull flew overhead, screaming, and she looked up then back to her new friend. They continued.

'Where are you staying, Suzanne?'

'Nowhere. I have nowhere,' she said quietly.

'Then you shall come to my home. For this day and the next, you are my daughter.'

They had crossed the bridge and were faced with a main road full of bicycles going in different directions.

Her thoughts followed the contrary, interlinking paths of the traffic until finally she said, in a very formal way, 'Your generosity is God's gift, and I am very grateful.'

'Good,' he said. 'That's good.'

She looked at the mild old man and saw at once that his eyes, which were crinkled at the sides by the smiling expression of his face, were gentle and kind.

Chapter Twelve

During the night after the exhibition Penelope dreamt again about an animal chasing her in the city. She could hear its paws hit the pavement with a rattle and a clatter like a dog's claws, but this was a bigger animal, a heavier animal. The rhythm of the paws was slow and lazy: an easy, galloping stride. Her legs began to weaken and ache and finally to seize up altogether despite her panic. Glancing back, she saw the tiger's orange stripes and huge haunches getting closer and closer. The first strike from its claws ripped through the fabric at the back of her shin and she fell forwards. The tiger pinioned her to the ground. Its jaws were around the nape of her neck and she could feel whiskers near her ears. Her legs were being roughly parted from behind. Then she woke up.

She gulped in some air then closed her eyes tightly to go back and investigate what had been about to happen, but the dream was gone. So she rolled over and sought out the comfort of Rolf's naked back. He smelt of turpentine and his hands were twitching and flexing: he was making art in his sleep again. What forms might he create, she wondered, if some malleable material was placed in his restless hands while he slept? D'Argent would acclaim it as the newest, most direct route to the creation of an object from a dream; a genuine shortcut to the unconscious.

So it was not the dream of the tiger but a fanciful plan to harness Rolf's restless hands during the hours of darkness that

Penelope thought about as she tried to get back to sleep. Years ago, Rolf had played around taking rubbings of rough wood or walls and called it *frottage*; well, she would invent *sleepage* or some other silly name and then maybe D'Argent would write about her in his next article. But no, she mustn't get sucked in. Surrealism was the creed she lived by and she would not reduce it to a competition for D'Argent's favour. But what about her fur cup with that appalling name? D'Argent had approved of that. Penelope felt a wave of nausea returning with the thought of it and decided to postpone the problem for another time.

She thought, instead, of that strange woman Suzanne who had claimed to be D'Argent's Natalia. The very fact that she had run off straight after making this outrageous statement seemed to prove that it was a lie, or some weird joke. Penelope tried to recall the details of D'Argent's portrait of the exceptional, inspirational woman he had met and then abandoned all those years ago. The make-up was right – that same smeary kohl around the eyes – and Suzanne's peculiar gnomic remarks. There was also her habit of appearing as if Penelope had conjured her up, and her maddening unworldliness. Could it be true?

Penelope watched the lights of a passing car move across the ceiling; their windows were curtainless. She was awake now, and a headache was taking hold of her temples. She went to fetch a glass of tepid water from the bathroom and allowed the night sky and crescent moon to detain her. The view from the window was obscured by the tall Scots pine which grew, unclaimed by any of the building's inhabitants, inside the railings that separated the house from the street. There had been a tree outside her bedroom at home, an oak, and family lore told a story of her being discovered by her mother at four years old about to jump from the windowsill onto a high branch – a leap of some five feet which, if she had not been found and prevented in time, might well have ended her life before it had really begun. She went back to bed.

She woke up the next day with a sore throat and a disgusting taste in her mouth. Rolf was in the next room clattering about and muttering to himself. She grabbed one of his shirts from the floor, rode out a brief wave of dizziness, and then remembered Suzanne running off into the night. She would try to find her later.

Rolf was tying up a white laundry bag with string.

'Oh,' she said, 'I have some clothes that need washing.'

'Good morning,' he said. 'This is not laundry. Jean has taken the heads off the leftover mannequins. He will not need them.'

She padded over. 'Let me see.'

Rolf undid the string and she looked into the sack where several bald heads with high cheekbones and heavily lashed, Marlene-Dietrich eyes jostled together. A dry sweat went over her. Then, a feeling of protectiveness.

'Can I have one?'

'A head?' He tipped them out onto the table. 'Of course.' He went to fill the kettle.

She lined them up and selected the least dented one, then returned the rest to the cotton sack. They were light to handle, being made of papier-mâché.

'Here.' Rolf gave her a mug of black coffee and kissed her, wrinkling up his nose at her foul breath.

He left with the sack of female heads, bumping them on the treads of the steep staircase as he went. She winced at each dull thud, then heard Rolf slam the door with characteristic force.

She turned to the salvaged head.

'Well, what have you got to say for yourself?' she asked it.

No answer.

Penelope dressed, then tucked the head into the crook of her arm. She needed to talk to another woman, almost any woman, after the sting of Rolf's name for her fur cup and Suzanne's desertion last night. It would have to be Una. There was no one else.

At the last minute, she grabbed a bath towel and wrapped the head with it. Una often let her bathe when she visited, since Rolf's was a cold-water flat.

Una was alone and welcomed her warmly, but Penelope realised immediately that their relationship was too distant for the confidences she had planned to share. If only she knew where Suzanne was staying. Might someone know? But Penelope would never divulge Suzanne's secret identity even if, and especially if, it was a fantasy.

'I thought you might let me have a wash.' Penelope indicated her striped, slightly grubby towel.

'Of course. But let me find you a new towel.'

Una went off and Penelope wandered over to the table, littered with empty bottles and the crystallised remains of unfinished drinks.

In a cleared space, there were some small cut-out pictures from magazines of naked women in balletic, active poses arranged around a golden cup with occult signs on it. Penelope remembered that Una had once been a dancer.

'This is an unusual subject for an atheist. Is it Jean's?'

'No. My own. A collage.'

'You are an artist?'

'No.' Una tossed back her silky blonde hair. 'But I make pictures.'

Penelope sighed. She was too tired to begin to explain how wrong that statement was and simply accepted the plump yellow towel.

'I think it will be a wonderful piece,' she said. 'Do you have a title?'

'No. Not yet.'

'Well, watch out with that. Someone might give it a name you don't want.'

'Like your cup?'

Una was clearly more observant than Penelope had given her credit for. She was about to reply when Alain appeared, barefoot, in a silk robe.

Una turned to him and her face lit up. Penelope waited until they had been kissing for a while, feeling awkward and out of place, then sloped off to the bathroom.

It was plain, tiled in white, and untroubled by the surrealist outrages of funeral crêpe and black leather shapes mounted on the other walls of the apartment by Jean. There were no horses' tails here and Penelope, comforted by the blankness, let her mind clear too. She placed the mannequin's head, still in its towel, on the floor and turned on the hot tap.

Lowering herself into the water was blissful and her headache dissolved with the steam. She relaxed all the muscles that had stored up the struggles and shocks of the day before and let the heat renew her. Her legs were bent and she stared, vacantly, at her vertical thighs, topped by the narrowness of her knees and, at the base, her pubic hair, which seemed to float like seaweed. She imagined her legs as massive rocks standing in the sea with a narrow, perilous passageway between. Then they became erect veined penises leaning towards each other in mutual attraction. She quickly brought her eyes back into focus and began planning colours, scale, background. The painting would be large, monumental, masculine.

Then Jean walked in.

'Ah ha,' he said. 'A strange creature has arrived in the bath, from the window? From the plughole?'

'From over the road. Now get out, I don't need an audience.'

'You'll be ready for me soon, though. It is into my hands you'll come next, I hope.'

She splashed him and he retreated, laughing.

What had she been thinking about? A boat, was it?

I'll cover the head with scarves or maybe feathers, or necklaces, she thought, as the water was draining away. Didn't someone say that her mother's face had been wrapped up after a violent death? But who had said it?

That evening Penelope was uncertain if more wine was good for her but it seemed to be the only thing to do; her headache had returned and was immovable. They were at a different place (meetings at Café de Flore were weeknights only) and Penelope was fascinated by the wealthy, expatriate crowd. She hoped that Ernest Hemingway would be here and planned to introduce herself then attack his love of bullfighting with arguments derived from her sympathy with horses. No animal deserved to be tortured for public entertainment.

'Will Hemingway be here?'

'I don't know,' shouted Rolf who was beside her as they entered the raucous crush of people. 'But I hear James Joyce is in town. Ah, there is Alain.'

Rolf put on a spurt of energy and left her stranded in the crowd. She followed his distinctive white hair, fighting through the mass of bodies with her shoulders.

When she caught up, there was no room left at Rolf's table but Gabriel had claimed one nearby.

'I got you some wine,' he said, offering her a place to sit.

Gabriel's behaviour since the party had been increasingly obvious. The others made fun of his infatuation with her and laughed at the way his amorous affliction caused him to become speechless or stutter in her presence. Rolf, in particular, watched with a fascinated, almost hungry gaze, as if the whole thing awoke in him new and compelling thoughts and possibilities.

Rolf sought complications of every kind. His art was motivated by the need for novelty and exploration and nothing he did was ordinary, or custom-bound. Even his clothing was a series of complicated interlocking layers: vests with different sleeves, scarves and ties competing for prominence around his neck, short socks outside his trousers and long ones inside. The only time he craved blankness and monotony was the time he spent sitting in a darkened room waiting for a picture to form in his mind. That was how he began any new work and even before this ritualised process in the dark he would for a time simply not see Penelope. Away from the studio, however, she often found that Rolf was watching her.

'How are you?' asked Gabriel, boldly turning to look at her. 'Are you well? Do you need to eat? Some water, perhaps, with your wine?'

Penelope threw back half the glass of red and felt immediately euphoric. She smiled back at Gabriel, dear sweet Gabriel, and on impulse, threw her arms around his neck. She pressed her face against his reddening cheek then placed an experimental kiss on his lips but he was too shocked to respond. She laughed and broke away, turning back to her drink. She caught sight of Rolf staring at her with his piercing blue eyes. Rolf bent his head to say something into Alain's ear. Alain looked over at her and she quickly dropped her gaze. She scanned the bar instead, lighting upon a group of noisy Americans who were teaching someone to dance.

Gabriel, belatedly reacting to his dream come true, moved closer to her and, in doing so, sent his coat and scarf to the floor. In his inept attempt to retrieve them, he managed to knock over both their drinks. He began apologising. He couldn't stop apologising.

Once she had mopped up the table and her skirt (which, luckily, was red too), Rolf arrived and placed two new drinks in front of them. He said nothing, but smiled then turned to rejoin Alain as if returning to the front seat of a theatrical performance.

Then Jean appeared and slid in next to her, the customary arm around her waist. Penelope looked from Gabriel to Jean on either side and then across at Rolf and Alain, both attending to her every move, and felt like a queen with her courtiers. How should she respond to this idea about her being passed between the hands of her fellow artists? To be angry was pointless, so she had better go along with it. It was only a joke, after all.

She lifted her glass. 'From one hand to another,' she said and took a mouthful before giving it to Jean.

He drank with glee, then gestured with the wine towards Rolf, who acknowledged it with a slight nod of the head.

Then the dancers appeared on the stage and Penelope allowed herself to merge into the sounds and sights of the nightclub, buoyed up by the music and the approval of these gifted men, all of whom appeared to want her. Each one was worth ten of those wooden idiots her mother was always arranging to meet her in the weeks after she came out. And she would make lots of new art. Then they would value her even more.

Chapter Thirteen

Paris, March 1938

The spring blossom was out and Penelope was once again in Place Dauphine, hoping to find Suzanne there. She went at least once a week, just in case. Today, the church bells were ringing. It seemed that they rang for her freedom because here, unlike in Oxfordshire, she had no obligation to go to Sunday service and suffer their vicar droning on, then continuing to talk through the roast lunch he came to eat with them at home afterwards. She had learnt to keep silent at these meals, not trusting her temper if she were to start to express her opposition to his views on 'a woman's place, as God has decreed'.

She knew, however, that she had absorbed some of the morality of the church and what faced her now was adultery of a kind, because Alain was courting her, in plain sight of Rolf and everyone, with gifts and bouquets. He wrote poems addressed to her, converting bizarre surrealist images of animals and plants into devastating passionate declarations. Her daydreams, conjured and nurtured by his poetry, returned again and again to that moment in the studio exactly two months ago, only this time neither Rolf nor Jean was present and Alain's hands did not leap away from her body at one look. Quite the opposite.

Alain was a restful companion. His melancholy moods were like a fragrant scent on the air which calmed her and at other times his seriousness amused her. His fragility made her feel strong. Unlike Rolf, Alain seemed unfinished as a personality; he could be broken by a harsh word and he believed in love as a force of complete transformation. He was offering her a passionate French romance, complete with hearts and roses.

What could she do?

Well, Suzanne was not here to help, although Penelope felt this strange, quiet triangle of Paris to be soaked in her unique spirit. It was as though she was watching from inside the dim interior of one of the restaurants, like a hare at cover in bracken.

Penelope came out of her reverie on Pont Neuf, which roared with traffic. She had to finish *Her Mother's Face* today: the wrapped-up mannequin head. It had not taken her long to recall that it was Suzanne who had told her about not being permitted to see the injuries to her mother and how her imagination had supplied horrors instead. Now, the work was beginning to represent Suzanne's withholding of herself and their nascent friendship. Penelope knew that she was motivated by anger with Suzanne as much as the drive to create art. But she would keep the title. Where could she get a black scarf?

On the Rue de Seine there were troops of churchgoers in hats and modest dress, making her feel like a streetwalker in her stained painting smock and Turkish trousers. She fought to think well of herself and throw off these antediluvian ideas of female purity. In truth, though, it was loyalty that she prized above all else and she feared that giving in to Alain would be disloyal to Rolf.

He had never said as much. Their partnership, so extravagantly physical at first, was now a pragmatic alliance between artists and making love was a realignment rather than an encounter, an invasion or a surrender. He supported her, but left her to work alone. Alain, by contrast, adored her. He would sit gazing at her as she worked, holding a pen lazily in his hand. His presence was loose and easy in comparison to Rolf's aggressive drive to create and make and know. And, unlike Rolf, he talked constantly about his feelings.

'I think I shall fall apart,' he once said. 'My heart has been sliced in two by your refusal to love me. I shall break into pieces, bit by bit.'

Penelope had laughed at that, but at the same time it made her feel potent and superior. With Rolf she always felt young and naive.

She turned right, into Rue Jacob, and soon reached home. There was no sound as she unlocked the door to Rolf's apartment but as she walked in she saw immediately that Alain's coat was on the back of the sofa. And there he was, with Rolf.

They were sitting with photographs and handwritten sheets strewn across the floor at their feet. Rolf cupped the back of Alain's head with his hand and laughed into his eyes. Penelope suddenly realised that this was love. For a moment, she felt jealous of Alain. How ridiculous.

'Come, little one.' Rolf had seen her. 'Look at what we're doing. It will be a book. A book about you.'

Rolf took her hand and she was led, mesmerised as ever by his touch, to view the spread of images and poetry.

She felt Alain's arm arrive very gently around her shoulders.

The next day, Penelope and Rolf went far north of their usual stamping grounds, all the way beyond the Saint-Ouen flea market to visit a jazz bar: Maurice's latest find.

They devoured their *steak frites*, watched by Una, who was reducing, and Maurice, who had been too busy asking about and anticipating the guitarists, fiddle players and singers to order anything. Jazz *manouche* was the music they played here. Penelope kept thinking about the flea markets in the streets around and felt a phantom crawling sensation beneath her blouse. She examined the scruffy carpet for jumping black dots.

Una had tagged along willingly, since Alain needed to work, and it had not occurred to Penelope until they all sat down that Alain's pursuit of her might make Una resentful. It seemed not. She was as sweetly smiling as ever, and Penelope noticed that she was directing all her attention very definitely at Maurice: laughing at his jokes, arranging his clothing.

'Have you finished your collage, Una?' she asked.

'Oh, that,' she replied.

'Here they are.' Maurice had spied some musicians he recognised.

Two men, one with a cigarette hanging from his lip, were getting out guitars and perching on stools at the front of the bar, with the windows to the street behind them. They began to play and Penelope immediately felt better.

A ray of March sunlight found its way between the two guitarists' shoulders and landed on their table. Near where they were sitting was a wooden horse from a carousel, which Penelope had noticed the moment they arrived. It was a white-painted merry thing, kicking out its front leg as it pranced, throwing its head up and to the side in the joy of movement. She reached into her bag for a sketchbook and without a word swivelled in her seat to begin drawing.

The music galloped on and she drew sketch after sketch in a child's style then began on a detailed study, showing how both back hooves were turned upwards.

Rolf went to the bar and, on his way back, peered over her shoulder.

'It's good,' he said.

He did not often praise her work, but the way he retreated and vacated the space around her, or arranged his day by taking her working routine into account, was something she noticed and valued.

'Thank you,' she said and looked tenderly at him.

He offered her the glass of wine in his hand and she smiled. He turned to signal to the waiter for a replacement.

It had been weeks since she had even thought about the horse-leaping-through-a-window project, but suddenly it seemed very urgent to begin it properly. She had the horse, and the dog or jackal with smears of blood where it had sat on the ground. She had the window and the field beyond. But what else was inside the room?

She looked across and lit upon Una's elegant shoes. They were high-heeled boots of an Edwardian style, and added height to her petite frame. Penelope didn't know how Una could walk so far or so easily in them. It had taken more than a quarter of an hour from the Métro to get here, but Una had smoothly matched the men's strides and Penelope's own pace in her trustworthy knee-high, flat boots.

She began to sketch the chair Una sat in and her feminine footwear. Then she combined the two together. Good. She could use this.

'Come on, little one,' called Rolf.

While she had been focused on her sketchpad, Maurice had been dancing with two girls who were with the guitarists. Una and Rolf had abandoned their card game and gone to join in.

After taking one last interior snapshot of the new geography of her horse-leap picture-to-be, she flung down her pencil. She touched the strangely warm head of the carousel horse on her way past and threw herself into the dancing.

She was here. In Paris. An artist at last, with a lover and friends who understood what she wanted because they wanted it too. To create was everything, and everything she had ever hoped it would be.

Penelope and Rolf arrived back home at seven, with aching legs and wide smiles. The only food they could find in the flat was a bag of squashed chocolate eclairs, which were sickly and unsatisfying. After one bite they went in the bin. The unwashed bowls from their breakfast were still on the floor. Penelope went to fill the kettle.

She came back and settled on the sofa next to Rolf who lifted an arm so she could nestle into his shoulder. With the other hand he was going through this morning's prints and dividing them into two piles.

'Una and Maurice were getting on well,' said Penelope, with a yawn.

'It was Maurice who found her in the streets of Berlin. I believe they married, to make it easy for her to come to Paris.'

'Una is married to Maurice?'

'Yes, or Alain. I forget. Jean, maybe.' Rolf's attention was on a shot of her naked back. 'Look, do you see a cello?'

'No, I see the scar from when I was thrown. It was the first time I used spurs. Never again.'

The kettle whistled and she got up to take it off the flame.

Rolf put aside the photographs and stood up. He suddenly seemed fully present.

'I have been talking about you with Alain,' he said.

'About the book?'

'No.'

Penelope spooned in some coffee and filled the cafetière with boiling water.

'I want Alain to move in here, with us,' he said.

'Why?'

'To share our space. To share our lives. Everything. And it would help with the book.'

'But where would he sleep?' asked Penelope, rubbing at the stains in their coffee cups. Rolf was so impractical when it came to household arrangements. There was not room for three in this two-roomed flat.

Rolf stayed her hand as she was about to plunge the coffee and looked pointedly, desperately even, into her eyes.

The penny dropped.

'You mean Alain and me and you would ...?'

'You seem surprised, I thought—'

'Is this what you want? To share me?'

'I want it if you want it.'

Penelope was saved from having to reply by a loud knock on the door.

It was Jean, who had arranged to go with Rolf to see a new photographic paper supplier. Rolf kissed her goodbye and his face was severe. She could not tell if he regretted his proposal or was irritated by her lack of enthusiasm for it.

Penelope sank down to her knees searching for a response to what had just happened, but all she felt was numb and blank.

The smell of coffee seemed to promise an answer but she remained motionless, staring at the dirty, empty breakfast bowls.

Chapter Fourteen

Amsterdam, April 1938

S uzanne was studying her reflection in a shop window. Butterflies landed on her face and covered her mouth and eyelids. Their delicate feet mingled with her eyelashes and explored her half-open lips. There were small birds perching in her hair and she thought she could feel their beaks denting the skin of her forehead, like unwelcome memories pecking at her brain. With a flash of fear she saw that thorny branches were wound around her throat. The brambles had pierced the soft flesh of her neck and she felt the blood dripping down over her clothes. But when she glanced down at her new dress, which was the colour of blood, she was surprised to see that it was completely dry.

Then she stepped back from the glass so that only the butterflies, stuffed birds and artificial branches in the display were visible without the ghostly shape of her reflected face mixed up with them. Restored to reality, she moved along the pavement to examine the other butterflies in the display which were pinned in crowded rows in traditional cases. Poor frail things, she thought. Some of these butterflies might once have flown across an ocean; sometimes resting in the arms of a blue sea wind, sometimes fighting onwards with all the remaining strength of their battered wings. She imagined the waves rearing up beneath, and energy ebbing away. She too had made a long journey to stand here, on the verge of another reckless gamble, near a bridge where the Keizersgracht met Nieuwe Spiegelstraat.

The surrealists were exhibiting just along the road at Galerie Robert and in her hand she clutched a note for Penelope. She stepped out from under the shop awning and sunlight bounced off the water making her eyes hurt. It brought back an image, a horror: a blade slicing an eyeball. She felt the fingers holding open her eye and saw the flash of metal coming near but she couldn't move away. Would there be pain? Or only afterwards? And sight? Surely sight would be lost. Unless, for ever after, everything was cut in two. 'I see a man, cut in half,' D'Argent had written. But surely the cut eye never sees again.

She started to look around greedily. Opening her eyes as wide as she could, she took in the broad, humpbacked bridge ahead and then the grey, padlocked bicycle chain on the black railings in front of her. She devoured the long view towards the Rijksmuseum and then the screw of newspaper on the kerb at her feet. A peculiar-looking bicycle appeared from behind and crossed the bridge. At first she could not work out what was odd about it but then she realised it was at least twice the height of an ordinary bicycle. A black man rode it; perhaps he was Surinamese, like her friend Sammy. How very proud he looked, high up on his homemade vehicle. But how would he ever get down? She imagined him pedalling on and on, day into night, night into day.

The Keizersgracht had well-appointed houses with smoothly painted doors and hanging baskets. Here was the doorway to the gallery; an ordinary-looking house like the rest. She went down and crouched on the sunken steps. Nervously, she turned back to scan the empty street. She even checked the road on the far side of the canal before pushing her fingers through the vertical brass letter box and letting go of the envelope. She heard it drop onto the floor inside then hurried away, like a thief.

Suzanne tried to imagine Penelope's face as she read the note. Penelope would frown at first to see the signature, *Suzanne. Please meet me at the Tuschinski cinema on Saturday at noon,* she had written. *I'm sorry I ran away.* And she was. It was a stupid thing to do after telling Penelope her secret that night in Place Dauphine. But perhaps it had been saying those words out loud that had conjured up this new life, or rather broken a curse and allowed her to live like others did. The young man who had guided her here and Isaac, who had taken her in, were all a result of finally confessing her true identity. Here, in this sane place of daylight and regular meals, she rarely slipped across into her other world: her Paris world. And often, just now with the butterflies, she could find her way back to the ordinary world, if she kept calm.

Isaac was always calm. Her duties were few: cooking his meals and washing his clothes. He called her 'daughter' (though she never called him 'father', only 'sir') and he loved nothing more than presenting her to his friends, none of whom seemed surprised at her sudden arrival in his life. She went to synagogue with him every week and the men were always blessing her. They would touch her head or squeeze her upper arm, and their wives would embrace her tearfully. She had never been handled so much in this way and each reassuring hand brought more and more steadiness: she could feel the ground under her feet now.

Isaac sold leather belts and other goods in the marketplace and one of his customers had managed to get her some modelling work at the art school. She revelled in the long periods of stillness that the job gave her. She learnt to watch her own mind as it began to stray beyond the here and now, and learnt to focus on a sound or the shape of one of the artists' hands or ears, and in that way to anchor herself, gently turning her wilful, wayward visions aside. It was like training a wild animal.

Isaac didn't know that she posed for a life class and she was sure that the idea of her being undressed in front of all the male students would disturb him. So the habit of half-truths was still with her and she had told a big lie about her past when Isaac finally questioned her about it. Perhaps, in time, when she had entirely aligned herself with the everyday, she would give up telling stories about herself, too.

It was Paris, and everything that had happened there, that had unmoored her. The memories of it were her most dangerous thoughts. But it had taken only three months for Paris to catch up with her and she had laughed out loud to see, in the paper that she was tearing up to hang on the hook next to the toilet, that D'Argent was arranging an exhibition in Amsterdam. Seeing Penelope's name alongside the other artists who would be exhibiting gave her a surge of pride, then excitement, then fear.

Penelope. What if she was angry? Vengeful, even? She imagined Penelope as Delacroix's Liberty, brandishing the flag. Penelope, formidable as a protector, would be terrifying as an enemy. On the other hand, look how she had crumbled over that stupid name for whatever it was she'd made in fur. She remembered Penelope's long, kinked hair and how it tumbled lock by lock over her shoulder when she leant forwards and the way she had of flicking it back or tying it in a loose thick knot which unfurled almost immediately afterwards. Penelope smelt of fresh air. There was always a half-smile on her face, even when her forehead was furrowed with fury or confusion. She knew that she would always be safe, she would always have a hold on sanity, as long as Penelope kept faith with her. When the time came to finally face D'Argent, Penelope would be her guardian angel as she walked in that dark valley again.

'They did not take my sight,' she said to herself, 'because I got away. And now I can see as high as I like.' She loved the dangling furniture-pulley hooks on the tops of the narrow houses. She wanted to jump up and grasp hold of one. It would be so easy to swing herself along to the next one, like a long-armed ape, and she would never need to touch the ground again until she reached her destination. She started to sing the 'Skye Boat Song' and matched her steps to the rhythm. With Angélique, she used to skip along the streets of Lille and had invented a game of hops and jumps just so she could hold Angélique's hand. Angélique had unthinkingly grabbed the hand of a sister, but Suzanne clasped her daughter's tenderly.

Suddenly, the way was barred. Metal fencing surrounded a house front, out as far as the gnarly tree across on the opposite side of the road beside the canal. Suzanne made her way carefully around the outside of the fence, trying not to look down at the stagnant water and steadying herself by wrapping her arms around the rough bark of the tree. How friendly it was, she thought, like the wrinkled, laughing face of an old woman.

On the other side, instead of going on, she turned to look back. There was a writhing shape on the ground that had not been there before. It was a dull gold colour and she squatted down to see. She watched it grow thicker and wider and expand into limb after thrashing limb. There were leaf shapes and distended pods and the legs were splayed open. It seemed to be screaming. The arms were flailing and the head was thrown back in a cry of agony. What cruel joke was this? Why was the horror of her past displayed here on the street?

As she stood up, her toe struck it and, in the jolt of cold, sudden pain, she saw that it was just a bit of twisted steel. Someone had driven over a piece of the fencing, perhaps, or it was just a piece of cast-off metal. Nothing to be afraid of. But her heartbeats thumped in her throat and ears. She started to run, and fixed her thoughts on the hope of seeing Penelope again. Speed, bonny boat, like a bird on the wing.

Chapter Fifteen

Amsterdam, April 1938

'But I thought it was all agreed. For the sake of the book, at least,' Alain said, as he and Penelope walked from Muntplein.

'So it's your precious book you care about most, is it?' said Penelope.

'How can you say that?'

'But you haven't even told me what it would mean for Rolf.'

'That is up to you. Surely it is easy to decide when it is all up to you.'

'No. None of this is easy for me,' said Penelope.

They reached the Tuschinski and Penelope halted. 'Here it is,' she said, looking up at the extraordinary art-deco facade of the tall, knobbly, tiled building. It resembled a creature with scales, motionless for now, but looking as if it might lumber off at any moment, webbed foot by webbed foot. Clinging to the articulated plates of its skin were bright orange, bug-shaped lanterns bringing warmth and colour to its venerable grey hide. She loved it and immediately felt a sense of encouragement returning. She would see Suzanne again soon.

'I'm meeting my friend here,' she said, 'so I'll see you when you get back from Utrecht. We'll talk more then.'

Alain took her hand. 'Tell me who you are meeting.'

'It's not my secret to tell.'

'More secrets? You are making things more complicated than they need to be.'

'No, I'm not. I'm going to sort it all out. With my friend.' She turned to go.

'Wait, please, wait a moment.' He pulled her aside into one of the smaller doorways. 'I need to know if this is going to happen.'

'Who knows what will happen,' Penelope sighed. Sometimes the whole business of her love life made her weary and struck her as an indulgence, or an irrelevance. What really mattered was that she had still not started the picture of the leaping horse. With things so up in the air with Rolf, she had not been able to turn her mind to it.

'Did you know that Hitler's troops marched into Austria without firing a shot?' Alain said. 'What if that was to happen in France?'

'Does Hitler have rules about what people do in bed?'

'No, but whatever happens, we would be safer together.'

'So now you're trying to scare me. You must be desperate.'

'I am. I am consumed. It is all I think about. I have enough material for two books, for twenty books. And it hasn't even happened yet.'

'Yet?'

'You cannot deny that you want to.'

'Can't I? How can you be so sure about what I want?'

Alain shielded her body from the gaze of the street and kissed her very carefully. Then he gently stroked his thumbs across her breasts. The thin fabric of her summer blouse moved against the silk chemise beneath.

'I know that you want this,' he said.

Tears of helplessness and confusion came to her closed eyes at the same time as a hot flame licked her from inside. She leant towards him and rested her forehead on his shoulder. He embraced her compassionately, as if she was a child who had braved a painful medical procedure. They had been to the tulip market earlier and she thought of the fleshy petals of the flowers that were, like this man, strange and familiar all at once. But the smell that lingered on her hands was of the black dirt clinging to the tubers.

'I have to go,' said Penelope, breaking away, 'or I'll be late.'

He kissed her forehead solemnly, looked into her eyes for a few moments, then left.

She watched him walk away. Despite the crowds he took great care to avoid stepping on the tram tracks. Such a careful man. An intelligent man. An idealistic, poetic, romantic man. And so very gentle. What on earth was she going to do?

Rolf was not in Amsterdam. Alain had driven her here in his blue Talbot and, as he stared at the road ahead, he had told her about being in a sanatorium at seventeen. He described his fear of tuberculosis, and the icy communal rooms, but most of all about the isolation. It was then that he had started to write poetry.

'Alone and palely loitering?' she had joked.

'What is that?'

'Don't tell me you never read Keats?'

'Why would I bother? With Baudelaire? Mallarmé?'

'For the colours of course.'

'Is that why you read poetry?'

'Always.'

'Then I will put a million colours into one poem alone for you, Penelope.'

After that, she never brought up the subject of his tuberculosis again. How would it change a person to know that their life was likely to be short? she wondered, stepping out of the flow of the pedestrians and drawing closer to the cinema's frontage. Should she show compassion by granting his wish? And if war did come, would she regret not yielding to him?

She tried to imagine the sort of art she would make as Alain's partner. Perhaps this was the next crucial stage in her artistic career. The key thing was to stay close to the surrealists: her chances of success were nothing without them.

Inside, the Tuschinski film theatre was sumptuous. She could feel the expensive carpet's yielding thickness beneath her feet and its warm colours were answered by a soft, rich, pulsating dome over her head which glowed from red to green. She wandered around the lobby and reached out a hand to caress the velvet nap of the black-and-gold-striped sofa chairs. She could not resist sinking into one. The lobby was large and empty but there was a tremendous, dense noise coming from behind the back wall which was flanked on either side by two sets of curving staircases. She surreptitiously stroked the carpet while sitting on the low, easeful chair. Everything would be all right.

She slipped off her shoes and tucked her legs up under her, Turk-style, which was easy, if not entirely ladylike, in her wide black trousers. The Dutch were more relaxed about dress than the Parisians and no one had raised an eyebrow here at her harem pants. The women wore sturdy shoes and carried bags for putting things in, not for show. Little dogs seemed to be unknown in Amsterdam and parks were for outdoor exercise, not showing off the latest fashions. Penelope liked it here.

She settled to watch the door, scrutinising every arrival. She glanced backwards each time the swinging doors opened, creating a surge of noise, and giving a glimpse of some very high-tiered structure. Opposite her was a counter staffed by a pleasant-looking woman who had smiled at her once then comfortably ignored her, seeming to understand that she was waiting for somebody.

A woman came in from the street, holding her little girl by the hand. The child was dancing and jumping and seemed to be repeating the word 'tart'. The woman paid at the counter then went towards the swinging doors at the back. As they went through, the little girl stopped her sing-song and pointed up at a picture of a leaping gazelle that was done in orange and gold above the doorway. Penelope felt a stab of desperation and envy because the beautiful animal was making the very same jump that, in her mind, the horse of her unpainted picture would make if only she could see how it was to be done. The movement was a light, buoyant clearing of an obstacle, a sure and swift escape from confinement in one supple, perfectly judged movement. The woman and child disappeared inside.

Originally, she had conceived her picture as an imaging of her flight from England to be with Rolf in Paris. The setting would be early morning with the pale misty light that had greeted her on arrival at the Gare du Nord. She was going to call it *The Horse of the New Dawn* but the picture would not compose itself, however long she stared at a blank canvas or made pencil sketches. Now she knew that to paint the leap, she would have to make another, greater one than she had done to leave her childhood home. Her legs started to ache and it was actually becoming quite painful to stay sitting in this position.

Unexpectedly, the woman from the counter came charging towards her, but no, it was not Penelope she was heading for, it was a large, roughly dressed man who had just come in, with a sludge-green cap crushed in his fist. The woman remonstrated with him and pointed at his feet. He was wearing heavy clogs and they were thickly coated in mud. He assented to wait while the woman headed off towards the roaring back room.

As the woman went through the doors she almost collided with a bellboy wearing a pill-box hat, who carried a wedge of yellow and white cake on a tiny plate. The bellboy came over to Penelope and said something to her. She smiled and began the well-rehearsed words to explain that she spoke no Dutch but he simply gave her the cake and left again. The man in the clogs gave her a wide grin and she gestured the plate towards him but he silently refused the offer with a wave of the hand.

The woman attendant came back and behind her a squat man in an expensive suit and schoolteacher's glasses held the door open. The woman signalled the clog-man to go in and he stooped to remove his clogs but she placed a hand on his arm and said something. The man straightened his back and, still wearing the muddy clogs, walked across the lobby with his head held high. He shook the hand of the bespectacled man, who threw an arm around his shoulder, and they went in together.

Penelope could not help scanning the carpet for brown smears, before turning her attention to the heavy, iced cake. As she lifted the fork to her mouth she continued to survey the lobby. The carpet did indeed seem to be a well-used luxury because across the way she saw two fashionable women, with hats perched precipitously on the sides of their heads, drop cigarette ash on the floor as they talked. Penelope's cast-off shoes lay on the floor, soles upwards and splayed apart. They made her think of Marlene Dietrich in *The Blue Angel*, straddling a chair with her open thighs. The cake was very rich and she set it aside unfinished.

She put on her shoes and started pacing about the foyer. What time was it? She had forgotten her watch but had been able to rely on the quaint clock of the Munt on the way here from the Schiller Hotel. She managed to catch the eye of the counter attendant and pointed at her wrist. The woman smiled and came over, pushing up her sleeve so that Penelope could see her watch. Five past.

'*Dank u wel*,' said Penelope. Suzanne would hardly not come. Might she be in the back, with all the cake and uproar? An organ was playing now and the swinging door revealed flashes of movement. Penelope decided to give it five more minutes and then go in.

Chapter Sixteen

P enelope saw Suzanne as she came into the lobby of the Tuschinski and headed towards the stairs.

'Suzanne!' she called, rather louder than she had meant to.

Suzanne turned, smiled brilliantly and ran to embrace her.

Surprised by the extravagant greeting, Penelope clung tightly to her thin frame, remembering her smoky, street-cat smell. Penelope felt a rush of love for this frail and separate person and she suddenly realised that the dragging of her spirits these last few weeks was in fact loneliness.

'It's so good to see you,' Penelope said, holding her at arm's length and reacquainting herself with Suzanne's delicate features. She wore that same heavy black kohl around her pale greenish eyes.

'Can you really see me? I'm so glad.'

Penelope merely laughed at Suzanne's strangeness, which no longer repelled her. Suzanne looked well, although still very thin. She wore a fluid red dress with a bow at the neck and black-barred shoes. Oddly, her legs were bare but not unattractive, being covered with a soft blonde down.

'How long have you been in Amsterdam?' Penelope asked, steering Suzanne out of the path of a well-dressed couple. 'Do you live here now?'

'Yes! Yes. I will tell you everything. Everything! Come on, let's sit upstairs. There's a lamp made of silk and we can go out on deck to see the ocean.' Suzanne was already mounting the stairs and Penelope had no choice but to go after her.

This was not the withdrawn, haunted creature she had rescued from a mugger outside Le Parisien and coaxed into smiling. Suzanne danced up the stairs like a little child or a girl in a musical show. When she spun around to check that Penelope was still following, her eyes were flashing with excitement. Maybe this was the real Suzanne: a woman at home in the world and full of enthusiasm.

At the top of the stairs was another jewel-like, carpeted space but this was in a curve surrounding an inner circle of wooden doors like the cabins on a ship. At intervals, warm yellow lanterns clung to the walls like glowing beetles. Suzanne ran up to one of the doors and pressed her ear to it. Penelope could hear the rapid fire of American voices filling the space behind the doors.

'Groucho is my favourite,' Suzanne cried out. She did a Marx Brothers silly walk back to Penelope then threw herself into one of the black-and-gold sofas with a sigh of pleasure. 'Oh how I love the movies,' she said, 'Dr Hackenbush recommends movies!'

'So where are you living?' asked Penelope.

'With Isaac. He is such a sweetheart. Isn't that what the Americans say?'

'Is he American?'

Suzanne snorted at the idea. 'No. He's Lithuanian.'

'An artist? A poet?'

'Oh no, Isaac is a beltmaker. But he is a teacher and a wise man and all of his thoughts go to God and back again. To God and back again.' Suzanne swayed slightly as she repeated the words. 'I'll take you to meet him.'

'Later, perhaps. Tell me how you came to be here.'

'I came to be a bird in the sky. I came to be a cat in the night. I came to be a breath on the glass. The wind is blue, Penelope, the wind is blue.'

Penelope followed Suzanne's eyes. She was staring at a picture on the wall beside the exit and, like some mesmerised acolyte, she got up and went close to it. It was of a woman with butterfly wings and dark-ringed eyes like Suzanne's. On the top of the butterfly-woman's head, long feelers sprouted from the midst of her lacquer-smooth black hair. After a few moments, Suzanne raised her arms to mirror the pose in the picture and suddenly gave a great, theatrical sob. Then she ran back to the top of the stairs, arms still held high, and jumped.

Penelope had no idea what to do. Suzanne lay in a heap at the first turn of the staircase and Penelope went to gather her up. She tried to absorb Suzanne's bewildering pain into her own body. At that moment a young man in shoes without laces came hurtling down the stairs and nearly tripped over them.

'What has happened here?' he asked, in German, which Penelope understood without thinking about it.

'My friend. She has fallen.'

'English? Come then,' he said, and together they put Suzanne back on her feet. Then they guided her down the rest of the steps, one on each side, and settled her into a chair. The man disappeared, returning almost immediately with a glass of water.

'Here.' He squatted in front of Suzanne and held out the blue glass, but she made no move to take it and simply stared at his face.

'You have come to show me my father's room,' she said.

'Of course, whatever you wish. Now, drink this. You will feel better.' He raised his hand to push the hair from Suzanne's face but she threw him off, sending the glass spinning to the floor and wetting the carpet.

'Not my eyes. Leave my eyes alone!' Suzanne bent over to shield her head with her arms.

While Suzanne cowered and murmured, Penelope and the man exchanged looks.

'Your friend is not well,' he said. 'What is her name?'

'I'm Penelope Furr, and this is Suzanne.'

'Friedrich Jacobs. To you, please, Freddie.'

They shook hands and stood looking at Suzanne in silence. It really was a rather absurd situation. Penelope became aware that the counter attendant, who had been watching every part of the performance, was coming towards them. The woman retrieved the glass and said something to Freddie in Dutch, which Suzanne clearly heard and understood because she raised her head and addressed Freddie in English: 'My name is Suzanne Levy and I live with Isaac Room.'

Freddie's face changed in a moment from a suspicious frown to a wide smile and he said something to the woman that made her shrug her shoulders and return to her post behind the counter.

'I would be glad, ladies, if you would accompany me,' said Freddie.

'Of course,' said Suzanne, as if nothing had happened. She stood up and smoothed down her dress.

'Please.' Freddie indicated the way with his shirt-sleeved arm and Penelope noticed a shiny band around his bicep which held the cuff away from his wrist. He led them to the opposite staircase and Penelope studied Freddie's good woollen trousers, which had frayed turn-ups, and admired his clean-shaven face and curly brown hair which fell pleasingly over one eye. He halted in front of the gentlemen's toilets and gave a cough of embarrassment.

'I am very sorry to ask you this, but if you will follow me?'

Penelope looked at Suzanne, who grinned back like a naughty schoolgirl.

'Lead the way,' said Penelope.

Freddie marched past the sinks and urinals and took out a key with which he opened a door at the back. He gestured for them to go in, followed them, and locked the door from the inside. It was a small, dark room with a folded blanket on the floor in one corner and a tangle of brooms and mops leaning against the wall in the other. The women sat down in the two folding chairs. Freddie pulled back the curtain to reveal a tiny window, which was of red-and-green glass like the grander ones downstairs. He produced a bottle of wine with Hebrew lettering and a single tumbler. This he filled and offered to Suzanne, who drained it easily.

'Thank you,' she said, returning the glass.

'How is Isaac?' asked Freddie. 'I haven't been to a meeting for quite some time.'

'He would say that he is all the better for being asked.'

'And business is good?'

Penelope began to feel a little left out.

'How do you come to be in Holland, Freddie?' she asked.

'I was born in Vienna but at eighteen years I went to work at the Ufa-Palast am Zoo, in Berlin,' he said, sitting on the linoleum floor with apparent comfort. 'Then in 1933 the new rules of membership in the Filmkammer came in and I lost my job. When my mother wrote that they had painted swastikas on the pavements in Vienna, I knew that she and my brother and sister might need my help before long. So my friend Georg wrote a lovely story all about my abilities and I came here. When I gave it to Abraham he hired me on the spot.'

'And what is your job here?' asked Penelope.

'I am one of the projectionists.'

'And you live ...?'

'Welcome to my humble abode. That is how the English refer to their castles, is it not?'

'You live here? How is it possible?'

'Entirely possible, I assure you, but not very comfortable. I have to pay the caretaker for his silence and the loan of the key. And I have to pretend to leave every evening. But it will do, until I have enough money for my family to leave Germany.'

Suzanne got up and circled the room. She swayed as if hearing music.

'Freddie, do you have any food?' asked Penelope.

'I have eggs. They are yours.'

'But where can I cook them?' Penelope searched the room for more doors.

In answer, Freddie sprung up and opened a cupboard. She heard him shake a matchbox. On the floor in front of her he placed a portable stove, a frying pan, a screw of greaseproof paper containing fat, a box of eggs and some salt in a bag.

'I have only one plate. But I have three forks. Hip hooray.'

Penelope got down on the floor and struck a light on the side of the Broches box. The stove was easy to use. It was a Perfectus exactly like the one she used to take on camping trips in Wales. The omelette was soon cooked and expertly folded. Suzanne's demeanour had changed and the whole room seemed warmer. Freddie refilled her glass and, as an afterthought, brought out a chipped cup and a plastic beaker with a smear of dried toothpaste on the rim and poured drinks for Penelope and himself. Penelope slid the omelette onto the warmed plate and they all toasted each other.

Suzanne knelt down to join them on the floor and helped herself to the lion's share. The omelette was a deep golden yellow colour and tasted surprisingly good. Afterwards they settled into silence. Freddie remained on the floor, sitting propped up against the wall and sipping quietly from his tooth mug.

'Would you like to see the projector?' he said, after a while. 'The next show's not until three, after the cabaret. Did you ever hear the Ramblers play?'

Suzanne and Freddie began throwing names around, none of which, except Coleman Hawkins, Penelope had ever heard of, so she gathered up the forks and cups.

'Wait, let me check first,' said Freddie as he unlocked the door.

But the wine had made them bold and Penelope and Suzanne charged out in front of him. They startled a man in a bow tie who immediately retreated back into the stall he'd just come out of and, once out in the corridor again, they shrieked with laughter. Freddie looked uncomfortable but Suzanne cuffed him on the arm as if he was her younger brother and he broke out into a broad smile. They set off through winding corridors until the gorgeous carpet and fittings were left behind. Finally, they mounted a narrow, steep staircase. Suzanne fell behind, dawdling in that annoying way she had, but Penelope kept pace with Freddie.

The projection room was spotlessly clean and the equipment shone. Freddie started explaining every knob and gauge to Penelope, who tried hard to look interested. She asked a few questions and dredged up some technical words from listening to Rolf describing his Deardorff camera. But Freddie needed no encouragement and was not afraid to assert the absolute superiority of the workmanship of the German projector. At great length. Finally he said 'and from here you can see the auditorium'.

Penelope went to the small window and feasted on the sight of the balconies and plush seats. The screen was curtained lavishly in yards of gold fabric and someone was in front of it, on the stage. Suzanne. Then came a beautiful voice, singing. The projection room was designed to convey the sound from below and Suzanne's sad notes filled their ears.

'Onward the sailors cry.

Carry the lad that's born to be king,

Over the sea to Skye.'

Freddie joined her at the window, craning his neck. 'Who is it?'

'It's her. It's Suzanne.'

'Let's go,' he said.

When they reached the auditorium Suzanne was sitting quietly on the edge of the stage, swinging her legs and looking up at the ceiling. She saw them come in and got up, waving cheerily. Then she began to sing a Cole Porter song and do a tap dance.

Penelope couldn't help smiling, but it wasn't just the song. Was this really the same woman who had tried to fly down the stairs an hour ago? The same one who was mortally afraid of being recognised in Paris and, after claiming to be someone impossible, had run off into the night three months ago without a word since? Freddie, also, was transfixed. He was standing with hands on hips, head on one side. A grin stole slowly across his face.

'Your friend is a very unusual lady,' he said.

They watched Suzanne shimmy and bump across the stage. She was a natural performer. She flirted with the empty rows of seats and winked mischievously at Freddie after every risqué line. The song came to an end and Suzanne took a bow as Penelope, Freddie and two cleaning ladies gave her a round of applause.

'It's time we went, Freddie,' said Penelope, when Suzanne had rejoined them. 'Thank you for everything.'

'Isaac would be glad to see you, Freddie. Why not visit one evening?'

'I would be glad to. Please give him my regards,' he said, and seemed to be about to say something else but then turned on his heel and hurried away.

'Do you need to be at the exhibition, Penelope?' asked Suzanne.

'No.' They were back in the curved lounge. 'What I need is to talk to you.'

'And I need to talk to you, too,' said Suzanne, meeting her eyes with a cautious but steady gaze.

'Come on, then,' said Penelope, 'Let's go somewhere quiet. Somewhere ordinary.'

Chapter Seventeen

T hey left behind the jewelled facade of the Tuschinski cinema and began to walk. Suzanne led the way, aware that in Amsterdam she was the one in charge. Penelope walked in that lively way she had, with firm steps ringing on the pavements. She took great lungfuls of air and swung her arms whenever there was room to do so. Penelope's hazel eyes were still bright and inquisitive, thought Suzanne, but there were traces of strain on her face and the line between her brows never did smooth out. Her cheeks were not such a healthy colour, perhaps, as before.

Emerging from this covert contemplation of her friend Suzanne realised, with a pang of anger at her own stupidity, that she had automatically taken the shortest route to where she lived in the Pijp district, meaning that they were walking back along the Keizersgracht. Unless she took a left turn very soon, they would pass the gallery where the surrealists were exhibiting. Suzanne craned her neck but the canal stretched on, unbridged.

'Wait,' she said, putting a hand on Penelope's arm, 'it's the wrong way. I'm sorry, we have to go back. The gallery is just ahead there.'

'Don't worry,' said Penelope, 'no one will be there until later on and then not even D'Argent, because he's in Utrecht for two days.'

'And Rolf, is he here?' asked Suzanne.

'No. I'll tell you later. It's complicated.'

'Oh. Well let's turn around anyway. I know somewhere you will like.'

'All right.' Penelope gave her a broad smile. 'Only you'll probably have to take me back to my hotel later. I'm lost already.'

'I think Amsterdam is easier than Paris. All the streets make squares with the canals, it's like a chessboard.'

'If you say so.'

It is true, thought Suzanne. This city is kind to me. The grid-plan of the streets I can carry in my head, and the small canals are edged with green and friendly to the wildfowl, not like the cold, steel-coloured Seine which cuts Paris in two like an anguished memory. Here the ghosts keep a respectable distance and, instead of laughing with ridicule, encourage me when I get up early and walk to work. They sing to me through the clocks that strike tunefully and helpfully, always when expected, when needed. And then there is Isaac. Suzanne conjured up an image of Isaac's soft white hair seen from above on the women's balcony. This morning, the synagogue had smelt of cigars and baking bread, just like home.

'What do you do here, Suzanne?' asked Penelope. 'How did you meet Isaac?'

'Mostly cleaning. Isaac recommends me to people. Some have bought his belts, some know him from the meetings. I've seen some beautiful places. Tomorrow I am going to a building that is shaped like a ship on the sea.'

Penelope gave her a quizzical look.

'No, it really is. You can come with me if you like. I'm going as a model. I used to sit for another painter,' she went on. 'He was German and he drank so much beer. All day long. He wanted to pay me in beer. It didn't work at all.'

'And Isaac?'

'I met Isaac on the day I arrived. He was coming back on the train with some new leather, from Utrecht also I think, and he saw that I was lost and on my own so he took me home with him.'

'But he could have been anybody.'

'I suppose so. Now I cook for him and I give him whatever money I have left over and in the evening I sing to him. In return he takes care of me. He doesn't know about Angélique.'

'You must miss her.'

The pain was strong. It stabbed hard as Penelope said the words. Suzanne didn't just miss Angélique, Angélique was missing from her like a part of her body. It was as if there was a gap where her stomach should be and instead you could see right through to the sky behind so that there was a piece of her that was blue and white or grey, according to the day, in the shape of a child.

'This way now,' said Suzanne, waiting for a fleet of bicycles to pass.

'Where are we going?'

'To the park. You'll like it. There are ducks.'

Penelope smiled. 'How do you know I like ducks?'

'Everyone likes ducks,' said Suzanne.

They walked on, then turned left onto a wider road, running parallel with a yet broader canal.

Penelope's thoughts went back to the exhibition. Alongside the fur cup she was showing the feasting and the running horses, and also the mannequin's head obscured by scarves and other materials. At first, the head was meant to be simply an interpretation of what Suzanne had told her about her mother's dead face being wrapped in cloth, but with Suzanne's continued disappearance, the feathers and fringes and shells and silk covering up a face became for Penelope the story of

Suzanne's strange and contradictory personality, and of her hidden identity.

What would the pragmatic Dutch people make of it? They would surely prefer Rolf's rayographs: the blurred but recognisable shapes of a comb, a hammer, the skin of a snake. Or the photograph of Penelope herself, standing at the printing press with her heavily inked arm resting on her brow. For her, that picture marked the last day of feeling at home with Rolf. But perhaps she had been living in a fool's paradise? Making art meant moving out of security into the unknown. Was Rolf's challenge to throw off the remaining conventions of their relationship a way for her to enter a new creative state? So far it had done the opposite. She was stuck.

'Suzanne,' she said, 'what you told me, last time, before you ran away,' but Penelope was cut off in mid-sentence by a shower of cold water falling on her head as, bizarrely, a horse was lifted into the air in a leather harness from out of the canal itself.

Just ahead was a large contraption of pulleys and weights, operated by two men in filthy leather trousers. *J.C. Sinck* was written on the side of a van nearby. Suzanne laughed at Penelope, who had taken the brunt of the deluge.

'What on earth?' cried Penelope, feeling her wet hair.

'They rescue the horses that fall in the canal. It's even worse than it used to be, they say, now that there are more cars to scare them off the road. Oh dear, it looks like this one will be ending up at the butcher's. But it's a profit for them, either way.'

The dead horse had been slung down on the ground.

'It's not even legal either,' said Suzanne. 'Come on, let's go to Berkhout. We can get a hot coffee for you there.'

The café was a rough place and heaving with men in blue overalls who gave off a strange, sweet smell.

'They're from the brewery. It's half day on Saturday,' explained Suzanne, squeezing past the knots of men who were all standing close together, smoking and shouting at each other.

They sat apart by a window at a bare wooden table and the seats were so coarse that Penelope could feel the grain, and a splinter or two, through her trousers.

A man with a harelip brought them two tiny cups of coffee.

'May we have apple cake?' said Suzanne.

She seemed to be asking Penelope, instead of the waiter. Of course, she's expecting me to pay, thought Penelope. 'Yes, you can have some,' she said, and Suzanne squealed with delight. Why must she always play the child? 'Who is looking after Angélique?' she asked Suzanne.

'My father. He's a complete idiot. He thinks that the Germans will take over France and that he'll have to bake pumpernickel instead of baguettes. Really, why would they bother?'

'I think he might be right,' said Penelope, but Suzanne was looking out of the window and didn't seem to be listening.

'And my French grandmother, my father's mother,' Suzanne went on, 'she is just as bad. She never liked my mother. She didn't trust her because she was Scots, although she would have been the same way about any foreigner. My family is a nightmare.'

'All families are,' said Penelope. 'But how did a Scottish girl come to marry a French baker from Lille?'

'I told you, my mother was singing the part of Mélisande. Her aunt was rich and used to pay for singing lessons. Then one day, when she was just eighteen, her aunt took her to the mainland and an opera promoter heard her sing at a concert. Instead of going home to Skye she began a tour of Europe. Why my father would go to see an opera by Debussy in Paris has always puzzled me; his favourite music is the klezmer, but he was young then.

He proposed that night and she stopped singing professionally when they married. But she used to sing in the house, and on the street, just like me. She sang to my father and now I sing to Isaac. But how will Angélique learn to sing our songs if I am not there?'

'Why don't you go back?'

'My grandmother won't allow it. She says I have become "a woman of no morals". Her family are very stiff. It comes from once being travellers; they go to the other extreme. But I am extreme, too. Perhaps it is better for Angélique to have just the boring ones while she is still little. What adventures we will have when she's older. But what about you? What have you been painting, Penelope?'

'I haven't. I can't.'

'Why? Have you been ill?'

'No, I just don't feel in charge any more. I can see what I want to paint in my head but I just can't get it onto the canvas.'

Suzanne sipped her coffee. 'I'm glad I can't paint what I see.'

'What do you see?'

'Terrible things, sometimes.'

'Have you always seen things?'

'Always. There was a time I couldn't make it stop. Now it's up to me, usually. And eating always helps.' Suzanne sighed with pleasure as an enormous slice of pastry and apples topped with billowing whipped cream was put in front of her. 'Thank you for taking care of me today.'

As Suzanne ate, Penelope tried to gather the courage to tell her about Rolf's proposition and her feelings for Alain, but she was too ashamed and confused. Did Rolf feel an attraction for Alain as well? Or did he want to observe closely what he himself felt for Penelope, in someone else? Instead of loving her, did he want to watch her being loved? Maybe he wanted to photograph it, or paint it. Or maybe he genuinely wanted to set her free to follow her desires.

'So, when we have seen the ducks,' Suzanne was saying, 'I will take you to meet Isaac and he will tell you why God made people.'

'Why did he?' asked Penelope.

'I didn't think you were listening. Here, try the apple cake.'

'No thank you. Why did you run away that night?'

'It wasn't safe.'

'Surely you trust me?'

'I do. I do, now. I'm so happy that you are here, Penelope, but no one else must know.'

'Why? I don't understand. Rolf, Alain and D'Argent too, they would all be happy to see you and to know that you are well again.'

'But I'm not supposed to be well. You see, they have never heard of a woman called Suzanne Levy. And Natalia is still in the hospital.'

'What do you mean?'

'Shall we go and visit the ducks now?'

It's like a dance, Penelope thought, as she counted out the unfamiliar coins. We step closer and then whirl away again. How long can this go on? One of us will have to change the music.

As they came back out into the brightness, Penelope noticed that Suzanne winced and gave a little whimper. She shielded her eyes from the sun and with the other hand held onto Penelope's arm. They walked on and into a road that had an empty market at the far end.

Then, without warning, Suzanne leapt away and called out, 'Sammy!'

An impressive black man in a checked cap and a brown suit sauntered towards them. His face lit up at the sight of Suzanne and he grasped her little hand in his huge one and shook it up and down until she laughed uncontrollably.

'Oh Sammy, what are you doing here?' Then, not waiting for an answer, she said, 'Penelope this is Sammy Kit Cat, the best barman in the whole world.'

'Hello,' said Penelope.

Sammy took off his cap. Suzanne shimmered with animation. She circled Sammy's waist with her arm and laid her cheek on his broad chest. People were staring.

'Sammy lost his job in the Wagenstraat, but it wasn't fair, so we will call him Sammy Kit Cat forever. Now he is in the films, and he can dance and box and play the trumpet.'

'I used to work in the Kit Cat Club, on the Wagenstraat,' explained Sammy. 'When I arrived in Amsterdam there were only ten of us Surinamese men here and people would show up at the bar just to take a look at my face.'

'I wish I'd been here then,' Suzanne said dreamily.

'But they had to let me go because I made the ladies too happy.'

'Sammy makes all the women happy.'

'Especially the beautiful ones like you, Suzanne.'

Suzanne coquettishly gave him a light blow on the chest and pulled away. 'What about Penelope, Sammy? Isn't she beautiful too? Take a good, long look before making up your mind.'

He scanned Penelope's body with his golden brown eyes and she felt a blush rising to her face.

'Well Sammy?' Suzanne asked.

'Very beautiful.'

'As beautiful as Greet?'

'More beautiful,' he said.

'Have you quite finished?' said Penelope. 'I feel like a prize cow at the fair.'

Suzanne ignored her. 'But what about Sophie? Surely my friend cannot be more beautiful than the perfect Sophie?'

Sammy and Suzanne rocked with laughter at their private joke while Penelope stood waiting.

'Come, we have made Penelope angry. She looks like a black cloud. What can you do to cheer her up, Sammy?'

'Well now, how about a song?'

'No, a kiss, I think,' said Suzanne with a wicked look. 'A kiss would be the thing to do it. What do you think, Sammy?'

'Sure. A kiss is the cure for a whole lot of things,' and he made towards Penelope.

'Leave me alone!' she shouted, springing back out of the way.

'Penelope, what's the matter?' said Suzanne, suddenly very still.

'How dare you?' she blazed at Suzanne. 'What gives you the right to offer me to your friend? You take everything and give nothing back, not even the truth.'

Suzanne stared at the ground.

'Who do you think she is, Sammy? Has she told you? Or is she playing with you too? Goodbye Suzanne, if that's really your name.' And Penelope, blinded with fury, struck out alone into the crowd.

I wish I'd never left home, she thought. I wish I'd married one of those wooden idiots instead. And as for Rolf, I never want to see him again as long as I live.

Chapter Eighteen

Amsterdam, April 1938

E very time the tram doors opened the smell was terrible. They were passing through the Jordaan and women in thin shifts were bringing out their families' night-buckets for the dung cart that progressed slowly, reeking. I've lived in some terrible places, thought Suzanne, holding her sleeve to her nose, but never that bad. She checked again for the envelope containing the key. Today was not a routine Sunday. Usually she cleaned at the art school where she also sat for the life class on Thursday. Instead, something of an adventure awaited. The instructor at the art school had asked her last week if she had heard of the workers' palace. He told her he had a friend there, a painter who worked in the Customs house at the docks. His friend was lonely. His friend needed a model. Could she help his friend? Her tram fare would be paid and he was sure that his friend, whose name was Jan Hatterman (perhaps she had heard of him?), would give her a present of money if she would be so kind as to visit him at 277 Het Schip.

Changed by the relentless work ethic of the Dutch, she heard only the offer of employment and agreed. It was only now, being shaken from side to side in the tram, that she considered the arrangements again and realised that there was an air of mystery, even risk, around the job. Her Paris self stirred and she felt her heart beat more strongly as the breath caught in her throat. She had been given a key to his door and she was to go in and wait for him. It would be fine, said the instructor, if you wanted to tidy up in the kitchen, and then maybe rest on the bed; Jan's wife died three months ago and he still misses her very much.

If Isaac knew what she was doing – going to the house of a man she'd never met – he'd be frantic with worry. And Penelope would almost certainly disapprove. Suzanne had not permitted herself to think about Penelope since yesterday when she had stormed off on Albert Cuypstraat like that. Sammy had taken Suzanne for several drinks afterwards and had the delicacy (or lack of curiosity) not to ask questions. Suzanne hadn't realised that seeing Penelope again would mean having to tell her story. She had trusted no one since the betrayal more than ten years ago. Concealment was the fact of her life now, the condition of her existence. To talk about that time again would be to change the laws of reality as she had grown to rely on them: it would be like something out of a book by H.G. Wells. But Penelope plainly would not settle for anything less than the whole truth.

The tram had reached the end of Marnixstraat and Suzanne got out. She hoped this place was easy to find. In a park, some children were dancing in couples to a street organ and a black-clothed woman clutching a hymn book glared at them as she stalked past. Suzanne tenderly watched the children who were concentrating hard on their feet. She wanted to give them some coins but felt shy. She moved on. The morning was fresh and she gave herself up to the scent of spring and the music of birdsong.

There was no trouble finding Het Schip. Suzanne's senses spun her into confusion as her imagination tried to respond to the pulsating, bulging shapes of the architecture. The buildings were funnelled and portholed and all but barnacled with their prows and slanting sides. To look up was to feel the lurch of a great vessel shifting into the water and Suzanne was launched onto the ocean time and again as she navigated the streets.

She located the apartment easily. The door was behind a grey wall and the building had a pointed tower of red brick. The key turned smoothly in the lock and in she went. Immediately to the right a face in a frame greeted her and she smiled stiffly before realising that it was her own reflection. She was wearing the new hat that Sammy had bought for her yesterday and she looked older than usual. She turned away from the mirror to look at the hallway but kept half an eye on her reflection in case it did not do the same.

Stacked neatly on specially made shelves were canvases of landscapes and children with dogs. So, Jan was what Louis used to call a 'Sunday painter'. She hung up her jacket and hat next to the mirror, giving herself a final questioning look, and went into the main room.

She had never been in a house so small that was so clean. The main room was warmed by a fire behind a shining black iron grill and was dominated by a rich red-and-pink tablecloth. A lampshade, skirted in cream-coloured silk, sent out a yellow glow. Everything in the room had a mellow, orange-brown tone, like the notes of a double bass. The kitchen made her gasp and a tear actually came to her eye to see the perfectly spotless grey countertops, green wooden cupboards and black-and-white-tiled sink gleaming with reflected light. At home in Lille there had been an honest, scrubbed appearance to their house (and she tried to keep this up at Isaac's despite the difficult sanitary arrangements), but here the quality of the materials meant that everything could be kept genuinely, hygienically clean.

In the small bedroom, she sat on the bed and smoothed the plump, stitched maroon coverlet and then, like a cat, dipped her head down and rubbed her cheek against the soft pink flannelette pillows, almost purring. Lying on the bed she looked up at the boiled-sweet colours of the glass lamp and imagined living here, with Angélique, and a noble, hard-working man who liked sugar in his tea and was kind to animals. This fantasy husband was still indistinct, his hair sometimes dark and sometimes fair, when the front door opened and a man's voice called out: 'Good morning, *liefje*. Here I am, back again.'

Bon Dieu. This must be the painter, Jan. She rolled off the bed and scurried into the main room, smoothing down her skirt and hair like an old-fashioned maidservant. The man smiled pleasantly and put his hat on the table. He moved naturally towards her and kissed her on the cheek. He too smelt clean and his newly shaved face was perfectly smooth like soft suede. He went to hang up his coat then returned, holding out his hands to the warmth of the fire. He was a neat, slender man, with close-cropped hair and he wore a red wool jersey tucked into flawlessly ironed trousers. She was still trying to think of what to say when Jan started to chatter on as if they had been speaking together only a few minutes before.

'I saw your sister, Bet. She sends her love. How are you feeling?'

'I am ... well.'

'Good. Here is the kidney and we have bread from yesterday. Shall I make our tea?'

'No, no, let me.' Suzanne took the brown packet and retreated to the kitchen.

She leant against the cool granite countertop and tried to get hold of her real life in Amsterdam: Isaac and Sammy, the filthy floors of the bathhouse she would have to clean tomorrow, the contemptuous art students who stared at her body then scrubbed with erasers and sighed as if it was her fault that they could not get a likeness. And Penelope, who she might never see again.

But Jan's apartment was where her life ought to be, where she really belonged. Nothing here was unfamiliar; it claimed her as its own. It was as if she knew already that the caddy on the shelf with the black, silver and green geometric pattern contained the tea and that the striped tea cosy would be hanging on a hook by the door where it always lived. With hardly any effort she could picture the peaceful evening she'd spend with Jan, by the fire, knitting and listening to the clicking of the clock on the mantelpiece. She went to the cupboard and took down the cups that had been washed and dried before bedtime last night.

As she waited for the kettle to sing, Jan came up behind and embraced her, kissing the back of her head.

'I'm so glad you are recovered, Bet. I've been so worried.' He released her easily and went to unlock the back door to greet a pale, fluffy cat which scooted in under the table then rubbed itself against Suzanne's legs.

'Did you forget to feed her?' he asked.

'I think I must have done.'

Jan gave a merry laugh, scooped the cat up in one hand and began telling it how absent-minded his wife had become. Suzanne smiled as she assembled the tea things on a tray and took them into the main room. Jan was pretending that she was his wife, which was absurd, but as she caressed the chenille tablecloth there was a small part of her that wished it was true, the part of her that was still a small child and a believer in fairy tales. It was so quiet here, an enclave: a haven. She heard Jan put down the cat's dish on the ground outside and close the back door.

'Are you warm enough, my love?' he asked, as he came in.

'Yes. Thank you.'

'What? What is the matter?' He rushed to her side.

'Nothing. I'm just ... happy.'

'I too, I too.' And his arms were around her again. 'Tea first,' he said, sitting her down at the table, 'then, if you are not too tired I shall make the first sketch and then, no arguments, you shall lie down and rest.'

'All right,' she said. It didn't seem possible to refuse such kindness.

Later, he placed her to sit in the light by the window and gave her a volume of school stories to read.

'Or would you rather talk?' he asked, as he sharpened his pencils.

'Would it not distract you?'

'No, of course not. Tell me about your big day yesterday.'

Suzanne knew she had been with Penelope at the cinema, and with Sammy all evening, and yet there was another set of events just as plausible, like two movies seen one after the other.

'Was Walt at the market?' asked Jan.

'Yes,' she answered, cautiously.

'Apparently his son Kees is a great fan of Dr Freud. Did you see Anneke?'

'Yes.' Suzanne was getting into her role with ease now. 'She invited me for coffee.'

'Good. But wait until May, when you are well enough to go back to work. The flowers are selling well enough without you.'

'Yes, I think I will. April can be so cold. Colder than November.'

Suzanne stopped speaking and stared instead at the book with its pictures of English hockey fields and pig-tailed, ruddy-cheeked girls. Angélique. Angélique was the unshakable reality. Angélique had been growing inside her all the time she was locked up. She had imagined the stiff leather straps making stripes across her daughter's curled-up body because they were so tight and left marks on her own, already-rounding stomach. The doctor always began by checking the restraints. At first it was all he did, but after a few days he seemed unable to prevent his hands from pinching her nipples and squeezing her bottom, and after that each time his invasions of her body became more intimate, painful and unbearable than the last. The nurses would not listen when she told them and simply gave her more frequent injections. Why was she imprisoned anyway? The time before was so jumbled in her mind. She remembered getting out of the taxi and Louis paying the driver but nothing after that. If I tell Penelope, maybe she will help me remember it all, but how will I ever find her again, and will she speak to me if I do?

'It's finished for now,' said Jan, putting down his pencil. 'You can relax. Walk around and get the blood back.'

She looked at Jan and saw him for the stranger he was. She knew nothing about him. Did he have children?

'Come, it is time to lie down now, my dear. Come.' He was kissing her now, full of confident desire and starting to unbutton her blouse.

She knew she must pretend; it was what women like her did for money, and besides, she couldn't help feel sorry for Jan. She wanted very much to bring his wife back for him and, more than that, to actually be the woman who had been loved so well and lived in this beautiful home. It was easy. He was kind and gentle and absolutely, perfectly clean.

Chapter Nineteen

Amsterdam, April 1938

'Dinges, oh Dinges,' Penelope sang in her head as she trailed down another long street in De Pijp. She couldn't shake that catchy Johnny and Jones song out of her brain. And who was Dinges, anyway? Someone people laughed at for being straight-laced: exactly the sort of fool she'd made of herself on Saturday with Suzanne and her Surinamese friend. Of course when she had calmed down, Penelope saw the funny side: Sammy had meant no harm, it was all in her own mind, and she had probably seemed to him the worst sort of racialist for recoiling at his touch in that way. What an idiot she had been. Now here she was, indulging in the sort of unhinged behaviour that was better suited to Suzanne by roaming the streets at random.

Penelope was hoping that she could somehow run into Suzanne by chance, or perhaps meet someone who knew where she lived. Freddie had been absent from the cinema so she couldn't ask him where Isaac's house was, and her only other idea was to look out for a synagogue where she could ask about him. She resolved not to give up for another hour. She located Albert Cuypstraat at last, where the tatty canvas structures of Saturday had transformed into a swarming food market, and decided to make forays in different directions using the market as her reference point. Yes, it was idiotic, but it was better than sitting about at the gallery and enduring Alain's plaintive looks and hurt silences. He was in such an emotional mess that she thought he might actually cry when an awful Dutch woman in a fox fur demanded her money back and started lecturing him on the Golden Age of painting.

The air of the Pijp district carried the perfume of tree blossom mixed with wafts of the sickly smell of the brewery nearby. Penelope saw a curved iron shelter ahead and it was only when a new, fishy stink took precedence over all the rest that she realised it was a Dutch version of a Parisian pissoir.

Penelope started to hurry past then stopped dead. The squawk of a duck came from behind the railings and trees by the urinal. This must be where Suzanne had been taking her on Saturday. Penelope found the entrance to the park, sat down on a bench and watched the ducks. But how did this help with finding Suzanne? It was hopeless.

Perhaps half an hour had passed when Penelope's gaze was drawn to a thin figure in a blue hat standing by the gate. At first she thought it was her imagination but, no, Suzanne herself came across the grass towards her. Suzanne sat down and without a word of greeting or explanation, began to talk in a calm, audible voice, as if she had long been suspected of a crime and this was her chance, before a judge and jury at last, to put her case and speak the truth.

'I met Louis d'Argent on 4 October, 1926,' she said, staring out at the water and not looking at Penelope. 'It was nearly two years after I arrived in Paris. I was twenty-four years old. I told him my name was Natalia.' But then Suzanne faltered and turned to Penelope who could see the fear in her eyes.

Penelope took her hand and nodded. 'Go on,' she said.

'Well, the truth is he had met me before, in January, when my friend Roger took me to the house on Rue du Château that some of the surrealists shared then,' said Suzanne, keeping hold of Penelope's hand but allowing her gaze to return to the trees in the distance. 'I remember there was a crucifix as a chain for the toilet and such a lot of mattresses on the floors. That evening we were playing Leaflets, the game you English call Consequences. It reminded me of a game I used to play on my own. I would close my eyes and think of a word, just any word and then another, and that way I would make up a story, so when it was my turn I said, "Just write anything", and the Exquisite Corpse was born. Everyone was delighted with the new game.

'Louis was shouting out, "This is it! The door is open." I can't remember who wrote "exquisite", but I was the one who put down "corpse" and it was a premonition, wasn't it, because now I may as well be dead to all of them, and to Louis too. But that was later, and I want to tell you about the beginning.

'On that day in October when I met him I was walking to the hairdresser in Boulevard Magenta from my hotel on the Rue du Cheroy. It was my second year in Paris and I was very happy. I was poor, but I was free: no more hot and heavy work at my father's bakery and no *grandmère* shrieking at me to sit up straight at mealtimes. I missed *Maman* but it was too upsetting to see her have to fight for everything. I blamed my father for being weak but his mother is a wicked woman, like a witch. She is still bullying her son, even though she is nearly eighty years old. In Paris I got bits of work: some dancing in the theatre. Once I worked in the kitchen of the Dôme for two weeks and lived on it for two months. And sometimes the street girls passed on a man who didn't mind doing it outside in the dark for less money.

'So I was free and what I liked most to do was to walk. I walked and walked with no aim at all and Paris got in through the soles of my feet, into my bones and my lungs and my liver. I breathed in Paris and I breathed out ... myself. I never knew myself at home in Lille, I was a shape made by the others, but in Paris I became a window. I saw the shadow of the writing on the tree trunk and the old man whose face has fallen through the years. I saw the iron balconies sprouting leaves and black fruits. I saw people made of stone and marble, sitting comfortably and watching me. I saw the horses' heads leaning over the awnings with their mouths open. I saw everything and I kept on looking until I started to understand the meanings that were hidden. Paris was alive and she was speaking to me. And when I met the famous Louis d'Argent I knew I had to tell him what she was trying to say.

'I expect you are laughing at me. People did. And sometimes I knew it was a little bit funny. I used to pretend that a statue in Place Villiers was talking to me, just to see the look on Maurice's face. If only it had been that easy to find out what Paris was saying. But I knew Louis believed me. He was the only one who did.

'So I was on my way to have my hair cut and not long after I had passed the church of Notre Dame de Lorette I saw him strolling along Rue Lafayette. He saw me and stopped. He waited for my little life of the side streets to meet his broad public life on the main road and we fell into step. He had the face of an angel, Penelope. So kind, so wise, so genuine. He introduced himself and I pretended not to have heard of him – or seen him in the Rue du Château – to spare his embarrassment. Of course I had seen his name in the magazines and I had heard of his book with Claude: the first automatic text. I knew he was a rare man, a creature apart, to have published this book of uncensored thoughts – such courageous nakedness. Men are so seldom bold in that way. Their courage is to attack, to strike a pose, not to undress or be undefended.

'He began talking, right then and there, about his passion to unite the reality that we have grown so lazily to accept with the dreams and desires of our souls. "But what if my desire is evil, or murderous?" I asked him. "That cannot be," he said, and smiled so gravely. It was like meeting a saint. He believed in goodness.

'I knew that most people, if they had heard of the surrealists, disapproved. Maurice and his friends were well known for spitting on priests in the street and for disrupting literary banquets. But for Louis it was different; he was looking for the gold.

'We went to a café, I can't remember which one, and talked until dark. He was married, of course. I could see in my mind's eye his intelligent, dark-haired wife and their apartment in Rue Fontaine full of books and paintings and African curiosities from the flea market, even though I had not been there. So I said goodbye because I know it is no good to be in love with a married man and I walked very far that night through the arcades of medical shops, bottle shops and shops that had walking canes with rabbit heads and chicken claws in the windows.

'I never meant to see him again, that's why I kissed him in the doorway of the café when we parted. He looked so solemn and so young. But the very next day we met by chance once again. I had been taking soup at the back of Sainte Trinité where they give it out for free at three o'clock and, on the Rue de la Chausée-d'Antin, there he was. I pretended I was out to buy some expensive chocolate.

'Again we went to a café and we talked about his work. We always talked about that. Then he offered to take me home in a taxi and we got into one but I couldn't bear to be separated so I asked him to go with me to where the voices of Paris are clearest: Place Dauphine. Do you remember I took you there, Penelope?

'I used to go nearly every evening, on my own. It was just like when I was a child, and I would creep into my parents' bedroom when they were out. I would smell my father's cigars and *Maman*'s perfume then I would jump up and run away in case I was found out and punished. It was with that same feeling of trespass that I used to hold my breath and walk into the square.

'It was always quiet, no matter if people were there, because their voices were made smaller by the shape of the houses in a triangle. Did you know that Louis once called Place Dauphine the female sex of Paris? That was very crude but perhaps he hit on a truth by accident; after all, ancient peoples used to worship the fertility of their goddesses.

'Every time I went there it was as if I had entered another time, another era. There were whisperings and a low, friendly murmur and the sunlight flashed behind the trees as if it was trying to hide and then jump out to surprise me. I soon realised it was not the sunlight because there was something moving even in the dark. No, it was the Parisians of the old time daring to take a peek at me and all the curious things of now.

'Don't worry, Penelope, I don't need you to believe me, because Louis did. We had our meal outside and an American banker I met during my first week in Paris came up and started calling me all sorts of names, but as you know, Louis has never learnt English so he just assumed the man was drunk, instead of angry about being ignored. The waiter understood it all and he got very nervous: perhaps he thought Louis would challenge the man to a fight over me. I remember the waiter spilled our wine on the tablecloth and, as I stared at the stain, I realised how the dead were getting behind the trees. A tunnel. It made sense.

'Louis was doubtful when I told him and he looked rather worried, so I tried to cheer him up with my game of guessing which windows would light up first. For a while none of the ones we picked lit up, but then I remembered one across the trees which had beautiful red curtains. I thought I saw a figure inside the room so I pointed it out and told Louis that it would be red in a minute. It was. When he looked at me as if I had performed some kind of magic spell, I didn't have the heart to tell him the truth.

'Later that night the river told me that there must be no more building. The red hand was over the water again and it was plain that it meant "stop". Then later, back in my cold room, I drew a picture of the faces of the dead from long ago, the curtain at the window and the star that hung over the red hand. And I drew Louis. I drew him as a lion with the sun behind his head and I drew him with his hair on fire because the voices had told me that he must become the one to make room for all the dead to return. I knew they wanted me to ask him to arrange this.

'When I showed Louis the pictures he said I was a true artist. No one had ever said that before, even though I have drawn pictures since I was a little girl. Sometimes I see things that are not obvious to others and sometimes it is the bad things inside me that get out. Like a window, you see, Penelope. I can see to the outside; my window is a clear and wonderful vantage point, but sometimes the glass has my own reflection in it and I don't want to see that. I don't want to see my own face mixed in with the world. My face is like a cracked plate; it cannot stand the use. I am broken but I can see more than you. I do not want mirrors in my bathroom. I do not want them to see me. My thoughts lie safe and soft on the water in the bath.'

Penelope touched her arm and Suzanne turned to face her.

'It's all right, I'm here,' Penelope said.

Chapter Twenty

Suzanne smiled back at Penelope and carried on speaking.

'The next day – or was it the day after? – we went to the Parc des Buttes-Chaumont. How I laughed: the logs were made of concrete. There were fences and railway sleepers and all sorts of things but everything there had been made to look like something else, just like in my waking dreams, but this time it was real. We climbed to the Belvedere and stood under the dome and Louis kissed me so desperately that I couldn't breathe. It was a cruel kiss; it was the kiss of a thief.

'I knew that he was writing down what I said, every night while his wife slept in the next room. I knew he would write a book about me but I shall never read it because I cannot bear his disappointment. He wanted me to be something unearthly, but the more time I spent with him the less money I had and the hungrier I got. The voices were everywhere, louder and louder, and I had to promise to do what they told me. Sometimes I just wanted to rest but they always had a job for me: I was to go to a bookstore and slap the red hand on the poster outside, I was to spin round and round in the entrance to Le Palmier, pretending it was a revolving door. And I could never step in a gutter, no matter how crowded the pavements became. It was such hard work, keeping them all happy.

'One day I was sitting in Le Palmier, waiting for Louis and looking at the tables with three feet. I was staring across at the windmill when a man came up to me and asked how much. Louis arrived at that very moment and he realised I was doing business so he turned and left. Things were never the same after that. But what did he think I did for money? I never asked him for it, although he did once give me a present of 500 francs. It's not easy for a woman alone in Paris. It was around that time that I was on my own at the Tour Saint-Jacques, looking up at the scaffolding and canvas it was wearing like bandages around an injury, when a man grabbed me from behind. I fought him off but he hit me on the head with something hard. I ran all the way to Brasserie Zimmer and threw myself on Louis. He was very embarrassed. I was still bleeding and my dress was torn. The bourgeois women with their earrings and hats pretended not to see and the waiters in their long white aprons were too appalled to come near. Louis took me outside. He didn't speak to me again that night, he just put me in a taxi and I had to go back to my hotel all alone. I should have stopped seeing him after that but I loved him. I still love him.

'We only ever spent one whole night together. I was cold with fear because I wanted to please him so much. We went to a hotel in Saint-Germain and I felt watched, from the moment I left Paris. There were no voices, just eyes in the dusk. I hoped that if I did it, it would put things right between us, put them back to how it had been at the beginning. But I knew he was thinking all the time about the men who had paid me, and maybe I was too. I felt as if I was outside my body, looking down at us both in that room under the golden bedspread and at the old-fashioned jug and bowl decorated with birds on the table beside the bed.

'He never came to my hotel in Rue du Cheroy. I used to lie awake hungry, night after night, and eventually the voices got inside the hotel. They were shouting every night and I started shouting back and in the end the manager called the police because I was in the corridor, I suppose, and keeping the others awake. And they took me in a black van to a terrible dark place.

'I don't remember the first few days because the drugs they injected me with made me sleep so well. I slept for hours and days, and one morning I woke completely clear in my mind and asked the nurse what the date was. Then I knew for sure I was going to have a child and I wondered if they'd let me keep it.

'Weeks passed and I can't remember much except for a scruffy little sparrow that used to come to my window and peer in through the bars at me. Then a new doctor arrived, Dr Augustine. I didn't like him. He wasn't kind to me. If I told you what he did you wouldn't believe me because no one wants to believe that about a doctor. He used to call me Isabel. This didn't worry me at first, after all, I had never told them my real name, just Natalia. Eventually I was well enough to be interviewed in his office and once, when he was outside the room, I looked at my file. The name on it was Isabel Castello, born in Figueres. There was a letter in beautiful handwriting, with a crest on it, attached to the file. When Dr Augustine returned I tried to tell him that it was the wrong file but he simply wouldn't listen. He just shook his head and sighed.

'Then one morning I was given back my shoes and a new, thick coat. "Aren't you pleased to be going home to Spain?" asked the nurse. "Yes," I said. I had learnt not to make trouble by disagreeing with the nurses.

'In the lobby a woman with thick ankles and a heavy, bored face was waiting for me. At last, I thought, it will all be sorted out. But she didn't seem surprised to see me instead of Isabel Castello and she picked up my bag without a word and made off, expecting me to follow. What sort of people would send a servant to collect their sick relative? The door was open and the maid was standing on the street waiting for me. I couldn't help it, I could smell the air, so I stepped outside. After all, no one would believe me if I said who I was. Do you think it was wrong? My identity had already been swapped with someone else's. A woman called Isabel who should be free is locked up because of me: a woman they are calling Natalia.

'Anyway, the servant woman took me to a taxi outside and then changed her mind and we walked to Gare Montparnasse instead where she started drinking the unspent taxi fare at the bar. I knew I couldn't go to Figueres and risk meeting Isabel's family so I pretended to have cramps in my stomach and said I needed the toilet. The woman let me go on my own, she was so stupid. It never seemed to worry her that I couldn't speak Spanish; perhaps she thought it was part of my illness. In the toilet I climbed out of the window and got out of the station. I lifted a purse from the pocket of a woman in furs who could surely afford to lose it and later that day I caught a train back from Gare du Nord to Lille.

'Angélique was born six months later. She is Louis' child.'

After Suzanne had been silent for a few minutes, Penelope said, 'But he wasn't disappointed. I've read D'Argent's book and he says that he was the failure, not you. He was not able to rise to the challenge you set him – to him you were the surrealist ideal in living form. You were the one who saw the Marvellous every day, everywhere.'

'Then why did he abandon me to the police? To the doctors?'

'We are never as strong as we would wish ourselves to be. I think his nerve failed, that's all. It is still forbidden to mention your name, or rather the name *Natalia*, in his presence. He's ashamed, Suzanne. He thinks you are still locked away.'

'I am. I am.'

Penelope watched as Suzanne bowed her head. It was too painful to see and Penelope turned away. Her gaze lit upon the nettles next to the bench. At first she thought her eyesight had gone wrong, or maybe she was having one of Suzanne's hallucinations herself, because the plants and the trees behind were entirely swathed in grey cobweb veils. Tiny black grubs were mindlessly traversing the fuzzy surfaces. 'What on earth is wrong with the trees?' said Penelope, getting up to see.

Suzanne snapped back into alertness. 'They are ermine moths, or they will be. Isaac told me about them. They weave a waiting place; warm covers to hide in while they change.'

'I've never seen anything like it,' said Penelope, poking a finger into the gauze.

'You can leave me now. Now that you know.'

'No. Now that I know, I can stay,' said Penelope, squatting down in front of Suzanne and taking her hand. 'I will always be your friend, Suzanne, and I promise never to let you down.'

'I believe you,' she said. 'And I promise that next time we see Sammy ...'

Just then a brown-and-white spaniel came hurtling along the path and knocked Penelope over sideways. Suzanne laughed as she hauled Penelope up again and they watched the dog making mad circuits of the grass and grey gravel paths. From the entrance a woman using a crutch to walk was calling to him: 'Bobbi! Bobbi!'

On the next circuit he came straight at them.

'Go on, boy, back you go,' said Penelope.

But the dog was merry and devil-may-care. They stroked his sides and he jumped up to paw at Suzanne's dress while she tousled his curly ears and smoothed his velvet head. Then off he went again, growling with exertion. The woman was getting closer and still calling plaintively.

Suddenly the dog stood still and seemed to be hunching his shoulders. His eyes were trained on the pond. Two black coots were ferrying about in the shallows. He raced in a straight line across the grass and into the water. One bird fluttered and splashed and got out of his way but the other was taken by surprise and Bobbi's jaws closed around its neck. Back he came, shaking the bird like a piece of wet rag. The dog's glossy coat was dark with water and slime. The woman started shouting in a language Penelope could not recognise and, sensing that his prize might be taken from him, Bobbi started to run back towards the gate, dragging the bird along the grass. The woman turned and began to retrace her slow, limping journey.

'Well, why does she not get her dinner from the market like everyone else?' said Suzanne.

'What? You are joking? She's not going to eat it, surely?'

'No, of course not. Well, I shouldn't think so. But such a darling little dog. Who would have thought he could turn like that?'

They got up and started to walk towards the monument on the other side of the park, crossing a bridge over the water. A family of moorhens had made a nest out of torn-up cardboard boxes. A little further on Penelope felt the grass with the palm of her hand and, finding it dry, sat down cross-legged on the ground.

'So why did you come back to Paris?'

Suzanne knelt down beside her. 'I wanted to tell Louis that I forgave him and to tell him about Angélique and,' she added very quietly, 'I thought he might still care for me.'

'So why run away without seeing him?'

'We are never as strong as we wish ourselves to be.'

'Yes, I did say that, but sometimes it can be the opposite: until we are tested we can't know how strong we really are. I'm puzzled though, about lots of things. In the book, D'Argent writes that Natalia had a daughter.'

'No. I told him that I wanted a daughter.'

'And there's nothing about a park with fake logs.'

'That's probably because he cried that day.'

'So much for the naked truth. And he said you'd never drawn before you met him.'

'That's not true. But I never considered I was any good.'

'Like me and Rolf.'

Suzanne waited for her to go on.

'But I can't talk about that. I'm not sure I can bear to tell you.'

'How bad can it be, Penelope? I went mad for love. I am on the run because of love. Love has ended my peace of mind forever and it was not even returned. Tell me a worse story if you can.'

'Shall we go? I think the ground is wet after all.'

As they made their way towards the other gate, Penelope said, 'You're Jewish, aren't you, Suzanne?'

'Not really. I mean my father is, like my grandmother, Françoise, but *Maman* was Catholic and it's the mother that counts.'

'But if you were in Germany now ...'

'Well I'm not. Besides, I have lots of German friends: the man who runs the life class, the man who sells me cigarettes, Isaac's friend Helmut.'

'And none of them would hurt a fly, I suppose,' said Penelope.

They paused to contemplate the monument. At the base, there were frogs spewing water and the bust of a Victorian patriarch was displayed under a dome.

'Who is that?' asked Penelope.

'It is Samuel Sarphati,' said Suzanne. 'A rich, respected, successful Jew.'

Penelope laughed. 'You win.'

'Will you come and see Isaac?' asked Suzanne.

'Why not? I really have always wondered why God made people.'

Chapter Twenty-One

By the time Suzanne and Penelope reached the market on Albert Cuypstraat, it was nearly packed up. As they approached, a man in overalls pulling a barrel stopped to chat with Suzanne, but it was all in Dutch so Penelope understood nothing and Suzanne did not introduce her. When they had finished speaking, the man lifted up the round lid on the barrel. Suzanne grinned and plunged her hand deep inside, bringing out a fistful of purple pickled cabbage. She offered some to Penelope but it smelt awful. Suzanne laughed and munched away gaily until it was finished. Then she started to dart about behind the skeletal frames of the vacant market stalls with an empty orange box in one hand. Penelope waited and in a few minutes Suzanne returned with a collection of limp-looking vegetables. She was jubilant with her loot.

'We even have good onions. And carrots! I think that the colour of a cut carrot is my favourite colour in the world.'

'You mean cadmium orange,' said Penelope. 'When I couldn't sleep at home I used to recite all my favourite names for colours: yellow ochre, viridian, cobalt, burnt umber, lamp black, verdigris, rose madder. I used to try to see the colours inside the words.'

'When we die,' said Suzanne, 'I think that the colours will be different but I can't say how. Perhaps they will be more like those words of yours because it's possible to describe something more perfect than we have ever seen.'

They walked on, through terraced streets, past a bathhouse and stopped abruptly on a street beginning with Q which Penelope could not pronounce. There was a canal at right angles to the far end. Suzanne retrieved a key on a string from inside the letter box of number 51 and in they went. The door gave immediately onto a room with a table and a crowd of mismatched chairs. There was a cooking range, then a sink and, immediately next to it, a covered toilet. It was hard to adjust to the gloom after the sun-filled street. Suzanne lit an oil lamp and the paraffin fumes combined with the faint tang of urine emanating from the wooden toilet. Suzanne put down the box of vegetables and plonked a bottle of gin and two glasses on the table.

'Now,' she said, as she poured two generous measures, 'tell me about Rolf while I cook dinner.'

Penelope took first a sip then a large gulp of the sour drink. It was tepid and tasted like a medical syrup instead of the iced cocktail she associated with the flavour of gin. Here in Isaac's home nothing was dressed up like something else. She watched Suzanne move purposefully around the small, dim room, gathering cooking implements, then got up to look at some pictures torn out of magazines that had been tacked up on the walls. One was of a man in a shawl with something strapped to his forehead.

'I'm listening.'

Suzanne was not going to let it go, so Penelope sat down again, and took a deep breath.

'Rolf wants to share me with Alain, and to have Alain move in with us in Rue Jacob.'

'What?' Suzanne put down the chopping knife and came to sit at the table.

'Crazy, isn't it? It started because of Gabriel.'

'Gabriel?'

'Of course, you didn't know him. His uncle is a friend of Maurice's. See how the new generation is coming up now? What is surrealism coming to? Hijacked by upstarts. What next? Women surrealists?'

'What did Gabriel do?' asked Suzanne.

'He fell for me, in a big way, and I played along.'

'And Alain?'

'Alain has been so kind. He says he's loved me from the start. Ever since I came to Paris.'

'Do you believe him?'

'I don't know.'

'Rolf visited me,' said Suzanne, 'when I was ... inside. They told me he waited nearly two hours before going away again. He was the only one who came.'

Penelope had not been shocked by any of Suzanne's story but she found it hard to control the strong waves of pity that she felt when she thought about this. To her, pity was a demeaning emotion to have about someone but she felt she could weep for Suzanne's loss. To have found the love of one's life and self-belief for the first time and then to have both of them taken away, it was so sad. So very, very sad. Goodness me, it must be the gin, she thought.

'Rolf did not desert me,' said Suzanne.

'He is an honourable man,' said Penelope.

'A horrible man?' repeated Suzanne.

'No, honourable!'

Penelope caught Suzanne's eye and they started to laugh.

'But how beautifully French,' said Suzanne, 'a *ménage à trois*.'

'The perfect solution,' said Penelope. 'I can have them both. And why not Maurice too? He has such lovely ears. Oh, what am I going to do?' She put her head on her arms.

Penelope felt Suzanne's hand rest briefly on her shoulder but when she looked up, Suzanne was back near the sink, peeling carrots.

'Tell me again, from the start,' said Suzanne. 'You wanted to make Rolf jealous.'

'Not deliberately. I suppose it was what he said about *Her Mother's Face*, the piece I made the day after you left. It's the head of a mannequin, wrapped in scarves. I was thinking of what you said about your mother, when she died.'

'Thank you.'

'Don't thank me. I used to shout at it when I got angry about how you ran off that night.'

'Oh. So what did Rolf say about it?' Suzanne paused her cooking preparations.

'He said his niece did something similar at school.'

'But that's good, isn't it? Louis used to say that the vision of the child is the essence of surrealism.'

'Only if it's a sexy woman pretending to be a child. All of a sudden it turns out I'm too much of a child for Rolf. He says I'm not mature enough to take two lovers at the same time.'

'And would he be taking Alain as another lover too?'

Penelope got up and started pacing around the room. 'I don't know. He's never explained that part. All I know is that when he and Alain are working in the studio together I might as well not be there.'

Penelope sat down again and took another swig of the warm gin. Suzanne came over and refilled her glass.

'And here's the best of it,' Penelope went on. 'They want to make a book about me. Pictures of me by Rolf, poems about me by Alain. I'd be immortalised. Everyone could stare at me then. Except it wouldn't be me.'

'What do you mean?'

'Well, wouldn't it be like D'Argent's book? *Natalia* is about a fantasy woman, a martyr to surrealism. It isn't you.'

Suzanne was quiet for a while. 'Maybe not,' she said, 'but who am I anyway?'

Penelope grinned. 'I thought we'd settled that.'

'We have,' she said, looking up again and smiling. 'So is that why you stopped painting? Because Rolf called you a child?'

'Yes, maybe. After he named the fur cup I felt he had taken my power away. Just like D'Argent took it from you.'

'No. Louis gave me the courage to see my world and to name it.'

'Then why are people reading his words instead of yours, Suzanne?'

Just then, the key on the string was jerked up and pulled out through the letter box from the outside.

'*Bon Dieu*, it's Isaac,' said Suzanne, leaping up and throwing the knife in the sink. 'Don't tell him I was using that knife to chop vegetables.'

Penelope was still trying to work out why not when Isaac came in and he must have taken her puzzled frown as a sign of guilt at being there at all. She rose to meet him.

'No, no,' he said. 'Any friend of Zuzanka's is welcome in my home.' He placed a hand on her shoulder to encourage her to sit back down.

The gesture reminded her uncomfortably of her first meeting with Rolf, but Isaac's wrinkled and dry hand was foreign to her; there was no kinship there. A heave of gin-fuelled sentiment overtook her. Rolf is my family now, she thought.

As if he had read her mind, Isaac intoned, 'And thy people shall be my people.' Then he went to greet Suzanne.

Penelope could not help but stare at Isaac's extravagant white beard and the soft cap he wore on the top of his head that seemed to have beads and sequins sewn on. His demeanour reminded her of photographs of Mahatma Gandhi in the newspapers. He was slight and bent but his humility had a commanding air. He wore an atrociously dirty coat over a neat tie and shirt collar.

'Tut, tut, Zuza,' he said, plucking the knife from the sink and waving it like a wagging finger.' Then he turned to the table. 'And drinking *chametz*, too.'

Penelope's frown deepened further. She felt very awkward, and rather responsible, but then she saw that Isaac's eyes were glittering, like the little buttons and mirrors on his cap.

'This is my gentile friend Penelope, Isaac, and she has no idea what you are talking about.'

'What a treat you bring me.' Isaac took off his coat and rubbed his hands together in anticipation.

'And,' continued Suzanne, 'it is possible she has no interest in hearing about Jewish customs.'

'Oh, no, please,' said Penelope, weakly. 'But won't you have a drink, sir, if Suzanne can find another glass, perhaps?'

Isaac was much amused by this and laughed in dry gasps.

'It's Passover, Penelope, and until the eighth night Isaac will not drink fermented grain, or eat bread, or scratch his nose for all I know, because we didn't bother about all this business at home.'

'Of course, I should have known that,' said Penelope. 'Daddy had an accountant who was always asking for days off. I'm afraid Daddy called him some names because he refused to work on Saturdays.'

'But he was allowed to keep the sabbath?' asked Isaac.

'Oh yes, of course.' Penelope didn't add that the man was in a union and had threatened a factory walkout otherwise.

'Then your father is a true friend of Israel and I raise a glass to his name. *Tok*!' Isaac pretended to toast Penelope's father by clinking an imaginary glass against her own, real, one. 'Cheers! *Proost*!' said Isaac and gave his rasping laugh again, much entertained. 'So you see, Zuzanka,' he said, 'it is not what is in the glass, nor is it the glass itself, it is the raising of the glass that joins us as friends around the table of God.'

'This isn't a meeting, Isaac, this is dinner, or it will be soon.'

'Dinner. You see how she cherishes me. You must cherish your father, Penelope.'

'I very much doubt if my father will ever speak to me again.'

'Why? Have you killed a man?'

'Never.'

'Have you stolen money, or cheated or told a large lie?'

Penelope shook her head to each in turn.

'Then you are still his daughter.'

'But I am an artist. I'm supposed to be at home, breeding dogs and children.'

'Every man wants his name to live on, that is true. Does your art honour his name?'

'I've never thought about it like that,' said Penelope.

'So, this is a new story for you, and for God also. Which is all he wants, Penelope. For why did God make people?'

'Because he loves stories,' supplied Suzanne.

'And does he know the end of my story?' Penelope asked Isaac.

'Perhaps. Perhaps.'

There was a knock on the door. Isaac looked anxiously at Suzanne.

'It must be Freddie Jacobs,' she said. 'I invited him.'

Isaac, stiff but sprightly, got up to open the door, and then spread out his arms. 'Freddie. Come in. Come in.'

'I hope it is a convenient time,' said Freddie, smiling at Suzanne from under his rogue lock of hair. 'Hello again, Penelope. Suzanne, these are for you.'

He had brought some white carnations which he presented very awkwardly. An image came to Penelope of Freddie pacing up and down outside the house, rehearsing his line. His eyes followed every move Suzanne made and Isaac had to ask him twice to sit down before he heard. Then he stubbed his toe on the table leg because Suzanne was still cooing over the flowers and smiling at him.

'Will you be drinking?' Isaac stood waiting for the answer.

'No, no, water only.'

'Zuzanka, some coffee for Freddie.'

Suzanne gave Penelope a look that said 'See what I have to put up with?' but smiled and went about preparing the coffee without a word.

'And now we can all sit down together,' said Isaac, comfortably ignoring Suzanne.

'Please, let me do this,' said Freddie getting up again.

'No, no, it's fine,' said Suzanne, who looked slightly puzzled and allowed her eyes to linger on Freddie's face for a moment.

Maybe, thought Penelope, he could heal the terrible bruise that D'Argent had left and which every memory darkened further. She imagined Freddie lifting Suzanne's little daughter high in the air and laughing as the copper curls glowed on his brow. Then the whole room slid sideways a few degrees and she couldn't put it right again.

'And some coffee for your new friend, Zuzanka. She is not used to strong spirits. Why, even I feel a little gladder for smelling it.'

The voices seemed very far away. 'You are speaking English, and yet you come from Lithuania,' said Penelope, clinging on to facts.

'Quite so. And we thought you were drunk, Penelope,' said Isaac with a mischievous look at Freddie. Then, with a serious face, 'My language was taken from me by the Russians. Lithuanian was banned in school so when I was older I taught myself English and Polish, as well as Hebrew, for spite. But I should not have done it for that reason, for to speak a language is to know the soul of a people. It is like eating their food or singing their songs.'

Penelope took a few thoughtful sips of tarry coffee and stared at a small, flat-backed tube made of brass that was fixed to the wall just inside the door. 'So, tell me about the soul of the British.'

'A decent soul, but always waiting for the other to ask, never holding out a hand first.'

'And the Dutch soul?' asked Penelope. She found it very comforting to be told what to think for a change.

'The Dutch are too conventional to admit to having such a thing,' declared Isaac.

'No,' said Penelope, rather belligerently all of a sudden, 'today at the cinema a man was let in with muddy clogs and you can't tell me that the man who let in this farmer with the manure still sticking to his shoes has no soul.'

'Ah,' said Freddie, 'that will be Abraham, the owner.'

'And he is Polish,' cried Isaac, triumphantly. 'He is Polish!'

'But what about the soul of Germany?' asked Freddie, staring down at his cup.

'I shall not speak ill,' was all Isaac would say.

'Well then, I shall,' said Freddie. 'I had a letter today. *Mutti*, Heinz and Anna are still in Vienna and things are as bad as can be. Mother is no longer allowed to teach the piano, not even to other Jews. She writes that it is not possible for Jews to get passports anymore and she needs a lot more money if she is to buy them on the black market. She says she is safe but our friend Renata and her two boys have disappeared. No one knows where.'

'Maybe they went on holiday,' said Suzanne, returning to the table and only just catching the drift of the conversation.

'I don't think so,' said Freddie, very gently. 'Anna was out shopping, or at least looking to see what was left in the shops, and she saw German officers forcing some men to wash the streets with a bucket and cloth. On their knees.'

'They must have been criminals,' said Suzanne.

'No. Jews.'

'Is it not possible to be both?'

'Suzanne, you are not hearing me,' said Freddie, still very tenderly.

'Do you have the money?' asked Penelope.

'Nearly.'

'How much do you need? I have a savings account.'

Freddie looked directly at her. 'I cannot take your money.'

'Yes you can.' She placed her hand on his arm. 'Yes, Freddie, you can.'

'So,' said Isaac, contentedly, 'they will come to Amsterdam and all shall be well.'

'Oh Isaac,' said Suzanne, 'tell about the Rembrandtplein, in '33.'

'The white doves?' asked Isaac.

Suzanne got up to stir the stew. 'They released white doves, Penelope, to protest against the fascists,' she said. 'Isn't that beautiful?'

'I think it's utterly pointless,' said Penelope.

'Zuzanka forgot to tell you that they released white mice also,' said Isaac.

'Well that's positively irresponsible,' said Penelope.

'You see,' said Isaac to Suzanne, 'your new friend is a realist.'

'Yes. I am. And Freddie's family must get out of Vienna. Immediately. Freddie, meet me at the British Embassy at ten o'clock tomorrow and I will draw out the money.'

'Thank you,' he said, studying her face.

'Your father's money?' enquired Isaac.

'In a way. That accountant I told you about, he was a friend of mine. He was very creative in his work.'

'*I sveikata*!' shouted Isaac, raising his invisible glass, and laughing until he coughed.

Suzanne was frowning, so Freddie got up and started slapping Isaac on the back, but the old man waved him away, unable to speak. When Isaac had recovered, Suzanne placed a huge pan of vegetables on the table.

'Now,' she said, 'let's eat.'

Chapter Twenty-Two

When the meal was over, the party broke up. Freddie had arranged to meet a friend, and Suzanne offered to walk Penelope back to her hotel.

'Because we wouldn't want you to fall into a canal and have to be fished out by Mr Sinck,' she teased.

All three set off together leaving Isaac standing in the doorway with his bony hand raised in a farewell blessing. At the corner, where the road met the canal, Penelope looked back and he was still there, staring across the road, lost in thought. With Isaac, Suzanne was sweet and compliant. Most probably, he had no idea of her visions and troubled past. Penelope could understand how this might help Suzanne, for if Isaac believed her to be a quiet, steady sort of person it would be easy to pretend to be so with him. The arrangement suited Isaac very well, of course, having Suzanne keep house for him, thought Penelope, then chided herself for having such thoughts about the kindly old man.

But Suzanne seemed to be whatever men needed her to be: the fey visionary for D'Argent; the guileless show-off for Freddie; the outrageous and scurrilous bar habitué for Sammy. With me, thought Penelope, she is all of these and she makes me happy. When I see her a weight lifts from my heart and a yellow glow takes its place, like sunlight in the centre of my chest.

Freddie was very quiet. He was walking ahead beside Suzanne and Penelope suspected that he was trying to gather up the courage to ask if he could see her again. Suzanne seemed to know it too and was giving him no help at all.

'Are you busy tomorrow, Freddie?' she asked, with a grin behind his back at Penelope.

'But don't forget, Freddie,' said Penelope, 'you are to meet me at ten.' She had reminded him of this several times during the evening but Freddie seemed unwilling to believe that this would actually happen.

'Thank you. Suzanne, perhaps you—'

'Yes, I'll come along. I don't have to work until two.'

Freddie beamed. The night was chill and Suzanne had thrown an old green jacket of Isaac's around her shoulders like a cape. When she saw Penelope shiver she dropped back and encircled her inside the jacket too.

'Well, ladies, it has been a pleasure. Such a pleasure. This is Prinsengracht and I must go my way. Until tomorrow, then?'

'Goodbye,' said Penelope, taking his hand.

Suzanne just smiled and Freddie turned and started to walk away. He looked back to see her once more and narrowly missed walking into a postbox. They laughed and continued on.

'I think you have an admirer,' said Penelope.

'Yes. How did you like my friend Isaac?'

'Very much. What have you told him about yourself?'

'That I ran away from my husband in Paris because he used to beat me. I borrowed that from you, remember, when you used to think I was Suzanne Müller.'

'Isn't it difficult, remembering all these different stories?'

'There is only one. And the truth is what I told you earlier today. I shall never forget that.'

'But you must put it behind you, Suzanne.'

'Why must I?'

'It can only do you harm, continuing to love ... that man.' Penelope suddenly found she was unable to say D'Argent's name.

'And is that how you live? Deciding who it is best for you to love?'

'I live only to paint.'

'That is a lie.'

Penelope set her mouth firmly and didn't reply. 'Isn't this Rembrantplein?' she asked.

'Yes, your hotel is just over there.'

'So it is, but what's this?' Penelope squatted down on the ground with her back to Suzanne and made little squeaking noises. 'A tiny white mouse?'

'What?' Suzanne scanned the ground with alarm.

'No, wait,' said Penelope, getting up. 'A whole family, a tribe, a nation, an army of mice. Beware all fascists!' and she skipped from foot to foot in pretend fear.

Suzanne laughed so much that she had to wipe her eyes.

'Let's never fall out over these wretched creatures,' said Penelope.

'Mice?'

'No, men.'

And that set them off all over again.

'Why don't I buy you a drink in the Schiller bar,' said Penelope, 'I haven't been in yet.'

Suzanne hung back but Penelope had already started to stride towards the small covered courtyard. 'Don't worry,' she called over her shoulder, 'I told you, D'Argent is in Utrecht and I'm not meeting Alain until tomorrow afternoon at the gallery. It's quite safe. Look,' she said as they reached the entrance, 'I'll go in first and have a look,' and she plunged into the revolving door, leaving Suzanne with her mouth open, about to protest some more.

Inside, Penelope just had time to gasp with pleasure at the huge lantern in the shape of a ship covered with lights above the bar before she saw Josephine sitting in a corner on her own. Penelope turned and, before Josephine could look up and see her, went back outside again. Suzanne had vanished. Penelope felt a swell of anger. Why must she always run off like this? Then Suzanne appeared again, emerging from the revolving door in her turn.

'This is like a scene in a Marx Brothers film,' said Penelope, a bit irritated but beginning to see the funny side.

'I thought you were waiting inside for me,' said Suzanne.

'No. Look, Josephine is in there. Does she know you?'

'Josephine?'

'D'Argent's wife.'

'I've never set eyes on her. He was married to Sidonie when I knew him.'

'So it's all right to go in then?'

Penelope doubted that it would be, but Suzanne surprised her.

'Yes, I'd like to meet her,' she replied.

The narrow room was almost empty. It was fitted with dark wood and golden lamps and had a medieval-style mural showing musicians in rich orange and russet colours. One table was occupied by a vociferous group of men engaged in the sort of political-cum-philosophical drunken conversation that needed no translation to be recognised. They were putting the world to rights, loudly, and would remember very little about who said what tomorrow morning.

Penelope led Suzanne to where Josephine sat.

'*Bonsoir*, Josephine. This is my friend.'

'How do you do?' said Suzanne, in a posh accent, with more than a touch of educated Scots. 'I'm Susie. Pleased to meet you.' She held out her hand.

Penelope was spellbound: another performance.

'*Enchantée*. From England, *n'est pas*, like Penelope,' said Josephine, getting up to reach across the table. 'My English is not very good. *Quel dommage.*'

'On the contrary,' said Suzanne.

'Please. Join me.'

So they pulled out two chairs opposite Josephine who then sat back down with an unladylike bump and hooked her smooth brown hair behind her ears. Penelope soon realised that Josephine was not her usual demure and contained self and sure enough there was a bottle of red wine two-thirds empty in front of her. Josephine picked it up.

'Penelope, ask the waiter to bring another of these for us,' she said in French, and Suzanne stared deliberately at the figure of a woman in flowing robes on the wall behind, pretending not to understand.

'Is Clara with you?' asked Penelope in English. She and Alain had travelled to Holland separately from the D'Argents.

'No, she is with Maurice and Una in Paris. I am free.'

'And what have you been doing in Amsterdam?' asked Suzanne.

'Do you want to see?' Josephine produced a portfolio from under the table and opened it, knocking the wine bottle which teetered dangerously until Penelope caught it. But Josephine was intent only on arranging the loose sheets in the folder. She turned it around and pushed the whole thing across the table for them to see.

'*Voilà*. What do you think?'

They were sketches of little girls in Victorian dresses near staircases and corridors containing many doors, in well-appointed homes. They had the bodies of children but postures that were knowingly sexual. In one picture a large sunflower emerged incongruously from a chink of light under the door.

'*Le tournesol* of Louis' poem,' explained Josephine.

'Has D'Argent seen these?' asked Penelope.

'He will not look.' Josephine lapsed back into French and Suzanne continued to turn the sheets over in silence, absorbed. 'He laughs and says, "Oh, we are an artist now, are we?" And of course they are naive. They are not very good. I have never been trained.'

'Stop,' said Penelope sharply. 'These are wonderful pictures.'

'What is this?' Suzanne, visibly shaken, held up another picture of a man whose hair streamed upwards as if on fire, or made of flames.

'It is from Louis' book. Do you know it? The book called *Natalia*?'

Suzanne, unable to speak, gave a shake of her head.

'Josephine, I want Rolf to see these,' said Penelope.

'Why?'

'They are wonderful pictures,' she said again.

'Perhaps. *Merci beaucoup.*' Josephine gathered the pictures together and stowed them away as before, under the table, out of sight. 'Do you live here in Amsterdam?' she asked Suzanne, but before Suzanne could answer, Josephine leapt out of her seat. Her eyes were shining; she had obviously recognised someone coming in.

Penelope saw D'Argent at the same moment as Suzanne. Josephine ran to him and stood by the door talking intensely with her hand on his sleeve. Penelope exchanged a wordless look with Suzanne that was a whole conversation and Suzanne reached for her hand under the table and grasped it tightly. Penelope could feel her thin fingers shaking as D'Argent approached.

'Louis,' said Josephine, 'this is Penelope's friend Susie, from England.'

Suzanne turned around to look at him, still gripping Penelope's hand.

D'Argent inclined his head politely and pushed up his glasses. 'Susie, I salute you. The English, unlike the Dutch, have an understanding of surrealism and also the courage to stand up for it.'

'Louis,' chided Josephine, 'Susie doesn't understand French.'

D'Argent apologised and turned back to Josephine to ask what they would like to drink, then wandered off to inspect the pictures around the walls. Suzanne looked back at Penelope with wide, panicked eyes.

'Actually,' said Penelope to Josephine, 'we really should be going. I have to meet someone.'

They got up to leave. Suzanne said nothing in return to Josephine's farewell and they walked quickly back to the door. Once they were outside again Suzanne put a hand on one of the covered chairs in the courtyard to steady herself.

'He didn't recognise you,' said Penelope.

Suzanne's face was hidden behind the curtain of her dull yellow hair. She began to cave in at the knees and Penelope grabbed the chair. In one moment she reversed it and pulled back the canvas over the seat while steering Suzanne into place. Suzanne sat and bent over, reminding Penelope of that day she had discovered her downstairs at Le Parisien.

Penelope leant over her and when she gently pushed Suzanne's hair away from her face, Suzanne did not flinch but looked up at her, ashen and revealed.

'Now you won't believe me,' she said.

'I do believe you,' said Penelope. 'D'Argent's Natalia lives for him only in his book. It was always that way.'

'And me?'

'You're not her. You are yourself.'

'Myself?'

'You are Angélique's mother, Isaac's daughter, Freddie's intended. My friend. But most of all, your own self.'

Suzanne's tears filled her eyes and started to spill down her cheeks. They were black with the make-up she continued to use, as if the shock of this hard lesson was finally cleaning and clearing her disturbed sight.

Chapter Twenty-Three

Paris, June 1938

Penelope had been basking in the summer sunshine all day.
Now she was in the Café de Flore: the café she loved most
of all. In England, the men's pubs and the women's teashops
repeated the exaggerated separation of the sexes like Victorian
costumes, but here, cafés were places for all. She watched a
coiffured woman feeding titbits to her little dog (tolerated
but covertly watched by the waiters). Nearby, a grumpy man
obscured by a newspaper grunted at the headlines. It had clearly
been hours since he had ordered anything: not even an empty
cup or glass remained on his table.

The cafés changed throughout the day. Very early, there were
the standing-up, hurried drinkers, then the prosperous idle who
could afford to sit through their empty mornings. Lunchtime
brought workers again, but this time office staff and managers
with money to spend on cassoulet and a glass of Bordeaux.
The afternoon was the most likely time for the less fortunate
to attempt to buy a sustaining Calvados by haggling, or better
still, by striking up a conversation at the bar with someone
who might buy it for them. And now, just before six, came the
irregular ones, like Penelope herself, or the woman with her dog,
or that young woman over there with her chic, radical haircut:
probably a student.

Penelope was still wrestling with the contradictions between
Suzanne's story and the fact that D'Argent had not seemed

to recognise her. Intellectually, Penelope knew that D'Argent's self-absorption could easily account for his behaviour towards Suzanne because his creation, Natalia, was safely in the past and, as far as D'Argent was concerned, still locked away. A random British woman who happened to be sitting in a bar in Amsterdam would not be likely to have any connection with her. But still it irked her to think that he could forget Suzanne's face so completely.

She secretly congratulated herself on the centrality of her role in the surrealist group. Suzanne had been, as far as she could tell, scarcely acknowledged and had remained on the extreme outer edges of the movement during that early period. But here Penelope was, waiting to take part in the six o'clock meeting as she had done all through her year in Paris. She had exhibited with them, been included in everything. And the jokes about the fur cup had, thankfully, subsided. What would happen, though, if the cup were to be exhibited again? Could she assert herself and ban the use of Rolf's awful name for it? Did she have a better title?

She was so absorbed in this question that Una's voice made her jump.

'I was asking if you would mind if I joined you, Penelope.'

'Of course. Of course.'

'The meeting is at six, is it not?'

'Yes.'

'Then I am not too late.' Una put her elegant handbag on the shelf behind the banquette and settled herself down neatly, beaming at Penelope. 'You are wondering why I'm here.'

Penelope smiled back and waited.

'Alain has been asking me to join the meetings. He keeps saying I should come. So, for him, I am here.'

'Not for yourself?'

'What do you mean? Shall we order some wine?' Una's attention was on one of the waiters, assessing her chances of capturing him.

'Our meetings are for artists and poets. Any surrealist is welcome, but I doubt they would interest anyone else. Are you planning to exhibit your collages, to develop them perhaps?'

'No, those are for my own amusement. But if Alain requires me, I will be here.'

'You're not his wife, Una. You don't have to obey his every wish.'

'But it pleases me to please him. The same with Jean. Rolf has also agreed I should come.'

'You'll have fun trying to obey all the men. What about doing what you want?'

Una laughed. 'My life is one long holiday now. Every day I am so happy to be safe and to eat well. I want nothing more.'

'Alain and Jean, they provide for you, then?' Penelope had never really understood the financial side of the three-way arrangement.

'Yes. Maurice, too. They all put money in my savings book. I owe my life to them. And if Alain were to decide to love another woman ...' Una's glance dropped to the table, 'it would make no difference. I would be cared for, still.'

Penelope thrust aside the alarming idea that Alain had discussed his feelings for her with Una, and went on trying to draw out how Una regarded her position in the group.

'But doesn't it concern you, not to have your own money? Your independence?'

'We are not all so fortunate as you, Penelope, to have grown up in a big house with servants.'

'We only had three: a cook, a chauffeur and there was Mrs Andrews. I'm not sure of her actual job, but she did everything else, even the gardening. I'd rather have had an ordinary upbringing – a father who had a trade instead of being someone who exploited his workers. I'm a socialist.'

'Indeed. But you really know nothing about real life, I think.'

Penelope bristled. 'What d'you mean? I left that big house. I gave up everything for art.'

'But not your private income.'

'That's what gives me my freedom. Having it means I can paint and do what I like.'

'You say you are free and yet you live on your father's money. I know I am dependent on Alain and the others. They saved me from a terrible life on the street. My freedom belongs to them.'

'But you don't,' said Penelope.

'Don't I?'

Una smiled at someone behind them.

Penelope turned to see Fabien wearing an inappropriate old raincoat – it was a warm day in June – coming towards them.

Fabien greeted Una warmly, seeming not to be surprised by her presence at all. He immediately went off to secure them a bottle of wine.

Penelope heard Rolf's voice before she saw him. He came striding in, with Alain following slowly behind, as he gracefully negotiated the tables and chairs.

My two suitors, thought Penelope. If only it were as simple as a choice between them. Rolf had never again referred to his proposal that Alain should join them in bed, but every time they made love she could almost hear him thinking about it. He remained staunchly supportive of her work, and concerned by the block she was experiencing.

Alain, obviously delighted by seeing Una, took his place next to her. Penelope got up and stepped into Rolf's path. She placed her hand on his chest, a strange beseeching gesture which was unlike her. He looked a question into her eyes then straightened up and moved to the side, giving her a mild, cordial smile as if she were merely a pleasant acquaintance with odd manners. He went to sit with Alain.

D'Argent arrived next, greeting Rolf and Alain with handshakes and performing the ritual of the finger-kissing on both of the women. Una became immediately subdued, her baby-blue eyes darting from one man to the other seeking reassurance. Conveniently, Fabien returned after D'Argent had sat down; Penelope had often noted how D'Argent preferred not to touch him. He gave Fabien a curt nod.

'Tonight we shall play Conditionals,' he said. 'I shall explain the rules for our guest.'

It took Penelope a few moments to realise he meant Una, who was smiling manically.

'First we shall all write a hypothetical sentence which begins with the word "if". We put these in the pot.' He held up a linen drawstring bag. 'Then we write a conditional: a sentence that begins with "then" or speaks of a future event, such as what will or would be. These are to be placed in here.' He indicated a second bag. 'Let us begin.'

'But—'

D'Argent turned sharply to Una, on his right. Penelope could see the fear in Una's eyes as his fierce gaze, focused through the flashing metallic glasses, fixed on her.

'How are the sentences to be matched up, please?' she asked.

'I shall withdraw them and follow where they lead.'

Una looked very perplexed.

'It will all become clear,' said Alain, pouring her a glass of wine.

D'Argent distributed slips of paper and short pencils. 'First write the hypothetical,' he commanded, 'and do not think.'

Penelope dived straight in: 'If snakes had feathers,' she wrote.

Alain smiled as he scribbled. Rolf had fixed his eyes on the mirror behind her, waiting for inspiration. Una leant across to see what Alain was writing and got a silent shake of the head in return.

Once both sets of slips had been collected, D'Argent ritualistically shook the bags in turn. He placed the contents in two columns, face down, on the table.

'First we have this,' he said and turned over the top row.

'If the printer's fingers blackened the steak,

Then letters would dance the polka.'

Penelope knew that Fabien had written the 'if' part because she knew about his lover at the Dijon Press. Everyone knew who had written the second sentence because Alain never contributed anything that did not have words or writing as its theme.

D'Argent went on to reveal the second pair. 'Rolf,' he said, 'we are of the same mind.' No doubt D'Argent recognised Rolf's handwriting. He read out their co-authored creation:

'If a train went into the tunnel of eternal darkness,

Then railway carriages would contain only ladies.'

Penelope could not determine which was Rolf's sentence and which D'Argent's, but found it significant that the sum result of this random collaboration was the abolition of women.

'Ah,' said D'Argent, turning over the next slip, 'here is Rolf's hand again, I think.

'If leather gloves knew the way to Wales—'

'Where is Wales?' asked Una.

'Next to England,' replied Rolf. 'I know of it because Penelope's mother was born there.'

D'Argent revealed the counterpart: 'Then two hats would fit on one head.'

He did not comment on the authorship of this sentence, which was Penelope's own, and now gave her an uncertain feeling: what two hats was she trying to fit on her head? Surely this life in Paris had given her a way to be truly herself in a way that a life straining against the conventions of her class and family in Oxfordshire never could. Penelope felt suddenly fraudulent and, when a look of severe disapproval came over D'Argent's face as he turned over the next slip, she thought for a moment that she was the cause.

'If I had money enough to fill a house,' D'Argent read out. 'Who has written this?'

All eyes turned to Una; no true surrealist would express such a mercenary sentiment.

'Have I done something wrong?' asked Una.

'Don't worry,' said Penelope, 'I'll explain later.' Poor Una, she looked so forlorn.

Luckily, D'Argent had already moved on. 'But here is the answer.' He laid down the companion slip which was in Fabien's unmistakable copperplate hand.

'Then death would cure it.'

Penelope wondered why Fabien would write about death. But she was immediately distracted from following her thoughts by the sight of her own contribution because D'Argent had turned over the next row.

'Ah, the mate for this is my own.

'If snakes had feathers,

Then knives would soften.'

'But what does this prove?' asked Una.

Alain prepared to speak, first hesitating to see if D'Argent would take up his position of spokesman for the group, but he was silent, perhaps considering the education of Una to be beneath him.

'The principle of surrealism,' said Alain, 'is to allow random connections to occur so that we may bypass rationality and manifest the unconscious. This is why we aspire to produce work by automatism or chance and thereby create art without the exercise of the will.'

'Freedom from the will releases the imagination and restores the primacy of love,' added Rolf.

'And not only that,' said Fabien, warming to the task of declaring their creed, 'we want to transform society, to throw over the old ways, make room for passion where only the constraints of law existed before. Down with all laws. Down with prejudice and oppression of all kinds!'

D'Argent gave Fabien a wary look and closed the meeting by leaving.

Alain left with Una, and Fabien said his farewells leaving Penelope and Rolf at the empty table.

'I am going away tomorrow,' said Rolf, without any preamble.

'Away?' asked Penelope.

'My Copenhagen exhibition has been brought forward. I must hang my work before July now.'

'Oh.' She wondered if Rolf would ask her to accompany him.

'When I return,' he said, 'I would like an answer.'

Penelope didn't need to ask what he meant.

'How long will you be gone?'

'About a month in all.'

Penelope found herself suddenly craving solitude with a desire so strong that it took her by surprise. Alone, she would be able to work again, and get some purchase on this confusing situation with Alain.

'Yes,' she said, 'when you come back, I'll have decided.'

'Good,' he said.

They scarcely spoke again that night and, in the morning, Rolf left for Denmark.

Chapter Twenty-Four

Paris, July 1938

As the weeks of Rolf's absence wore on, Penelope began to feel that she was being punished. Rolf had withdrawn both his love and his presence in order to exert pressure on her. She drew a rough portrait of him in her sketchbook and added a small cage dangling from his hand in which a miniature white horse was enclosed.

Alain came back into the kitchen where they had been having lunch. With Jean away helping Rolf in Copenhagen (another rebuke to her) and Una on a road trip with Maurice to Cannes, Alain had implored her to visit. Fabien had left too, finally deciding to move back to Dijon after losing his job at the bookshop and all his boxes were gone. They were alone.

'A surprise,' Alain said, holding a basket with a domed lid.

Inside were two adorable black kittens.

Penelope threw aside her drawing and plunged in her hands, able to enclose a kitten in each. She rubbed their silken fur against her face and for some reason felt tearful.

'But we have no milk for them,' she said.

'On the contrary,' said Alain, opening the Frigidaire where a row of small milk bottles stood next to a paper bag she recognised from her favourite patisserie.

After the cats had been fed and lunch was over, they went into the other room. Alain returned the kittens to the basket where they yawned, displaying their delicate pink-ridged mouths, then settled to clean their whiskers and doze.

Penelope leant on Alain beside her on the sofa and felt her body go loose. She imitated the cats and stretched her limbs luxuriously, full of good bread, wine and cream cake, and shut her eyes. She knew what was going to happen and merely smiled as she felt Alain gently unbuttoning her shirt then slipping off her harem pants. But, before he led her to the bedroom, she moved away and dropped his hand.

'It is you, or him. Not both.'

'And you choose me?'

'I choose you.'

'Then you are all I want, Penelope. Let me show you.'

A few days later, Penelope discovered that Una's clothes had gone. The closet was empty apart from a pair of white high-heeled shoes.

'Una thought you might like them.' Alain came up from behind to embrace her.

His step was so light that she never knew where he was in the flat. Rolf, by contrast, made a noise whatever he was doing: even when sitting still he would be tapping a pen or twisting a cup on the table. Alain was as silent as the kittens when they played at hunting, sinking close to the ground and tautly hunching their back legs and shoulders.

Alain reached around and held out a bag of pastries.

'I'll get fat,' said Penelope, leaning back against Alain and feeling his erection fitting into the cleft of her buttocks. She broke away, plucking the cakes out of his grip.

In the kitchen the cats, named Fire and Brimstone, were tumbling together in mock battle.

'Una has moved in with Maurice,' said Alain as he splashed milk into the two saucers on the floor, 'and I have suggested that Jean should take Fabien's room, so ...'

'We would be alone together here.'

'Yes.'

'I'll think about it.'

'Rolf will be back next week.'

'I know.'

Alain looked at her and she went to him but something touched her bare foot. It was an injured mouse, lying sideways with its tiny white belly rapidly working up and down.

'Oh no. What have they done?'

'Who?' Alain asked.

'These darling cats have caught a little mouse.'

'Here.' Alain got a dustpan and scooped up the disjointed, oozing body. He went to deposit it in the rubbish bin.

'No,' said Penelope, 'you must kill it first.'

He stared at the pathetic mouse, which Fire and Brimstone had apparently forgotten about, but he seemed unable to move.

Penelope took the dustpan from him, turned on the tap and filled the kitchen sink.

'I'm sorry,' she said to the mouse as she slid it into the water.

Blood bloomed out and she saw it was scrambling desperately to escape so she pressed the dustpan over it and waited. After a few minutes she looked underneath and the body was floating free.

She turned away. The decision was made. She went to pack up her things at Rolf's apartment.

Living with a poet was very quiet and orderly. Alain kept his work to himself until it was finished and Penelope had the strange sensation of huge worlds and journeys going on in a reality that was both beyond her and very nearby, inside Alain's head. Compared to the paraphernalia of art-making, literature was tidy and simple: a pen, a bottle of ink, a typewriter and some paper. It all fitted on one half of a table. With Rolf, Penelope had lived in a sort of landscape of things: paints, materials, canvases, bits of tree bark, sandpaper, scraps of cloth, old books with torn-out illustrations, hammers, varnishes ... the list was almost endless. She had learnt so much from watching the construction of Rolf's art but there was more space for her here with Alain.

She had brought only a few tubes of colour but no larger canvases; they scared her. Instead, she brought glue, ribbons, scissors; things a child might enjoy. She played with the kittens, scrunching up paper and making pretend mice that she attached to pieces of wool.

Alain put down his pencil and she turned to meet his gaze from her place on the floor with the cats. She watched him return to the present time and moment and to register her reality again.

'Shall we go out? Or I could buy some cheese?' he asked.

'Let's have lunch at home again. Like before.'

Alain knew this was an invitation to bed later and came to kiss her.

'I won't be long.' He kissed the kittens, too, as if they were naughty toddlers, and picked up the cotton shopping bag he used.

Penelope sighed, looking forward to the treats he would bring back. She was being looked after. She was the centre of his life, and this meant she could stop giving all her energy to figuring out her relationships and use it instead for art. She had made the right choice and for once it was the easy choice.

Penelope wandered into the bedroom. The wardrobe door was open and Una's left-behind shoes were on show. She put her feet in, tentatively. The shoes were too small, of course; she was a good six inches taller than Una and at least a stone heavier. She took them into the kitchen, where her box of art materials from Rolf's was stored temporarily.

On the draining board was the oven dish Alain had roasted a chicken in last night. He was the first man she had known who could actually cook. She turned the pan over and settled the shoes inside, heels pointing upwards and outwards. She laughed.

When Alain returned she had cut out white paper frills and glued them to the tips of the heels. He frowned.

'I don't understand,' he said, putting the bag, which clinked invitingly, on the table.

'I had a nurse when I was very little. She used to carry me when I was upset and I remember we saw a man once and she squeezed me tight. Somehow I knew that she was squeezing her legs together in pleasure.'

'A connoisseur of love, even as a child?'

'Not really. It wasn't till Rolf – Oh!' Penelope was embarrassed. How stupid of her.

'He is already back, Jean has seen him.'

'Rolf is in Paris again?'

'Yes. Are you hungry?'

'I think I'll have a bath first.'

Alain smiled. He loved the soaps and scents that she used.

In the water, Penelope tried to work out how she felt about Rolf coming back, but her mind wouldn't fix on it. Maybe she felt nothing.

Suzanne had written again this week, and Penelope watched the pictures inside her head of Suzanne, first as the woman she knew and then, flickering like an old movie, turning into D'Argent's Natalia. It was like one of Púbol's double images: the one with a head in profile which, turned at 90 degrees, became a group of villagers outside a hut. Somehow, Suzanne was both. Her letter was all about films too: how she was swooning over the dashing Errol Flynn as Robin Hood and delighting at Katharine Hepburn in a funny story about a tame leopard that got mixed up with a wild, savage one. *It reminds me of what we talked about that night after the Beaux Arts exhibition, Penelope,* she wrote, *and how easy it is to confuse tame and wild creatures. Also, how dangerous.*

Penelope opened her eyes and looked at her knees. The idea for the painting she'd had here in the bath before came back, complete in every detail. She struggled out of the water, not bothering to wash her hair, then threw a towel around her middle. This time, she promised herself, the idea wouldn't get away.

But in the kitchen, where her sketchbook was propping up one of the wonky table legs, was Rolf.

He smiled and came towards her, then checked the movement when he realised she was practically naked.

'Hello,' she said. 'How was your trip?'

'It was good. And you?'

'I'm fine.'

'You look well. I am glad.'

So that was it. No recrimination? No anger or jealousy? Nothing?

'I'll go and get dressed,' she said.

'Penelope,' Rolf called, as she turned. 'I brought your things.'

In the corner were her easel, a stack of canvases and enough paint to last the next six months.

'Please,' said Alain to Rolf, 'eat with us. There is plenty.'

'And I see you are serving an unusual dish.' Rolf was grinning at the shoes in the oven pan.

Penelope felt goosebumps on her shoulders as a summer breeze came in underneath the sash window. The shoes were lewd, suggestive. And trivial. She couldn't bear the sight of them any longer and rushed out of the room.

I need Suzanne, she thought. I think I'm going crazy. I need Suzanne to tell me I haven't gone mad. The irony of this did not escape her.

She pulled her suitcase out from under the bed then stopped. She was famished and if Rolf could behave normally – he was, after all, what a court would call 'the injured party' – so could she.

The case went back, she put on her oldest clothes and returned to the kitchen.

But Rolf had gone. And so had Una's shoes in the roasting pan.

'Rolf is taking them to show Púbol,' explained Alain. 'He is making commercial work, and someone christened Púbol "Pay the Bill" so that's what D'Argent calls him now.'

Penelope imagined D'Argent's refined French accent struggling over the English phrase.

'Why do you men always run off with my artworks? They belong to me, not to anyone who fancies showing them.'

'But Rolf was very impressed.'

'And what if D'Argent cuts me off, too? I can't put on a solo exhibition. Oh, never mind. Let's eat. I can't think straight when I'm hungry.'

Alain embraced her. 'Forgive me for handing over the shoes before asking you. It is good, though, that you are working again,' he said.

'Yes. I suppose so.' She broke away and tried to smile at him. 'Yes, it is.'

Chapter Twenty-Five

Amsterdam, September 1939

Penelope now divided her time between Alain in Paris and Suzanne in Amsterdam, spending a month with each. In Paris, she sketched the cats and made surrealist objects constructed from things she found at the flea market. They were not always successful, but they salved the place in her soul that was aching and still unable to paint. In Amsterdam, she drew Suzanne or the wildfowl on the water, or the people in cafés. Sometimes a tourist would try to pay for their portrait but Penelope would tear it out and give it away for free. Her allowance easily covered her room at the Schiller Hotel and all her needs, since Alain, like Rolf before him, refused to accept any contribution to the rent.

This afternoon she had sought out a Jewish bakery on the way to Quellijnstraat and was carrying a moist, heavy honey cake. She still hadn't grasped all of the kosher laws but enjoyed Isaac's delight at her attempts to learn. He was even more stooped and seemed to Penelope to have slowed down over this last year, but Suzanne contradicted this. 'He has been selling more belts than ever, and still leads the Shema at synagogue,' she said, when Penelope had remarked on Isaac's incessant coughing.

Penelope knocked loudly on the door before using the key attached to the letter box. Suzanne was coming down the stairs to greet her and Penelope rejoiced again at the change in her friend and in her home. Freddie was the reason for both. The toilet was screened off from the kitchen now, and light flooded in through newly fitted windows. Freddie had fixed the leaking roof and painted the walls a bright white with yellow on the window frames. He had brought sunlight to the house and to Suzanne's life. The courtship, however, was agonisingly slow: Freddie would tackle any practical job, it seemed, but hung back from expressing his feelings.

'Hello. Where is Freddie?' asked Penelope, embracing her friend and endangering the loosely wrapped cake which swung in her hand.

'At Max's,' said Suzanne, eyeing the brown paper bag.

Freddie was no longer stowing away at the Tuschinski. He lived legitimately rent-free in return for working on the home movies of a film distributor called Max Prins. He also looked after Max's two daughters when needed, and fed and exercised his two Doberman dogs.

'And Isaac?' Penelope started to look in the cupboard for some plates.

'I thought you had come to see me,' teased Suzanne.

Penelope smiled. 'Yes, of course, but the cake is for Isaac. And for you.'

Suzanne grinned. 'Coffee?'

'Yes. If we are allowed. With the cake.'

'Don't be silly,' said Suzanne. 'It's meat and milk that don't go together. Coffee is neutral.'

Penelope laid out the plates, forks and cups on the table. 'Did you go out with Freddie last night?'

'No. And stop going on about me and Freddie.'

'I will not. It's my job to make sure you are happy. It is the chief responsibility of a friend.'

'But I am happy. I can scarcely believe now that once when Louis was driving me to Versailles I dared him to drive blind. I covered his eyes with my hands and the car swayed to the side before he threw me off. But now I want to live. And I am so happy that you're here.'

Suzanne fell into a reverie as she waited for the water to rise in the coffee percolator. Freddie hadn't asked her to go to the theatre, but he had hinted, for several days beforehand. They were locked in a strange relationship, both imagining an affair but perhaps both enjoying the fantasy too much to risk turning it into a reality.

Isaac came carefully down the stairs, using the wall to steady himself. Perhaps Penelope was right and he was too old to work. How would they manage then? Well, she would have to go back to the art school and do more days a week cleaning the bathhouse. Freddie had demonstrated real industry to her, and her father's working day had paled into insignificance in comparison. Apart from the sabbath, he crammed in hours of work at Max's, or repairs to the house here or fixing up his own place: a shed at Max's which he was now connecting to electricity. It made her realise how little time in her life she had spent actually doing. Thinking was what her life had been about. Maybe that was her problem: to do, and not to think, was the answer.

'That coffee pot will burn through,' said Penelope, snatching up a cloth and taking it off the flame.

Suzanne laughed at herself.

'I brought you a honey cake, sir,' said Penelope, waiting politely until Isaac had arrived at the foot of the stairs and slowed his wheezy breath.

He reached up to place his hands on her shoulders and said a blessing which Penelope, of course, did not understand.

When Freddie arrived an hour later they were still sitting around the table with the much-depleted cake.

He came to join them and Suzanne could see how he had to stop himself from reaching out to touch her. She felt a ghostly kiss on her lips as if he had done what his eyes betrayed he wished to do. Soon, thought Suzanne. Soon.

Freddie ignored their pleasant greetings and waved away the offer of cake. 'It has started,' he said, placing a newspaper on the table for Penelope to read. 'Britain and France have declared war.'

Penelope grabbed the paper, all in Dutch, and scanned the photos of Chamberlain and Daladier.

'What should I do? Should I go back to Britain?'

Suzanne had never seen Penelope look so pale and uncertain.

'I don't know, but I am sure Poland will fall very soon,' said Freddie. 'Perhaps you had better go back to your friends in Paris.'

'Yes,' said Penelope, vaguely. She was frowning and still trying to read the newspaper. Then she threw it aside. 'And you, Freddie, did you send the false papers to your family?'

'No, I never had an address I could be certain of. I was thinking of changing them.'

'For yourself?'

Freddie nodded, then turned to Suzanne. 'Do you still have that Spanish passport?'

'Isabel Castello's? Why?'

'We can replace her photo with yours,' he answered.

'But why should Holland be involved with Poland's war?' said Suzanne. 'Surely the British and the French governments are making a gesture of support, that's all.'

'I hope you're right,' said Penelope, 'but I fear you're not. Freddie, please, as soon as you can—'

There was a knock at the door.

Suzanne put a hand on Isaac's arm to reassure him then got up.

It was a postboy, getting something out of his satchel.

'Furr?'

'Yes,' Penelope answered from inside.

'Telegram.'

'Good lord!' she said, then, 'Sorry, sir,' to Isaac.

At the door, Penelope dug out some coins from the pocket of her jacket.

They all sat down again, looking at the piece of grey printed paper that was folded and sealed.

'How has it come here?' asked Suzanne.

'Alain has the address. In case.'

Suzanne was terrified of the piece of paper. She saw black tendrils of smoke coming from it and pictured the contents as smuts of soot. It was alive with bad stories.

'Open it,' she said. 'Quickly.'

Penelope lifted the flap and read the message.

'It is from Alain,' she said. 'It says, *Rolf taken to internment camp at Meslay-du-Maine. Stop. Going there tonight. Stop. Will write.*'

'Rolf? Why would they take him?' asked Suzanne.

'Is he German?' asked Freddie.

Penelope nodded.

'Then that is it. It has started.'

'Stop saying that, Freddie.' Suzanne got up and went to stand behind Penelope, putting her hands on her shoulders. 'It is all a misunderstanding, surely.'

'I need to go back to the hotel,' said Penelope, faintly. 'Don't worry,' she turned to Suzanne. 'I won't leave without telling you.'

'I'll come with you.'

'No. Don't. I need to think. Come later, we'll have dinner. You too, Freddie. We can have that schnitzel that you like. And,' she put some notes on the table, 'if you'd like to join us, sir, here is something towards a taxi.'

Isaac bowed his head.

'I have to go now,' said Penelope.

A few days later, the letter arrived. Suzanne put it in her pocket and set off for the Schiller Hotel. It was nearly nine. At the reception, she was directed to the bar where Penelope was sitting at one of the round tables, alone, reading a book and leaning back against the red-striped seating with one knee bent under her. She smiled brightly when she saw Suzanne.

'It's Alain's letter.'

'Let's go up to my room,' said Penelope, draining her glass.

Suzanne marvelled again at the sumptuous decor of the hotel; her old haunts had been threadbare affairs in comparison. It even smelt expensive.

They sat on the bed side by side and read the letter together. After Alain's brief opening endearments he wrote:

Rolf is with some fifty others in makeshift huts in an open-air cage. I tell you Penelope, this is the truth, I'm not exaggerating. They are all men, some from Austria and some have pointed badges sewn onto their clothes. He looked thin, but not sick. He tried to come to the fence but there were guards, so we threw the clothes over and then the paintbox, even though it seemed foolish. Others got the clothes, but he managed to retrieve the box of gouaches and brushes and so on. Tomorrow we will try with food, but it will be very difficult. I am writing to all the councillors and to the president of the département. *One of Púbol's dealers is helping with money. I shall stay here for as long as it takes. Do not*

go back to Paris, it might not be safe. The concierge is feeding the
cats, at least I hope so. Greetings to your Dutch friends.

Penelope, stunned and expressionless, looked as if she had
been dipped in wax. Then she started to beat the bed with the
letter in her fist.

Suzanne was afraid for her, and of her. 'Stop,' she said.
'Stop!'

She looked back at her through messy locks of black hair and
Suzanne saw herself reflected in Penelope's wild brown eyes.

'I can't stand it,' she said, getting up to pace the floor.

'I know,' said Suzanne. 'I know.'

'It's the end. I can't stand it.'

Suzanne put her arms around Penelope: her source of
strength, her rock. She felt the sobs heave through her friend's
body and tried hard to absorb the pain, as Penelope had done
so often for her in the past. 'It will all be all right,' she said.

'How will it?' Penelope broke away and went back to pacing
up and down on the thick red carpet. She bashed away the tears
on her cheeks with the backs of her hands. 'The group will fall
apart. Without freedom there is no surrealism. No art.'

'Surely they will release Rolf when they have questioned
him.'

'What about Una? Tristan? They are German, too. Suzanne,
wake up. You are Jewish. What if the Germans come here?'

'Don't be ridiculous. Why would they? And France has an
army, doesn't it? Let them fight it out somewhere while we go
on living, and you go on making art.'

'But without the group I'm not even an artist. Surrealism is
everything. It's the source of my ideas, my place, my reason to
create. And my sole opportunity to exhibit and sell.'

'But you have plenty of money.'

Penelope gave her an almost contemptuous look, as if she
was a child with limited comprehension.

Suzanne tried again. 'Is it Rolf? Do you still have feelings for him?'

'Feelings? Of course. He is one of us, he is the one who created me as an artist. He's my parent, my brother. Alain has the same bond with him.'

'Alain's bond is with you now surely?'

'Yes, but it goes further.'

Suzanne began to feel excluded. Why didn't Penelope acknowledge the importance of their friendship? 'You could live here instead. If France is taken.'

'You haven't heard a word I've said. Being part of the group is the only way for me to be myself.'

'Well, they don't paint your pictures. Or mix your paints. They don't do your sketches, or imagine the animals and magic places. You do that. You could do it anywhere, and do it alone.'

Penelope was scarcely listening. She had sat back on the bed and was looking at the crumpled letter. 'An open-air cage. Imagine it,' she said.

Suzanne sat beside her. 'I don't want to.'

'And I can't even be there to see him. I have to go back to Paris.'

'But Alain said—'

'I have to, Suzanne. But if I feel I'm in danger I'll come back to you, and we'll see this out together. I promise.'

Chapter Twenty-Six

Amsterdam, October 1939

It was awkward to press the foot pedal and at the same time bend down to see into the metal-edged screen of the Moviola, but gradually Suzanne became absorbed in the pictures she had made through the black-and-silver eye of the Bolex camera belonging to Freddie's employer. First there was a series of black-and-white diamond-shaped tiles repeating in a star pattern, then arrested by a broken brown scar where the city's grime and indifference had claimed one of the tiles as its victim. Then the rain. Rain in puddles, in guttering and on the railings of the bridges. Rain on the water of the canal in repeating circles going out and out and renewing themselves perpetually, rhythmically. Next, the slow, elegant dance of the raindrops on the tram window.

Each raindrop began alone on the window, at the top. Some drops remained static, they had no desire or attraction, but others were rounding and filling with extra moisture and swelling into full, teary roundness. At a specific moment of critical weight and need, they started to travel down the glass, sometimes steering in zigzags, making themselves conspicuous, tragic. In the journey downwards they joined with others, becoming heavier, and descending more quickly all the time until they reached their ultimate annihilation in the trench at the base of the window, or they were torn away mid-journey by a sudden gust of wind.

Then the film sequence switched to an image of Suzanne herself holding the camera, which was a reflection in the window of a green car. She was outside the car but her arms, shoulders and hair were superimposed on the steering wheel and dashboard on the inside. After this came the wilder ideas: her head in a mirror ('You can't go in there,' they had called, as she marched into the back of the restaurant) then a round clear lamp and then (oh, the ecstasy of reversing time) both of these together: her face looking out from inside the glowing lamp. Then another experiment: some steps upside down, and the drunken sky turning and falling into the river. To finish, several long, slow sequences tracking through the beloved streets of Amsterdam on the way back to the front door of this house where Freddie's employer Max lived in luxury and had this room full of the most wonderful machinery for making films.

Movies were solid dreams. Dreams you could rerun. And the film itself was alive: it crackled and hissed when Freddie unspooled and crushed it into the processing tubs. It curled and flipped with tensile joy around the wheels and clips of the projector. Suzanne had always regarded herself as an enemy of machinery. Whoever would have guessed, she mused, that I would find my salvation in this masculine assemblage of metal dials and a cold, stiff substance like fish scales?

'And now,' said Freddie, 'you must decide which parts to keep and which to throw away. It's up to you.'

Suzanne didn't answer. I would keep all our times together, she thought, suddenly embarrassed to look Freddie in the eye. And I would throw away everything before this, except Angélique and Penelope. I would jump from the time I shared a birthday cake with my daughter in our room above the bakery to the day in Paris when I met Penelope and she ran after that man to get back my mother's hat. I would keep the first time I met Isaac, and all our walks, Freddie, every film we've seen sitting in the soft seats at the Tuschinski, and every cup of coffee I would keep, most of all, the day the new cantor arrived in the synagogue and you looked up at the women's balcony and smiled at me. If only I was younger, Freddie, if only we had met before.

'Here is the splicer. Do you want to try to do the editing yourself this time?' he asked.

'Yes, all right.'

'First rewind the film. Here, it is this pedal.'

'Like this?'

'Yes, but slow down, Suzanne, we have plenty of time.'

Suzanne chose to cut from the raindrops on the window directly to the double exposure of her head in the lamp.

'I think you are making a mistake,' said Freddie, but he helped her line up the celluloid and make the cuts. Then he showed her how to tape it carefully back together on both sides.

Once the film was reloaded onto the viewer, he started to roll it again and the genius of her idea became apparent. The last falling water drop landed perfectly in the lamp containing Suzanne's face, then this dissolved into a steering wheel with the ghost of her body hovering around inside and outside the car at the same time.

'Tonight I'll process this,' he said, 'and then we can watch it with the projector.'

Suzanne savoured the pleasure of expectation: they would watch her film together.

'What is in Max's films?' she asked as he started rewinding the spool.

'Usually his daughters playing in the park or on the way to school. Or Ruska hanging out the wash. Or the dogs.'

'Ordinary things, then.'

'Exactly. He doesn't have your vision.'

Suzanne smiled, but avoided his gaze.

'How is Isaac today?' he asked.

'Very bad. In fact, I had better go. I promised to make him some soup.'

'That's a coincidence. I think Ruska wanted to give you some soup to take home.'

'I'll go and see her then. Tomorrow?'

'Tomorrow.'

Suzanne hesitated a moment, then turned and left the room.

On her way back to Quellijnstraat Suzanne thought about Penelope, now back in Paris with Alain. Rolf's confinement had taken a terrible toll on her friend and she worried and missed her daily. Freddie had suggested asking Max if she could use the telephone to speak to her but Suzanne held back, waiting for Penelope to return. They would talk then, late into the night and eventually they would laugh; always when they talked there was laughter by the end, no matter how bad things at first seemed to be.

Suzanne went in and called out to Isaac. There was no answer so she went through to the back where a bed had been set up for him since he'd become unwell. He was sleeping. Illness had made his slight frame shrink to the size of a child and his face was strangely blotched and stained. His beard had thinned. She pulled the many covers back around his bony shoulders and stroked the sparse silky grey strands of hair lying close to his pink skull. Then he came alarmingly awake with a phlegmy, bubbling implosion followed by a volley of coughing. The will to breathe was so fierce that he sucked at the oxygen coming through his lips like an addict, or a starving man. After a few reedy breaths he fell back on the pillow panting and exhausted.

'Do you need the doctor, Isaac?'

'No. No. Bring Moshe.'

'The rabbi? He has no medicine.'

'Yes, he has. He has what I need.'

'I don't know what you mean. There's some soup. Good soup from Max's kitchen. Shall I get you some soup?' Suzanne rested a hand on his bony shoulder.

He jerked away at her touch. 'No. No. Moshe. Moshe and Hermann.'

'Who is Hermann?'

'Posek. Posek. He will write for me. I want you to have—' but Isaac was overtaken again by great assaults on his lungs. His shoulders shook and Suzanne was afraid that his chest would snap like the wishbone on a cooked chicken.

'Try to sleep,' she said, which was a stupid thing to say but it helped her to stay calm.

'Bring Moshe, my daughter. Hermann, the papers,' Isaac gasped on.

'All right. I'll be back soon.'

Only as she turned to lock the door did Suzanne realise that Isaac believed he was about to die.

The night dragged on. Suzanne couldn't sit still, and wasn't allowed at Isaac's bedside. Sorrowful men in big shawls crowded the house with candles and books, and chanted in low voices. Then there was a terrible silence. Suzanne lifted her head and saw the rabbi come through the curtain that divided the rooms. There was no need to say anything. He made as if to allow her through but she leapt up, turned on her heel and left the house.

Out into the night she ran, with the echoing space of the canal in her ears and she couldn't slow down, she couldn't breathe properly or calm her heartbeat, and she didn't want to. All of her body was alive to the night and she ran on and on. She pulled the cold air deep into her lungs and felt with gratitude the strain on her calf muscles as she kept on running, running.

At last she was on Prinsengracht. The school next to Max's house had a gate it would be possible to get over, as long as no one saw her. She tied up her skirt and began to climb, foot over foot. The leap down to the other side gave her a jolt but not enough to slow her down. Now the garden wall. Easy. There was a tree next to it and a few bricks missing at the top. She remembered Freddie telling her how he had broken his ankle stealing apples as a boy. But such a thing was impossible tonight: no harm could come to her because she was alive. Alive.

She heard a bark. Max's Dobermans were loose in the garden. Once over the wall, Suzanne ran to squat beside them, murmuring their names and rubbing their ears. They snuffled and quietened, thoroughly satisfied with her familiar scent. Freddie's hut was dark. The covered way made of scrap windows glinted and for the first time Suzanne looked up at the moon. It was full and surrounded by a silver halo as bright as a scratch on celluloid. She tried the handle to the shed, without knocking first.

He lay on his front, in black pyjamas, with the covers thrown off. His arms were outstretched as if he'd landed from a great height. The side of his face was lit by the moonlight coming in from the windows he'd added to the roof. The bed was low: he slept on wooden pallets. Max had given him some carpet and a smelly old oil lamp which made Suzanne think of the sanctuary lamp at the synagogue that had to be kept burning all the time, even when all the candles on the huge chandelier were extinguished.

Why didn't he wake up? Suzanne had a chilling thought: were all the people she loved going to die tonight? Was it some sort of special gas coming from the German army? What if there was a chemical, an invisible, odourless chemical, calibrated to her heart's particular construction that was travelling into the rooms of all her beloved ones and killing them in their sleep?

She knelt down by Freddie's bed and touched his arm. The pyjamas were silky smooth but perhaps not black after all, that might just be because of the darkness. Then he turned over and opened his eyes. The lock of hair that always fell across his brow had fallen aside and he looked more solemn and exposed than ever before.

'Isaac is dead,' she said.

'And you are here. Come.' He opened his arms.

So she lay down and the warmth of his body came burning through to her skin until her heart slowed to a steady strong rhythm. Her skirt was still tied up and her bare legs moved against the dark smooth material covering his hot, solid body. Carefully, he kissed her and she clung on, for dear life. All night they kissed and held each other desperately. It was one moment playing over and over again. Time on a loop: time repeated. Time, suspended.

Chapter Twenty-Seven

Lille, May 1940

F reddie and Suzanne arrived in Lille on a Sunday afternoon when she knew that the bakery would be closed. It was a surprise visit, made possible by the loan of Max's old car. Suzanne had not written in advance, knowing that her grandmother, Françoise, would refuse to see her or let her spend time with Angélique. How old would her daughter be now? Thirteen. Was it possible that she had detected the lies told her about her birth? Would Suzanne finally be able to claim her as her own? With Freddie by her side she felt stronger, and more able to speak.

Her father came to the door of the house and let them in. He kissed her briefly and gave her a look that betrayed he was seeking his lost wife in his daughter's face.

In the sitting room, Suzanne said: 'This is my friend Freddie, Papa. He has helped me a lot. I live in Amsterdam now, and I have a house of my own.'

Daniel extended a hand to Freddie but was interrupted by the arrival of Françoise. Suzanne felt the temperature of the room fall by several degrees.

'You,' she said.

'Hello, *Grandmère*, I have come to visit you.' She handed her a wrapped cake.

Françoise surveyed the peace offering and huffed. 'Angélique is out,' she said.

'Oh. I did want to see her. And stay for a few days, perhaps?'

'If you must.' Françoise took a quick, critical survey of Freddie, but said nothing and left the room.

'Come and have some tea before I start tomorrow's loaves,' said her father. 'Angélique is doing her homework in the kitchen.'

'But I thought *Grandmère* said she wasn't here.'

Daniel simply gave her a weary look and led the way.

Freddie had not understood anything that had been said.

'It's OK,' Suzanne reassured him, 'we can stay. Angélique is here. Come on.'

As they made their way to the back of the house, behind the shop, Suzanne began to feel nervous. Her grandmother's bad opinion and spite was constant and expected, but how would Angélique react to seeing her again after two years with no word?

She scarcely knew the tall, dark-haired young girl who stood to greet her as Daniel said: 'Look who's here, Angélique.'

They embraced, and Suzanne fought down the tears that threatened to rise out of her throat. 'Hey, little angel,' she said, using the old nickname, 'how are you?'

'I thought you'd forgotten about us, Suzette.'

'Never.'

'Is this your husband?' Angélique had spied Freddie hesitating in the doorway.

Suzanne took her by the hand. 'Angélique, meet Freddie.'

'*Bonjour, monsieur,*' she said, nodding.

Suzanne saw how her daughter had a new reserve, and a certain self-possession that had not been there before. She was becoming the woman she would be: steady, discriminating, perhaps a little unimaginative.

'Freddie doesn't speak French,' said Suzanne. 'He speaks German, English and Dutch.'

'Very good,' said Angélique in English. 'I started to learn English two years ago,' she boasted, turning to Suzanne. 'I got top marks on vocabulary last week.'

'Come and tell me everything.' Suzanne pulled out a chair and beckoned Freddie to join them.

Daniel put a teapot, a plate of rolls and some jam on the table and came back with cups and milk. Suzanne watched her father open his mouth to say something to Freddie then close it again, defeated. He gestured at the supplies on the table instead.

'Thank you,' said Freddie.

Daniel went off to the bakehouse and Freddie attacked the rolls with enthusiasm. He poured tea for them all and got another flash of a smile from Angélique.

Suzanne asked about Angélique's new school and heard all about her new friend there, Michelle.

'And *Grandmère*, is she kind to you?'

'Sometimes,' said Angélique. 'But tell me what it's like in Holland. Do you go to the pictures?'

'Yes. Freddie is a projectionist and he makes films.'

Angélique looked at Suzanne's companion with undisguised awe. 'He makes films?'

Freddie, recognising the words, smiled back.

Suzanne let her shoulders drop and breathed easily for the first time that day. Everything would be all right.

One morning, Suzanne came down the stairs to find her grandmother waving the newspaper with a look of savage satisfaction.

'They have surrendered,' she said, and called Queen Wilhelmina a name that made Suzanne blanch.

She had only just begun to get to grips with the possibility of a German victory after the campaign had begun a week earlier and actual defeat was unthinkable. What would it mean? German money? Different sorts of food? Suzanne had no knowledge of such situations.

She pushed past her grandmother and went to the kitchen.

Her father was making coffee and picking at breakfast between bakes. He looked tired as usual and gobbets of hardened dough were stuck to his fingers and arms, making it seem as if he had a skin disease.

'Holland has fallen,' she said.

'I know. It's bad, very bad,' he agreed. 'Better to end your friendship with that poor man now.'

'What do you mean?'

'He can never go back to Amsterdam and if you have been going to synagogue it would be better for you not to return either: there will be reprisals.'

'But it's nothing to do with me. I work at the bathhouse and the art school. The German soldiers won't go there.'

He snorted and went off to check on the loaves.

Freddie's face appeared at the window and Suzanne let him in.

'Where is your grandmother?' Freddie looked around nervously.

He hadn't been invited to stay. Even if Françoise could have communicated with him (Freddie had very little French, and Françoise had nothing else) she would have spurned him for accompanying Suzanne without the benefit of marriage. Daniel, overruled as usual, had nevertheless taken pity on Freddie when he found him sleeping in the car and allowed him to use a camp bed, set up by the big ovens in the cigar-scented bakehouse at the back. Once again, then, Freddie was in an annexe, a shed, a temporary place, but he never seemed to mind.

He was not welcome at meals either. Suzanne set up a plate for him at each meal and made a big show of taking it to him.

'I made a call,' Freddie told her. 'It's very bad news. Max is dead.'

'How?'

'I spoke to Ruska. She said the girls are with relatives, in Texel. Max took them there last week. His body was found in the canal. I think he meant to do it.'

'But why?'

'He has family in Poland, in Lodz. A neighbour of theirs was shot for refusing to go behind the fence. Perhaps he thought that would happen to us, in Amsterdam.'

'I don't understand. A fence?'

Freddie put an arm around Suzanne's shoulders. 'You know we can't go back, don't you?'

'Of course we can. Isaac made sure of all the documents. The house is legally mine.'

'No. Ruska said the Germans are taking over empty houses. If it's the same as in Austria, the Jewish homes will be re-registered for German families.'

'They can't do that.'

'It has already happened, Suzanne. We must think very clearly and plan. What a good thing I brought the passports with us.'

Suzanne's mind went into a mad whirl of scenarios. She imagined living in Lille again and pushing Freddie into her abrasive, misshapen family, or running away with him to somewhere remote where the Germans didn't care about them.

She hit on it at last: 'We could go to Penelope. She would take us in.'

'Are you sure?'

'Entirely. There is no question. That's what we'll do. We'll go to Paris. Paris is my home, much more than this place. But I want to take Angélique. How will I ever rest unless I know she is safe?'

'This is her home.'

'But I am her mother.'

'You're right. She must come to Paris with us.'

At that moment Angélique herself appeared, harried in by Françoise who was ordering her to drink milk and eat properly before school.

'Good morning,' said Suzanne. 'Let's all sit down together because Freddie and I have something to discuss.'

Her grandmother refused to acknowledge Freddie, but sat at the far end of the table where she could police Angélique's behaviour. Angélique awkwardly pushed the jug of hot milk towards Freddie but he smiled and said he had already eaten at the café. Suzanne suspected this was a lie but she didn't press anything on him because she needed to keep the old woman in a reasonable mood.

'Freddie and I are going to stay with my friend in Paris. How would you like to come with us, Angélique?'

'Oh yes. I want to climb the Eiffel Tower. Michelle has done it three times.'

'Not possible,' said Françoise. 'She cannot miss school. Or her rounds.'

Angélique collected money from the wealthier customers who had monthly accounts.

'But I have rights, *Grandmère*,' said Suzanne.

'No. You have none. None.'

Freddie said nothing but looked concerned. Suzanne could see he was struggling to catch the meaning of the words but she was sure he could interpret the emotions behind them.

Daniel ambled back in and Françoise shrieked at him: 'They want to take her. Take her to that filthy city.'

'But, *Maman*,' he said, 'Angélique is older now, it is her decision. If she knew that—'

'Stop!' barked Françoise. 'Angélique, time for school.'

'But there's half an hour yet.'

'No. Time to go. Get your coat. Now.'

Angélique slammed down her cup and flounced out.

At least her spirit isn't broken, thought Suzanne, and then she launched all the fire power she could muster at her grandmother.

'It is wrong to keep the truth from her.'

'It was wrong to be so stupid that she came into existence at all.'

'Love is never wrong.'

'Idiots should not breed.'

Daniel started to rise from his seat. '*Maman*, please.'

'Oh, you are no good, either,' Suzanne shot back at her father.

'Suzanne,' said Freddie, sensing the possibility that she might say things she would regret, 'does your grandmother forbid Angélique to come with us?'

'Yes, she forbids it,' answered Suzanne, casting evil looks at her grandmother across the table.

'It might be better to leave things as they are for the moment, with the war getting so close.'

'The Germans cannot defeat France,' said Suzanne, as if Freddie was a child.

Daniel had picked up enough of the English words to catch the drift. 'The Netherlands is just the start. Your friend is right to be anxious.'

'What is your father saying?' asked Freddie.

'He says the Germans are busy enough with the Dutch. One day,' Suzanne said, turning back to Françoise, 'I will come for my daughter and you will have to let her go.'

'I'll die first.'

'Die then, witch!' cried Suzanne getting to her feet. 'You brought nothing but sorrow to my mother. I will not let you ruin my daughter's life as well.'

'And how would you have looked after a child?' shouted Françoise, standing toe to toe and poking Suzanne's shoulder. 'You can't even look after yourself. This idiot man you go with has no job, no home. The car he drives is not even his own. And you tell me I am a bad guardian to Angélique.'

'You don't love her.'

'Love. Always you say *love*. Love is no use. Love is for songs and movies. Love is not for food, or money, or a bed to sleep in.'

'Then I choose love.' Suzanne grasped Freddie's hand.

The men were on their feet as well now.

'Go!' shouted Françoise. 'Out of my house. Once before I sent you away. Why have you come back? Go! Do not try to come back again.'

'*Papa*?'

Her father sighed, threw up his hands and turned away.

Freddie made as if to step forward but Suzanne held him back.

'We need to leave now,' she said to him. 'There is nothing for us here.'

Chapter Twenty-Eight

F reddie waited in the car while Suzanne gathered her things. They drove towards Angélique's school but she was nowhere to be seen. Suzanne wanted to go into the school itself to say goodbye but Freddie persuaded her that this was a bad idea so they set off for Paris. Suzanne's tears eventually began to give way to sleep. On the tree-lined roads, the spring sunshine stroked the car windows and behind her closed eyelids the light flashing through the leaves made a pattern like the flickering white blanks at the end of a reel.

When she woke up on the outskirts of Paris, she was hopeful again. Penelope would put everything right, even this silly war that was making everything so awkward. With her help, they could go back and collect Angélique from school perhaps, and tell her grandmother only afterwards, when they were all safely away from Lille. What a lovely time they would have in Paris. Penelope, Freddie, Angélique: all her dear ones. They could live together. Alain was a problem, of course, but surely his refined, restrained character would not suit Penelope for long and they would soon break up.

Freddie drove well; the workings of all types of machines were second nature to him. He seemed to be unaffected by the hysterical scenes in the kitchen but he looked frequently at her, as if checking her emotional weather.

They stopped to ask for directions to Rue Bonaparte where Penelope lived, then continued on.

'Have you been to Paris before?' asked Suzanne.

'I don't know. My mother played the piano in all sorts of places when I was young and sometimes she took me too. The cities all seem the same in my memories: hotel corridors, concert halls, railway stations.'

'But she must have played in Paris.'

'I expect she did. After Heinz was born I didn't go with her anymore. To take two children was too much to manage.'

'I wonder where she performed in Paris.'

'Please, I don't want to talk about her anymore, I—'

'Here it is! Look, you can stop over there. Oh, I hope Penelope hasn't gone out somewhere.'

'Is it a good idea to simply turn up? Maybe we should have stayed somewhere overnight and sent a telegram,' said Freddie, manoeuvring the car into a parking space.

'Don't be silly. Telegrams are only for bad news. And she'll be so happy to see us.'

Suzanne ran up to the blue double doors and rang the bell.

The concierge opened the door and asked what they wanted.

She had a most bizarre accent, thought Suzanne. Perhaps she was from Algeria? She wore beaded slippers with pointed toes along with a dull overall.

'Mademoiselle Furr, please. It's a surprise visit.'

'She's not here.'

'When will she be back? Has she gone to the café?'

'No. Catalonia.'

'What?'

'You heard me. Spain.' She went inside and came back with a piece of paper. 'Here, it says it here. *Monsieur Púbol, Post Office, Cadaqués, Catalonia, Spain.* Who are you, then?'

'I'm Suzanne. We live in Amsterdam.'

'Wait.' She ducked back into the hallway again. 'Is this letter from you? It came after she left. Are you Suzanne Levy?'

'Yes, that's me. But how long will Penelope be away?'

'They said not to keep the rooms, but I've not told anyone yet. Less to clean. Quieter too. All those parties, what a mess they made. Goodbye.' And she shut the door.

Suzanne was too shocked to react but Freddie's face said it all. They were homeless.

'She must have written to tell me but it would have arrived after we left Quellijnstraat. What are we going to do, Freddie?'

'We'll have to find a place to stay. I have enough for a few nights if we can find a cheap hotel.' Freddie began to walk back to the car.

'But I need to see Penelope.' Suzanne was still by the door.

'It would take days to drive to Spain, and the car has nearly run out of petrol.'

'We could write. Penelope would send us some money.'

'No, I must find work. Then in a few weeks we would have enough.'

She went to join him. 'Let's do both. I'll write and you look for a job.'

They crossed the road.

'Maybe we can stay in my old place. It didn't cost much. And there's always Isaac's money,' she said.

'True, but first let me ask for work. It is for me to look after you now, because ...'

'What?' Suzanne turned to him.

Freddie looked down at the pavement and said: 'I care for you. And I want—'

'To marry me?'

'My love, this is not the place, not the right moment.'

'So you don't?'

'I do. I do.'

'So do I,' cried Suzanne, and she grasped both his hands and twirled him into a dance on the street.

As they got back into the car, Freddie gave her a look of adoration mixed with confusion, as if he couldn't quite decide if she was the most wonderful or the most peculiar woman he had ever met.

The tender grass under her bare feet changed into cold pavements strewn with grit. People seemed to be staring at her. Suzanne realised she was naked but this did not alarm her because she knew it was a dream and she was often naked in dreams. It was when she saw herself (a second self) lying on a couch, sleeping, that she started to panic. She looked down at her own unconscious body, with the arms flung back and the exposed white belly. She was afraid that some cabal of surgeons would take advantage of this vulnerability and plunge their hands into her stomach, opening it up by peeling back the skin to display the red, beating organs for all to see.

She rose up into her consciousness far enough to turn herself over and try to start a new dream, but she slid into a solid wall and bumped her nose on strong-smelling leather. Then she remembered that she was not in bed at all but in a car, on the roadside. And that the danger was real.

After two weeks in Paris, they had heard on the radio in a café that Lille was occupied. Suzanne was frantic, but Freddie would not hear of going back. Then last night there had been bombing on the outskirts of the city. The exodus from Paris had begun: handcarts, bicycles, suitcases, birdcages. Shouting women and crying children. Swaying cars with mattresses tied on top, looking like massive, mobile mushrooms. Paris buses leaving the city.

Suzanne and Freddie joined the cars on the road to Orly that were four abreast and stationary for longer periods than when they were moving. Many cars were old and had been pressed into service for the first time in years. Some even had hand-cranked starters so progress was slow, but spirits were still good and people were tolerant of each other. All were slightly ashamed but Paris was no place now for Parisians with self-respect. The trains were no longer running.

When they reached Fontainebleau Suzanne imagined that the forest was protecting them, and that they were like animals panting with relief under the sheltering trees. Many, including Suzanne and Freddie, stopped on the road for the night and got out camping stoves. In the long dusk of the warm June evening they sat in a daze of holiday memories which, for a time, muffled their fears.

Freddie said he would sleep on the ground, and Suzanne tried to find a comfortable position in the back seat of the car, where there was barely room for her knees when she tucked up her feet. She had been sleeping lightly, taking little sips of unconsciousness and going in and out of dreams until the horror of confronting her own sleeping body had chilled her into wide-eyed wakefulness.

Still lying on the seat, she gazed at the pale grey sky and searched for stars. How long now until morning? She looked through the window of the car, upside down, and it made her feel as if she was travelling through space. The window was open a little and the leaves in the trees shuffled and made the sound of water falling. Behind their hiss she thought she heard a church bell which comforted her because it reminded her of the sound of the cathedral on Sunday mornings as a child. She remembered how she had once asked if she could go to

Mass with her friend from school. Her father had slapped her and Françoise didn't speak to her for a week. But her mother whispered comfort, like the beech trees were whispering to her tonight. 'There are many ways to God, Suzanne,' she had murmured, as she tucked her into bed.

Outside the car figures were moving about. They crossed and recrossed the window, blotting out the sky. Suzanne lay rigid. She could not see their faces, or their feet. It was as if the gods of the zodiac were manifesting and travelling from star to star. Suzanne felt small, earthbound, insignificant. But then she heard human voices.

'This is the one. He was driving this one.'

'A German? With a French woman, you say?'

'*Bien sûr*. We must go to the police.'

'Wait till it gets light.'

'But he might get away.'

'Look, we can make sure he doesn't get far.'

Their petrol. Suzanne felt the car rock as the boot was banged shut. Silence.

Had they gone? Suzanne sat up slowly and endured a flare of fear as the beam of a torch swept the car. Briefly, she saw the disembodied reflection of her own eyes in the rear-view mirror looking at her. She imagined rows of the same eyes, one on top of the other.

She cowered in the seat, wishing it could all be pushed aside, like a bad dream. After a while, she steeled herself and scrambled out to find Freddie.

He was sleeping squirrel-like in a curled-up ball under a grey blanket a little way off.

She shook his shoulder. 'Freddie. We have to go. They are coming for you.'

Chapter Twenty-Nine

Cadaqués, June 1940

It was dangerous to sleep in the sun, but Penelope didn't care. Her safety was no longer precious because the once-living creature of her creativity was dead inside her. It was a slowly putrefying corpse shrinking into a hollow heap of fur and bones. As they travelled through Spain scarred by Franco's victory, she felt nothing except a dull ache at the loss of her own dreams of becoming an artist. Everything that played out on this immense stage was merely an illustration of the desolation and division within herself. She was the bombed city; she was the defeated, maimed revolutionary. This kind of self-pity was new to her and she was ashamed of it.

Yet she managed to fool people that she was still the same. Even Alain. It was he who had persuaded her to leave Paris nearly a month ago and come here to Púbol's strange and hidden world, a white-washed fishing village called Cadaqués, which was sequestered from the ruined towns. Here, sustenance had always come from the sea and it was possible to ignore much of what had happened. But she could not stop worrying about Suzanne.

After the invasion of Holland at the end of May Penelope had tried frantically to contact her with no success. She continued to send letters and telegrams to the address in Amsterdam but had little faith in the post. It was quite likely that the man in the local post office was simply delusional in believing that the letters would reach their destination. Since the convulsions that had brought Franco to power and placed Hitler's ambitions at the centre of everything, all the old systems, like the postal service, had ceased to function properly. But here on the beach all remained as it had been millennia ago. The same water returned from sky to sea. Even the seaweed carried some infinitesimal spore of ancient plants and the same sun continued, dangerously, to shine on the foolish, changeable creatures beneath.

Penelope yawned and stretched out her bare arms behind her head feeling the sharp stones prod into her back as her weight shifted. She breathed in the clean sea air. It had been good to escape the city but the land here was so different from the place of her birth that, instead of reminding her of the green hills and forests of rural England, it might have been another planet. In place of country hedgerows there were outsized cactus bushes. The children used knives to score their names into the big, fleshy paddles of the cactus leaves. At least the olive orchards, kindly in their classical silver, afforded coolness and a vague resemblance to the shelter of apple trees.

She tried to read the landscape for reassurance; nature was all that was left to believe in, but here was a perverse beauty. The coast towards the Cap de Creus became more and more barren. The cliffs were yellow, pockmarked, jagged and bare: a moonscape. Yesterday, she had fallen at the top of a path and the rocks had clawed the skin from her knees and fingertips. But then, turning back to the sea which was laid out in a succession of bays each more perfect than the next, she had gasped at the blue splendour which shone with piercing glory. Púbol's paintings had answered these clean-picked rocks with shit-daubed bodies and replied to their diagonally slashed edges with rounded, ruddy, fleshy protuberances. But how could she respond to this place? Its starkness rebuked her.

So much had changed. Once, the idea of living under the protection of a supporter of Franco like Púbol would have been unthinkable, but where else was there to go? No one knew how much longer it would be safe to stay in France and returning to her parents was out of the question. She could see that Púbol did not actually espouse the fascist cause; he simply had to be able to live in this landscape that was the life-blood of his art and the explanation of his personality. Perhaps Penelope also would sell her soul in exchange for paintings as exceptional as his. As for Alain, he was shelter of a different kind. She did not love him but she needed to be loved at this time when it was impossible to love herself. He was obsessive about describing her in his poems and she clung to this as a temporary identity, like a plaster cast protecting a broken limb.

There was a crunch as Alain sat down on the pebbles beside her. He said nothing. The silences between them had continued to lengthen since the beginning of their affair, now over a year ago. Certain topics were off limits, and one of them was Rolf.

'Be careful of the sun, *chérie*,' said Alain, at last. 'Here.' And he draped a towel over her legs. She kicked away the towel. He shrugged and lit a cigarette.

So this is what we have come to, thought Penelope. A bickering couple. But perhaps it was enough merely to survive. Holland and Belgium had been lost since they left Paris, and France could surely not hold out much longer (news was hard to get). As for Britain, it was small and vulnerable, and surrender could not be far off.

She had written to her parents, but had got no reply and had lost sleep trying to decide if they were in trouble or just still angry with her. Auntie Carys had responded with a telegram, which was typically extravagant of her, but not very informative. It had been so thrilling to throw off her British identity during the early days in Paris, but now she hungered to hear English voices and news of her homeland. A conversation with Alain in which she proposed that they attempted to go to England had ended in shouting and the subject was now another one on the taboo list. And how could she leave Europe, not knowing what had happened to Suzanne?

There was talk among the group of going to America. Púbol's buyers included an eccentric millionaire who could pay for tickets on a plane from Lisbon to New York and there was a shady-sounding Turk who could arrange things, if it came to that. So would they just run away then, leaving Rolf behind?

Click. It was Una, who had arrived just a few days ago, taking pictures with her camera. She looked like the perfect holidaymaker sitting in her striped deckchair, wearing her sunglasses.

'May I?' asked Alain. 'Penelope,' he said, 'sit near Una so that I can take your picture. Now, both of you, close your eyes.'

So Penelope lolled against Una's chair and hid her weary eyes behind sun-warmed lids. At last, she thought, I am the object of the picture. After all my striving to meet the gaze of the camera eye, and the man behind it, I am now supine. I am now the sleeping beauty. I am the artist's model and no longer the artist. This is my surrender.

'Now you, Alain. Now it's your turn.' Una was as cheery as ever.

She watched Una and Alain play-fighting over the camera, noting Alain's uncharacteristic looseness and gaiety and saw in a moment what would happen. The bond between Alain and Una had been merely in abeyance. Una had been waiting patiently, with a charming lack of spite, for Alain to get over his obsession with Penelope and had taken refuge with Maurice in the meanwhile. Curiously, Penelope felt nothing at the prospect of losing Alain. Then came a flash of illumination. It had all been vanity. Alain had fawned on her and she had allowed herself to be flattered. And I left Rolf, she thought. I left my comrade-in-arms for a bunch of roses.

A shout from the water cut off her thoughts.

'*En Miguel*!'

'*L'Eduardo*!' Púbol answered, scrambling to his feet and waving his arms at the incoming vessel. A small weather-worn fishing boat puttered up to the shallows and Púbol turned to beckon at Alain.

'Come. It's time to fish.'

'Aren't you going?' Penelope asked Alain.

He looked in turn at Una.

'I'll stay here,' Una said.

Alain looked from Una to Púbol and back again, but in the end it was the call to his masculine pride that won the day. He gathered his things.

'Wait,' called Penelope. 'I'm coming too.' At last, something to take the place of her depressing thoughts. She pulled some trousers over her bathing suit and rolled up the legs to wade out to the boat.

'*Com et dius*?' asked Eduardo as he pulled Penelope onto the boat. She looked to Púbol for help.

'He is asking your name.'

'Penelope,' she said, keeping hold of Eduardo's hand which was as steady and dry as a rock in the sun. She found that she didn't want to let go of the old man's hand; the motion of the boat was a little alarming. Then she collected her wits and sat down. Eduardo grinned. He was missing several teeth and the crucifix swinging at his neck glinted in the sunlight.

Púbol braced his foot on the side of the boat to pull up the anchor and she marvelled again at his naturalness in this place compared to his awkward behaviour in Paris. He continued to indulge in schoolboy tricks and puerile humour, but Púbol's character made sense here, especially when she heard about the wind that sent people extravagantly mad for a season. Púbol was wearing the same laced espadrilles as Eduardo and the shoes, with their flexible rope soles, were perfectly adapted to the terrain. The boat turned and they left the cove.

Alain was not a good sailor. He sat twisted around to face the direction of travel, as if in a car, and clinging with both hands to the side of the boat. Penelope saw him furtively kick away a coil of rope for fear, presumably, of his feet becoming entangled in it. His face became pallid. Púbol, by contrast, stalked the boat as nimbly as a cat, altering his gait to fit the motion with a lean grace. As soon as he noticed Alain's fragile dignity he began to dance up and down the boat, circling the store box and making the boat rock drunkenly from side to side like a steam swing at the fairground.

At length, Eduardo cut the motor and they stopped in the open water. Púbol went across to help Eduardo spread the nets, trampling the floor of the boat like a cow in a lorry. Then all was still and very quiet. The boat swayed gently now, like a soothing crib. An immense silence spread out around them and was broken only by the soft cuffing of the waves against the outside of the boat. Alain relaxed a little and took out a notebook and pencil from his shirt pocket.

Penelope felt the sun consuming the skin on her bare shoulders. She would be burnt away, down to the bone. She would be cleaned by the sun, like the rocks on the shoreline. Everything would become stark and the truth would emerge. She returned to the moment of clarity on the beach. Had she been wrong to leave Rolf?

Rolf's continuing imprisonment was the background to each meal or everyday comfort and every thought of freedom. He had been moved south to a slightly better place on the French side of the Spanish border at Pau, which was full of captured Republican fighters, and Alain went on trying to secure his release with letters, petitions and appeals to government officials, all to no avail. Penelope would find him sitting at his desk late into the night, staring at the mounting correspondence in despair. She would place a hand on his shoulder and he seemed glad of her sympathy, but if she mentioned Rolf's name his face closed off. He did not like her to speak about Rolf.

They were pulling up the nets now and the sun was no longer overhead. The fish were disentangled and thrown into a red bucket where they slapped their tails against the sides until their labours decreased and then stopped altogether. Púbol clapped Eduardo on the back and seemed delighted at their catch, but Penelope suspected that Eduardo regarded him as a rich man at play. Púbol had hinted that there would be some sort of extravaganza on the beach later, meaning that the fish were merely the props for some game. They turned for home.

Una's jaunty red-and-white bathing suit gradually came into focus. As Eduardo dropped anchor she got up to greet them, throwing a cardigan around her shoulders. Alain disembarked first and plunged his plimsolls into the shallows with a groan of relief. Una took one look at him and began to pour out feminine sympathy for his seasickness, making Penelope feel like a brute in comparison. Eduardo started up the motor again and gave them a wave in farewell.

During the boat trip, a boy had come with a letter to Una from D'Argent. Púbol prodded spitefully at the fish in the bucket with a stick and pretended not to be listening because D'Argent had publicly denounced Púbol as a Franco sympathiser and excommunicated him from the surrealist group at last.

'D'Argent is in Marseilles,' Una said, after scanning the letter, 'Josephine and Clara are with him and an American committee is trying to arrange their passage out of France. Louis says it is only a matter of time until Paris is occupied and he writes that those who wish to leave France, and are able to do so, are absolved of all blame.'

Penelope remembered the cadences of D'Argent's speech in these words and she smiled, quite fondly, at this characteristic dispensation given to all true surrealist believers.

'So, D'Argent is leaving Europe,' said Alain, trying to accept the full import of this new development. It seemed more significant to him than the news about the progress of the German army. Alain and Una wandered off, still discussing the letter, leaving Penelope to sit and stare out at the sea.

She feared even more now for Suzanne and for Suzanne's daughter, Angélique. Could Freddie keep Suzanne safe, not only from the Germans but from her own demons? Last night, in Púbol's bizarre and uncomfortable house, Penelope had woken sweating from a dream in which she was on a high mountain overhang, gripping a rope which Suzanne, unseen below, was hanging on to. In the dream, she pulled on the rope to raise Suzanne to the ledge to join her, but it was slack and Suzanne had gone.

Penelope realised with a jolt that there were ants crawling over her toes. She got up, cursing the angular stones that bruised the soles of her feet. She put on her sandals and retrieved her cigarettes and matches from a jacket pocket. Alain had started her smoking. Now she felt restless between cigarettes but the imagined pleasure, often inspired by the smell of someone else's smoke on the air, never quite measured up to the real thing. She took her cigarettes to a flat rock higher up the beach and settled down to monitor the lowering sun.

She remembered the smell of cigarette smoke clinging to a rocking horse that Rolf had brought back for her from the flea market when they lived in Rue Jacob. They had to wait for Jean to come and help take it up the stairs. The rocking horse had whorls of grain on its buttocks and was missing its lower jaw.

Rolf had intended it as a help for painting horses but of course he had missed the point: she could draw a wooden horse; it was a living, breathing, twitching, turning, dancing horse that she wanted to capture. Sometimes she would shut her eyes and imagine being a horse galloping on toothsome, springy grass, just like when she was a child and her feet had seemed actually to turn into hooves as she ran faster and faster downhill. What had become of that rocking horse, she wondered?

Púbol was assembling his entertainment near the water. He had collected firewood and assembled a rack for grilling the sardines. He called for Penelope to bring her matches. He lit the fire and they both settled down in silence to wait. The sun relinquished itself and fell slowly into the sea. Penelope watched it faithfully until the last slice of the golden disc was lost to view.

When the others returned, Púbol handed round some red wine which was so sour that it brought tears to the eyes and then produced a triangular loaf of bread with bulbous corners from a red cloth bag that might actually have been a hat. His brown, dirty fingernails piercing the dough looked faintly obscene. Like some swarthy, Iberian Christ at the Last Supper, he solemnly broke the bread and gave a piece each to everyone around the fire. Una immediately placed a piece of fish inside the bread and handed it to Alain as if she were a sort of automated housewife, while Penelope helped herself to one of the sardines and enjoyed the crackle of the bones snapping between her teeth.

'To absent friends,' said Alain, raising his beaker.

They ate in silence with the greying fire collapsing gently into the sand, part by part. Rolf was the spectre at their feast, of course, as at every meal. Penelope remembered the bread and sausage on the floor of the studio on the day she had made the fur cup. It was her claim to fame now, everyone knew it, and it had fixed her to that day in the past – the last time that she had shaped her own desires in the free space of unqualified love.

'D'Argent also wrote of something very sad,' said Una, into the dusk. 'He says that Natalia is near death. She was moved to a hospital some years back. There is no family, so it was to Louis that they wrote. Of course, he cannot go and see her now.'

'But he could before and he didn't,' said Penelope savagely, aware at the same time that it was just as well D'Argent had never visited and found out that his Natalia had been replaced by some raving Spanish aristocrat. Penelope had continued to air her vendetta against D'Argent, hoping that one day Suzanne would become infected by her anger and manage at last to throw off her emotional dependency on him. Alain was looking at her strangely, as if he wasn't quite sure who she was.

'I'm sorry,' she said, then mumbled under her breath, 'but not very.'

She remembered the way she and Rolf used to call D'Argent 'the Perfect One' behind his back and felt a stab of loss. Rolf, I need you, she thought. I need you to give me back my strength. I can't manage any longer without you.

Chapter Thirty

The phone call finally came through. Ironically Alain, who had worked so hard for this, had left early for Figueres and still did not know that Rolf had got out of the camp and, by some means or other, crossed the border. He was in Girona. The message was that he would be on the cathedral steps at noon. So it was Penelope who was going to meet him. Eduardo had offered the loan of his truck for the return journey because he was going to Girona to collect a car for his cousin. Penelope wondered what Púbol had told him about her relationship with Rolf. What was that relationship, anyway?

Bumping along in the truck, Penelope repeatedly scanned Eduardo's profile, searching for clues to his mood and imagining a pencil in her hand as she followed the deep-cut creases in his sun-browned skin. Conversation on the three-hour journey would be impossible due to the lack of a common language, so communication was restricted to nods, smiles and the sharing of some bitter green olives from a paper bag. Eduardo spat the stones out of the open window. Now and again he would turn and give her a reassuring toothless grin, as if she were a little girl. He coaxed the long gearstick into place and expressed no surprise or reaction of any kind, as the truck bumped from side to side on the roads which were, in some places, entirely broken up. Rocks were strewn about and there was evidence of explosions. Some of the farmhouses were perfect, like picture postcards, but some were little more than heaps of rubble or had doors missing and blackened windows.

The disorder and alarm spreading across Europe was a far cry from the idealised image of a place of freedom and good living that she had cherished as she crossed the Channel three long years before. She recalled the thrill of that first journey to France to meet Rolf; a journey so different from this one. When she had first travelled to Paris she was certain that he was the answer to everything she wanted in life: love, art, friendship and ideas. And now? She had thrown all of that away because of some failure in herself, of generosity or trust. Now it seemed that Rolf had always been the key to her happiness and his love was surely the catalyst for her own creative gifts, which had languished and died in his absence. She had no idea what she would say to him when they met.

Eduardo rolled a cigarette while turning the wheel with his elbows and then, perversely, pulled over to smoke it. Penelope got out an old map that she'd found among Púbol's things and proffered it to Eduardo as a way of asking where they were. He looked at it with a sort of blank awe until it dawned on her that he could not read. Eduardo offered her his leather pouch of tobacco but she shook her head and lit one of her own. She inhaled and sighed at the tranquillising effect of the nicotine and Eduardo smiled back, in perfect accord. They smoked in silence. The road was deserted.

An hour later they were stopped at a barricade made up of old wire fences. A gaunt man wearing a smart blue uniform leant in through the open window to scrutinise the fuel gauge. He was missing a hand and the stump was neatly bound in the same coloured cloth as his uniform. He ordered them out of the truck. Penelope could not understand what he was saying to Eduardo, or Eduardo's curt replies. Two other men appeared. They had filthy, torn clothes that were reminiscent of uniform, but a travesty of the one-handed man's peaked-cap efficiency. Eduardo frowned and threw his hands up and down as the one-handed man wrote something in a notebook on the bonnet.

Then a shout came from one of the men who had opened a sack on the back of the truck. The smell of smoked fish rose up in the heat. The one-handed man flicked his head to one side as a signal to his inferiors to remove the sack and Eduardo shook his head with resignation. Then they moved the fences and Penelope and Eduardo got back into the truck and drove off. Once out of sight, she placed her hand on Eduardo's sleeve. He did not turn to her but tightened his arm muscles and pressed his lips together.

They crossed a wide river. Eduardo pulled up as they came in sight of the tall, honey-coloured walls of the old city. He nodded and pointed at the bell tower of the cathedral, then handed her the keys to the truck. She helped him to unload the remaining sack of mackerel and to retrieve his grey bedroll which was strapped to a knapsack. At the last moment, she held out her hand and the firm, friendly grasp of his handshake threatened to bring tears to her eyes. To avoid Eduardo's look of bewildered concern she turned and fled into the narrow streets.

She found herself stumbling and sliding in an alleyway of long, shallow steps that were worn smooth with use. The ancient stones of the walls were interrupted by two modern windows and a black metal gate with bars in a grid, like a prison entrance. Cowering in a doorway was an emaciated cat. Penelope suddenly felt all the strength leave her and she sank down next to the cat, which froze in terror. Everything bore down on her. She didn't know why she was crying. Perhaps it was for the state of things in this warring world, or perhaps it was simply because this was the first time she had been really alone for weeks. The cat finally made a break for the open but it could not run fast or properly. Its back legs were dragging along the ground. The horror of the cat's deformity stopped her crying, in the manner of a child whose weeping is arrested by a fascinating sight. She heard bells chiming. Surely it was not noon already? She got up and began to walk, pulling her thoughts together.

It was nine months since she had spoken to Rolf and he had been a prisoner all that time. He would be changed: ill, perhaps, or altered from brutal treatment. Maybe he would have aged. As she drew closer to the flight of wide steps leading to the cathedral, she saw him. He looked exactly the same. His white hair waved across his brow and his shoulders were straight and firm. Penelope had a strong memory of his arm around her and of his intelligent hand cupping her shoulder, shaping it, knowing it. She started to run.

When she reached him she saw that Rolf's trousers and grey shirt were appallingly dirty. He was talking to a young man in a cap sitting beside him on the steps. She waited while Rolf read out the wording of an official letter in French for him, leaning over to point out each word with his finger. When they reached the end the man shook his hand gratefully and Rolf turned aside.

'Thank you for coming,' he said, and began to walk off.

'Where are we going?' she called out as she hurried after him.

'I want to see the gardens once more before I leave. There is a fountain there I admire very much.'

'How are you?' she asked, struggling to keep up.

'I am fine. Where is Alain? Is he not with you?'

'No, he's in Figueres, with Una. He doesn't know that you are free yet. I've got a truck. And a map. It'll take three hours to get to Cadaqués.'

'Good. And will Alain be there?'

'Yes, I expect so. But aren't you glad to see me?'

He stopped and looked at her for the first time. 'Of course I am glad.'

She moved towards him, but at the same moment he turned again to continue on up the hill and their shoulders clashed.

'What was it like, at Pau?' she asked after a while.

'Here. Here it is,' he said, ignoring her.

They were in a quiet garden of tall cypresses and palm trees, surrounded by yellow-gold medieval brick walls. The sound of running water came from a little way off and Rolf went to the fountain and rested his hands heavily on the rim of the stone bowl. For a moment she thought that he would return to his normal self, but instead he squatted and, in a businesslike way, inspected the designs on the stoneware.

'Moorish,' he said. 'No figurative representations.'

'Rolf. Talk to me.'

'What is there to say?'

Penelope could not answer.

'Where is the truck?' asked Rolf.

By the time they started out on the road, the sunlight was beginning to soften. Rolf drove the truck badly and very fast, exclaiming German oaths each time the gearstick crunched with resistance. Penelope was apprehensive about being stopped again. She didn't know, and dared not ask, if Rolf had been released legitimately or if he was fleeing. When the road straightened out on the long stretch towards Figueres, Rolf's driving improved and Penelope cautiously let go of the handle she had been gripping to brace herself.

'What has Alain been working on?' asked Rolf.

She explained that Alain had been writing very little since leaving Paris. Rolf wanted to know why. And what about Púbol? She described his latest picture: a molten telephone in a Greek temple.

'And what of Louis?'

When Rolf heard that D'Argent was in Marseilles awaiting passage to New York he slapped the steering wheel.

'Yes. That is it. America. A clean slate. A new canvas. It must be so.'

Then Penelope told him about the chance that Púbol could get tickets for them to fly out of Lisbon and he praised Púbol as 'the best of us, always'.

'That's not what you used to say,' said Penelope. 'You used to call him an idiot and a dangerous narcissist.'

Rolf shrugged.

When she looked back at him after a few minutes he was sitting up straighter in the driving seat and his narrowed eyes were fixed on the road ahead with an even greater hunger to cover the miles. He drove faster.

All this time she had been waiting for him to ask about her work. But he never did, and she felt unable to bring up the subject herself.

The final few miles to Cadaqués were on a long, curving road in a hairpin shape, first along one side of a ravine then back along the other. The road twisted and meandered to follow the contour of the mountainside and in contrast to Eduardo, who drove with a steady, mature knowledge of the terrain, Rolf turned it into a roller-coaster ride. He refused to slow down in response to the road's demands, slamming on the brake and skidding on the loose stones. Penelope began to fear for her life.

'Rolf, be reasonable. There's no hurry,' she pleaded, at last.

'Not for you, maybe,' he replied, but he did moderate his speed a little after that.

On the second half of the long curve she looked back at the ravine, seeing the same scrub on the slopes and the same abandoned buildings with cacti flowering through the piles of glinting rubbish. She was seeing it all from a new angle but it was the same landscape as before. Rolf seemed scarcely to notice her at all. His own thoughts occupied all his attention, his focus on what might happen next to him. Had he always been like this? One thing was for sure: her romantic dream of a reunion with Rolf was laughable and naive. She was confused, and carsick.

They reached the outskirts of Cadaqués and Penelope felt an enormous sense of relief, as well as of homecoming, when she spied the sea between the white buildings. It was shimmering with the glamour of the lowering sun. She directed Rolf to stop at the square near Port d'Alguer and they walked back along the sea road, with the evening churchgoers passing by the other way towards Santa Maria. Across the road from the Casino bar, Alain perched on the wall. He jumped up and embraced Rolf. They remained like that for some time, like lovers, then they went off into the café already deep in conversation and without a second glance back at her.

She was stunned for a moment, and then became very clear-headed. What did she feel? It wasn't sorrow, or jealousy, or exclusion. She tried to imagine how she would express it to Suzanne, bringing to mind her intelligent, mild green eyes. She remembered Suzanne's bowed head, cut down like a flower by D'Argent's rejection. But that was not what she felt at this moment.

She began to retrace her steps back to the square, then out of the village, climbing higher and higher into the hills with their fascinating shelves of granite making horizontal slashes in the earth as if newly stacked by a recent ice age. Further and further towards the lighthouse she went, and then began the descent to the empty beach, slipping sideways in her town shoes, which she soon took off. Then off came her skirt, her blouse, then her underwear. She was in a sort of trance in which her intentions were not clear even to herself and yet at the same time she knew she was doing exactly the right thing. For the first time in many months, she felt at liberty.

The sharp pain of the stones under her bare feet made her yelp out loud but she limped on, picking her way into the water, and launching herself into the cold sea with a grunt. She began to swim out, towards the sun on the horizon.

There was a pull under the water, to the right side, always the right, and even when she tried to compensate, she drifted with the current. I am going to drown, she thought, quite calmly, and took an experimental mouthful of seawater. Then she coughed and splashed and flurried up the water experiencing only the pure desire to stay alive. But she soon tired and, for a few moments, stopped striving and began to fall, feet first. Her hair flowed upwards as she sank down into the water. It was as though time was falling away, or dividing into two. She opened her eyes under the water and saw something massive and striped with orange.

Then the strength came back into her limbs and she swam upwards until she broke the surface. She struck out fiercely towards the shore as if the power and the muscular force of a wild animal had entered her legs and back from deep beneath the water. Nearing the beach she found she needed only to paddle easily, like a large, four-legged beast, to reach her destination. She lay at the edge of the water and panted. There was seaweed covering her legs as if the human skin had been replaced with something of another species. She threw the tawny brown kelp back into the sea.

After a sound night's sleep, in which she dreamt only of a pleasant visit with Suzanne to a sunny zoo, where the animals roamed freely and harmoniously in a flowered field, Penelope woke refreshed and ready to begin. She painted a rocking horse with a missing lower jaw inside a room next to a cat with a broken spine. Outside the window a white horse galloped away through the trees and, instead of hooves, it had furry, clawed paws.

Chapter Thirty-One

Fontainebleau, June 1940

Suzanne and Freddie were preparing to abandon the car. They quickly repacked one each of Isaac's old suitcases and at the last minute Freddie ran to collect the road map from the dashboard.

'We won't need that,' whispered Suzanne, thrusting in Ailsa's old hat, then havering between two pairs of spare shoes and choosing the smarter ones. 'We can go by train.'

Freddie gave her a look and added the map to his case along with a torch and a screwdriver that had been rolling around loose in the boot of the car. He threw a tartan blanket around Suzanne's shoulders and jettisoned a book in favour of an umbrella. Suzanne experienced a flash of alarm in some remote corner of her mind and then quickly dismissed it. They were going to Spain; it would be an adventure.

The sky was almost light by the time they had walked beyond the most crowded part of the road. It was strange to see these civilised Parisians sleeping outdoors with their pets and possessions and it took Suzanne's mind off the uncomfortable, cracked handle of the suitcase which had begun to rub and blister the inner creases of her fingers.

The sun gained strength and they rolled up the blankets. Freddie brought out a ball of string from his pocket and tied up the blankets to wear them like the panniers of a bicycle, one on either side of his hips. Suzanne laughed at him.

They passed through a small village and stopped to buy water and a large pork sausage: clearly Freddie's dietary rules were being cast aside. They sat by a duck pond to eat and study the map.

'Look,' said Suzanne, licking her finger and tracing the blue line of the Seine.

'Yes,' said Freddie, 'it will be better not to use the road.'

'Why?' asked Suzanne, offering him the water bottle.

He took a sip, and said nothing, then: 'Prettier?'

She smiled. 'Come on.'

The route was indeed enchanting. They went through trees along a woodland path and then there was the river, curving and shining before them. As they walked beside the water, Suzanne imagined the voices of Paris muttering within it, carried there from her city of spirits and noble buildings. Hand in hand with Freddie, with the tuneful birds in the forest around them and the ripples carrying messages from her beloved places, she was entirely happy.

Then came the sound of explosions, far off. They stopped to listen.

'Where is that?' she asked.

'A few miles? On the road, perhaps.'

'Where are we?' asked Suzanne.

'Close to Saint-Mammès,' said Freddie, showing her the map. 'The rivers join here.'

'But we must go south. This is west, towards Germany.'

'If they have broken through, we are already lost, but we stand a better chance off the main routes. Come on. We are nearly at Montereau. It's past lunchtime.'

They reached the town by around three and Freddie refused Suzanne's appeals for a meal in the charming restaurant by the square, instead loading up a shopping bag with biscuits, dried fruit and more sausage, plus a second bottle of water. Suzanne was about to throw the other empty bottle away but he stopped her, saying that he had seen a drinking fountain by the church on the way in.

After another roadside meal and the awkwardness of finding a public toilet, they set out again, following the road at first.

A car pulled in. 'Need a lift?' asked a large, red-faced woman accompanied by two hysterically barking sheep dogs.

Freddie glanced at Suzanne, and at the hand she had wrapped in a scarf to hold the suitcase. He nodded.

They got in, Freddie in the back with the dogs who sniffed him and whimpered at the scent his clothes still carried from Max's Dobermans.

Freddie was careful not to speak so it was Suzanne, in the passenger seat, who received the flood of the woman's talk: all about Germans. Suzanne said 'Yes', 'Really', 'Incredible', 'Terrible' to her questions about their journey, the news from Paris, the people who had already left Montereau and the price of bread which had gone up. The woman was a farmer's wife, widowed, and her sons now ran their dairy farm.

'My neighbour is a seamstress and she has gone to stay with her sister in Nice. It's not so easy to pack up a herd of Friesians,' she joked bitterly.

'No,' said Suzanne, as realisation began to dawn: France would not be safe for much longer. Penelope must have known. She did know, of course; she had been telling Suzanne since Christmas to be ready to leave if necessary. Suzanne had not listened, nor told Freddie what Penelope had written. Was this a mistake?

'And where are you sleeping tonight?' asked the farmer's wife. 'Do you need a bed?'

'Yes,' said Freddie, picking up one of the French words he knew. 'Yes, please.'

'Fine. Achille is in Troyes tonight. You can have his room.'

The farm was sprawling and smelly, but the house was clean as a pin. They were given cassoulet and wine. Freddie said very little, relying on his boyish good looks and smiles to get by. Suzanne didn't know where the farmer's wife might think he was from. Later, she made hot chocolate and took them to her absent son's room.

'I hope you will be comfortable,' she said, as she left and Freddie nudged Suzanne into thanking her.

Squashed between the wall and Freddie in the single bed, Suzanne sipped the rich, sweet drink and remembered making it for Angélique in the kitchen at the bakery. Her mother used to put Angélique to bed, but it was Suzanne's job to carefully make her bedtime chocolate.

Her mother had never spoken of Angélique as Suzanne's daughter, not even when she and Suzanne were alone. There had been just a single, difficult conversation before Angélique was born, when she had told Suzanne that she could go on living at the bakery in Lille. 'You may stay to watch her grow up as my daughter,' her mother had said, 'but if it becomes too painful, then you must go.'

The baby had been born on the Isle of Skye at her Scottish grandmother's croft; far away from the prying eyes of their customers and acquaintances in Lille. After the birth, which the women managed between them, her mother wouldn't give the baby to her, even though she pleaded to be able to hold her. Granny Campbell wrapped her in strips of cotton to stem the flow of blood from between her legs then held Suzanne's face against her own soft, flabby bosom to absorb her tears. Suzanne had closed down her heart then, until Penelope's smiles and Freddie's devotion had opened a crack to let the light back in like a slice of yellow brightness.

In the morning, Suzanne tried phoning Lille while the farm dogs barked at her side. There was no answer at the bakery. After a breakfast of hot milk, cheese and yoghurt, and the gift of two enormous haversacks which were big enough for all their things including food and blankets, Freddie and Suzanne set off again.

They arrived at Troyes just as the shops were closing. Freddie eyed up the passers-by, trying to assess if they belonged here or were travellers like themselves. They headed out to a tennis court and squatted on the hard reddish clay to eat some more sausage. Suzanne was getting very tired of sausage. They rested for an hour then hoisted the canvas sacks onto their backs again.

Freddie found some well-appointed houses on the road behind the tennis club and made Suzanne wait with the bags. He came back a few minutes later looking embarrassed.

'You will have to go and ask instead,' he said.

'For a bed?'

'Yes. Be polite.'

She left him and selected a shiny red door halfway down the street.

The woman who opened it wore an overall and headscarf. A maid?

Suzanne swallowed hard. 'Please, my husband and I would be very glad of a bed for the night.'

The door was shut in her face and Suzanne turned away almost with relief: it was unthinkable to be doing this. Then the door opened again and the woman held out half a loaf of bread.

'She says no. She said that to the others, too. Not just you. Here,' she put the bread into Suzanne's hand, 'don't tell her I gave it you.'

'Thank you,' said Suzanne with an uprush of gratitude that alarmed her. 'You are very kind.'

The door closed again.

Suzanne took the bread back to Freddie, then tried the next house.

It was getting dark and she had lost count of the houses she had been refused at, each one stiffening her voice unrecognisably with injured pride. 'Perfectly understandable,' she would say. 'Please, it's not a problem.'

'But Freddie,' she said, 'why don't we go to a hotel?'

'And give what name? Come.'

She followed him to the back of the houses and watched as he examined each garden in turn.

'This one,' he said.

They waited until complete darkness.

Freddie crept through the gates and attempted to release the padlock on the shed door.

'Come on now,' he pleaded softly. 'Open for me, that's right.' His toothpick magically released the workings and they were in.

The shed floor was hard and oil-smelling, and the sweep of Freddie's torch revealed rows of spiked gardening tools. He cleared a space, got out the blankets and filled a sack with clothes for a pillow.

'I can't,' said Suzanne. The place frightened her. It was dark and pungent and there was something scrabbling at the roof, or maybe at the door.

He made her sit down and stroked her arms until she quietened. Then he persuaded her to eat the tough, unfriendly heel of the stale loaf she had been given at the first house, sawing off the top of a can of soup to dip it in.

They slept, fitfully.

The next day was beautiful. They played guessing games and walked through fields, jumping off walls like children and running downhill. Suzanne felt as if she was flying. The scent of the grass and the flowers was exhilarating and later when there was a sudden, summer shower, they sheltered in a barn breathing in the scent of the dry earth soaking up the rain. She remembered what this perfume was called: one of her favourite words.

'Do you have a German word for petrichor?' asked Suzanne.

'No. It is the same. Perhaps in French, too?'

They slept in the barn and in the morning, Freddie found two bicycles leaning up against the gate outside. Without a moment's hesitation he grasped the handlebars of one and told her to take the other, silencing her protests.

They ran on to the lane and Freddie mounted his bike not noticing at first that Suzanne was still pushing hers.

'Quickly,' he shouted back.

But she shook her head. 'I can't ride. I don't know how.'

Once they were a few fields away, the rest of the day was spent teaching Suzanne to ride. She laughed and laughed, wobbling and sashaying her front wheel then falling in an explosion of giggles into the long, soft grass as the cows stared and chewed. By the evening she could pedal for a few yards and they went back to the lane.

The next day they began a three-day ride to Lyon. They were back on the main road with an endless line of tell-tale cars with cases and boxes tied to roof or bonnet, and a few horse-drawn carts, all travelling south. There was even a bus that belonged in Paris.

Suzanne saw a little girl sitting on the verge, crying, and went to her.

'Where is your mother?' she asked, her arm around the girl's shuddering shoulders.

The child just kept crying, and Freddie pulled Suzanne sharply away.

'No,' he said. 'No.'

Freddie was so rarely like this – imperious and hard-faced – that Suzanne's surprise allowed him to lead her away.

The villages on the road to Lyon were busy and the shops, if open, were nearly empty. Freddie gave her the last two inches of sausage which she broke in half to share with him but he shook his head.

'It is time to spend some of our money,' he said. 'We need to get on a train.'

They saw the crowd outside before even reaching the forecourt. Lyon railway station itself was a mass of shouting and baggage and there was a choking stench coming from the sidings where streams of people had used the tracks as a toilet. Freddie was overwhelmed by a sea of bodies and harsh words that threatened to carry him away. He fought with arms and shoulders and Suzanne gripped onto his hands to stop him being separated from her. There was no question of staying to queue for a ticket. It was too loud, too violent.

It was warm enough to sleep outdoors that night, but in the morning some uniformed men came and kicked them awake. It turned out there were soup kitchens in the centre of town and this was why they were being rounded up. So they went to wait in line, herded like cattle and stupefied with hunger and another bad night's sleep. Suzanne had begun to lose her hold on day, night, forward and why.

'Free soup.' 'Please wait.' 'Wait in line.' Always waiting. The first shall be last, and the last first. The feet move before the line does. People stand and look to the front and nothing happens. A bell strikes in the church tower and an engine revs. Children shout. And here we are, birds who don't migrate but are moving all together, changing their ways, wearing the same clothes for weeks, speaking less every day.

In a theatre, the seating had been cleared and the floor was covered in straw. Some people were directed to the stage to bed down under huge, dusty curtains, but she and Freddie were told to take their blankets to a space in the auditorium. A man had a newspaper and was reading it aloud: the Germans had occupied Paris. Some wept at the news, but most were too tired and had already gone to sleep. Suzanne didn't like sleeping with other people nearby. The straw was crawling with fleas and in the dark, she remained rigidly awake, trying to distinguish the movements of the sleepers all around from the scuttle of rats. Freddie took her hand. As long as he was with her, it seemed he could keep up his courage and take the part of the one in charge, the one able to cope and plan and manage.

Earlier, she had watched him sitting on the ground when he couldn't see her, and his whole body had collapsed inwards, his eyes were empty and she could see how much weight he had lost from the hollows in his face. Then he noticed her watching him and rebuilt himself quickly, asking how she felt, how she was.

In the darkness, the confinement and fear rose up in Suzanne's chest, suffocating her. The worst nightmares were becoming real: this was danger, hunger, desperation. Freddie was her only hold on safety now and if she could not trust her mind, at least she could rely on him to protect her.

Chapter Thirty-Two

Cadaqués, June 1940

Since Rolf's return, Penelope had spent more and more time alone. She tramped around the dry hills, turning back to look at the white houses of Cadaqués that were reassuringly reduced to the size of toys in the distance. She had commandeered an empty room in Púbol's enormous nonsensical house, which had tiny corridors, high-ceilinged rooms and an outdoor pool, and there she kept the completed picture of the leaping horse (unnamed as yet), a stack of canvases, paints and a chair on a box to use as an easel. She would get up very early, leaving Alain to sleep off the rough wine he had drunk at the Casino bar the night before, and paint until breakfast, which she bought on her way through the town. Then she would climb up, away from the houses, sometimes spending whole days on deserted beaches that she had half-walked, half-slid down to reach. Walking and swimming in silence. Waiting, and watching internally for new pictures to come.

She scarcely spoke. Twice now, Eduardo had taken her out with him on the boat, waiting outside the house in Port Lligat then springing up off the wall at the sight of her. He would raise an eyebrow and make a motion with his hand like a fish in the water. She would laugh and nod, as if given a present. The second time he had indeed brought a gift. It was a pair of espadrilles, just like his own, and he showed her the complicated knots and method of tying them. She had never worn such soft, comfortable footwear and they gave her a firm grip on the boat and the rocks alike.

Eduardo had a talent for expressing both information and emotion without the need for words. By contrast, in the evening, Penelope would listen to Alain, Púbol and Rolf, shouting-drunk, debating the value of art in circular, meaningless arguments. Once she would have joined in, now she simply sat and watched. Then, she would wander out to look at the sea again. The sea meant something stronger, something clearer. She would paint the sea. But how?

Una, too, was present for these evening gatherings in the Casino or by Púbol's pool. Like Penelope, she watched without speaking, but she smiled or did some sewing; she was happy to be near her men, and looked up frequently, especially at Alain. He often absently put an arm around Una's shoulders as he lifted a drink to his lips. Alain was once again paying attention to his appearance: his top button always done up and his shirt as white as the walls of the church of Santa Maria.

Alain was eloquent and writing poetry again, but for all his words Penelope could not really understand him. Eduardo, however, in his red-and-blue jersey, ragged-edged shorts and sun-creased skin, flooded her with his passion for the sea and the pride he felt in his boat, his nets, his home and his language. She could say a few words in Catalan now. Why Eduardo called her '*mi bitxito*' she didn't know, but he said it kindly, with a grin, so she liked to hear it.

As for Rolf, they scarcely exchanged a word other than 'pass the salt' or similar. Understandably, Rolf was focused on food and sleep. He often slept till midday which would have been unthinkable during their old days in Paris together. She didn't know if he was working again or not.

She often returned to the beach where she had come close to giving in the day that Rolf came back and where she had had that peculiar experience of strength as if possessed by a tiger. It was called Sa Conca and this evening she had come to it again, leaving Alain and Una to wait at the Casino for the others. It was obvious that Alain wanted to be released and reunite with Una, but Penelope's pride would not quite allow it. She sensed that everything was in a state of precarious balance and that any move would bring it all down on her head. But something would have to happen soon; she couldn't live for much longer as an observer of her own life, waiting only for the next chance to be alone.

It was getting late. The sunset colours were appearing in the sky above the water as if an invisible brush had painted a wash of orange across the horizon. Penelope sat at the top of the beach, wearing her espadrilles and wishing that Eduardo had come for her today. Perhaps tomorrow. She thought about Suzanne. About Fabien. About the exhibition in London where she had first seen Rolf and called him insufferable. The pictures rolled on and she drew up her knees and put her forehead down on her arms to try to block out the procession of scenes from her life since leaving home three years ago.

A few minutes later she jerked upright at the scraping sound of a boat being pulled on to shore. Eduardo. He came up the beach with that lively, jerky, old-man movement that reminded her of Isaac, now long gone. Oh dear, where were these tears coming from?

Eduardo saw her dry her eyes and he held out a hand to her. She took it and he pulled her up to standing. He indicated the boat and she understood.

The journey around the two bays was like stepping into a fairy tale and being taken to a magical land. The lights from the harbour and the town sent lines of gold across the water and the dark settled around them.

At Es Pianc, Eduardo handed her out and tied up the boat. She followed him along the path on the top of wall and then into one of the narrowest streets of the town. After a short while he stopped at a door covered with foliage – it was too dark to see what kind – and opened it.

Inside, it was even darker but there were two places illuminated. One was lit by the flames of a brick-built oven in the corner, where pots were sunk into depressions in the stone and piles of pine branches spilled over the surface next to it. The other bright area was a table lit by a lamp and covered in a patterned cloth that hung low on all sides.

Sitting at the table was a large woman with black hair tied up in a chignon.

'*You-sia*,' said Eduardo to Penelope.

He so rarely spoke to her that she knew it was important. Of course – his wife's name.

'Ah,' said the woman, getting up. She used that same word that sounded like '*bichito*', and laughed affectionately with Eduardo, as Penelope found herself tightly enveloped in the woman's arms.

Eduardo said something to his wife and, as if by a miracle, she addressed Penelope in French.

'Good evening, mademoiselle. Have you eaten?'

Penelope looked so amazed that Eduardo and his wife began laughing again.

Over a meal of sardines and bread Penelope learnt, from drawings by Eduardo and spelt-out words by his wife, that *bitxito* meant 'little bug' and that *You-sia* was Llùcia: the Catalan name for Lucy. She was made to practise the pronunciation – with the emphasis on 'You' – many times, and each attempt provoked more amusement.

Penelope, now christened 'Penelopito', let out a surreptitious yawn and after another conference between Eduardo and Llùcia she was taken to a back room where there were stacks of baskets smelling of seaweed and a table covered in small shapes. There was a couch with ugly metal arms but it was long enough to stretch out on.

Llùcia covered her with a soft cotton quilt, pointed to a covered bucket, then left her in darkness.

The chances of sleeping in such a strange place seemed very slim but the next moment she woke up again. It was still dark. She heard the sound of Púbol's voice at the front door talking rapidly with Eduardo and started to get up, but then sat still, listening to the discussion. She didn't understand a word and wondered if Púbol expected her to return with him. Must she go?

At length the conversation ended and she heard the door close. Eduardo's light footsteps moved up the stairs and above the room she was in. Then came the low notes of his voice interspersed with Llùcia's gentler, higher tones.

Penelope lay down and allowed the alternating voices to lull her back to sleep, feeling all the tension drain away from her arms, legs, back, shoulders and skull. She began to dream of a gallery with wonderful, huge, coloured pictures on the walls. Each one hung low enough that you could step right into it. She found one of Suzanne and Freddie sitting in the Tuschinski cinema and joined them to watch a film all about a riding school for winged horses.

Penelope woke up, stretched and banged her arms on the cold iron of the couch. The room was much larger in daylight, though the window was small and the branches hanging over it made for even less illumination. She got up and immediately went to the table. The shapes that she had not been able to make out last night were carvings, most about two or three inches high, of various creatures: snail, bull, fish, horse, dog. Selecting the best of the horses, she took it into the other room.

Eduardo was at the table, working with a knife on another piece. They exchanged greetings and conversed as usual with gestures and facial expressions. Penelope held up the horse, showing her admiration for it, and was given it to keep after an initial, half-hearted refusal for form's sake. Then she enquired what Eduardo was working on and he explained that it was a rabbit. He wondered if she was hungry and she readily agreed. There was bread, which he sliced. He then demonstrated how to add olive oil and salt and then rub tomato on top. She loved it, and ate three slices, which he found amusing.

Penelope asked where Llùcia was and Eduardo, making sure Penelope had put on her shoes, took her outside. The sunlight was blazing and the foliage turned out to be a rampant, violet bougainvillea in full bloom. Eduardo nodded in agreement with her ecstasy at the colour, then took her next door: a house with an open front and an old woman in black sitting by a table on which was a heap of crusty white loaves and a jar of money. After a respectful greeting to the old woman, they went to the back where Llùcia was surrounded by the heat and smell of baking. There was a long table covered in flour and Llùcia, similarly whitened from head to wrist, had her hands full of wet dough.

'Have you eaten, my Penelopito?'

'Yes. Yes. Is this your workplace?'

'Yes, it's all mine.'

A girl of maybe fourteen came in with a sack of flour half her size.

Llùcia was jubilant. 'It's so hard to know if we will get more,' she told Penelope, then launched into a string of instructions to the girl.

Penelope turned around, but Eduardo had gone.

'Come. Beside me,' said Llùcia.

Penelope then spent two hours copying Llùcia's movements, kneading the dough then leaving it aside while they worked on other, already-rested dough to form long sausage shapes. These were spiralled up and finally slid into the oven in sets of six. Next they paused to drink water, step outside and smoke a cigarette. Then they did it all again. And again. It was easy, and Llùcia slowed each time she saw that Penelope was uncertain.

The pastries came out golden and were then covered in icing sugar. They left them on the table next to the old woman who had not moved. She had taken the opportunity of having no customers to take a nap. The villagers knew to wake her up if they needed change, explained Llùcia, although many would leave money without bothering her at all.

Penelope straightened her back and realised she had some letters in her pocket that she had never got around to posting yesterday.

'I need to go to the post office,' she said.

'Come back for lunch,' said Llùcia, indicating one of the pastries that she had put in a paper bag.

At the post office, Eduardo's brother, who spoke his own variety of English, greeted her.

'Pen-lee. The money is yours.'

Finally, her letters must have found the right person and she could now collect her allowance from the post office in Figueres. Eduardo's brother had been on her behalf and brought back as much cash as could be scraped together for her. He apologised for not being able to bring the full amount. Things were still difficult.

Penelope suppressed an ungenerous thought about the missing third of her allowance and rejoiced over her reinstated financial independence. She sent her traditional weekly letter to Suzanne in Quellijnstraat, which had become a sort of diaristic exercise on her part, and another letter to the French embassy in the Netherlands appealing for help with locating her friend. The chances of seeing Suzanne again were lower every day and Penelope tried not to dwell on it.

As she walked back past Port d'Alguer, towards Eduardo and Llùcia's, she wondered if they meant her to stay. The idea of spending her time baking bread with Llùcia, learning to carve with Eduardo and going out on the boat, and maybe even setting up a sort of rudimentary studio in her room with supplies raided from Púbol's vast store of materials, was the most wonderful thing she could imagine.

When she reached Carrer Hort d'en Sanés, Eduardo was excited and took her by the hand to her room. The carvings on the table had been packed into a box and instead there was exactly what she had envisaged: a stack of blank canvases, bags of paint tubes, a heap of brushes, a bottle of spirits and some rags. On the floor, wrapped in cloth were the pictures she had done since the night Rolf returned: the leaping horse; a picture of Suzanne as a butterfly at the top of the stairs in the Tuschinski, and the one depicting her legs in the bath as if massive rocks in the sea, which she had only just started. Not for the first time, she had the strongest feeling that Eduardo was her soulmate: the one person in the world who understood her completely.

He pointed at the horse picture and then at the pocket of her skirt where she had put his carving that morning and nodded sagely.

Chapter Thirty-Three

Lyon, June 1940

Despite the dirt and noise, Suzanne found that she was not keen to leave Lyon. She felt a perverse pleasure in being part of a group, and the continual exchange of news and comparing of stories became addictive. Freddie sat silently while she swapped tales with families from across France and beyond, from Belgium and the Netherlands. Many had waited and hesitated until armoured vehicles began passing through their towns, or lines of refugees gave a living demonstration of what the future held for them. Some of them had been bombed or shot at on the road. Some had seen their elderly relatives die and had been forced to bury or abandon them along the way. But the worst were parents whose children had become separated from them.

Freddie, now picking up more and more French words, would intervene and take Suzanne away from conversations about missing children. She knew he was right: this unnatural hunger of hers for stories of lost sons and daughters was dangerous because she would replay the scenes in her head over and over, feeling the anguish. Feeling the guilt.

When news came of German tanks in Dijon, Freddie said: 'Enough. We go tomorrow.'

Many of the families had determined to return north and see what was left of their homes in the wake of the Germans, but Suzanne and Freddie never discussed going back. Freddie, in fact, spoke less and less. Suzanne knew that he was beginning to fail, and she also knew that he was stronger when in the service of her needs, so she encouraged him to believe she wanted to go to Spain more than anything else. In fact her heart was torn equally in two: one half yearned to go back and look for Angélique; the other half to be with Penelope again. But Freddie had put everything into getting them this far and the only way to buoy him up was to go on, further south.

The bicycles had gone missing on their first day in Lyon when they were at the station, so it was on foot once again that they set out. The next chance of a train was in Grenoble and they had good luck with sleeping places: a garage, and then an attic in a small farm run by a single woman who had already taken in two families, one from Rouen, and the other from Joinville-le-Pont. A French soldier on the road had given them some dried food and they foraged for raspberries in the hedges.

On the third morning, the road into Grenoble felt very different: people were nervous and silent. Then a volley of bombing came from the air and the rattle of gunfire from all around. Suzanne and Freddie threw themselves into a ditch by the road and others who were cowering there told them that the Italians were beginning their attempts to take the south-eastern areas of France. Someone said it was the Germans attacking them but others were sure it was the Italian army.

That night they slept outdoors. Freddie was pale, unsmiling and still shaking from the danger, now reduced to far-off rumbling. Strangely, Suzanne found she was calm and able to focus on their present needs. She had found a tatty but clean blanket in a bush by the road earlier and she tucked it around them and pushed Freddie's hair from out of his eyes, then waited for him to fall asleep before giving in to the extreme fatigue that always followed a crisis.

In the morning Freddie was back to his old self: he had, after all, the gift of sleeping soundly anywhere. Close to the town, by great good fortune, they found an abandoned house. There was even some food left in the pantry. Freddie nailed up boards over the doors and windows, but attached them to the large window on the ground floor very loosely in case they needed to escape. There were books in the house, and running water, and Suzanne spent her time reading Flaubert and washing.

They slept in a bed: it was so unfamiliar, so soft. Suzanne dreamt she was back in Paris, wearing only a slip and barefoot. She had become separated from two nameless companions and was pacing back and forth outside a theatre entrance, shivering in her thin petticoat. She had no money and no idea where she was.

Then she woke to find the cover had fallen on the floor. In her dream, the sky had been almost light but, with all the windows covered, it was impossible to tell if morning had come or not. She found Freddie in the kitchen.

'It's time,' he said, and she knew that their brief respite in this dim, safe retreat was over.

It had taken a few days to buy tickets but the Italian invasion had been halted many miles away and now the armistice had been signed, there seemed to be a brief time when everything went back to normal.

To travel by train was extravagantly fast and comfortable. Suzanne laid her cheek against the headrest, crushed in by a sweaty large man who was dozing against her arm, and listened to the sound of the engine as if it was the heartbeat of a mother and they were safe in the womb for a time.

Freddie slept.

They could only afford to go as far as Montpellier as nearly all their money had run out now. Suzanne suggested writing to her father to ask him to send more, so they went to the post office and joined the queue that stretched out along the road. After an hour, they were inside. There was a lot of jostling and angry words, and someone pushed Suzanne backwards. She trod on a black cat that yowled then sank its teeth into her shin. Freddie shot down to scrutinise the punctures and made her spit on her hand to wet the place.

By the end of the day, there were blisters on the wound. In the morning, as they waited by the road, she shivered in the July heat. After that, things got very strange. Freddie's voice moved away to the back of him, or maybe off to the side, or over his head. She saw a split-second, sideways view of the opening door of the bus and then a bright nothing.

Waking in the dim, dog-smelling room, Suzanne found herself on an operating table. There were hands restraining her arms and ankles and she struggled to escape. What if they had straps here, like before? What if they wanted to tie her down?

Then she saw Freddie's face directly above her.

'Stay still, now,' he said. 'The vet has some medicine that will bring down your fever.'

She didn't believe a word of it. 'Let me go! Let me go!'

He looked sorrowfully at her then nodded to the figures she could sense but not see in the room with them. Freddie always thought too well of people, it was one of the best things about him but now one of the most dangerous. She gave one massive heave away from the table and then, again, everything was gone.

She woke next in a proper bed, with Freddie asleep in a chair pulled up close. His forehead rested on her stomach and she ruffled the copper curls of his hair, so reliably strong and springy.

He looked up and smiled. 'Welcome back.'

'How long?' she asked, as he poured some water from a jug for her.

'Three days, but don't you remember the soup? The songs we sang?'

Suzanne examined her recent recollections and could only remember the barking of dogs and a sound like gravel being tipped from one side of a tray to another.

Freddie opened the shutters to a blue sky so bright it made her wince.

'Look,' he said, 'we are by the sea.'

The vet who had saved her life and taken them in was called Emmanuel. He spoke English and knew all about Freddie's identity. They had bonded over a broken coffee-maker that Freddie had repaired in two minutes and had drunk the last cups of real coffee together. There was no more to be had.

Emmanuel lived with his young son who drew immensely detailed pictures of farm machinery and seemed too young for his size. He immediately took to Freddie who gave him rides on his back. While the vet continued to treat the sick animals of the wealthy tourists who were extending their holidays indefinitely while waiting to see what would happen next in France and beyond, Freddie set about earning his keep by rebuilding a wardrobe, fixing the plumbing and making a model aeroplane out of balsa wood for the boy. Emmanuel had managed to persuade the owner of a local restaurant to give Freddie a job washing dishes in the evening.

Before leaving that night, he sat and watched Suzanne eat every mouthful of the stew he had made and she was then properly introduced to Emmanuel.

She tried to get out of bed to greet him but he stopped her and put his hand on her forehead.

'Good,' he said. 'All over. Now, the recovery period.'

'How long must she rest for?' asked Freddie, getting up and putting on his new cap, a gift from Emmanuel's son.

'It will be a week, maybe two. Bed rest.'

'But I don't want—' said Suzanne.

'Bed rest,' said Emmanuel, then he smirked a little. 'No walks. No treats.'

Freddie roared with laughter and it was such an unfamiliar, welcome sound that Suzanne lay back and, looking about her, began to enjoy the pleasant yellow bedclothes, the picture-postcard view and the glowing sensation of good, sufficient food in her stomach.

Then Emmanuel's son came running in and jumped on to the bed, closely followed by a black poodle. The boy jumped from one side of her feet to the other, making the bed bounce, while the dog barked.

'Out!' shouted Emmanuel, herding them both. 'Bed rest,' he said, as he shut the door behind him.

'I'm going to work, now,' said Freddie, 'but I'll come and check on you when I get back.'

'Wake me up if I'm asleep,' said Suzanne.

'Certainly not,' he said, grinning. 'No walks. No treats. I'll sleep on the floor as usual.'

Suzanne saw that he had made a typically cosy nest out of a padded pink eiderdown on the floor and she was content that he would return and sleep close by. In fact, sleep was a lovely idea, a gorgeously tempting ...

Chapter Thirty-Four

Cadaqués, July 1940

The days began to blur as a routine imposed itself on Penelope's life: in the morning, baking with Llùcia; after lunch, painting or carving till dinnertime. Penelope was trying to carve an insect to give them as a joke about her pet name. Llùcia was teaching her the Catalan names for things but advised her not to use them outside the village where the ruling party's influence was stronger. Penelope had long since ceased to underestimate Llùcia's knowledge and abilities. She had assumed, when she knew only Eduardo, that he was the provider, but now it seemed to her that the bread was their main income and Eduardo's fishing merely supplemented it.

After an evening they had all spent eating at Eduardo's brother's house, Llùcia came to give her a clean pillowcase just before bed. Penelope plucked up the courage to ask if any shops sold Kotex because her period was due and she had no idea where to buy them (at Púbol's, the housekeeper had produced anything they put on her list).

Llùcia sucked her mouth in and shook her head. 'We use only cloths,' she said. 'You can wash them.'

'Oh, all right,' said Penelope, and she kissed Llùcia goodnight.

In the morning, Penelope volunteered to collect the drinking water. She took the green water jug, holding it in front of her body rather than balancing it on her head as all the women and girls did, because she was afraid of breaking it. Llùcia had shown her the special loop low down on the jug that she could hold onto to keep it stable on her head, but Penelope still didn't think she should risk it. She would never really fit in here. Her clothes were not modest enough and she could not bring herself to go to church. No one was outright in their disapproval, but she knew she would always be an outsider.

The light was already illuminating the little waves as she left Es Pianc. She tracked in away from the sea for a short distance then emerged to follow the promenade, passed the bar and then went on to Port d'Alguer. Under the archway on the opposite side she paused and thought again about how she would manage without disposable sanitary pads. Well, she had mastered washing herself from a basin and doing without mirrors. Llùcia would help her. She thought yearningly of the blue-tiled bathroom and deep, scallop-edged bath at Púbol's large house.

Today was the twenty-fifth. Penelope realised with a jolt that her period was three and a half weeks late. At the same time, a high-pitched screaming heralded a flock of young children who were running through the arch. Penelope jumped back, out of their way, clasping the water jug to her stomach. The children's shrieks bounced off the walls. Then, as they ran out from under the arch, their cries escaped into the open air along the curving road by the town beach. The jug, though empty, felt very heavy and awkward.

Stowing the water holder under one arm, she went on. Was she pregnant? If so, what did that mean? She had religiously used the Dutch cap all the time since being fitted in the early days of Paris – in Cornwall she and Rolf had taken a chance – and with Alain, too, but as Rolf's imprisonment had driven her and Alain apart she had stopped bothering to wear it at night.

But there was that one time, just before Rolf was released. Did she want a child? A child of Alain's?

More likely it was a disruption and the result of all these upheavals to do with the war: moving here, losing touch with Suzanne, the worry over Rolf in the internment camp and now, her separation from the small surrealist group here. Penelope had heard of menses stopping in women who experienced shock or stress. That must be it.

Later, Penelope was alone and working on her new picture. It was the representation of her legs as massive rocks coming out of the sea: that image she had seen in Alain's bath, forgotten and then remembered again, just before Rolf had come back from Copenhagen. She patiently coloured in the spaces between the two upright objects that were legs, rocks and penises all at once, and tried very hard not to picture a baby's head emerging from between them.

She thought back to the tribe of children in the archway that morning, the biggest leading and waving a crude sword made of two pieces of driftwood tied together, and the little ones running along after. All went barefoot, with old, frayed clothes. There was no school here, only lessons with the priest, but not all families approved of the church, which they felt was too close to the Falangists.

Penelope had never pictured herself as a mother. The role was a distant one in her family, with nannies taking care of day-to-day needs. Her brothers were older and had been dispatched to boarding schools before she was of an age to be a playmate, so she had grown up as if an only child. Her companions were dogs, horses and storybooks, and time with her parents had been restricted and stage-managed by the successive nannies. To discuss with her mother anything so personal as menstruation in the way she had with Llùcia was unthinkable.

Llùcia's mother was French, hence her knowledge of the language, but had died when she was young, and her father came from Figueres. This was where she and Eduardo had met. Llùcia was the mother Penelope had never had: she advised, hugged, encouraged. Sometimes, when she embraced her, it made Penelope tearful, which worried Llùcia greatly. 'I'm happy,' Penelope would explain and this, like so many things she said or did, made Llùcia smile. Llùcia could teach Penelope how to be a mother, but how could she stay here as an alien, unable to speak the language?

The paint had dried on her brush as she had been sitting, staring and thinking. She took off her painting apron and went to pour some water to drink. The door was open – it was still very warm – and Una stood nervously outside as if trying to decide whether to knock.

'Una. Come in.'

They sat down at the table and Una accepted a glass of wine.

It was some time since Penelope had drunk anything. Her hosts, who had bought the wine out of the money she had forced on them for her keep, used it to sprinkle on bread with sugar added on top. So the wine went straight to her head and it was suddenly so good to speak to someone from her Paris world.

'How is everyone?' asked Penelope. 'How is Púbol?'

'He's in Barcelona trying to arrange to put on a show. Rolf says it's delusional. I think Rolf misses you,' said Una, seeking out Penelope's face.

Penelope took another large mouthful of wine.

'So am I in trouble for leaving?' she asked.

'Not in trouble exactly, but Rolf is rather angry. I came to ask if you were coming back because, you see, Alain and I ...'

'Of course. I knew it would happen. Are you happy?'

'Very happy. But are you? I mean, leaving and living here like this.'

'I'm fine. Fine. Apart from ...'

'What?'

Penelope poured out the rest of the bottle. 'I'm late.'

Una caught on immediately. 'A baby? Is it ...?'

'Alain's, yes. But I don't want anyone to know.'

'We could look after it. I can't have a child but a child of Alain's, I—'

'Why wouldn't I look after it myself?'

'On your own? Here?'

At that moment Eduardo came in.

Penelope leapt up and embraced him, then made introductions. He could see that she was drunk and for the first time ever there was disapproval in his eyes.

Una sensed the atmosphere and got up to leave. Penelope went with her.

They walked together along the wall by Es Pianc.

'Come back with me now, Penelope.'

'No. But it's good to know you are there.'

'That's just it, we might not be for long. Alain is talking about trying to go back to Paris.'

'That's madness.'

'I know. But he feels he must. Maurice and Gabriel are going to try to reach Lisbon by car, via San Sebastián. Púbol still hopes to get to America. And Rolf is going with him. You should be with Rolf, Penelope.'

'Rolf and I have finished, Una.'

'No. No, that's not true.'

Una held both of Penelope's hands in hers before they parted and made a final appeal for her to join them.

How kind she is, thought Penelope. I would not be that kind.

Telling Una had made the pregnancy real. Who could she turn to now? And how had she ended up here, alone among strangers? To return to her own country was impossible; her parents would certainly not take her back in this state. To get rid of a pregnancy was illegal and hard enough in a city, let alone in a remote Catholic place like this. She would have to tell Llùcia eventually, and that would be very hard. A great desire came over her to go to a café on her own, as she used to in Paris. Well, why not? She had some money in her pocket.

The Casino bar was almost empty this early in the afternoon and Penelope took a seat near the window. There was one other man, accompanied by a dog with bald patches in its fur. The man had a large stick propped up by his table and he gave the dog a sharp tap on the rump every time it whined.

In return for a few coins, Penelope was given a clay jar of wine and a thick stumpy glass. Both the owner and the man with the dog ignored her.

She stared at the wall outside, remembering how Rolf had been reunited with Alain there and that she had left them behind, intent on finishing herself. How melodramatic. But her strength and ability to paint had returned to her after that gesture of relinquishment.

After a while, some men came in, from a fishing boat by the smell of them. They were boisterous, laughing and slapping each other's shoulders. Penelope failed to catch even one word of their rapid, overlapping speech.

One pulled his cap at her, presumably recognising her as connected with Eduardo, whose family spread through the town like a spider's web with his mother, the black-clothed old woman who sold the bread for Llùcia, at the centre of the kinship net. Would her child grow up speaking Catalan? Where would she get her painting supplies once Púbol had gone? Was it safe for her to stay here?

One of the fishermen came to sit with her, without asking permission. He sat right next to her, pulling his chair close. He had brought another jug of wine and started filling her glass. She shook her head but he grinned, revealing blackened teeth and a pad of tobacco lodged beside his tongue. Then he started to stroke her forearms with the back of his fingers and when she sprang away he leered at her, undeterred.

Another of the men came to stand behind the table and then made a lunge at her breasts. She stood up, scraping her chair, which made the mangy dog bark and receive another cruel blow to its side. The men at Penelope's table turned towards the dog and in that moment she swerved smoothly past them and out of the door.

She hurried home. How stupid to think she could behave like that, here. She had never seen a woman in a bar alone, in fact, hardly ever in the street without a husband, child or female relative.

Eduardo was at the door and, reading her face, placed an arm around her shoulders. He clicked his tongue as if he had seen everything that had happened at the bar, and comforted her with a kiss on the side of her head. He smelt of the sea, of salted fish and fresh air, and the aroma of the warm loaves travelled towards them from the doorway of the bakery.

A solution was impossible, and Penelope suddenly found herself remembering the iron with nails attached to its base at the London exhibition. She was safe and well, and also in complete and utter crisis, but the surrealist game of defeating rationality by entertaining a contradiction was not going to help her now.

Chapter Thirty-Five

Cadaqués, August 1940

I t was an ordinary Sunday afternoon: Llùcia and Eduardo were visiting and Penelope was painting. She had tried many arrangements of books, planks and baskets to prop up her canvases on Eduardo's carving table but in the end nothing worked, so she sat, cross-legged on the floor with the new canvas leaning against the couch. This way she could make the most of any light that did make it in through the window past the luxurious bougainvillea which Llùcia had promised to prune back hard once it had stopped flowering.

A knock on the door. She frowned.

As she got up, something scuttled into a corner. The house was inhabited, like the places she had lived in Paris had been, with a variety of life: mice and cockroaches. They were part of her latter-day world just as bats and moths had been in her parents' massive echoing mansion. A composition of creatures attendant on the rooms of her old home presented itself for consideration in her mind's eye as she went to the door.

'Rolf.'

He stood, scanning the upper end of the narrow street.

'Una told me,' he said, turning his blue eyes on her like an interrogator's light.

'Come in, then.'

Rolf examined the table heaped with proving baskets that needed mending, the cast-off espadrilles by the door, the keys on the hooks and the black wool visiting cape that Llùcia had left behind this hot August day. He wore shorts, and his legs were brown and healthy-looking again. His movements were slower than before, though, and there was a wariness mixed in with his habitual acuity. For the first time, his white hair suggested agedness instead of incongruity.

'Do you want a drink?' she asked.

'Nothing. Show me what you've been working on.'

'All right. How is Alain? Púbol?'

'Well. They are well. Alain wanted to come. I said no. He said he would write.'

They really are ridiculous, these men, thought Penelope, as she showed Rolf through to her bedroom-cum-studio. She realised that she had begun to think of the surrealists as two-dimensional and trivial. In contrast, the community she now belonged to, with aunts and weddings, children and goats, recipes, bedspreads and stories of human towers at carnival time, was a life with all the senses engaged. Hot pungent beaches, wet fishing nets, astringent pine needles, warm loaves and sweet *ensaïmadas*. Words in Catalan were bright, solid things like red wooden toys. Her French was receding as if into a well-behaved past and she spoke it now with Llùcia's curious, vigorous inflections.

'But where can you work here?' asked Rolf.

'I sit on the floor. And I'm painting the walls, too. Look.'

Penelope had begun a mural: a sea scene with Eduardo in his boat.

'Portraiture?' said Rolf, incredulously. 'Let me see those.' He indicated the pictures stacked upright in the corner.

Penelope was suffering agonies as he took them one by one to examine in the window light so she went back into the other room.

He came and joined her at the table, making Penelope remember when Una had sat in the same chair just a couple of weeks earlier.

'Una was very good to come,' she said.

'Alain has heard of an organisation against the Occupation and they are determined to go back to Paris, but getting themselves arrested won't help anyone. It is just a plan, as yet. I have pleaded with him to come to Portugal. I thought that now you will have to come with me, he might change his mind.'

'What do you mean?' said Penelope.

'Well, you can't stay here and have your baby.'

'Why not?'

'It's obvious.' He gestured at the room around them.

Penelope wasn't having this. 'I am living on an allowance that I share with my hosts,' she said, 'who love me as their daughter. The war is not going to reach us here, thanks to the charming General Franco, who is Herr Hitler's best friend. We have a roof, money and enough aunties to start up a babysitting school. I can get paint from Barcelona via the post office. Llùcia has no children so it will be a grandchild for her, when she finds out, and I know she will be happy.'

'And what about you? You will soon stop painting. It is what happens when a baby comes. You will be resentful. Then, when you are able to start again, who will see it? Your fisherman and his friends? The local priest? Púbol will be gone. No one will come here who cares for art. You have no contacts, and there will be no galleries interested in your work, or people to approach them for you. And in any case ...' he hesitated.

'What? Let's have it all.'

'Your work is no longer good,' Rolf said.

'What?'

'You paint allegory, not the surreal. You are painting little stories of your life, sweet enough, but with no edge, no force.

It is a long way from your cup of fur which changed us all – it was a breaking through.'

'Not for me. I hate it. I never want to see my name next to it again.'

'Why do you say that?'

Penelope got up and paced as far as the small, cluttered room allowed.

'That awful name you gave it made it into a sign that I was for men, that I was available, that I served your needs. The cup was all of it together: comfort, home, sex. It was everything you wanted in a woman. But I had nothing of my own. Only—'

'What?'

'Never mind.' Penelope had never talked to Rolf about Suzanne, only to Alain, and neither had met her again.

'But take the picture of the horse,' Rolf continued.

Penelope began to feel sick and yet she couldn't bring herself to stop him. She had to hear it all.

'It's true that the lemur is good,' he said.

'It's a cat.'

He brushed aside the correction. 'That's fine, but to show the horse twice, it is like a nursery rhyme. When I drew you as a horse with flowing hair it was surreal: two at once, neither dream nor life. Both. It is our creed. We are part of a movement, Penelope, a movement which will remake the world.'

There was someone at the door again.

It was a little girl come to pick up two farm loaves that had already been paid for. Penelope gave her a twist of sugar in paper as well, and kissed her head. Children were caressed and handled so much here that they expected it. The child skipped off without a word.

'You desire motherhood more than art?' asked Rolf, who had watched every move.

'Rolf, please.' Penelope suddenly felt completely weary. 'Let's go for a walk,' she said.

'All right.'

She locked the door behind them and turned to go towards the water but Rolf had already set off up the street in the direction of Púbol's house.

She followed.

They walked through sparsely planted conifer trees that were clinging to the hillside, some, near the larger houses, shaped in the Moorish style to tall points. It was steep at first and neither spoke. They paused, by mutual impulse, at the highest crag, looking down to Port Lligat where Púbol's kidney-shaped pool could be made out, as well as the white oval of the egg sculpture on his roof.

'I am willing to be a father to the child if you want to give it birth,' said Rolf. 'I will even marry you if you wish it, although I would have to get a divorce first, of course.'

Rolf was still legally bound to Helga, who he had met ten years before Penelope and married when she was seventeen.

'I don't want to marry you, Rolf.' She started to laugh.

He looked uncomfortable. 'What is so funny?'

'My parents would have been so pleased: at last, a proposal I really did consider.'

'I am honoured,' said Rolf.

'Oh, don't act like that,' said Penelope. 'You don't have to marry me. It's not as if the baby is yours.'

'I know. But I promised Alain.'

'I might have known you and Alain would have discussed it all first. You'd like to share my baby too, would you?'

'You never used to be bitter.'

'Maybe I had to paint *allegories* in order to get things straight.'

'You know I am right. You cannot become the artist you are meant to be if you live alone, here. No one will see your work, Penelope, do you not understand? In America there is freedom. Money. Opportunity. This chance will only come once, especially for a mother-to-be. And—' He stopped, turned away, then picked up a stone and threw it savagely away.

'What?'

'I still love you.' He spat it out, as if it was an accusation or a disaster.

She winced.

'I'm going now,' he said. 'We are travelling to Lisbon in two weeks. In the convertible. There is room for you and one canvas each. I will wait for your answer for two days only, because it will take some time to arrange the papers.

'All right.'

'Goodbye.' Rolf had clasped her before she even saw his arms move. For a moment it was all back again, flooding into her body. The strength and knowledge of him. She melted into his bones and desire flared up.

He pulled away angrily and swivelled on his heel, almost sprinting into the distance.

Penelope sank to the ground and sat down hard. Those dim, blurry images of a baby on her hip as she painted while, in the distance, Eduardo's boat came back to shore or her paintings hung along the street, strung up like washing in between the houses, and members of Llùcia's family pointing and smiling at them, were an impossible fantasy. Rolf was right. It was ridiculous. She started to trudge home.

Llùcia was making stew. A skinned rabbit lay on the table.

Penelope took one look at the grey-blue flesh next to the pelt, heaved and went out the back in case she was sick. She wasn't.

The rabbit was in the pot when she got back. Llùcia gave her a glass of cold water with lemon juice and sat down.

'Was the baby's father here?' she asked.

So she knew. Of course she did.

'No.' Penelope burst into tears.

'My poor child.' Llùcia came over and rocked her.

'I th–thought you'd disapprove.'

Llùcia snorted. 'A child blesses all.'

'But not me. It won't bless me for having no father. One of the artist-men at Púbol's has offered to marry me and take me to America. He wants me to go on painting.'

Penelope was waiting for Llùcia to implore her to stay but she said nothing for a long time.

'Penelopito, my house is yours, but our country is not a place of freedom anymore. I will love your child but our neighbours will hate it and your life would be very hard here. You belong with your own people.'

'But who are my people?'

Llùcia shook her head then went off to the other room. She came back and propped up the leaping horse picture on an empty chair.

'This is you with us here.' Llùcia pointed to the rocking horse inside the room in the picture. 'And this,' she pointed to the wild white horse galloping free outside, 'this is you in America. Which do you choose?'

Llùcia gave her one last hug, took off her apron and left.

Penelope gave a deep, ragged sigh. It was obvious that she must go to Lisbon. She stared at the picture as the tears dried on her cheeks.

Chapter Thirty-Six

Cerbère, August 1940

On the same day that Penelope said her farewells to Llùcia and Eduardo, Suzanne and Freddie made it to Cerbère. The French border with Spain was close, in the mountains up ahead. They had stayed a whole month in Montpellier with Emmanuel in the end, until Suzanne was strong again. The line to the bakery in Lille was dead and Suzanne's attempts to get a call through to the post office in Cadaqués had all failed. Freddie, still earning good money washing dishes, had moved on to fixing things for members of Emmanuel's extended family and had undertaken to refit the kitchen at the restaurant. His final repair job was to a rusty Citroën C4 van that had been left in a field for years by Emmanuel's uncle. He had also repaired the uncle's tractor and in return, was given the Citroën. So they had a car again, and money for fuel when they could get it.

They said goodbye to the vet and his son, who cried a great deal and had to be given barley sugars. Suddenly, they were back in that terrible game with the Germans coming up behind in search of displaced Jews like Freddie and herself, and Penelope waiting ahead of them, perhaps giving up hope that they were still alive. At Cerbère, there was one room left in the Hôtel Canal and they were hoping that visas, and a guide, could be arranged before their money ran out again.

On the first night they arrived, Freddie declared that they would eat properly and they were shown to a table in the deserted dining room, lit by candles. They ate herbed chicken, or what they assumed was chicken, heavily flavoured with lemon, and drank absurdly good wine. There was custard afterwards – powdered for sure – but sweet, which was all that mattered. Freddie talked about the risks of trying the train: without visas it would not work. But the mountains he felt confident about.

'We could go on our own, if only I had a compass and the map was better,' he said.

Suzanne had grown to hate the ripped, stained map that had been with them since Fontainebleau, stuffed into Freddie's coat or resting, like a rebuke, on top of his shoes at night. Every night he tracked their progress and added to the pencilled line that showed how far they had come.

After it was cleared, Freddie spread the map out on the table and a drop of wax added another new feature.

'We are here.'

'And where is Penelope?'

'Here. Not far from the border. Look, there is the Cap de Creus. It's not far now.'

She tried hard to picture Penelope, with her long hair and smiling mouth. But all Suzanne could see were roads and paths at her feet and the creased, dirty skirt she had worn every day since June covering her bare, scarred legs.

'We can swim in the sea when we reach Cadaqués. It will still be warm enough in September.'

Suzanne tried to smile but she couldn't believe him anymore. Life would always be sore feet, grimy fingernails, dirty hair and sweaty clothes. It would only ever be roads full of filthy crowds and crying children, railway stations teeming with people, hard floors to sleep on, and Freddie's map with its tiny, weak pencil line.

'You are tired,' he said. 'Let's try for a bath and then bed.'

'All right,' said Suzanne, looking at him in the watery light.

Freddie went to run the water. They had been given the attic room, next to the bathroom, and no one seemed to be around.

'Is it hot?' asked Suzanne, joining him in the small, fumy room lit with an oil lamp.

'I don't understand why, when there's no electricity, but yes.'

They watched the water bobble into the big, claw-footed bath then stutter, trickle and finally bulge out again.

'We had better share,' said Freddie.

Suzanne had never bathed with a man before and turned away to remove her clothes while Freddie stripped off and got in with a satisfied sigh.

'Come on,' he said.

She stepped into the water, placing her feet carefully between Freddie's ankles and lowered herself down, facing him. His large feet encircled her hips. Naked, he looked wiry and thin. His white, bare chest clashed with his sun-browned forearms, and she saw again how much weight he had lost. His legs, however, were still strong and solid.

He bent forwards and took her hands, making the water chop sideways.

She had not realised that she was shielding her body from his gaze. They had only been together in the dark, and had so rarely been undressed during their journey. He had never shared her bed at Isaac's house, and there had been no privacy at Emmanuel's.

There was a bar of perfumed soap on a dish by the bath and he plunged it in the water then proceeded to wash her hands and arms as she watched. At first it was as if she was an observer of her body but gradually the lavender-smelling lather brought her skin to life and she felt the dirt loosen and dissolve into the water. With it went all the grey despair of the past months.

She looked directly into Freddie's creaturely brown eyes and felt herself going deeper and further into them. He moved closer, bending his knees up around either side of her and turned the soap in his hands again. Then he washed her neck and her breasts.

They held each other's gaze and Suzanne urged her eyes to take an imprint of his face, like a photograph but one that would never fade. She recorded his sturdy hair that stood up in waves and the faithful lock that always fell over his forehead, making his eyes so friendly and soft. His narrow shoulders troubled her again but his arms were veined and muscular. He had never had rough or labour-coarsened hands even after the hard work on their journey and they were smooth as silk on her body now: warm, and soapy.

Foolishly, tears came, so she started to play about and trickled water on his head until he laughed and said he would get out so that she could wash properly. He gathered up their clothes and left the towel where she could reach it.

Suzanne thought of him getting into bed in the room next door and waiting for her. She slid under the water and raked her fingers through her hair to release the final pollutants, then got out and wrapped herself in the towel, only slightly damp from where Freddie had used it.

In bed, they lay together watching the light of a streetlamp shining through the leaves of a tree and making patterns on the sloping ceiling.

'Let's make a film,' she said.

'How do you mean?' He drew her into the crook of his arm.

'Up there,' she pointed to the shifting shadows on the ceiling.

'What is it about?' Freddie rested his ear on the top of her head, undeterred by her still-wet hair.

'You choose,' she said, rearranging herself against him.

'It will be a scene in Cadaqués.'

'When we meet Penelope again?' she asked.

'No, a long time in the future. There, do you see my very nice Buick?'

'Yes. Do you use it to go to the seaside?'

'Sometimes,' he said, 'but mostly I motor into the city where our film studio is. And next to the car is a house.'

'I see it. With a balcony. And pots of red flowers.'

'And there are two children playing there.'

'Our children?' Suzanne turned towards him.

'Yes, one is. The other is Penelope's.'

'Where is Angélique?' she asked, lying back again to gaze upwards.

'She is there too, inside. She has been looking after the children while we made our new film and later this evening we will all have a meal of schnitzel and potatoes in the kitchen.'

'We are all together then.'

'Yes. We are.'

Suzanne began to kiss him and gradually he began to take charge of her cleansed, softened body, transporting her to a warm, safe future of love and home.

It took Freddie another week to find someone to help with their documents. A Hungarian woman who knew an American at the consulate had acquired transit visas for them. Oddly enough, these were for Portugal but would work to get into Spain, apparently. Now all they needed was a guide to take them over the mountains because they had no exit visas for the train station (to apply would be to attract far too much attention). Their money was getting low again, depleted by the cost of the visas. They ate less and less, aware that a guide would be another large expense.

Freddie came back one afternoon from a walk, full of excitement. He'd met a man in the cemetery.

'The cemetery?' repeated Suzanne.

'Yes, his name is Ansell and he says he will take us over the mountains tomorrow and he doesn't want much money. His English is very good. He's a forester but he grew up in Scotland.'

'Like my mother.'

'Yes, I told him you were half Scottish.'

'You shouldn't tell people about me. How can we be sure that he can be trusted?'

'We have very little money left, my love. We shall have no choice soon but to trust somebody.'

'What time do we go tomorrow?'

'Very early. We are to mix in with the vineyard workers to avoid attracting attention as we set off. And there must be no luggage, only a day bag, as if for a lunchtime meal.'

Suzanne had again grown used to their temporary lodgings and she savoured their new privacy in a room of their own. She had become attached to the little village with its church and the forest sheltering at the foot of the mountains.

The journey Freddie proposed, even with the ultimate reward of finally seeing Penelope again, terrified her and she suspected that her intuition on this should be trusted. But Freddie was enthused, purposeful, excited. He kept smiling at her and she hadn't the heart to question this decision that had brought such a positive change in him.

They would go tomorrow.

Chapter Thirty-Seven

The next day at dawn, Suzanne and Freddie put on as many of their clothes as possible and added their documents to the small bags containing the last of the cheese and almonds they had been living on for three days.

'Suzanne,' said Freddie, 'your Spanish passport will give you a good chance. It's not so easy for me to hide who I am.'

'So what? I know all this.'

'So, if I give you this signal,' Freddie made a sign with his left hand, forming a circle with thumb and forefinger, 'I want you to leave me, to separate. Without arguments, and without speaking. Will you do this?'

'Never. I will never leave you.'

'Suzanne, I will not make the journey without this agreement between us.'

'But why? If you are identified I shall explain, I'll tell them—'

'No.' It was that commanding voice of his again: so rare, so different.

'Come on,' she said. 'We'll be late.'

They crept down the stairs of the hotel and hurried along the road to the edge of the village to find Ansell. He stood on the corner kicking stones and puffing on his pipe.

Suzanne shook his hand, but there was a hardness in his eyes that disturbed her. She also seriously doubted that he had any connection with Scotland at all: he had no trace of an accent.

'We should be going,' said Freddie.

'Money first,' said Ansell.

Freddie and Suzanne exchanged a look, then Freddie pulled out the last of their funds and gave it to him.

The vineyards in the foothills made for pleasant, easy walking and the few workers picking the last grapes accepted them and threw them a greeting or two, whether acknowledging them as fugitives or fellow workers, she was not sure.

As the terrain changed, the sky clouded over and Suzanne shivered. They saw no one. Soon all her attention was taken by tackling the stony, uneven, steep climb. She was wearing a pair of man's hiking boots that they had found on the roadside near Béziers and their grip was good, even if they were too big for her. Just as well. The ground continued to rise up, sheer and loose-stoned. Thistles tore at her clothes and bloodied her legs or ripped through her hands when, sometimes, the only way to steady herself was to grip onto them.

Suzanne focused remorselessly on the immediate situation, glad almost of the pain from climbing and the scratches on her wrists and knees. She refused to allow her imagination to work on any of this. Progress was all. She pictured Penelope standing outside Cadaqués, a place she visualised as a walled city, and she crawled, slid and slogged towards her.

Ansell climbed nimbly and silently but Freddie was sweating: the sun had come out again. She felt terribly thirsty. They should have brought water, like Ansell, who had not offered to share his leather bottle with them.

They were high up now but beneath an overhang that hid them from the road above. She marvelled at a road being built so high. Higher, even, than the scruffy mule tracks and dry water gullies near them. There were voices in the distance above them and Ansell did not need to tell them to be quiet.

Then a figure in grey appeared against the clear sky on the edge of the overhanging cliff. He shouted something in German and Ansell raised his hand and waved. The man acknowledged him in return.

Freddie grasped Suzanne and made the signal with his hand.

'Remember what you promised,' he said into her ear.

One moment she was feeling the scratch of his hair on her temple and the next she was watching him moving away, heading back the way they had come. Freddie broke into a run and began to leap like some two-legged goat down the slope.

Ansell reached into the pocket of his coat and the next moment a shot rang out all around them.

Suzanne watched Freddie jump from one stone to the next then fall, face first, on to the ground. Even from this distance she could see his extreme, complete, stillness.

Ansell turned to her, still holding the gun, and she willed him to shoot her too.

'Now what will you do, Jew's whore?' he sneered. 'Not even the Germans will pay for you.'

Then he spun around and began looking for a route up to the road above.

Suzanne stood still, unable to speak or move.

When Ansell had disappeared, she forced herself to go and look at Freddie, lying on his front. She remembered, in a flash of sickening memory, that he was lying just as he had that night at Max's after Isaac had died. Their first night together.

Not daring to go too close, she could see one hand turned up at his side, resting in an already-drying circle of brownish blood. His thumb and finger were touching: he had continued to make the signal for her to leave him, even as he fell. Their map had fallen out of his pocket and she watched it twitch in the wind. In a bizarre reversal, the map began to come to life while Freddie lay still and Suzanne watched it turn and tumble then eventually take flight away into the distance.

The sky began to revolve and she staggered then went down on hands and knees. After being sick, she managed to stand up again, hands propped on her knees.

Then something inside her moved her on. One step, then another. She must get help. The clouds were low now; the mist was coming down and hiding everything, including Freddie behind her.

Suzanne's mind became as blank as the whiteness in front of her eyes. She walked because walking was all she could do and when she could walk no more she tumbled to the ground and cried until she slept.

When she woke again, a white of an even greater intensity assailed her eyes. It seemed to be an angel in a white gown bending over her. The angel had solid, rough hands and was forcing her to sit up. There was a wall of people around her, all talking at once in different languages.

A young man in glasses squatted down, reached into her bag and opened her passport.

'*Espagnol*,' he said.

'Spanish, huh?' echoed an American voice.

'Isabel Castello.'

'Isabel.' The woman in white took hold of her shoulders and rocked her back and forth.

The voices were getting nervous now, and she felt their urgency, their need to hurry. Was she Isabel again? Was a servant of the Castellos here to take her away again?

'*Kannst du stehen*?' said a kind woman, wearing a fur coat and carrying a small brown suitcase.

She tried and when she swayed, hands caught her and supported and pushed her on. The kind woman gave her some whisky from a hip flask.

The light was fading.

The men took over and she enjoyed the sensation of a strong arm around her waist and the relief of no longer having to climb. She remembered climbing, then the sound of a gun and ... oh!

'Freddie! Freddie!' Suzanne began to struggle against the two men holding her.

The white-dress woman and the one in fur came back to remonstrate with her until together, the party persuaded her to continue. Suzanne wondered if she had imagined Freddie's death. He had made the sign, she knew, but was that in Cerbère, or much earlier in Montpellier, with the vet? Freddie was maybe coming another way? And she couldn't remember his face. No. Wait, his hair, she remembered his hair. He was lying face down, but was that at Max's, or where was it?

'D'you have a visa, Isabel?' asked the American. 'We're getting close now.'

'Yes,' she said, 'we have visas for Portugal.'

'That should do it. Don't speak English though, your accent sounds wrong.'

'Wrong?'

'Yes. Just stick to Spanish.'

'But—'

'There.' The fur-coat woman pointed to a road and, not far away, some buildings clustered around a barrier. The place was brightly lit and when Suzanne looked back down at her feet, her eyes struggled to readjust to the darkness. Would they have to sneak through?

The border was a barrage of talk. Suzanne proffered her visa and was bustled through with the others, all speaking at once. The American handed over three cartons of cigarettes and a bottle of whisky and suddenly they had left the border station behind. All walked at a careful pace, neither too fast to betray relief or too slow in case they seemed to be trying to hide their guilt.

When they were far enough along the road they began whooping and embracing each other.

Suzanne was caught up in their joy which fought against the desperation inside her: that gap where Freddie should be.

Several hours later they parted in Portbou as the American took charge and ordered the others to a hotel where they would wait for their luggage to arrive by train.

'Share our room,' said the young man, 'you are tired.'

Freddie had said that. When?

'No,' said Suzanne, 'I have to get to Cadaqués.'

All at once, she came back to herself. Penelope was waiting. But oh. Oh, God. Freddie was dead.

'My name is Suzanne Levy and my fiancé is dead,' she said. 'My friend is waiting for me in Cadaqués.'

'Well, good luck,' said the American, shaking her hand.

They left her as dawn began to show in the sky. She was at the top of the little town which curved around a bay, and she sat down by the road to wait for passing traffic, hoping to be helped once again.

Miraculously, after maybe half an hour, a farmer in a truck pulled up and she got in.

Chapter Thirty-Eight

Lisbon, September 1940

P enelope looked out across the roofs of the city: a network of sloping surfaces in tangerine and salmon-pink.

'St George's Castle was held by the Moors from AD 714,' said the English guide. 'In 1147, Afonso Henriques, the first king of Portugal, gained the assistance of some Crusaders who were on their way to Jerusalem and, after a seventeen-week siege, they ended the Muslim rule of Lisbon. Now we will go on to see the remains of the royal apartments. This way, please.'

She tried hard to ignore the man's droning, nasal voice and the shuffling and murmuring of the English tourists with him. Who, in their right mind, would take a holiday in Europe now? But maybe that's what I look like, she thought: a rich, eccentric Englishwoman who likes to travel and do a little sketching. Her notebook was full of attempts to record the panorama of the city before her because, nearly every morning since she, Rolf and Púbol had arrived here three weeks ago, Penelope had come to the castle. She had seen the romantic ochre walls with perfect turrets from her hotel window in Rossio Square on the first day. She later found out (from overhearing another tour guide) that these towers had been added just a few years earlier, when General Salazar ordered a full-scale restoration of the castle battlements. Even if it was partly fake, the notion of a fortified place attracted her. She loved to stand on the walls and stare out over the city, picking out the roads she knew and feeling a sense of control that was impossible when trying to navigate the streets on the ground.

It was a breathtaking view of coloured roofs, church spires and the grand Tagus river widening and curving out to sea. She could see the white dome of the Basílica de Estrela in the distance, and, down by the water, the classical arch of Black Horse Square. Further out were the docks and the preposterous Monument to the Discoveries which could just about be seen, way off in Belém.

This wooden monument, featuring the massive figures of Vasco da Gama and Henry the Navigator on a caravel, was part of the Exhibition of the Portuguese World, the brainchild of Salazar and it was, she had heard, the last sight on European land seen by those departing on the great ocean liners for America. It was a perfect example of swaggering, lumpen, fascist art, but at the same time, a reminder of the long chain of history from which the emigrants were detaching themselves, perhaps forever. It was ironic, she thought, that thousands were setting sail for America to flee from persecution and death while being watched over by heroic, oversized models of the historic European conquerors of the New World.

She turned over a fresh piece of paper and roughed out a representation of the triangular monument towering over a ragged refugee who held out a beseeching hand. Then she crossed it out, seeing how simplistic it was. Her own departure was set for four days' time and the emotions with which she contemplated leaving for New York could scarcely be reduced to such a caricature. So why would any of the hundreds of people she had seen queuing at the consulates or milling about at Santos docks be any different?

They would fly to the United States on a Pan-Am Clipper. Púbol's contact, a Turkish man called Griggi – his name was Aran Grigoryan, but he had been educated in Oxford where he acquired his nickname – had bought tickets for them and arranged exit visas. All but Rolf had entry permits to America, but Griggi was confident that the letters from the British and Portuguese embassies he had obtained would be enough. Five of them then, would be travelling together: Penelope, Rolf and Púbol; and Maurice and Gabriel, who would soon arrive from Porto.

But it felt wrong to the very marrow to be leaving when she did not know where Suzanne was. Penelope had left a forwarding address in Cadaqués, but she had still heard nothing. She had been half-hoping that Griggi would fail to secure their passage to New York, but apparently he had friends in the highest of places (or maybe the lowest, at the level of issuing the many documents needed for travel these days). It was now four months since Suzanne's last letter from Amsterdam, and she had nearly worn away the thin paper rereading it and trying to detect some clue to her intentions. But what could she do? To travel back through occupied France and Holland would have been pointless and dangerous. She had no idea of Suzanne's whereabouts.

She closed her sketchbook, got up and wandered along the walls. She loved to look at the blue-and-cream tiles on the ground which were laid in irregular patterns and framed by brown earth and heaps of pine needles. Two old men were playing chess on a purple cloth under the shade of the olive trees. Nearby was a garden full of tumbling pink bougainvillea that made her heart yearn for Eduardo's house in Cadaqués. The garden also contained an elaborate outdoor altar with a brass statue of the Virgin and an ugly, underperforming fountain constructed of rubber pipes in front of the figure. It looked like something Púbol, with his mania for mixing banal objects with religious icons, might put together.

Rolf had begun to work again also. Partly because of the scarcity of materials, he was making charcoal pictures of stark, violent traumas: injuries, malformations and heartless, aggressive pornography. He scarcely deigned to comment any more on Penelope's incessant iconography of animals done, these days, in modest watercolour since oils were hard to come by. The mild colours made her feel like a Sunday painter, a maiden aunt, a dabbler. But underneath she was a warrior again. Rolf's opinion, though still painful, no longer mattered. She still had a warm, comradely affection for him and a feeling of gratitude, but the rest had been burnt away, or maybe washed away that day in the sea at Cadaqués.

She sat down again and reached for a pencil sharpener. As she hunted around in her bag she realised her purse was missing. She darted across the main terrace looking left to right and spied a boy running on the lower level. She easily caught up with him and stopped him by grabbing the tail of his jacket, which was already torn. He had no shoes. Penelope grasped him by the scruff of the neck and held out her other hand to demand the return of her purse. The boy said nothing. He could only be seven, maybe eight years old. His trousers were too short for him, while the jacket was large and loose.

The boy slowly pulled out her embroidered purse from the depths of a pocket in the outsized jacket and once he had handed it over, his whole body slumped. While she checked the contents of the purse, the boy sat down and started to cry. Penelope examined him closely. She was no longer angry and the histrionic weeping, like some operatic aria, was really rather ridiculous. Penelope squatted down and put a hand on the boy's shoulder. He flinched automatically and then stopped crying.

'Are you hungry?' she asked.

Unlikely to have understood what she was saying, the boy nonetheless nodded vigorously. Penelope let out a laugh. She opened her purse once more and took out one of the notes which she stuffed into his hand. He was up and gone in a flash.

It was time to go. She had to get back to pack her things. She, Rolf and Púbol were sharing a room at the Métropole Hotel. Griggi lived in the hotel and had a suite on the third floor but he had only been able to get them one room. They were lucky to have that; some people were paying to sleep in laundry cupboards while they tried day after day to get tickets on one of the ships. The men agreed that Penelope should have the bed, Rolf slept on the floor and Púbol curled awkwardly in a chair and shouted in his sleep.

She was heading down the hill now and leaving Castelo São Jorge behind. The only way that Penelope could manage to find her way around Lisbon was to return to the water each time and get her bearings before going on to the next place, so she dropped down to the narrow alleys and steps of the Alfama instead of cutting across directly back to Rossio. These little streets with houses crowded together had been left by the Moors. This district had escaped the great earthquake of 1755, whereas the royal palace had been completely swept away. Maybe the Moors had won in the end then. Perhaps, but these streets, so narrow that only two people might walk side by side, were not a noble monument. They stank of fish and bad drains. The walls were peeling, the doorsteps were rough and battered, and the pavement dipped up and down and tripped her with false, broken kerbs.

There were shouts, clattering noises and a shrieking voice that Penelope finally identified as belonging to a grey parrot high up on a half-derelict balcony. But the washing was white and the sky, seen from below in small, triangular portions, was blue and clean of clouds. There were flowers in pots and flags on strings, and trees flourished in the small squares even though they grew out of tiled, slanting ground. A dog enthusiastically gnawed an enormous pink bone that had been thrown outside a doorway.

Penelope passed a thin man wearing a yellow shirt tucked into cheap, shiny black trousers and he raised a bottle of wine to her in hazy acknowledgement. Nearby, an old woman held out a baby on a level with her face and sang tunelessly at it. She was watched on and off by its mother, or so Penelope assumed, who was bandaging her leg with dirty strips of grey sheeting. A man in a white vest came out of the door and sat next to the mother. When the bandage was secured in place they beamed together with pride at the puffy baby held in its grandmother's arms. Looking at the human group, Penelope felt like an anthropologist, or a birdwatcher. Every infant she set eyes on now horrified and obsessed her. There might still be time to find a way to terminate the pregnancy in America, but she felt no confidence in this city of propaganda posters and derelict roads.

Turning away from the family on the doorstep, Penelope felt a strong, familiar stab in her belly. Could it be? Suppressing the outrageous idea of hiding at a street corner and secretly inspecting her underwear, she began to hurry down the lumpy, tangled pathways of the Alfama. Once she was in sight of the wide road leading from Santa Apolónia train station, she reoriented herself and struck out in the direction of the Baixa, from where she would climb again to reach Rossio and the hotel.

It was all over: her periods had resumed. Penelope went to find one of the cloths Llùcia had given her and returned again to the hotel bathroom, mercifully without a queue now, in the middle of the day. She could feel her spirits rising and never before had she welcomed so much that well-known dragging pain in a region of her body that only became tangible once a month. Her life was once more her own and the desire to paint flared up like a raging hunger or sexual urge.

Now there was some chance of dealing with the chaos brought by war. She would go to America, then find her own way, leaving Rolf and Púbol to try to reconvene the surrealist group with D'Argent. But immediately, she felt the strings attaching her to Europe pull tight. Where was Suzanne? And what about Britain? Did she care nothing for the country that had borne her, and the family she belonged to?

Rolf was coming back to their room and called to her in the corridor as she emerged from the bathroom.

'Any luck?' she asked.

Rolf shook his head. He was still attempting to get a visa.

'Could we talk somewhere?' she asked. 'The bar, maybe?'

Rolf gave her a wary look. He had ideas about alcohol and pregnancy and had become disapproving of almost anything she did: if she walked too far, or did not take enough exercise; if she ate too much, or starved herself. They had not told Púbol, who had a phobia of both children and doctors.

At the hotel bar, Rolf climbed onto a high stool and ordered a bottle of red wine on Púbol's account.

'Let's go over there.' Penelope led him to a table by some black iron patio doors where they couldn't be overheard.

'There will be no baby after all, Rolf.'

'What? Have you found a doctor to do it?'

'No. There never was a pregnancy. Just a gap, a blip, a disruption. Don't make me say any more. I thought … and now …'

Rolf visibly let the tension fall from his shoulders.

The wine arrived and both drank deeply. Penelope felt a hopeful glow spread into her heart and soothe her cramps.

'Do you regret it? Did you begin to want a child?' asked Rolf.

'Never. I'm so relieved, you have no idea. But what about you?'

'For me, it was a gesture of hope in this nightmare we are living through. I would have stood by you, even without your love.'

'I believe you, but you are free too, now. When we reach New York, I'll go on somewhere else. I need a clean start, although some help with finding a dealer would be welcome and, well, if we could speak sometimes, or meet up now and then?'

'No, you are part of the group. We sink or swim together.'

'Goodness, I hope you aren't talking about the Clipper. It sounds like a very dodgy way to travel. But thank you. You've been good to me, and I've been ... well, I've been unfaithful in many ways.'

'You have followed your heart. We shall always be friends, but I would like us to be as we were at the beginning again, one day.'

Penelope looked at him and saw the man she had met at that first exhibition in London, when he had taken her hand and led her into his new world. With clarity surging through the waves of the welcome ache at the base of her belly, she saw that she had never really loved him as a man. He had been her passport to a new life, her guide and protector. Could they forge an equal partnership, in a new country where neither had a history, a name, a foothold?

Then she heard Púbol's cracked voice calling out, 'Look! They are here.'

Maurice and Gabriel were in the foyer, putting down suitcases and looking around at the colonial splendour of the hotel with tired, bewildered expressions.

Penelope ran to Gabriel and nearly knocked him over with the enthusiasm of her welcome. Then she grasped Maurice's hand and pumped it up and down, tears on her face.

Her people. That's what Llùcia had called them – these eccentric, earnest, crazy men, who spurned jobs and respectability for poetry and painting, and had dedicated themselves to art like the Romantic poets of the nineteenth century. This was her tribe and they would go together, taking the best of Europe to a new continent. Eventually, it might be possible to return, with new ideas, new sights and sounds.

Penelope's excitement and happiness was not even punctured when she found out that Maurice and Gabriel would have to share their room for the three nights before they all boarded the plane to New York.

Chapter Thirty-Nine

Figueres, September 1940

T he farmer stopped his truck and left Suzanne in the middle of a city. She waited for the shops to open and went into a poky place with unplucked chickens hanging in the window. With the last few coins in her pocket, she bought a sausage, having been trained by Freddie to choose the item that had the most sustenance for the least money, rather than what she would prefer to eat. She asked how to get to Cadaqués.

'If you will travel with the meat,' said the butcher, in a mix of French and another language which sounded similar to Spanish, 'you can go with me and my son in the van. Come back at two.' He held up two fingers to make sure that she had understood.

So later that day she found herself bouncing around on the hard floor of a closed lorry with pale, frightful pig carcasses swaying from hooks on rails above her. She shut her eyes and clung on to the locked door handle.

The image of Freddie's body lying unprotected on the mountainside repeatedly invaded and overtook her mind, bringing a piercing pain to the middle of her chest. She could not cry, so instead she summoned as many visual memories of Freddie in life as she could: Freddie at Isaac's table listening and smiling; Freddie next to her at the Moviola; Freddie trudging through a field or bicycling downhill with his legs extended, laughing; Freddie, focused on picking the lock of a garage or shed; Freddie, holding her at night and talking about the films he loved the best.

He had reinvented her. He had simply chosen not to look at her faults or eccentricities and instead he had found a way to translate them into gifts: her obsessiveness became loyalty; her strange vision became sequences of film. Became art. Where, now, was D'Argent's Natalia, that frail, otherworldly child of the Paris night-time? D'Argent had also been fixated on her strangeness, but he had colonised it. Taken it for his own.

Without Penelope, I would never have broken free from D'Argent's spell, thought Suzanne, but without Freddie I would not have become a new person. Freddie died for me. He died so I could live. And now Suzanne was crying. She gasped and retched as the smell of the dead meat was sucked into her nose and lungs by the violence of her grief. She vowed one day to bury what remained of Freddie, and to make a film of his life.

Thinking about the scenes in this story, beginning with his job as a projectionist in Berlin, stopped her tears, and when the butcher unlocked the doors in Cadaqués she was dry-eyed and ready.

The butcher's son helped her down.

'The post office?' she asked him.

He pointed the way.

Cadaqués was a gleaming white town full of grubby, frowning people. The post office was large and well appointed and when Suzanne reached the front of the queue she showed the man the address that the concierge in Paris had given her.

'Púbol,' she said. 'I need to speak to Monsieur Púbol.'

But the man at the counter shook his head and tried to move on to the next customer.

'No!' she shouted. 'Monsieur Púbol. Now!'

The man shook his head again, but with resignation rather than annoyance. Then he called to another man to take his place and motioned for her to follow him.

He took her in a delivery van on a long detour around the back roads of the town then down to a large house near a cove where small boats were tied up. He turned off the engine.

'Gone,' he said. 'Not here.'

Suzanne refused to believe it. She got out and hammered at the door, leaving the man to shake his head again.

The door opened and what seemed to be a servant (a butler? a chauffeur?) stood in readiness.

'Please. I want to see Monsieur Púbol,' said Suzanne. 'Señor Púbol.'

'Sir,' called the servant.

A man came forward, expensively dressed in pale purple linen and holding an immaculate Panama hat.

'Monsieur Púbol? Please, I've come for Penelope Furr. She is my friend. I've come all the way from Paris.'

'I'm sorry, miss,' said the man, in perfect English, 'I'm not Miguel Púbol, and I have never heard of your friend.'

The post office man had joined them. 'Penelop? Penel Furr? I know him.'

'You do?' Suzanne swung around and grabbed his arms in case he tried to get away. 'You know Penelope?'

'Come.'

'Wait a moment,' said the linen-suited man. 'Please explain your connection to Señor Púbol.'

'You sound Scottish,' said Suzanne, then realised how abrupt she sounded. 'Forgive me.'

'James MacConnell,' he said. 'At your service. I look after Púbol's affairs, and I have a gallery in Edinburgh. I'm here to collect his work because he will soon be in America. I shall wait to hear what to ship and what to keep. Is your friend an artist too?'

'Yes. She was part of the group. She lived here. Oh, please, I have to hurry. I must see her. I've been travelling for weeks to reach her.'

'Let me assist you,' said the man called MacConnell. 'Smith, a package of sandwiches and some coffee in a flask, please.'

He asked the man from the post office something in Spanish and told Suzanne he would follow on behind them.

Suzanne and the post-office man drove back to the town, left the van and walked through narrow streets with tiny windows. They stopped at one covered in trimmed foliage.

The man opened the door, which was unlocked, and called out a name.

'Brother,' he explained to Suzanne.

A woman came into the room. She had a mole on her chin and her glossy black hair was arranged in the French fashion with a long comb.

'Please,' said Suzanne, 'I'm looking for Penelope Furr.'

The woman replied in French. 'Are you Suzanne?'

'Yes, I am.'

'I'm so sorry. Penelope left us more than three weeks ago. Come. Come in. She told me all about you. Come, child.'

Suzanne went inside the dark house and the woman dispatched her brother-in-law after a brief, rapid conversation.

She gave Suzanne some water and made her sit down at the table to drink it.

'Where has she gone?'

'Lisbon. To go to America. I don't know when they will leave.'

'They?'

'A man called Gantz, and the mad one, Púbol, they all went together.'

'James MacConnell will know. Where is he?'

'I don't know this name. Calm yourself. You are upset. Come, I have her pictures. Will you look?'

'Penelope's pictures?'

The woman took her into the back room where the walls were hung with the most wonderful paintings.

Suzanne went from one to the next, stroking the edges of the unframed canvases as if it was Penelope herself she touched.

The woman went to answer a knock at the door.

James MacConnell, stooping slightly to enter the room, appeared. In the other room, his man unwrapped the food he had brought and Suzanne could hear the woman enthusing over it.

Nodding briefly in greeting, James MacConnell joined her in inspecting the pictures. First he examined a picture of a rocking horse inside a room and, in the distance through a window, a white horse running free. Suzanne recognised it, having heard Penelope agonising over it repeatedly.

Next he moved on to one showing two vertical rocks rising out of the sea, and chuckled at it. The third picture was of Suzanne herself, depicted as half-butterfly at the top of the stairs in the Tuschinski cinema.

'They are exceptional,' he said. 'Entirely exceptional. Let's eat while we talk.'

They sat at the table, a mismatched collection of people: James MacConnell in his pristine linen jacket and yellow cravat, Suzanne in her old coat and oversized boots, and the woman of the house with her scruffy black skirt and stylish hairstyle, all waited upon by the sombre Smith.

James MacConnell managed the introductions, switching effortlessly between languages as they drank hot sweet coffee with cream and Suzanne tore into her ham sandwich without regard for manners.

The woman was Llùcia, wife of a fisherman called Eduardo, who had become friends with Penelope. She had stayed with them for weeks.

Once the niceties were over, the Scottish man started to make his pitch, speaking in French so that Llùcia could follow.

'Your friend's work is highly saleable, mademoiselle,' he said to Suzanne. 'I would like to represent her and, if she will allow it, I would like to take these pictures to Scotland for safekeeping. I will buy them, or sell them on her behalf, or keep them until she can return. I would buy all her future work, too. Will you make this offer to her on my behalf?'

'Of course, but she might have already left for America.'

'Indeed. It's possible. Miguel has not informed me of his plans in detail, only that he wished the house to be emptied.'

'I shall go to Lisbon as soon as I can,' said Suzanne, on her fourth sandwich.

'And you will ask her?'

'Yes. I have to find her. I have to reach Lisbon before she leaves.'

'The train is the quickest, quicker even than Smith could drive, supposing we had the fuel. You must go by train.'

'But I haven't any money.'

'Money is not a problem. Smith, go and buy the tickets. She will need to break the journey in Zaragoza, Madrid and Badajoz. And draw out enough for a good hotel for three nights. When can you travel, mademoiselle?'

'Tonight?'

'No, Suzanne,' said Llùcia, 'you must rest. Stay here and recover.'

'I think that's wise,' said James MacConnell. 'The service will be better on a Monday. Leave all this,' he said to Smith. 'I'll clear it up. Go on.'

'Yes, sir.'

'All right. Monday, then,' said Suzanne. 'But I must write to Penelope immediately and send it today. Where is Monsieur Púbol staying, Mr MacConnell? And do you have a stamp, please, madame? And some paper? And does anyone know of a good place to meet in Lisbon? A café, perhaps?'

Chapter Forty

Lisbon, September 1940

T he day before they were due to leave for New York,
Penelope was crossing the hotel lobby which was full as
usual with people hoping for rooms, or looking for their friends,
when someone called out her name. It was Púbol's fixer, Griggi.
He was holding an envelope and grinning under his perfectly
trimmed moustache. Griggi was always very dapper. He wore
a bow tie and Argyle socks with polished brogues; only his
dark complexion and the aroma of hashish smoke that lingered
around him marked him out as anything but the stereotyped
English gentleman.

'Here is a letter for you, dear girl,' he said. 'Who can it be
from?'

Penelope looked at the handwriting. Suzanne!

'Are you quite well, Miss Furr?'

'It is my friend Suzanne. My very good friend.'

Griggi raised an eyebrow. To him the word 'friend' signified
a lover; he made no attempt to hide his preference for his own
sex.

'Let us sit,' he said.

'No, I have to go to my room. I must read this now.'

Griggi's curiosity was barely disguised: 'But you are so pale,
perhaps I should come too?' It was plain that he would not leave
her alone until he had found out what news the letter contained
and if it could be used in his games of diplomacy: Griggi's wealth

had originally come from oil but latterly he dealt in what he called 'international information'.

'Oh, all right, if you really want to,' Penelope relented. She couldn't wait any longer before opening the letter.

In the lift, Griggi was all concern. Penelope held the unopened letter crushed against her chest and felt her heart beating underneath it.

In the room she sat on the bed and tore open the envelope. She flashed a warning look at Griggi, and he went to stand tactfully at the window with his back to her. Suzanne was in Cadaqués. Llùcia and Eduardo were looking after her until she could set out by train to Lisbon. There was no mention of Freddie.

'Thank God, oh thank God. She is alive,' said Penelope.

'But who is this precious girl?'

'She is my friend. Griggi – may I call you Griggi? – would you be willing to help me?'

'I would, dear Miss Furr, I would. Dear girl, what is the matter?' Griggi sat next to her and took her hand.

Penelope looked at his black, greased-down hair and steeled herself.

'My friend Suzanne is on her way here. She will arrive on Saturday. She is alone, and she's come a very long way to find me. She is Jewish, French, well, half-French, and it's not safe for her to use her real name. Nothing is safe for her.'

'We live in dangerous times.'

'Yes, yes,' said Penelope impatiently, removing her hand from his, 'but Suzanne was in hiding even before the war. She stole someone's identity to escape confinement, and then she went to Holland and began a good life, until ...'

'Until our present troubles began.'

'Griggi,' she said, getting up, 'I can't leave on the Clipper tomorrow, not now. Could you get someone else to go in my place?'

'There are twenty people I could name who would take it in an instant.'

'And the money for the seat?'

'That should be yours, dear girl. Our patron would surely agree.'

'This is the mystery man who buys Púbol's paintings, is it? The one who's paying for us all to stay here?' She returned to sit beside Griggi on the bed, but he didn't meet her eye.

'The very same,' he said.

Griggi was clearly not going to divulge any name he didn't have to give away.

'But, dear girl, is this good for you? Your friend will be hoping to see you, of course, but when the others of your party have left, and I too leave – I am expecting to rejoin my employers in October – you would be alone here. I have been in contact with your father, of course.'

'Really?'

'We have some business together and he was glad to know your latest address.'

'My allowance.'

'I have opened an account for you in America, but I could draw some money out and alter the arrangements before I leave.'

'How is my father?'

'Well. All are well. Your brothers are in Norway, however, and rarely in contact, I believe.'

She tried to imagine the gangly teenagers who used to pull her hair transformed into young men in uniform and she found herself wishing she could go back to England just once more. The newspaper she had found in the lobby had described the bravery of the Londoners during the repeated nights of bombing, and she felt proud as she read about people sharing flasks of strong sweet tea as they sheltered in underground stations. She was glad that her parents, and Auntie Carys, lived in the countryside.

Someone tapped lightly at the door. 'Señhor Grigoryan?'

'Excuse me.'

Griggi exchanged some words with a bellboy then said: 'I won't be long, dear girl. Wait for me.'

Penelope went to the window and gazed at the square below trying to ignore the ugly putto carved on the pillar by the balcony. As she watched people, cars and carts revolve around the column of Don Pedro IV, she tried to imagine the Boeing boat plane leaving tomorrow without her.

The Clipper took off and landed in water and yet it was a luxurious way to travel – first class only – with a silver-service dining room and bedrooms almost like the one she stood in now. She struggled to picture herself watching it take off and tried to predict her feelings at being left behind as Rolf, Púbol and the others set out for America without her.

Would they take her hopes for a career as an artist off into the sky with them? Or would she always be overshadowed and restricted by the feminine role they expected her to play? The only work she was proud of had been done in spite of them, in reaction to them. Rolf was plainly hoping that their affair would resume once they had a private room again and a new, intimidating, unknown country brought them closer together.

Then she played a different movie in her head: Suzanne arriving in Lisbon to find her gone. It was more painful than anything she'd yet envisaged, including being left alone in Lisbon without even Griggi to speak to. She imagined Suzanne's despair, her desperation.

No, to leave without Suzanne was impossible.

Griggi came back, barging in without knocking.

'Continue,' he said, sitting back down on the bed.

Penelope ignored his presumptuous behaviour and turned towards him.

'Could you arrange for Suzanne and I to leave Europe together?'

'To do that I would need to know who this woman is.'

'Could she use a false identity? She has the passport of a dead Spanish aristocrat with her own photograph substituted.'

'Dead, you say? What name?'

'Castello. Isabel Castello.'

'It depends.'

'On what?'

'Money, of course. Everything depends on money. And I would need a little incentive.'

'All right, but is there enough in my account for Suzanne's papers and our tickets?'

'Not on a Clipper. There is a ship, though. The *Nea Hellas* liner is sailing again in October.'

'Can you do it, Griggi?'

'I can try, dear girl. I can try.'

About an hour after Griggi had left, Rolf returned in a tearing rush.

'We must pack,' he said. 'Are you well?'

'I'm fine.'

'Where are the cases? We must be ready to leave early tomorrow.'

'Rolf,' said Penelope, scarcely able to look him in the face, 'I'm not coming to New York.'

'Not coming?'

'No. I can't. I can't leave, not yet.'

'But why?'

'Because of … It's a friend. She needs my help. I have to stay until I know she's safe.'

'And then you will come?'

'I don't know, I'd better not promise anything. I'll try.'

'But Portugal will not remain neutral forever, and it is easy to see which way Salazar would go. You would be trapped here on your own. You must come with us.'

'I can't. I really can't.'

'But why?' Rolf was beginning to raise his voice. 'What is this woman to you?'

'She is my friend,' said Penelope quietly. 'She needs me.'

'Pah!' Rolf threw his hands up and Penelope thought for one moment that he was actually going to hit her.

Instead he knelt at her feet. 'Little one, I do not want to lose you again.'

'Then you'll have to stay too,' she said.

He got up. 'No, I have to go.'

'Then that's it. That's the end.'

'But Penelope, please.'

He sat beside her and his arms encircled her. His strange white hair spread across her cheek and obscured the vision of her left eye.

She felt once again that melting and draining of will that she had loved and craved in the Paris days and she let her head rest on his shoulder. Then she saw that he was sitting on Suzanne's letter and an image of a man in a black coat running across a roof with a young girl in his arms flashed before her eyes.

She broke away. 'It's no good. I'm not going with you.'

Chapter Forty-One

'Penelope Furr, Penelope Furr, Penelope Furr.' That was what the train had chanted all night on the way to Lisbon from Madrid. Suzanne had nearly exhausted her inner resources and the thought of Penelope was all that was holding her together. The dream she'd had last night of a worm living in her hair and consuming her brain with gummy, sucking lips kept breaking in and her vision, too, was starting to fracture. So, as she walked towards Rua Garrett following the directions given by the newspaper boy, she struck her feet hard on the ground to the rhythm of his call ('*Século notícias. Século notícias*') and then, when pictures began to form around those words and stalk her, she changed her mantra to the name of the place she was going to meet Penelope: 'A Brasileira at twelve o'clock. A Brasileira at twelve o'clock.'

Repeating the words was enough to keep most of her brain occupied so she allowed her eyes to explore the texture of the small square stones, or tiles, on the ground which were dirty brown if old, or creamy white if new. Among these were patterns on the pavements picked out in blue china tiles forming swirls and crosses and, sometimes, stars. The streets were busy, but Suzanne kept her eyes resolutely on her feet. Occasionally she glanced up to check that her route was correct. 'A Brasileira at twelve o'clock,' she whispered.

Then she almost tumbled over a man in grey overalls who was crouching on the pavement. She stepped around him then saw that he and another man in similarly dusty clothing were actually laying the tiles. They had pegged out strings attached to long nails as a guide and were banging the tiles into sand with lump hammers. Before Suzanne could do anything about it, reality tilted and shifted. The surface she had depended on fell down into empty space because the tiles were not flat at all: each was a stub with only the top face showing and each was buried, standing upright. Suzanne thought of teeth being pulled and the whole of this bewildering city was revealed in a moment to be paved with blunt carious stumps, all leaning at a different angle. Once again the world threatened to snap its jaws around her. It reared up, ready.

'A Brasileira at twelve o'clock,' she said out loud, as if it was a magic spell, and the second tiler looked up and gave her a silly grin. When she did not move, the man must have assumed that she was lost and he got up and pointed along the street. But Suzanne could not take her eyes away from the open mouth of the exposed earth, so he placed an arm around her shoulder and turned her firmly in the right direction. She moved on.

As she walked away she noticed that he had left a dusty handprint on her sleeve. She had been jostled, she had been pushed in line and squashed against bodies in carriages, but no one had laid a hand on her since Freddie had held her that one last time before running away in the mountains.

She looked around her. The shops in Lisbon were a marvel. The profusion of food and clothing was like that of a fairy-tale land in comparison to the places she had been through. She fell helplessly into thoughts of Angélique and the pure pleasure she used to take in buying cakes and hairslides and dolls' dresses for her. She passed a sweet shop and smiled at the shiny, stripy jewels in their jars, but the smell of sugar made her feel sick because it brought back a memory from one of their lowest times on the way to Cerbère, when all they'd had to eat was a box of Algerian dates squirming with white maggots.

On Rua Garrett there was a huge department store called Eduardo Martins. It had a series of grand windows separated by black columns with vertical signs describing the variety of goods on sale. Suzanne paused and leant against the rail outside one of the windows. At first she genuinely sought to examine the blouses and hats and perfume bottles on display, but then along came her old companion, the ghost that travelled with her, her witness, her accuser: her reflection.

She scarcely recognised herself. No wonder the tiler had been so casually familiar: she looked like a man. Her hair was shorn (the lice had become too much to bear), she was wearing Freddie's overcoat belted with some rope from a barn, and she still had on the hiking boots. Her heavy bag made her hunch forward and she looked, all in all, like a rough farmer of fifty or so. Suzanne smiled when she thought about the way D'Argent had described her in his book. What would he say now? Had she ever been the things he called her: beautiful, mysterious, mad?

She took off the pack for a moment and looked back into the window. Suzanne imagined D'Argent's writing covering her naked body and her eyes peering through the spaces between the words. It began to rain in great, hot drops and the sound was like cellophane crackling. Suzanne lifted up her arms to hold the coat over her head, bunching the material in her hands. As the rain increased, she started to imagine that the snapping sounds were coming from the fabric of the coat that she was crushing in her raised fists.

Then she understood in a flash that D'Argent's words were never part of her at all; instead it was as if they were printed on a sheet of transparent plastic that she had been holding up in front of her for so many years that she had lost the ability to lower it and look at her own plain, honest body. She picked up her pack and walked towards the grand entrance of the shop, treading on a discarded wrapper in the street that popped underfoot as she flattened it.

The heavy treads of her boots skidded on the polished wooden floor inside the department store so she went very slowly, looking at the glass case of jewellery on one side and the hats arranged on one wall on the other. The shop assistants were watching her, she knew, and her pride suffered from the awful dirty coat she wore and her bald head. It had been so long since it had mattered how she looked.

She remembered the smart boots she had worn when arriving in Amsterdam. Would Isaac have invited her home if she'd been wearing these cast-off men's clothes then? Yes, he would. The more time that passed since his death, the more often Isaac's personality and words were coming back to her. 'Do not delay to be good, Suzanne,' he had once said. 'We do not have long on earth for all the kindnesses we were sent here to do.' All that time when she had been wrapped up in the drama of her life, she had neglected to understand that Isaac was that truly rare thing: a wise man, and a wholly good man. I was lucky to know him, she thought, slipping into the lift and electing to go down to the basement.

It was easier here, among the lingerie, to be unobserved. She walked idly along rows of slips, cabinets of stockings, ranks of bras. For some reason, she began to think back to the last phone call she had made before they came to lock her up all those years ago. It was in the afternoon and she had gone to a public phone, impelled by the terror that had overtaken her after D'Argent had failed yet again to meet her as arranged. She'd had that same sick premonition the night before she and Freddie went over the mountains, but then of course there had been good reason to be afraid. Back in Paris on that day so long ago, when D'Argent was her whole world, she had known something bad was about to happen: to him, if not to her.

Rolf was the one she had chosen to phone. Perhaps that was why he had tried to see her after she was taken away: he had not heeded her warning and felt guilty.

'Natalia,' he had said when he heard her voice, 'I haven't any money.' He sounded annoyed.

'It's not money I need,' she answered. 'Something is about to happen.'

'What?'

'I don't know. I feel it. It is black. It has a dark face.'

'Where are you?' Rolf had asked, in a different voice, not angry now.

'Just in a street.'

'A street where? Tell me where you are.'

Suzanne had not replied. She stood, listening to his voice with her eyes closed.

'I cannot be reached,' she had said, and then put down the phone.

But years later, she had been reached: Freddie had loved her, and Penelope had befriended her.

What time was it? Suzanne started desperately searching for a way to find out and went back up to the ground floor.

Just when she thought she would have to ask one of the assistants, or a kind-looking woman who was trying on a hat, she saw a large clock on the wall above the double doors at the entrance. It was all right: she wasn't late. Penelope wouldn't be there yet.

When at last Suzanne found the café it was very beautiful. It had a wide arch with the name in iron lettering above the entrance and a model of a man sipping a cup of coffee amid moulded curlicues of foliage. Black statues of two women leant from either side of the arch to peer with interest at the man and his coffee cup. Suzanne envisaged a shot with the camera Freddie had taught her to use: she would begin by zooming up close to the face of one of the figures and then gradually pull back to reveal its insecure position curled around the top of the facade with knees braced for balance.

The café had three sets of double glass doors. The furthest two were open and hooked to the green pillars outside. Suzanne went to the set of closed doors and peered inside. There was a bar stocked with pastries along the right-hand side, stairs descending to the left and black-and-white squares on the floor. The seats were almost empty; there was just one old man at the very back. Suzanne put down her hands and allowed her eyes to refocus on the surface of the glass once again. Her own reflection had become at last an ordinary copy of an intelligent Frenchwoman in her thirties facing some difficulties.

Then, reflected in the window next to her own image, she saw the exuberant wavy hair and lively smile of Penelope's familiar, long-missed face.

Chapter Forty-Two

Half an hour earlier, Penelope had burst out of the hotel entrance into Rossio Square, trying to shake off Griggi and frantic to keep her appointment with Suzanne at A Brasileira.

'Here, dear girl, please, buy yourself some nice clothes. A dress perhaps? Here, for a hat too.'

'Griggi, my old stuff is fine. Keep your money to help people who need it.'

He gave her a barely disguised, disapproving up-and-down look. 'Please. Take it. It is your money, dear girl.'

'How so?'

'I have done a very nice deal with your father, as it happens, dear Penelope.'

'Well, in that case.' She took the money. 'Did he ask after me?'

'Not exactly.'

'Meaning what?'

'He wrote that he hoped you would still be comfortable even though he had fired an old friend of yours. I did not understand it.'

She laughed. So that's why her allowance had been reduced: her father had taken a closer look at the books kept by his troublesome Jewish accountant.

'But if you need more funds, dear girl ...'

'Thank you, no, I never spent half of it. It's all under the mattress.' Enjoying Griggi's scandalised expression at this cavalier treatment of his god (money), she took advantage of the fact that he was speechless to make her farewell and slip away.

'Wait!' he called out.

Too late. She had already crossed to the centre of the square and a tram was clanging along, intercepting them.

The trams fascinated her. In the narrow streets the tram wires crossed and recrossed at the height of first-floor windows and she could never follow one set of wires and match it to the grooves in the road. It was the sort of thing Suzanne might become obsessed with and unbalanced by. Penelope had tried but failed to become an expert in the study of Suzanne's peculiar mind, which seemed to her (as it had to D'Argent) to contain the original blueprint of the surrealist way of looking, and thinking. The real world and the dream world were like two overlapping circles in Suzanne's mind. She could move freely from one to the other or, on occasion, occupy both at the same time.

There was no telling when Suzanne might fall through to the other dimension. How frightened she had been at first when Suzanne took that leap down the staircase of the Tuschinski. The changes in Suzanne's perception always came out of nowhere, with no warning. Penelope was very afraid that the stress of Suzanne's long, dangerous journey might have destabilised her irreversibly. With so much fear of imaginary scenarios how would she cope with real crises? Penelope knew that Freddie was no longer with her, but Suzanne had not explained why.

At the other end of the square there was a great knot of girls in loud, checked skirts, most with the flat woven baskets used by fish sellers. They were laughing and throwing around the padded rings that they used to cushion and balance the baskets on their heads. One fell at Penelope's feet so she threw it back. The girls gathered around her and pointed at her trousers and the old boots she wore, more in merry entertainment than mockery. She stretched out the material either side to show how widely her trousers were cut. One of the girls pulled off her own scarf and draped it around Penelope's head. Penelope tried not to blanch at the powerful fishy smell, but the girls were bright and quick and they saw her wrinkle up her nose. They all laughed again. Penelope gave back the scarf and the group of girls parted to let her go.

Well, that's something I'd never have seen if I'd stayed in Wallingford, she thought. She found herself thinking about home more and more. The out-of-date English newspapers that Griggi sometimes got hold of contained images more surreal than anything in an exhibition: houses sliced in half vertically by falling bombs; crowds of people sleeping in the tube station. What would her mother say? They would probably have people from London staying in the house and maybe with Auntie Carys who lived in Llantrisant.

Penelope used to stay with her aunt at Christmas time when she was little and the first time she ever drew a horse was at Auntie Carys's dining table, with the loud clock ticking on the dresser. Then her aunt had frightened her by bringing out a horse's skull draped in a long white smock with a necklace. Auntie Carys had put the smock over her head and cantered about the room singing a song in Welsh from behind the skull. Penelope was afraid but fascinated. Thinking about it now, Rolf's sketch of her as half-horse wasn't so original after all.

It was Carys's husband, Gwyn, who had first lifted her onto a horse's back. Penelope longed to ride again. It was as if she had not been able to see properly all this time, moving slowly on her own two feet and travelling so close to the ground. Perhaps she could ride in America? Griggi had managed to buy tickets to New York on the *Nea Hellas* for both herself and Suzanne. Her papers were in order and he was working on getting an exit visa for Suzanne, who would have to present herself in person, as Isabel Castello. Penelope wondered if Suzanne had managed to learn any Spanish. Suzanne didn't know yet that the real Isabel was dead. Penelope hoped it wouldn't upset her; it was the sort of thing that might.

So they would go together. Surely America was large enough for them to keep away from D'Argent and Rolf, and from all the others in exile. Penelope had not gone to see the others off and she was learning to shut down any thoughts about Rolf, or Alain and Una, who were now back in Paris. She wondered if Josephine had carried on making those vivid pictures in spite of D'Argent's contempt. As for Fabien, no one had heard from him for months.

She had reached Rua Garrett. The rain had stopped. There was plenty of time. She went to the *tabac* at the side of A Brasileira and idly, desirously, examined the blue-and-yellow cigarette packets. The café was her favourite. She loved the spinach-coloured columns outside and the sulphurous yellow of the mock-gold decorations of the facade. The mirror inside was a bit disconcerting, of course, running the whole length of the long room. She gazed across at the entrance and saw a figure in a long, brownish overcoat speckled with rain, squinting at the closed doors. Could it be? Penelope went closer and stood behind the person in the baggy coat.

She stared hard at the back of their closely shorn head. First she caught the scent of the familiar smoky essence that she associated with a blue haze in the air. Then she saw the unmistakable eyes and brow of Suzanne reflected in the glass door as a smile of recognition lit up her face. Suzanne turned to her. There were tears in her eyes and she threw her wiry arms around Penelope's neck.

A few minutes later they were sitting inside the café. Without the huge coat and with her massive, muddy boots hidden under the table, Suzanne could just about pass for normal, apart from her progressive haircut. They drank *aguardente* and hot chocolate; Penelope had forgotten how singular Suzanne's tastes could be. She looked up at the gilded ceiling fan and then back at Suzanne, enjoying the silence. Not speaking was part of the luxury of being able to talk at last and it was a round, warm silence, full of possibility and ease. How different to that first meeting in Paris when Suzanne had refused to speak.

Suzanne sighed with pleasure as she drained the cup of hot chocolate then got out some battered cigarettes.

'Can I have one of those?' asked Penelope.

'You've started smoking?'

'Yes, it was Alain.'

Suzanne waited as Penelope lit a cigarette.

'He's gone back to Paris, with Una.'

'I'm sorry.'

'Don't be. I was an idiot.'

'And Rolf?'

'He's fine, Griggi had a letter. But we're finished for good. And I'm over it.'

Penelope thought about the picture of Rolf she had drawn when he was away in Copenhagen showing him standing in a frozen landscape and carrying a cage with a miniature horse inside it.

'That's good, and I can see that you are warm again.'

'Yes, I am. So, tell me, how did you get from Paris to the border? And how did you meet Eduardo?'

'It was the man at the post office – he remembered you. Eduardo was so kind. His wife treated me like her own child. It was her idea to cut my hair to get rid of the lice.'

'Llùcia was good to me too. I thought I was going to have a baby, and she helped me so much. Oh, don't worry,' said Penelope, registering Suzanne's alarmed expression, 'it was a false alarm.'

'I would give anything to be carrying Freddie's child.'

'Will you tell me what happened to him, Suzanne?'

'Ah, I nearly forgot. I have the most wonderful news for you, Penelope.' Suzanne stubbed out her cigarette and beamed with pleasure. 'A man called James MacConnell came to Eduardo's and he saw your pictures. He was there to take away Púbol's work. He owns a gallery in Edinburgh. Look.'

Suzanne dug out a business card and handed it to Penelope.

'He wanted to take your pictures back with him and keep them safe. He will sell them if you wish, and he said he would buy all your future work.'

'But this must be Púbol's dealer: the man who paid for our hotel and the places on the Clipper.'

Suzanne nodded. 'He has a lot of money. He paid for my tickets here and gave me such a lot extra for hotels, though I didn't use it. I don't think a good hotel would let me in looking like this. But I've eaten so much, Penelope, more than all the time we were travelling from Paris.'

'So, in France, you travelled with Freddie?'

Suzanne flinched at the repetition of the name. 'He never left me. We stayed in some terrible places. And we could never get enough food; there was never hot food, you know, real food.'

'Are you hungry now? What about some pastries? Have you tried the custard tarts they have here?'

'Penelope, really—'

'Just a minute.' She got up to order more drinks and a plate of *pastel de nata*.

When Suzanne had finished eating, she lit another cigarette.

'What happened to Freddie, Suzanne?' Penelope said.

She did not answer straight away.

Penelope studied her clean-scrubbed face, older and more lined than before but with a new dignity in the absence of the ridiculous kohl. Her eyes seemed larger, and braver. Suzanne tapped the ash from her cigarette.

'We were in the mountains, near the border. Our guide betrayed us and Freddie ran to give me time to get away. Everything he did was for me. All the time we were in France, when we were trying to get to you he never stopped taking care of me.'

'What happened?'

'They shot him. I saw him fall. But then the mist came down and the next thing I remember is an angel coming to me, and then the angel turned into a woman, with others. They took me with them to Portbou.'

'Was Freddie...? Was he dead, Suzanne?'

'Yes. I think so. I don't remember if I touched him. He looked so strange on the ground. He must have been.' She covered her face with her hands. 'I left him, Penelope, I left him lying there.'

'I'm so sorry.'

'It's been so hard, just to keep going. I haven't really been able to think about Freddie.'

'That's probably for the best. There'll be time to grieve when we get to America.'

Suzanne looked up again. 'America?'

'I have a new friend called Aran Grigoryan, Griggi for short. He's a fixer, quite a shady character, but he's helped all of us and he seems to like me. I'm not sure why, unless my father is worth cultivating. Griggi has managed to get us tickets on a ship to New York and we'll be sailing on 10 October. It will be a new start for us both, and you will be safe.'

'But, Penelope, I can't leave Europe. I can't abandon Angélique.'

'You can't go back for her, it would be far too dangerous. Do you even know where she is?'

'I've been trying to get a call through to the bakery but the lines are down. I went to see her before, with Freddie, but Françoise threw me out.'

'So she wouldn't let you take Angélique even if you did make it back to Lille.'

'She is a horrible woman.'

'But she will protect Angélique?'

'With her life.'

'What about your grandmother on Skye? If Françoise has any sense she will get her away from France. But if not, maybe Griggi could help. There are still some child refugees making it to Britain. I saw it in the papers. And Angélique's mother was British. If Griggi can find her, will you go with me?'

'Yes.'

'All right then. I think I need another drink,' said Penelope

She went to the bar and tried out some more of her very bad Portuguese, then went to buy some more cigarettes as well.

Suzanne chased the last crumbs of pastry round the plate and licked her fingers, realising too late how dirty her hands must be. But the food Penelope gave her had always had magical properties: it could drive out demons, and cure loneliness too.

To go to America was a terrifying prospect, but Penelope would protect her and do everything possible to keep Angélique safe. The least Suzanne could do was to get on a ship. When the time came to board one of the huge ocean liners that she'd seen only in newspapers, she would pretend it was really the beautiful red-bricked building of Het Schip in Amsterdam. The memory of the painter who lived there, and whose wife had died, came back suddenly, mingled with the recollection of Freddie's soft kisses. For once, she had guided and led a lover and never once had she felt that Freddie was using her for his own pleasure or casting her as a character in his own story. Her need for him surged up and she searched desperately for a memory that was strong and encouraging.

Film had been Freddie's gift to her, as precious as his love. All her life, Suzanne had been afraid of the shifting planes of her sight and the reversals of reality she encountered when her mind was disordered. But when he showed her how to use the camera to focus and compose and connect one image with the next, the curse had gradually transformed into a blessing, a talent. The knowledge that he had given her by teaching her to film what she saw would be with her always. 'Suzanne, you have an eye,' she remembered Freddie saying, 'you really do. It is not something that can be learnt although all the rest can.' Maybe in America she could sell this skill. After all, weren't all the big films made there? If only Freddie could have lived to come with her, surely he could have made his name there, working in the movies.

Penelope had been gone a while. The familiar panic of not being able to reach her started to return. But no, here she was.

They sat in silence, imagining the future.

Penelope looked again at James MacConnell's card and felt a rising excitement at her strange stroke of fortune: she had a patron, a buyer, someone to make sure that her work was seen. Being part of the surrealists had been life-changing, but it had taken the chance coincidence of Suzanne, in flight, to connect her with an opportunity that had been there all the time: Púbol's patron. Púbol had never thought to show her work to him, and probably never would have done.

Penelope could not see very far ahead into the future but she knew that once they had left Europe she would be able to breathe easily again and to have Suzanne with her meant an end to these months of anxiety about her safety. One day, perhaps, they could go back together and live on the Isle of Skye with Angélique and Suzanne's Scottish grandmother. Once there, she would paint and spend time with her new dealer in Edinburgh. It was a rich, golden, possible future and Penelope knew that this vision would give her strength, just as that strange, orange-striped visitation in the sea at Cadaqués had strengthened her before.

She watched Suzanne dig around in her dirty rucksack then pull out a piece of matted wool. It was Ailsa's old beige cloche hat with its yellow-and-red flower clinging on by a thread, the one that she had saved from the mugger outside Le Parisien.

'Remember this?' Suzanne was smiling. 'To think, I didn't like you when I met you: I thought you were a snob, a real spoilt English bitch.'

'Well, don't worry about it. I thought you were a con artist on drugs; your hands were shaking you know.'

Suzanne laughed. 'And all you would talk about was Rolf, the wonderful, perfect Rolf who had turned you into a real artist.'

'Because of course you knew better than to worship some man or other.'

'*Touché*. It is the mirror that teaches us best.'

'I was blinded for a while, it's true,' Penelope said. 'When I met Rolf it was like coming out of a dark night into a brilliantly lit tunnel. No genuine artist had ever praised my work before. It was rather fun in bed with him too.'

'Yes, you told me. Several times. But now you know your work is good, don't you?'

'I'm beginning to believe it.'

Suzanne reached across the table and took her hand.

'You have saved my life, Penelope.'

'No,' said Penelope, clasping Suzanne's thin fingers, 'it's the other way round.'

Author's Note

Swimming with Tigers is based on the real people associated
with surrealism in the 1920s, 1930s and 1940s, but I have taken
great liberties with the details of their lives and artworks to
create this fictional story. By giving the following descriptions
of some of the instances in the book where I have diverged from
historical fact, I aim to set the record straight and also hope
to inspire readers to learn more about the women artists who
were part of one of the most important and far-reaching art
movements of the modern era.

In my novel, Penelope Furr is a composite figure combining
the lives and works of several women, including Leonora
Carrington, Meret Oppenheim, Eileen Agar, Ithell Colquhoun
and Lee Miller. Penelope paints a version of *Self-Portrait: Inn
of the Dawn Horse* (by Carrington), makes the famous cup in
fur (by Oppenheim), swathes a dummy's head in scarves and
feathers (Agar's *Angel of Anarchy*) and also invents solarisation
by mistake in the darkroom (as did Miller).

Leonora Carrington's father, like Penelope's, was a wealthy
textile manufacturer but they lived in Lancashire, not
Oxfordshire. Carrington, a debutante, did not meet Max Ernst
at the 1936 International Exhibition of Surrealism, but did
meet him around that time (June 1937) and knew his painting
Two Children Threatened by a Nightingale. Carrington's
Self-Portrait from 1937–38, is Penelope's *Horse of the New*

Dawn (with a slightly different small animal), but doesn't come together until 1940 in my novel. Carrington's painting *Portrait of Max Ernst* (1939) provides the basis for Penelope's sketch of Rolf holding a cage with a horse inside.

Meret Oppenheim made the fur cup, *Object*, in 1936, not 1938 as in the book. I made up D'Argent's title for it (*From One Hand to Another)*, but Breton did rename it *Breakfast in Fur*, as a nod to Edouard Manet's *Déjeuner sur L'Herbe* and *Venus in Furs* by the Marquis de Sade. It was Oppenheim who allegedly peed into the top hat of a pompous man on the terrace of a Paris café (see Whitney Chadwick's groundbreaking account of women and surrealism, *Women Artists and the Surrealist Movement*, 1985). Oppenheim also posed for the photograph by Man Ray at the printing press (*Veiled Erotic*, 1933). The shoes lying open at the Tuschinski cinema foyer and then as a surrealist object assembled in a roasting tin at Alain's apartment are from Oppenheim's *My Nurse* from 1936.

Eileen Agar made the object *Angel of Anarchy* in 1940, not 1938, which is when Penelope makes the equivalent *Her Mother's Face*. Ithell Colquhoun's *Scylla,* of 1938, is the model for Penelope's painting of her legs in the bath. Lee Miller co-created solarisation much earlier (around 1929) and not in 1937, as Penelope does in the novel.

Suzanne occupies the place of the woman described by Breton in his book *Nadja* (1928). She was known for years only as 'Léona D.' and many supposed her to be an invention of Breton's. There were rumours that she was seen in France in the 1970s (see Mark Polizzotti's 1999 introduction to the Penguin edition of *Nadja*), but it is far more likely that she never regained her freedom and did indeed die in 1941, in a hospital near Lille, where she, like Suzanne, was born. Recently, Nadja's full name was revealed as Léona Delacourt and a biography of her has been written by Hester Allbach, currently available only in French. Léona had a daughter, but there is no possibility that she was Breton's child because she was born before Léona went to Paris.

Suzanne has Nadja's memories, as documented in Breton's book, of an argument with another diner, and of predicting that a window will light up and appear red in Place Dauphine. She also recounts the story from Breton's book of arriving covered in blood from a sexual assault at Brasserie Zimmer. Her recollection of a disastrous night at a hotel in Saint-Germain is based on Breton's account, but her drawing of D'Argent as a lion is my own invention, inspired by the fascinating sketches attributed to Nadja and reproduced in Breton's book. Suzanne shouts in her hotel like Nadja and is taken away and locked up as she was.

There is now some evidence, uncovered by Hester Allbach, of Nadja's physical mistreatment when confined. I was unaware of this when writing my novel, and the sexual abuse that Suzanne endures is a product of my imagination. I have borrowed the name of the doctor, Augustine, as a nod to Jean-Martin Charcot's best-known female hysteric patient and to indicate the surrealists' troubling fascination with sexualised images of madwomen.

In my book, Louis d'Argent closely resembles André Breton and Miguel Púbol is a fictional portrait of Salvador Dalí. Alain is loosely based on Paul Eluard and Maurice bears some resemblance to Benjamin Péret. Fabien Sadoul makes paintings in the style of Yves Tanguy. Other male characters are mixed: Rolf Gantz combines Max Ernst and Man Ray.

Ernst invented frottage and was included (as is Rolf) by the Nazis in the exhibition of Degenerate Art in 1937. His *Bride of the Wind* pencil sketch was created later than in the novel, in 1940. Man Ray's photograph *The Primacy of Matter over Thought* is the one Penelope recalls depicting her as a melting body. Man Ray created rayographs of many things including a comb, but not a hammer or the skin of a snake, as Penelope credits Rolf with doing for the Amsterdam exhibition.

There are references to many other surrealist works throughout the novel. Some are included directly, such as Dorothea Tanning's painting of girls and sunflowers *Eine Kleine Nachtmusik* (1943) which, in the book, is made by D'Argent's wife Jacqueline. Tristan Müller's dolls, objected to by Penelope, are Hans Bellmer's. Some references are less literal, such as when Suzanne experiences her body as the metal sculpture by Giacometti, called *Women with her Throat Cut* (1932). The iron with nails discussed by Penelope and Suzanne is clearly Man Ray's *Gift* (1921). Suzanne has a vision of herself in an Amsterdam shop window as Roland Penrose's *Winged Domino* (1938) and relives the notorious eye-slicing moment from the film *Un Chien Andalou* (Luis Buñuel, 1929).

Suzanne's dream of the lemur is from Valentine Hugo's *Dream of 21 December 1929* (1929), and her dream of seeing her own sleeping body was inspired by Paul Delvaux's *Venus Asleep* (1944). The dream that haunts her as she arrives in Lisbon is from a story written by Gisèle Prassinos sometime between 1934 and 1944, called *Venda and the Parasite* (reprinted in *Surrealism and Women*, edited by Mary Ann Caws *et al*. 1993).

Suzanne's method of escape from her guardian in Paris is the one used by Leonora Carrington to give the slip to her nurse when being transferred to a different asylum, and I heartily recommend Joanna Moorhead's 2017 biography of Leonora Carrington for an account of this and other episodes in her life. Suzanne's brief awareness of a double in the mirror is my homage to Claude Cahun's *Self Portrait* (1927) and her final hallucination of being covered by a sheet of transparent plastic at the department store in Lisbon is from Eileen Agar's *Ladybird* (1936).

My recreation of the 1936 First International Exhibition of Surrealism at the New Burlington Galleries in London refers to Humphrey Jennings' *Mountain Inn with Swiss Roll* (1936), and the object wrapped in a blanket is Man Ray's *The Enigma of Isadore Ducasse* (1920). It was the poet Dylan Thomas who wandered around offering tea made of hot water and string, and the composer William Walton attached a kipper to a Miró painting. Dalí famously wore a diving helmet to deliver a lecture and nearly suffocated when it became stuck.

At the Paris exhibition, much of the detail matches the real event of 1938 including the rainy taxi (Dalí's) which did not have live frogs but did have snails. The street of mannequins contains versions of the actual exhibits, although the mannequin with zips on its eyes owes more to Marcel Jean's *Spectre of the Gardenia* (1936). The large room was indeed hung with stinking coal sacks. As in the novel, visitors were given handheld torches and experienced a surrealist dance in a pond by Hélène Vanel.

Una's life story is based on Nusch Eluard (born Maria Benz), who made the collage of naked women dancing around a chalice (1936). The book of poems and photographs that Rolf and Alain work on as a celebration of Penelope is similar to *Facile*, the book about Nusch by Eluard and Man Ray (1935). Finally, the poem Alain writes for Penelope resembles Breton's well-known 'Free Union' (1931).

I hope that all the dedicated scholars of the history of the surrealist movement will forgive me for making these alterations and transmutations in my quest to create an absorbing fiction.

Reading Group Questions

1. How would you characterise the position of women artists in the surrealist group as depicted in the novel?

2. Why do Penelope and Suzanne form a strong bond?

3. What events cause Penelope to change her attitude to the surrealist group and her relationship with Rolf? How do the different stages in her friendship with Suzanne feed into this?

4. Suzanne begins by distrusting men but gradually gathers supportive male figures around her such as Freddie and Isaac. Penelope's trajectory is the opposite: she begins by expecting solidarity and assistance from men and ends up realising that self-reliance is her only option. Why do you think these two opposite stories are placed side by side in the novel?

5. Suzanne and Freddie's hazardous journey across the Pyrénées is based on the experiences of real-life Jewish people fleeing persecution. Using your own knowledge or online research, discuss how these escapes were made and why they were necessary.

6. What is the significance of the title of the novel?

7. Can fictionalised, composite portraits in historical novels such as this one help preserve the memory of people and achievements that might otherwise be lost?

8. What, if any, are the dangers of fictionalising the past? Is it defensible to alter the facts for the sake of a satisfying story?

9. The novel ends as Penelope and Suzanne are about to embark on new lives in America. What do you imagine in their futures?

10. How many women surrealists could you name before reading this book and how many do you now know?

Acknowledgements

Firstly, I would like to thank all the feminist art researchers, curators and critics who have worked to restore the women surrealists to visibility. I could not possibly name them all but, in particular, Whitney Chadwick for her pioneering work in the 1980s, Joanna Moorhead for her biography of Leonora Carrington, Katharine Conley for her subtle theoretical work and Mary Ann Caws for her long service to the critique and anthologising of women surrealists. Penelope Rosemont's monumental collection of surrealist writings by women was the book that began everything for me and the 2009 exhibition in Manchester, UK, entitled *Angels of Anarchy,* was an inspirational experience for which I would like to thank curator Patricia Allmer.

Many people have read and commented upon the successive incarnations of this novel and I thank them all, especially if they have read more than one version or, like David and Liz, have read every single one. They include Annie Williams, Sue Wilson, Zoë Skoulding, Rhys Trimble, Harriet Tarlo, Bryn Hopewell, Julie Perren, Richard Hopewell, Beth Bithell and Julia Ozanne. I am also grateful for the professional advice given by Rebecca F. John and Caroline Oakley at Honno Press, and by Samiha Meah at Lucent Dreaming.

I would like to thank my amazing editor Gale Winskill whose excellence knows no bounds and Louise McGuinness, my super-efficient proofreader. All the errors are mine and the elegance is theirs. Thank you to the University of Michigan Press for permission to quote from Breton's *Second Surrealist Manifesto*.

The enthusiasm of my students on the Women's Studies MA degree module *Women and the Arts* motivated me to develop my material on women surrealists and I thank all of them for being so open and engaged with what were probably the strangest things they saw at university that year.

It only remains to thank the two pillars that hold up my world and stop me from falling into self-doubt and despair, namely my dear friend Liz Cross and the best husband anyone ever had: David Hopewell. Liz, your intelligence and friendship have inspired and encouraged me for forty years, and our long conversation will never end. David, you have made this book possible. Thank you for making me happy.

About the Author

Dr Kathy Hopewell lives in North Wales with her husband and books and has a view of the mountains of Eryri (Snowdonia) from her study window.

She taught at Bangor University from the 1990s onwards and established the first community courses in women's literature in the area. She ran degrees in Women's Studies and in Literature and Creative Writing at the Department of Lifelong Learning, then left the university to run independent courses on freewriting and to create her online resource *The Freewriter's Companion*.

She regularly performs at local festivals and events as one half of *Hopewell Ink*, a spoken word and music band with David Hopewell, and they have produced four CDs.

Swimming with Tigers is her first novel and you can learn more at https://kathyhopewell.com